A Love So True

This Large Print Book carries the
Seal of Approval of N.A.V.H.

TEAVILLE MORAL SOCIETY

A LOVE SO TRUE

MELISSA JAGEARS

THORNDIKE PRESS
A part of Gale, a Cengage Company

Farmington Hills, Mich • San Francisco • New York • Waterville, Maine
Meriden, Conn • Mason, Ohio • Chicago

LIBRARY OF CONGRESS CATALOGING-IN-PUBLICATION DATA

Names: Jagears, Melissa, author.
Title: A love so true / by Melissa Jagears.
Description: Large print edition. | Waterville, Maine : Thorndike Press, a part of Gale, Cengage Learning, 2017. | Series: Thorndike Press large print Christian historical fiction | Series: Teaville Moral Society
Identifiers: LCCN 2017018216| ISBN 9781432842055 (hardcover) | ISBN 1432842056 (hardcover)
Subjects: LCSH: Large type books | GSAFD: Love stories. | Christian fiction.
Classification: LCC PS3610.A368 L68 2017b | DDC 813/.6—dc23
LC record available at https://lccn.loc.gov/2017018216

Published in 2017 by arrangement with Bethany House Publishers, a division of Baker Publishing Group

Printed in the United States of America
1 2 3 4 5 6 7 21 20 19 18 17

To Naomi,
for having to deal with a rather difficult-to-please critique partner, yet valiantly remains friends with her anyway, who deserves more gratitude than she gets, more encouragement than she hears, and all the strawberries in the world.

1

Southeast Kansas
September 1908

If David Kingsman had any chance of making his father proud, this next decision could be it. Of course, Father was just as likely to disown him for it, but if David's projections were correct, it would be worth it. Hopefully.

Closing the last ledger, David looked across the room at the factory manager of A. K. Glass. Mr. Burns stood by the window, stroking his gray beard while staring out over the industrial part of town, as he'd done the whole time David had pored over the factory's books.

The fact that the manager had done nothing for several hours was as telling as the numbers in these ledgers.

Mr. Burns should be glad Father wasn't the one here right now. Though he wouldn't like him either once he heard his decision.

"Mr. Burns." David released a breath and pushed himself out of the chair. "After today's examination, I'm afraid I need to let you go."

The man blinked but didn't move.

"I understand you'll need time to gather your things." He gestured toward the man's desk before striding to the door and entering the front office, where several men handled the glass factory's paperwork. The stacks of papers on their desks were but a draft away from fluttering to the floor already littered with boxes, crinkled papers, and glass jars. He tapped his hand on the empty desk closest to Mr. Burns's door. "Does anyone know where Mr. Carlisle is?"

The three other employees in the office looked up and shook their heads.

"Men," Mr. Burns's voice boomed from behind him, "I'd suggest you find a job elsewhere before it's too late. After only one day's assessment, the owner's son here thinks we aren't doing our best. If he'll fire me, he'll fire you."

David held up his hand. "That's not true. Workers who earn their pay will not be fired." He turned to glare at Mr. Burns. "I suggest you leave peaceably."

Mr. Carlisle's tall, thin frame sneaked in through the outer doorway, his thin mustache twitching. "I heard Liberty Glass is hiring."

"Better to work under someone who cares about the people in this town rather than some outsider." Mr. Burns shuffled through the crowded office, holding his box high above his paunch. "Come, George. I'll put in a good word for you." He gestured with his head for Carlisle to follow, then stomped out the door.

The three men behind their desks glanced between Mr. Carlisle and the outsider who'd dared to fire their boss.

David took his time to look all four men in the eyes. "I can't promise anything, but my intention is not to fire anyone who's competent. If you've been hardworking and —"

"Well, my uncle did the best he could with this place, and if that wasn't enough . . ." Mr. Carlisle shuffled through the mess toward his desk. "I'll pack my things."

His uncle? No, no, no. He needed Mr. Carlisle! "Now wait. I know how difficult it can be to work with family, the pressure to remain loyal no matter what. But I'm willing to raise your salary since I need to make this place ready . . . er, I mean . . . start to . . ." *Argh.* What could he say that wouldn't offend but would convince him to stay? Especially since he wasn't sure how long Mr. Carlisle could keep the position. "I'd appreciate your help in turning this place into what my father and I have envisioned."

The man dumped the contents of a filing box onto the floor and snatched the lone photograph off his desk. Before packing it, he stopped to give David a smug look. "Good luck doing that without me." He opened a drawer and retrieved a sweater and a tin box.

"Is Liberty really hiring?" The youngest of the three remaining men ruffled his red hair.

David clamped his jaw to keep from begging the man to stay. His father would have immediately handed the kid a box for uttering such a disloyal question.

But why would these men feel loyal to Kingsman & Son? Father had only visited once after he'd received the deed from the former proprietor, who'd signed it over to clear a debt. He'd then left the place to run on its own, expecting the same diligence from his Teaville manager as those who ran his holdings in Kansas City.

As soon as these workers found out Kingsman & Son planned to sell this place, what reason would they have to be loyal?

David refused to let his body posture

slump an inch. "You're free to go, of course, but I won't rehire you."

"We'll put in a good word for you." Mr. Carlisle waved a beckoning hand toward the redhead.

The two other men stared down at their desks. The one to David's right pulled an invoice toward him, focusing on it as if fascinated.

The younger man stood and shrugged. "It's closer to home anyway. I resign."

David gave the redhead a curt nod and tried not to fist his hands while he and Carlisle finished clearing their desks of personal items.

How would he fix this place up quickly without the secretary he'd been counting on to know the ins and outs of the company?

Uncle and nephew. How he wished that information had come to light earlier.

After the two men exited, David turned to the remaining two employees. "Continue on, I'll be asking for your help shortly."

They both gave him a nod before he returned to Mr. Burns's office. Shutting the door quietly, he wilted onto one of the office chair's cushioned arms.

Good thing Father had already banished him to Teaville, for it seemed he'd be here awhile. He stared at the papers and ledgers piled on the desk, then looked at the clock. Three fifteen.

As if his stomach could read time, it rumbled, reminding him how he'd skipped his lunch hour while agonizing over the right decision.

Which now seemed to have been the wrong one.

He grabbed the jacket he'd left draped over a chair and shrugged it on. Working on an empty stomach was foolhardy, but he really couldn't blame this fiasco on hunger.

"I'll return, gentlemen." He strode through the office and out onto the metal balcony that overlooked the main floor of the factory, where men sorted, boxed, and hauled all the various iterations of A. K. Glass canning jars. Thankfully the furnaces were clear across the building and the heat was only mildly stifling here.

His hard soles clanged as he descended the narrow metal staircase, like the pinging of a hammer pounding nails into the coffin where his business prowess now lay.

Outside, the early-autumn air was almost as muggy as inside the factory, but at least the sun was shining. He closed his eyes against its bright rays.

Lord, I need help. In more ways than one.

Thankfully the same God who made that

very sun rise knew his predicament. He could take comfort in that, if nothing else.

The scent of something fried wafted on the slight breeze, so he took a left turn at the end of the building and attempted to follow his nose. He glanced around at the industrial area surrounding his factory — bland brick-walled alleys, rutted roads, and tall buildings. Why hadn't he asked the men where he could get something good to eat?

As he passed by another massive factory, the sight of a street a block ahead crowded with buildings better suited for small businesses made him rub his hands together, especially since the fried smell was stronger now. He passed an abandoned building on his way to the shops and squinted to make out the well-painted wooden signs hanging from the storefronts up ahead. Where was the smell of food coming from?

He slowed as he finally reached the sidewalk.

The Dutch Tulip, the California, the Pink Lady, the Charlatan.

The faint sound of a piano playing and subdued laughter somewhere down the street gave him pause. He looked into the nearest two windows. Saloons or inns, maybe, both dark at the moment. He really should've asked the man who'd picked him up from the train to tell him about the area, but David had been so focused on accomplishing Father's request, he'd paid little attention to his surroundings.

He had never stepped foot in the seedy areas back home. Should he just go back to work?

A young man walked out of a nearby building and tipped his cowboy hat. He'd exited from someplace called the Hawk and Eagle Soda Fountain.

The youth looked respectable enough, so David returned the nod and pulled out his pocket watch. What harm would it do to grab a plate of food and take it to the factory? He needed to return in time to ask someone to recommend a few boarding-houses or hotels lest he end up somewhere less than savory tonight.

He crossed the fairly empty brick street and headed toward the soda fountain. Even if the delicious smell was coming from somewhere else, he should at least find something edible here.

As he stepped onto the sidewalk, a tall, dark-headed woman emerged from the alleyway. The pale blue of her simple, high-necked dress was not the vibrant color he'd expect of a woman who frequented the bad areas of town. Perhaps he wasn't where he thought he was after all.

She turned into the Hawk and Eagle before he did. Should be a decent place, then.

Inside, a few men sat at smoky tables surrounding the square counter in the middle of the large room.

The woman was halfway across the floor. She wasn't calling attention to herself with a seductive sashay or suggestive glances, so he headed for the counter.

A flash of brilliant red caught his eye. A female at a back corner table was wearing the exact kind of dress he would have expected in a brothel. The woman's painted lips curved as he met her eyes, and she ran a hand across her bodice, tempting him to look at the skin her dress failed to cover.

This sort of woman made the lady in blue stick out like a sore thumb.

He glanced back at the lady he'd followed in, who was ascending the stairs of a balcony lined with several doors. Why had she come in such a place?

She strode across the balcony without a glance toward the players groaning about losing a hand of poker or the woman in the red silk sitting on a man's lap.

Though average in looks, the woman in blue's uncommon height, if nothing else, should have caught people's attention — yet a quick glance around told him no one seemed to notice the out-of-place woman except him.

She stopped at the second door on the balcony and knocked.

What could she possibly be doing up there? Was he wrong? Would upstanding people rent rooms in a place where this woman in red worked?

When the upstairs door opened, the tall woman said something with a smile and then disappeared into the room.

He rubbed his eyes and glanced around the main floor. Not a single man was looking in her direction with a puzzled expression — or one of baser interest.

Should he do something? What? She certainly didn't appear to be in danger. But could he go about his business not knowing how she fared?

"You wantin' something?"

The man at the counter had finished drying a glass and stood staring at him with an uplifted eyebrow.

David looked around and saw no food. "Um . . . what sodas do you have?"

The man picked up another glass. "Ginger ale and club."

"That's it?"

"If you want fancy, try the soda fountain on Main Street. Frilly flavors like cola, cherry, and lemon-lime there."

David waited for a few seconds, but the man didn't ask him if he wanted something harder to drink, though maybe he was just being cautious with the newcomer since alcohol was illegal in Kansas.

"Club soda, then."

In a matter of minutes, the woman in blue backed out of the room and headed downstairs. A young man who'd been busily shucking peanut shells between sips of what appeared to be whiskey seemed to notice her for the first time. The red-freckled youth looked her over with a shy smile and quickly abandoned his seat and headed for the bottom stair. If he meant for the silly tilt of his brows and his puffed-up chest to convey confidence, he failed by combining it with a nervous swagger.

Without so much as a how-do-you-do, the lad cut off her path and took hold of her left arm. "I've heard there's nothing in this world like being held in the arms of an angel, and I'd like to find out for myself."

She backed away, giving him a patronizing glare. "You should go home, young man."

The boy's lips curled into a snarl as she tugged against his grip.

David left his soda and hurried forward.

"Let her go," the man behind the counter hollered. "She ain't one of my girls."

The youth glared at the soda jerk, and the woman took the opportunity to pull away. She gave the man behind the counter a nod before heading out.

David stopped, but she didn't even acknowledge him as she blew past.

The freckled miscreant huffed as if he were ten and his momma had told him he couldn't bring frogs into the house, then slogged off to his seat. The two groups of men at the corner tables hadn't stopped jabbering. The red silk woman had disappeared.

David looked back at the soda jerk or bartender — whatever he truly was — but the man had resumed polishing the rows of empty glasses on his counter.

A woman was almost assaulted and he goes back to cleaning?

David turned to follow the lady out.

"Hey!" the bartender hollered. "You didn't pay for your drink."

David dug a coin from his pocket and tossed it onto the counter, then rushed outside. To his left, the tall brunette was walking east, seemingly *farther* into what had to be this town's red-light district.

18

Had she no idea where she was either?

He sped up and then kept pace far enough behind not to draw attention, but close enough to sprint to her if needed.

A sudden flurry of black flew out of the alley. A muddy-haired kid ran straight for her.

David's feet flew just as quickly as the young one's. A pickpocket hadn't been the fate he'd expected to save her from, but he wouldn't let her be mugged if he could stop it.

The boy slammed into her and wrapped his arms around her legs, throwing the woman off balance.

One of her arms twirled for a second to save herself from a fall, and then she laughed.

David pulled up short. Laughed? He couldn't help but wrinkle his brow.

What kind of decent woman came into a red-light district with a smile for a prostitute and a laugh for an urchin?

She leaned over to embrace the boy, dirty clothes and all, then ruffled his matted hair.

After getting a tweak to the nose and a reply of some sort, the boy dashed off so fast the brunette's attempt to pat his back failed.

Perhaps this woman didn't need an escort

after all . . . and yet, that made her all the more intriguing.

She shoved one hand into a side pocket and whirled around, her eyes narrowed, her chin tilted in question. "Is there a reason you're following me, sir?"

Was there anything about this woman that wouldn't surprise him? He'd expected a big-boned woman like her, who was likely a smidgen taller than he, to have a deep, husky voice, and yet it was as soft as an angel's, even with challenge coloring her tone.

He glanced at the stiff arm disappearing into her skirt. At least she wasn't completely unprepared for the bad section of town. Hopefully she had something more substantial than a jackknife in her hand.

"No need to worry about me." He walked forward slowly, his palms out. "You, on the other hand . . . I mean, it looks as if you're doing just fine, but the people who frequent areas like this . . . Well, if it's all right with you, I'd like to make sure you get out of here safely and meet up with someone you know."

Her hand didn't leave her pocket. "You do realize I saw you in the saloon."

"You mean the Hawk and Eagle Soda Fountain?"

She snorted.

All right, so that wasn't the sound he would have expected from an angel.

"Not a soul believes that's a soda fountain." She rolled her eyes, and yet her smile was more amused than anything. "You might think me less than bright for visiting this part of town, but I assure you, I'm not that stupid."

He pulled at his tie, feeling a little less than bright himself, since it had taken him a while to figure out this was indeed the bad part of town. "I only went in because you did. I was looking for something to eat."

He threw her the grin that made most women duck their heads and flutter their eyelashes — didn't work on her, apparently. "Regardless, would you mind terribly if I escort you home? Considering where you are, I doubt many men will stop to ask you who you are before they make assumptions."

She straightened and threw back her shoulders. "Your escort is not necessary. I'm fine, thank you, and good day." She turned and strode away.

She was obviously not fine, but she sure was interesting.

He waited until she was farther ahead this time before following.

In just a few blocks, she turned onto a much busier street with plenty of well-dressed ladies strolling among the passersby before she disappeared behind a shiny new streetcar. The green monster of a contraption rumbled down its tracks, heedless of horse or human and the rare automobile.

David's stomach cramped, but thankfully the woman had led him into a section of town he wouldn't have to worry about being seen in. At the hotel across the street, a couple — framed by a large picture window — ate what looked to be a gigantic slice of meringue pie.

After one last glance toward where the mystery woman had vanished, he made his way across the street for lunch. Too bad Father's glass factory would keep him busy until it was sold and he could return to Kansas City. Trying to figure out what the woman in blue was about would have been a great way to entertain himself during his banishment.

But he couldn't work every hour of the day. Maybe he could find a way to run into her again.

2

Swaying beside Caroline on the wagon bench, Evelyn Wisely could see a small group of the red-light district's neglected children awaiting them under the scrawny tree they picnicked under each Saturday. Unfortunately, there wasn't a single redhead wandering among the industrial castoffs in the overgrown field.

Where was Annette? Her little brother, Lawrence, had been moping about the orphanage for more than a month now. If she didn't turn up soon, what hope was there that she ever would? Annette had been so diligent to check on her brother every week before disappearing without a word.

Evelyn turned to Caroline O'Conner, the housekeeper for the orphanage they both worked at. "I don't know what I'll tell Lawrence if we find out Annette has succumbed to the pressure of the district. She was so adamant she'd never leave him the way their mother did."

"You tell him the truth. That regardless of his sister's whereabouts, you and your parents will dote on him until a good family adopts him." Caroline steered the horse toward the children. The housekeeper's thicker figure, tight posture, and out-of-style auburn curls made her seem older, though her thirty-three years weren't much more than Evelyn's twenty-seven.

"And if we never find her?" The knot in her throat from yesterday's disappointing search came back in full force. The prostitute she'd visited at the Hawk and Eagle had promised she knew everything that went on in that part of town, and if she didn't, she could find out. But it had been three weeks, and Miss Lily White had not one iota of information worth the ten dollars Evelyn had paid her.

Caroline stared off into the distance. "Most people would probably encourage you to help him forget her. Many advise me to do so with my own sister, but I can't, and likely neither will he. All you can do is let him know you still care."

Did Caroline feel as hopeless as Lawrence? At least she knew where Moira was. Though the ache of having her sister trapped in prostitution had to overwhelm Caroline

24

from time to time.

The team slowed, and the handful of children swarmed them, climbing onto the sides and into the back before the wagon stopped.

"Good afternoon, children." Evelyn hopped down and was immediately clobbered by ill-washed bodies and big, desperate hugs. Though her job and this ministry wrung her heart, she couldn't think of anything she'd rather do with the years that stretched out before her.

Three-year-old Jesse pulled at her skirts, so she picked him up. "Guess what, Jesse? We've brought your favorites today: roasted chicken, mashed potatoes, and split pea soup!"

The little boy's wrinkled nose and pout were adorable. Every time they brought his least favorite soup, she purposely tried to coax that expression out of him. Though only three, he roamed the red-light district and the surrounding area seemingly at will, but unlike the other children, he wasn't skin and bones. His father must feel some burden toward him, since he gave Jesse's mother money each month. And somehow she heroically resisted using those funds to feed her opiate addiction. The sacrifice these two wayward parents made for Jesse kept

Evelyn from begging the woman to let her take him to the orphanage.

"Then I guess Jesse won't mind if I ladle out his portion to the others?" Caroline pulled the kettle closer to the back of the wagon and gave him a mischievous look. "Unless you want to taste it again to make sure you still don't like it?"

Jesse shook his head vehemently.

None of the others would refuse, even if they agreed about the taste. They were usually so hungry they'd eat slug soup without complaint.

Evelyn put Jesse down and passed out the food she wished she could distribute every day. But thankfully she could come once a week when Nicholas Lowe, her boss, and his wife, Lydia, her good friend, took over the orphanage on Saturday afternoons to give her and her parents a break.

She handed one of the older boys a loaf of bread to pass around while a few girls took the blankets off the wagon. The brightly colored quilts the Teaville Ladies Moral Society donated to the poor always made their sunshiny picnic spot feel a little homier.

While grabbing the stack of plates, Evelyn caught a glimpse of vivid purple off to her left.

Scott, a lanky youth of near twelve, was walking straight and tall beside a slightly taller woman. Her voluminous purple dress was trimmed with black lace at every imaginable seam and hem. Her free hand tightly gripped a delicate black fringed shawl around her neck. Her chin was tilted to the side and her eyes downcast, as if expecting a blow. However, Scott's bright face almost overpowered the sunlight. Evelyn couldn't help but respond with a matching smile.

How many weeks had Scott prayed for his mother to come and hear the Bible stories they discussed after lunch? Evelyn left the plates and walked forward to meet them. "Mrs. Jones, I'm pleased —"

"I've never been a Mrs. anything."

Evelyn winced at her mistake. "Miss . . . ?"

"I don't go by my old name either." Scott's mother's knuckles tightened on the shawl she held closed at her throat.

"What do you wish to be called?"

Her shrug was noncommittal. "Amy works."

"All right. May I have the children call you Miss Amy?"

"Don't know why you'd bother since they've heard me called worse." The woman's eyes practically dripped with defensiveness, as if she believed being turned away

27

was inevitable and figured she might as well do her worst to deserve being so.

Evelyn held out her hand, as if a wounded animal cowered in front of her. "Won't you join us for lunch?"

Scott's smile widened, and he squeezed his mother's arm.

The woman's stiffness disappeared, and then she looked at her son. "I suppose, since Scott wants me to. But I got nothing to give you for it."

"That's all right, we're not asking for anything."

Amy lifted her chin a little higher as she let Scott escort her closer to the wagon.

Evelyn exchanged glances with Caroline, who wordlessly handed the woman a plate. Caroline wouldn't be as excited as she was about this turn of events, since the housekeeper seemed uninterested in the Bible lessons, always busying herself with cleaning and repacking after everyone finished eating, but Evelyn couldn't help the tingle of excitement.

Lord, please let today's story help Amy. No wonder I didn't feel right about skipping the story of Rahab even though I thought it might hit too close to home. You knew Amy was going to be here!

With a bounce in her step, Evelyn distributed the last of the food, then finally got a plate of her own. She was pleased to see the children had left the spot beside Amy empty.

She lowered herself next to Scott's mother, trying to avoid crushing the wads of purple fabric ballooned around her. "I'm glad to have you, Amy."

The woman continued chewing whatever she'd taken a bite of and gave Evelyn a quick nod.

Sitting on his mother's other side, Scott leaned forward. "I told her Jesus would want her here, though she thought you wouldn't."

Amy stopped chewing and turned to glare at her son.

"We welcome anybody's parents to join us." Hopefully that would entice Amy to return and the other children to bring a parent who needed the food just as much as the Bible lesson. She gave Scott a little wink in response to his ear-to-ear grin.

Amy stared at her lap. "That's kind of you. More than kind."

"Yes, and if you have any other —"

"Boy, something smells good!" A man's voice boomed from behind them, startling Amy.

Evelyn looked over her shoulder to find the man who had followed her from the Hawk and Eagle earlier that week approaching. Her hand reached for her pocket pistol but stopped short since she never brought it with her on Saturdays. She'd never had men pester her amid a gaggle of children.

Amy began to stand and got tangled in her skirts. Evelyn struggled to rise as well, making it onto her feet about the same time as Amy did.

She reached out for Amy's arm. "Please stay."

"I have to get to work." Despite her food being mostly untouched and Scott frowning bigger than a catfish, Amy picked up her skirts and rushed off.

Evelyn closed her eyes and blew out her disappointment. Why hadn't God kept this man away?

3

Evelyn turned from the picnicking children to face the man who'd stalked her in the red-light district the day before yesterday. Funny how her heart wasn't palpitating with trepidation, but rather annoyance.

Her father often lamented she hadn't a healthy amount of fear, considering how often she visited the district with only Caroline as an occasional companion. But she understood the danger, especially after one incident where a man had followed her all the way home. If Daddy ever found out she now carried a pocket pistol, he'd forbid her to return to the district again.

But when women and children were in need, how could she not go?

Besides, most people knew who she and Caroline were and gave them a wide berth, and the man in front of her would have already had an opportunity to do something to her if he'd wanted to. "What do you want?"

The man took a step back and held out his hands. "I heard you say if anyone was looking for food —"

"Poor people! I meant poor people looking for food." What man in a three-piece business suit wandered around the factory section of town looking for food?

He winced, yet his eyes glistened with merriment.

The exasperation in her voice *had* sounded a mite funny. She relaxed her shoulders and forced herself not to shake her head at her outburst. Did this man really want something to eat? "Why would you be looking for food in this part of town?"

"I'm staying at a boardinghouse that doesn't provide lunch, and I smelled chicken." He threw a thumb over his shoulder toward the industrial building looming over them. "My office window is up there."

So he'd be perched right above them every Saturday?

But the factory looming over them was normally quiet on the weekend. "You're working today?"

"Yes." He sighed and stuck his hands in his pockets, but instead of looking displeased with his situation, he threw her a most attractive smile. And coupled with those intense blue eyes under that mop of dark blond hair — well, he was too good-looking by half.

"And your name is?" Not that she needed to know. What she really needed to know was how to keep him from returning, especially since his presence had driven Scott's mother away.

Did Amy know him? What if this man hadn't been worried for her safety in the district two days ago as he'd claimed? What if his smile had been meant to disarm her? But surely, with children here, he wouldn't be so bold as to —

"I'm sorry, I haven't introduced myself. I'm David Kingsman." He put the side of his index finger against the brim of his dark gray homburg hat. "Might I ask who you are?"

"Miss Wisely." She gestured toward Caroline on the blanket with little Jesse in her lap. "And this is Miss O'Conner."

"Pleased to meet you both." His eyes glanced at Caroline for only a second before returning to her. "Now that we're acquainted, may I join you?"

He probably expected his smile — which likely melted many a woman — to gain him a seat on her blanket.

"I'm afraid —"

"I'm willing to pay." He took out a money clip.

"We're not selling anything."

He stopped pulling out a dollar bill, and his expression turned hesitant. "But your food smells better than what I had at the hotel yesterday, and the company — I'm willing to bet — will be much more interesting." He gave the children that same lopsided smile he'd given her.

Men were usually scared away after seeing her embrace "dirty scamps," as one want-to-be suitor had called them. "I'm afraid —"

"That there are no green beans left." Caroline had somehow eased Jesse off her lap and stood. "But we have enough of everything else for a paying customer." She gave Evelyn a sharp look, likely signaling for her not to argue.

Whatever did Caroline want his money for? The richest man in Teaville was their patron; they didn't need this man's coin. Though she shouldn't be rude to him in front of the children. "I suppose twenty cents would do."

He didn't move, his eyes searching hers. "Unless you are truly opposed to my join-

34

ing you."

Evelyn gave a slight shake of her head. Now that Amy was gone, why should she fight Caroline over having him stay? "It's all right."

"Thank you." He walked over to take the plate Caroline had filled for him and put two dollars into the housekeeper's hand.

Two dollars! They weren't serving steak with all the trimmings.

And Caroline took it.

Evelyn narrowed her eyes at her friend, who didn't even look at her as she stepped around the silent children to return to her spot.

With plate in hand, Mr. Kingsman glanced about the two blankets, his lips scrunched to the side as if he couldn't decide where to sit. There wasn't enough room for them to sit together near Scott without looking cozy, so she pointed toward the opening on the other blanket. "I believe there's room for you over there."

The two girls sitting where she pointed squished closer, but more from wariness than trying to create space for him.

He smiled at the two girls, but they didn't smile back. "I think I'll sit here if you don't mind." He settled into Amy's empty spot, then tapped Scott's knee. "If that's all right with you, that is."

The boy shrugged and plopped another piece of bread into his mouth.

Theodore, a skinny boy she'd only met last week, ogled Mr. Kingsman's shiny pocket watch as the man took a bite of chicken and closed his eyes as if he too were underfed. Did this man not realize he oozed wealth? Not that he was a dandy by any means, just very nicely dressed. His gray three-piece wool suit, fine blue silk tie, and minutely patterned vest were a far cry from the ill-fitting clothes the children wore, Caroline's black dress and white apron, and Evelyn's work dress. Hopefully none of the children were considering helping their mothers gain a little extra money by lifting something off him.

Mr. Kingsman took off his hat and settled it on his bent right knee. He lifted his spoon and then glanced around at the silent crew. "Don't let my presence spoil your conversation." He tried the soup and smiled. "No wonder you come to Miss Wisely and Miss O'Conner to get lunch. This is delicious."

Jesse's face screwed up so comically at someone enjoying split peas that Evelyn couldn't stop the little snort of laughter that escaped.

Mr. Kingsman looked at her, eyebrows

raised in question.

Evelyn turned back to the wagon to add another dollop of potatoes to her plate. Why had his look made her squirm? A snort wasn't anything to blush over.

She didn't bother to even look at the vacant spot next to him and crossed over to sit with the two girls on the other blanket.

The children weren't normally talkative while they filled their shriveled stomachs, but silence now reigned deafeningly. Mr. Kingsman tried to make small talk with the children — though hardly any of them responded.

He turned to Theodore, who'd finished his entire meal before Evelyn had even sat. "What's your name, young man?"

"Theo."

"What do you have there?" He pointed to the tarnished watch hanging from his belt on a bit of twine.

The boy clasped his hand around it, hiding it from view. "Just my grandfather's pocket watch. Nothing fancy like yours."

"May I see it?" David took a monogrammed handkerchief from his pocket, wiped his fingers, and held out his hand for the watch.

The boy untangled it, then set it on his open palm as if afraid it might break.

Mr. Kingsman flipped the cover open, which was indeed in danger of falling off since its hinge was broken. He studied it with narrowed eyes, then glanced at his own watch. "Good. I was hoping mine wasn't losing time. This one's so troublesome; the old ones are always so much more reliable." He handed Theodore's watch back. "I wish I had my grandfather's — that's for certain."

He smiled and winked at the boy, then looked over at Alexandria across the blanket. The girl was near six yet still sucked her thumb unless she was occupied with eating, but she'd abandoned her food the moment he'd arrived. "What's your name?"

She shrugged, but her older sister Jocelyn answered for her. "She's Alexandria. Alex for short."

"Nice to meet you, Alexandria. You remind me of a beautiful woman who came to talk to my church a few years ago — her name was Scholastica. She had the prettiest smile. I wonder if you do too?"

Jocelyn smacked her sister's hand from her mouth. "The man wants you to smile for him, Alex. He wants to see if you're pretty enough."

Mr. Kingsman's eyes widened and Evelyn stiffened. It was always so unnerving how these children could take things the wrong way — in ways she wouldn't have thought of herself, even at the age of seven and twenty.

"Oh no." Mr. Kingsman shook his head. "You don't smile unless you want to, Alex. No man should make you do anything you don't want to do, all right?"

Jocelyn rolled her eyes. "I don't know where you're from, mister, but that ain't the way things go around here." She took a bite of her roll and repositioned her dirty skirt around her long, thin legs.

Alexandria gave Mr. Kingsman a shy smile before sticking her thumb back in her mouth.

"All right, children." Evelyn wiped her hands, hoping they'd pay attention to her Bible story despite Mr. Kingsman showing no indication of leaving. "Let's continue reading about the Israelites fighting for their Promised Land, shall we?"

The children sat quietly enough, but after she told the story and started asking questions, only Scott seemed to have paid any attention. Caroline passed out the peppermint sticks they brought to entice the children to stay through the lesson, and then they all quickly scrambled away.

Without asking any of his customary questions, Scott picked up little Jesse and, with a heaviness in his step, returned to the red-light district.

She sighed and gathered the remaining plates and added them to Caroline's pile in the wagon.

"I hope you aren't too irritated with me." Mr. Kingsman stopped beside her, rotating his hat in his hands, crushing its brim. "I didn't know the woman wouldn't stay."

"It's the first time she dared come." Evelyn swallowed her disappointment. The man had behaved gallantly among their uncouth little crowd. His presence hadn't been unpleasant. "Her son's been praying she'd come for weeks now."

"I see. What's your connection to these children?"

"No connection, just the hope that with a modicum of guidance, they'll choose to leave their parents' world before it's too late."

"Do you do more than this Bible story lunch thing?"

She turned to look at him. Had she noted some censure in his voice? "It's all I have the time and provision for at the moment. I help run the orphanage for the children who were once more needy than these." Why hadn't he left yet? Was the chicken the real reason he'd come, or was it her?

Because if he was interested in her, he might as well give up now. "I know we had extra today, but that's not always the case. It would be best if you pack your lunch next time, so —"

"He gave us two dollars." Caroline stopped folding one of the blankets to look at her pointedly. "He paid for everyone's meal."

"But we don't need charity."

"We don't?" Caroline frowned at her as if she'd said they weren't in need of oxygen.

"We have a benefactor."

"Who could use freed-up funds for something else worthwhile."

If she read her friend's look right, Caroline was seconds away from lecturing her in front of this man. And likely for good reason.

But there was a reason he shouldn't return, a very good one. "Thank you, Mr. Kingsman, for the money. But truthfully . . ." She stopped and forced herself to look into his mesmerizing eyes. Were there actual purple hues in those dark blue irises? She dropped her gaze the second she realized she was staring and he was smiling. "The thing is, I want Amy to return, and unfortunately, your presence drove her away. My gut says you've heard plenty of

Bible stories, but I bet she's not heard a one."

"I understand, Miss Wisely. Thank you for your hospitality." He tapped his finger against the brim of his hat, his smile a little lackluster. "Give my compliments to your cook." And then he was gone.

Caroline tsked once he got out of earshot. "That man could have helped these children. Did you not see how Theodore looked at him after they talked about his watch? I don't know who this Mr. Kingsman is, but when has any man other than Mr. Lowe given these boys some decent attention?"

"But what about Scott's mother?" How could Caroline ignore that need?

"That's one person who might not be helped, but what about the others? Mr. Kingsman could show these boys some good manners as long as he was willing to come. Scott's mother could have returned later." Caroline picked up a stray spoon off the ground. "Mr. Kingsman didn't come here for you, you know."

Evelyn halted on her way to the wagon seat. "What does that mean? And how would you know that anyway?"

She shrugged. "It just means every time a single man comes near you, you act as if he'll fall in love with you if you so much as talk to him — even if he's not looking at you with any interest."

Her cheeks heated. Was she turning as vain as that sounded? No, her response to new men was a safety measure. She'd had to tell one too many that she would never be interested in his court, and she was loath to do it again.

She busied herself with wiping her hands with a handkerchief. "I'm obviously not so beautiful or cultured that I'd believe a man falling in love with me was inevitable, but men . . . well, they complicate things." More than Caroline might ever know.

4

Taking one last look at Scott and his hopeful eyes, Evelyn knocked on the door to his mother's surprisingly quaint little cottage. It had been only three days since Mr. Kingsman had scared Amy away, and Scott had been to the mansion twice already to ask her to talk to his mother.

Amy opened the door with a scowl. Her frown disappeared for a second as she took in her visitor but returned as she stepped outside. "What am I supposed to do for you?" Amy swept her dark unbrushed hair off her shoulder, seemingly not the least bit embarrassed by still being in her nightclothes at nearly ten in the morning.

Evelyn gave Amy a smile. "I wanted you to know I was glad to see you Saturday. Mr. Kingsman doesn't plan on returning, so I hope —"

"Scott." Amy looked past Evelyn's shoulder toward her son. "Go get us more wood."

He squirmed in place for a moment, but after giving Evelyn a quick pleading look, he pivoted and ran off.

"Now look." Amy leaned casually against her doorjamb and crossed her arms, more the stance of a rebellious youth than a lady. "I know you're putting all this God talk into my son's head, and maybe it'll do him some good, but I don't need you begging me to come listen to your Bible telling too."

Evelyn's lips twitched. That wasn't the only reason she wanted her to join them. "I'd be happy just to have you come eat, if you'd like. Your son wants more time with you."

"Well, I do what I can . . . sometimes." She shrugged. "I went with him on Saturday, didn't I?"

"Is there a reason you don't want to return?"

"Frankly, I'm not interested in spiritual things. And I'm afraid Scott thinks that if I listen to some preaching, I'll be able to give him the life he wants. But that ain't going to happen."

"I know how uncomfortable hearing God's Word can be sometimes, but I —"

"Ma'am, I know what you think of me. Frankly, I don't have a high opinion of myself either." She straightened and took a step back into her home. "So I'm not eager to hear what your God thinks of me too — not when I can't do nothing about it."

"But He offers a way out."

She raised an eyebrow. "Show me one former prostitute getting along in good society, and I might believe you."

The door's slam ended the conversation.

Well, that hadn't gone well. She stared at Amy's door for a minute, but she couldn't think of anything to say that would make Amy thankful she'd answered her door a second time.

With a sigh, Evelyn turned away. What hope could she offer Amy in regard to joining good society? Queenie was a well-known former prostitute in Teaville, but she still lived in a small shack on the edge of the district. Despite the woman's adherence to Christianity and tireless hours serving the hurting, her past profession marked her unfit for good society.

Lydia and Nicholas Lowe's housekeeper was a former child prostitute who had escaped, but anyone who knew had been sworn to secrecy, since she'd be shunned if her history came to light.

If only she had a success story to share — but she knew of none.

"Miss Wisely!" Scott came running out

from behind a nearby house, no wood in his hands. "Is she going to come?"

"I'm afraid not."

His face drooped, and the light in his green eyes disappeared.

She couldn't help but pull him into a side hug. "We'll keep praying, all right?" She felt him shrug against her, and after a few seconds, she let him pull away. "Let's not give up hope. I'll think some more on how to help your mother, and you be the best boy you can be. God will honor that."

He nodded slightly.

"So go get some wood, and I'll go see Mr. Lowe." He'd helped a few women out of the red-light district; perhaps she could convince him to try again. But what could he do for Amy if she didn't want to fight for a way out?

Evelyn consulted her timepiece. Before heading back to the orphanage, she could drop by the Lowes' to see if her best friend's husband was at home.

She didn't exactly know what she hoped Nicholas could do, but if anyone could help her figure something out, it would be him. And if he agreed to help, she'd not have to worry about the finances.

With a swiftness in her step, she chugged along the sidewalks and skirted passersby on her way to the upscale part of town. Her friend's gorgeous Queen Anne house sat across from the new library. If she'd had more time, she would have checked to see if there were any new books the children might enjoy, but she couldn't leave her parents longer than necessary.

Evelyn knocked on her friend's beautifully carved front door, closed her eyes, and inhaled. Lydia had planted even more roses this year, and the scent of their yard was spectacular. Oh, to have the money to not only create a fence out of roses, but to have them imported from Europe.

The door opened many minutes later, and the Lowes' young butler, a boy who'd grown too old to stay at the orphanage, waved her in. "I'm so sorry, Miss Wisely. I was clear across the house."

"I assure you, it is no hardship to stand out here with the last of the roses, Mr. Cleghorn."

Franklin rolled his eyes. "You don't have to call me Mr. Cleghorn."

She tugged on his lapel as she walked by. "Yes, I do. It befits your new vocation."

"Still feels funny."

She tugged off her gloves and handed them along with her hat to Franklin. A tittering of laughter sounded somewhere in the house, but it didn't sound like little Isabelle Lowe's giggles and it certainly wasn't Lydia's laugh. "Is Mr. Lowe in?"

"He's expected any minute. Mrs. Lowe's in the dining room, I believe."

"Thank you."

The laugh sounded again, and she couldn't help but smile at the gaiety. Who did Lydia have over? Whoever it was sounded as if she might help brighten Lydia's day. With newly walking Isabelle getting into everything and Lydia sick with her newest pregnancy — despite being six months along — she'd been having a rough time of it.

Evelyn headed for the dining room and lost her smile the second she got a glimpse of the occupants through the open doorway.

Mr. Kingsman was leaning against the wall, grinning at Lydia's housekeeper, Sadie.

Evelyn hesitated beside the doorjamb. She should have known such a smile hadn't been anything special for her, but rather a practiced one for wooing the ladies. It was indeed too perfect to be real.

"Are you sure they didn't name these after you?" Mr. Kingsman winked, then popped the last bit of white candy into his mouth. He closed his eyes and groaned.

"Oh stop — divinity's good, but not that

good." Sadie shook her head as she finished wiping down the dining room table, a light blush staining her cheeks. "I found the recipe in the *New York Times* — had nothing to do with me."

Sadie was right; her divinity fudge wasn't nearly as good as Mr. Kingsman's groans indicated. The young housekeeper had taken up candy making since she'd come to work here, sending batches to the orphanage every Saturday, determined that the children would have sweets despite Nicholas's declaring orphans didn't need candy — at least not weekly.

Was Mr. Kingsman interested in the Lowes' seventeen-year-old housekeeper? He was likely in his midtwenties, so Sadie wouldn't be considered too young to court, considering most wife-seeking bachelors started turning up their noses when a woman hit twenty-three or twenty-four. But what if he learned Sadie had been a child prostitute Lydia rescued from the red-light district?

But Mr. Kingsman hadn't seemed bothered at the prospect of eating lunch with Scott's mother, and Amy had clearly been dressed as a woman of ill repute.

Perhaps Caroline was right. She was intent on thinking ill of him for no good reason.

But if she let herself think too well of him, she might become as taken with his smile as Sadie seemed to be.

Mr. Kingsman snatched another little white square from the sideboard. "The *New York Times,* you say? Could I get a copy of the recipe?"

"Of course, I'll go get it for you." She smiled at him and he smiled back.

Evelyn spun on her heel and left the room, hoping they hadn't seen her.

She slowed to keep her footfalls from drawing attention and stopped in front of a mirror, placing a hand on her cheek where the pox scarring was most noticeable. She should be happy she was only decent-looking and too old to be of much interest anymore. So why had she left before bidding Sadie good morning? Jealousy?

Surely not. She was not allowed to be jealous over some man she'd only met twice. And definitely not because he simply smiled at someone else.

The heavy scent of roses was perhaps too thick around this place, and her brain was muddied up.

Hopefully he wasn't going to get too chummy with Nicholas. A handsome, single friend of Lydia's husband would inevitably be seen as the next best person to pair her up with.

Of course Lydia only wanted her to find the same happiness she had, but no matter how nice Mr. Kingsman might be, she would resist his charm.

5

"Lyd!" Evelyn called as she took the stairs up to the nursery. Hopefully her friend's housekeeper's sweet disposition and divinity candy had kept Mr. Kingsman from noticing how she'd fled.

Evelyn peeked into the nursery, but no one was there.

Though Lydia could afford a nanny, a governess, and whatever servants rich people employed to keep children out of sight and mind, Lydia had only employed a maid who would watch Isabelle whenever Lydia and her husband spent time together on the town or with guests.

Would Isabelle be with her mother when there was a guest downstairs? No, more likely the maid had taken her for a walk or something. Evelyn turned around to head for Lydia's sitting room. "Lydia?"

Before she got there, her friend popped out into the hallway with a hairpin in her hand. "I'm sorry I wasn't downstairs to greet you, but I got" — she cringed — "sick in front of a guest, and my hair . . . Oh, it's too embarrassing." She shoved her pin into her beautiful dark hair behind the pouf she'd created at the crown of her head and patted her hands against her coiffure. "Do I look all right?"

"You're as pretty as ever." Except for her having no color in her cheeks and purple smudges under almost-transparent light blue eyes, but she wouldn't tell her that.

"You're such a dear." Lydia slipped under Evelyn's arm to give her a hug. "I just looked at myself in the mirror, so I know you're lying."

Lydia's huge stomach made it difficult for Evelyn to give her friend a good squeeze. Not that it wasn't always a bit awkward to hug her friends, since most were at least a half foot shorter.

Lydia took a step back, locked an arm around Evelyn's, and pulled her toward the steps. "I have a guest I'm eager for you to meet."

"If you're talking about the man downstairs eating a plateful of candy as if he's never tasted sugar before, I've met him."

She pulled up short. "You have?"

"I came across Mr. Kingsman in the

district last week. Wanted to make sure I made it out safely."

"And what was your impression?"

That first day, Saturday, or ten minutes ago? They'd been far, far different reactions. Strangely spontaneous reactions to a man she'd been around for less than an hour all together.

"Well?" Lydia's intentions weren't at all hidden by her nonchalant tone of voice.

Evelyn pinched the bridge of her nose but quickly pretended to have an itch to hide the frustrated gesture. Which birthday would have to slip by before the matchmakers gave up?

If she answered Lydia with anything even remotely sounding like she didn't think well of Mr. Kingsman, her friend would know something was wrong. And it wasn't that she thought ill of him, but she didn't want Lydia thinking she thought too well of him either, lest she get the wrong idea. "I don't know him well enough to have reached any conclusions, but the fact that he's your guest speaks well for him."

Lydia shook her head at her. "You can't tell me you haven't noticed what he *looks* like."

"Well, he has a mesmerizing smile." Which he evidently flashed at every living, breathing woman. "And his eyes are striking, but I thought Sebastian Little's eyes were striking too, and you know what a snake he was."

Lydia winced and closed her eyes, despite taking another step down.

Oh, why had she brought up his name? Making her friend feel badly about her former suitor to discourage her from match-making was a rotten thing to do. And it wasn't as if Sebastian had completely duped her, for Lydia and Nicholas had both gone through a lot to expose the shady lawyer and his corrupt mayor father. Yet despite saving the town from the Littles' crooked-ness by getting them convicted and behind bars, Lydia still questioned her discernment when it came to others.

Evelyn shrugged when she reached the bottom of the staircase. "But I'm sure there's a reason besides his features for your entertaining Mr. Kingsman."

"Yes, well." Lydia blew out a breath as if abandoning the idea of stirring up a romance between her guest and her friend.

Good.

Lydia headed across the foyer. "Nicholas met with him earlier about some lumber deal and sent him here for lunch. He's evidently new in town and was wondering where to get something good to eat."

They stepped into the dining room, and Lydia called to her guest with a lilt in her voice as well as a pretty grin lighting her face.

Evidently this man's smile could charm away all vestiges of pregnancy sickness too.

"Why didn't you tell me you'd already met Miss Wisely?" Lydia walked toward Mr. Kingsman with her hand trailing behind her, gesturing toward Evelyn.

They'd been talking about her?

"I assure you, Mrs. Lowe, she is not a woman I'd forget. But I didn't know her Christian name, which is how you referred to her."

Before Evelyn realized it, Mr. Kingsman had taken her hand and pressed his lips to her knuckles. What kind of man did that anymore? And why on earth did the gesture make her feel like melted butter?

He dropped her hand and gave her that smile. And, boy, did it work — despite her now knowing how he plied it on everyone. Heaven help her, she needed a fan. Was a pair of beautiful eyes and a cheeky smile all that was needed to keep her discombobulated? Surely not. She'd never had trouble directing men's attention away from her before.

What she needed was to put some space

between her and his distracting charm. She walked over to the sideboard. "I see Sadie made candy."

"Try that white stuff there." Mr. Kingsman pointed to the divinity. "It's fit for an angel."

Surely he hadn't just called her an angel, for she hadn't acted much like one in his presence. If only new men never came to Teaville — then she'd never have to get through those initial months where she had to make certain to do nothing that might encourage them to pursue her.

Even if Caroline was right about her overdoing the iciness, it saved everyone trouble.

She filled two plates, then handed one to Lydia.

Her friend held up a hand. "I can't." She appeared ill just looking at the treats.

"I'm sorry." How could she have forgotten about Lydia's sickness in the space of a minute?

Lydia cringed as she turned to look at Mr. Kingsman. "I believe I need to apologize."

"No need to be sorry, Mrs. Lowe. If I'd known what was wrong, I would have tried to help keep . . . things from getting so . . . messy."

"Oh." Lydia clamped a hand onto her

mouth. "I'm mortified. I'm very sorry —"

"Again, don't apologize. Your maid took care of things."

Lydia sank into a chair and covered her eyes while pinching the bridge of her nose.

"Here, let me get you something to drink." He turned for the sideboard but then pivoted sharply. "Unless that's not a good idea."

"Probably not."

"Is it all right if I have something to drink? I don't want to drink or eat in front of you if that will make you suffer in any way."

Evelyn looked at the piece of candy she'd just crunched into and stopped chewing.

"I think I'll be all right."

Evelyn set down her plate and scurried to Lydia's chair. What kind of friend was she that a stranger was being more sensitive than she was?

His smile hadn't just mesmerized her, it had confounded her brain. "Can I get you something from the medicine cabinet? Sugared ginger, perhaps?"

"No, I'm fine. No need to worry about me." She looked up at Evelyn for a second and actually winked. "But why don't you tell us more about yourself, Mr. Kingsman?"

Unless Mr. Kingsman was dense, he

would likely catch on to what Lydia was trying to do.

And why would Lydia think a man like him would want to be paired with a woman like her anyway? Evidently, he only need look at a woman and she turned into a pile of ridiculousness.

She shook her head a little. She was twenty-seven, not eighteen. She could wind herself up tight enough to prevent his smile from befuddling her thinking, to keep from reliving how the brush of his lips against her hand had made her want to melt into the carpet.

"Nothing much to tell." Mr. Kingsman swept a chair out from under the dining table and slid into it as if it were a lounge chair. "I work with my father, who sent me here to deal with the A. K. Glass Factory. He obtained it three years ago and now wants me to . . . make sure we're getting our money's worth from the investment. I'll head back to Kansas City afterward."

There, he wasn't a permanent resident. Lydia's matchmaking hopes would be dashed.

"I bet Evelyn hasn't told you much about herself, has she? She's a dear and too modest by half."

Evelyn held in a groan. If only Lydia knew

60

that Caroline accusing her of vanity was closer to the mark. But truly, she wasn't modest or vain, just . . . cautious.

Why did you have to give him those eyes and that smile? Quite unfair, actually. Maybe I should take up matchmaking myself. Maybe he'd do for Caroline. She seemed quite defensive of him.

"My friend here is an important part of our moral society." Lydia patted Evelyn's hand, then turned to see Mr. Kingsman better. "She helps us women see true needs and meet them with humbleness and sincerity. Has no qualms about getting her hands dirty or working with hard cases, and she has single-handedly turned some of our hardest orphans into the sweetest cuddlers. She's —"

"Please." Evelyn placed her hand against the heat in her cheek. "You'll make him think I'm a saint."

Lydia chuckled. "Because you are."

Oh, how she was not. As he'd likely already divined after how she'd treated him at Saturday's lunch gathering. The fire in her cheeks quickly fled as if doused by a thousand waterfalls, and she wished for something to fiddle with. She turned to stare out the window, focusing on a peach rose smashed against the pane.

"I can see compliments confuse the lady." Mr. Kingsman's voice even sounded as if it contained a smile. "At one point she blushes, another she pales."

Was she always this easy to read, or was Mr. Kingsman watching her that intently? The thought that he could see something so subtle made her cheeks heat again.

She needed to stop with this blushing nonsense and get his focus off of her. "Actually, if you want to get to know a saint, that would be Miss O'Conner, whom you met on Saturday. She has selflessly given up her life for others. I think you'd like her."

Lydia turned to her with a quizzical look.

She shrugged. Why must she be the only one pushed toward eligible men?

A child's cry quickly escalated from somewhere in the house.

"Excuse me, that's a hurt cry." Lydia pushed herself out of her chair, skimming Evelyn's shoulder as she passed. "I'll be back."

Mr. Kingsman tried to stand but didn't make it an inch out of his seat before Lydia disappeared through the doorway. He resettled himself in his chair with a content expression.

Evelyn folded her hands in her lap. "Did you hear when Mr. Lowe was —"

"I've been wondering about you," he said at the same time.

"Why?" She hadn't exactly been congenial. Her behavior around single men was likely as awkward as Caroline considered it. But after having to explain to several bachelors that her only goal in life was to help orphans, saving any future men the discomfort that discussion caused seemed to be the right thing to do.

But didn't Mr. Kingsman say he was returning to Kansas City? If so, there was no danger of him wanting to get involved with her.

"After how we first met?" He sat back a little. "How could I not be intrigued?"

"I suppose it's not every day you see someone like me traipsing about a red-light district."

"Honestly, I wouldn't know. That's the first time I'd ever found myself in one. However, you definitely aren't the kind of woman I'd envision in such a place."

"I suppose not." How could she bring up Kansas City again to be certain he wasn't staying? "So you never went to a similar place in Kansas City?"

He frowned. "I do hope, Miss Wisely, that you don't think every man frequents such places."

"I'm sorry. I didn't mean to insinuate you do, but you would be surprised and perhaps saddened by the men I've seen there. I just imagined Kansas City's red-light district would be huge."

"I know where it is, but I've never gone. I have plenty enough trouble at home. I don't need to add more to myself."

"I'm sorry your home life isn't what you'd like it to be. Are you married? Do you have many children?" If he was married and flirting with Sadie, it'd be all she could do to sit and talk with him any longer.

He only smiled and shook his head. "No. Just me and my father."

"Oh." Well, at least he wasn't a married flirt. "How long until you return?"

"I hope to return home in two months, but realistically three."

Three months? She took a deep breath and settled back against her seat. No one's heart would be in danger whatsoever. "I hope things go well enough at A. K. Glass that you can return in two. I actually didn't know it had changed owners."

"The owner owed my father, and since the man had no cash, it was all he had to settle the debt. The former management has run it ever since."

The front door opened and shut, and a

man's purposeful stride sounded on the wooden planks. Nicholas appeared in the doorway soon after. He was taller and leaner compared with Mr. Kingsman's stocky build, and she'd always considered Nicholas's hazel eyes to be uncommonly attention-getting — until Mr. Kingsman's dark blues showed up, anyway.

Nicholas put a hand through his wavy dark hair. "Ah, Mr. Kingsman. Ev— Miss Wisely, I didn't know you'd be here. Did Lydia invite you to lunch?" He flipped open his pocket watch, then looked at Mr. Kingsman. "I did inform you lunch wasn't until noon, yes?"

"You did, but I didn't want to be late."

If there was a man who could lose his heart through his stomach, it seemed Mr. Kingsman was such a man. She'd make sure never to cook for him.

"I'm not here for lunch." Evelyn stood. "I have to return to the orphanage, but I wanted to ask you something."

"Certainly." He backstepped out into the hallway, glanced toward the stairs, and then came back in. "Is Lydia not here?"

"She went to check on Isabelle and hasn't yet returned."

"All right." Nicholas went to the sideboard and grabbed some divinity. "What did you

65

want to ask?"

She glanced at Mr. Kingsman. He shouldn't be too surprised about what she was going to ask after seeing her in the red-light district. Hopefully he'd not add a negative voice to the conversation. "I wanted to discuss the possibility of you trying to help prostitutes escape the district again."

He stopped chewing for a second, then swallowed. "You know how disastrously that went for me."

He turned to Mr. Kingsman. "I tried to help some women out of the district by allowing them to work at my mansion until we found them a safe place to go, but when the town discovered them, I was accused of running a brothel. That's why we're focusing on the children now."

It had been quite the mess three years ago, but they couldn't let one failure keep them from trying again. "But because of those children, maybe we should start thinking of ways to help the women they're connected to."

"I think she's right." Lydia came in with one-year-old Isabelle on her hip, the little girl's riotous dark curls framing her chubby face. "People have not opposed our work with the children as much as we thought, and none of the disasters the townsfolk

66

predicted have befallen us, so maybe it's time to try again."

Nicholas swiped his hands on a napkin, shaking his head a bit. "I know your moral-society ladies and many in our congregation are coming around — and I'm glad of that — but I'm not sure we'd have a lot of the townsmen on board. Many are entrenched in the district's darkness or have friends who are. They'll not be happy with us messing with their vices, and there's no way I could do so in secret again. And secrecy is vital to getting the women into some kind of normal life."

"But we could try to think of something, couldn't we? At least for the women who are interested?" Lydia turned to Evelyn. "Who's interested?"

She shrugged a shoulder. "Actually, none I know of, but one of my Saturday boys' mother came to lunch for a little bit. I talked to her this morning, but she wasn't willing to return for lunch again. Said she didn't want to do anything that made her feel guilty about her life since she has no way of escape."

"And she wants to escape?"

"She didn't say so exactly, but if she knew there was a way . . ."

Nicholas's jaw was clamped so tightly, he

67

had to be forcing himself not to say no.

What could she ask him to do that he hadn't already tried years ago? "Maybe we could, um . . . create some kind of women's home inside the district? No one would complain about former prostitutes living inside the district."

Nicholas ran a hand through his hair. "Queenie already takes in women."

"They need more than a place to bandage their wounds and leave as soon as they're healed. Besides, Queenie only has two beds. No one can stay long. Maybe we could set up a building where they could stay until they felt confident enough to go out in the world."

"And where will they go where they'll be accepted?" Nicholas put a hand against his chin and rubbed against the dark stubble. "That's been the crux of the problem all along."

"I don't know. Perhaps we need to teach them a vocation. Then they could go anywhere with their new skills."

Mr. Kingsman cleared his throat. "There are housemaid positions available in innumerable towns. Cleaning doesn't require an education of any sort."

The fact that he hadn't scoffed at them this entire conversation had been surprising enough, but he was actually attempting to offer ideas?

She shook her head. "Housemaids are paid so little. I'm not sure we could convince them to give up their way of life — which is lucrative for many of them, even if it is terrible — to know nothing but the drudgery of housework when they will have no family or friends to support them, and no one to help with their children. But if they could run a bakery, millinery, or seamstress shop — those positions might convince them they could be free and happy, even if they made less. And of course, they'd live longer, happier lives."

Isabelle toddled to Nicholas, and he swooped her up. "I'm afraid I'm not willing to do anything by myself again. Having no community support was hard enough when I was single, but now . . ." He stopped, closed his eyes, and sighed. "If you could gain the support of two other large business owners — with more than just a promise not to talk badly about our efforts, but to support with actual assets. If you could do that . . . I'll consider it."

She tried not to deflate. If Nicholas wasn't one-hundred-percent behind her idea, how was she going to convince anyone else in this town to help?

6

"Come on in, Mr. Black. I'm happy to see you." David got up from his seat and gestured for Mr. Lowe's secretary to take a chair. The manila envelope the man carried was a good sign things might be looking up for A. K. Glass. "Is that the contract?"

"Indeed it is, sir." Mr. Black handed him the envelope but didn't take a seat.

Since the thin man with a nose too big for his face sported a smile, that should mean the contract inside held good news. "Thank you for delivering this to me personally." David broke the seal and pulled out several pages. "May I ask you something before you leave?"

"Of course."

"Do you do the hiring for Mr. Lowe?"

The man leaned on the back of the chair nearest him. "Mr. Lowe personally hires everyone, from his managers to his house-maids, but I often winnow the applicants for him."

"I'm needing someone to take over the management of this place. Have there been any men looking to hire on as management that Mr. Lowe thought qualified but passed over for some reason?"

"I might be biased, but I'm not sure I'd hire Mr. Lowe's rejects. He's quite fastidious."

"I'm afraid I can't afford to be as picky." Not if he wanted to leave Teaville any time soon. "What about someone he debated over but lacked experience or education?"

Mr. Black looked off into space somewhere behind David's desk for a moment before shaking his head. "I can't think of anyone. I'll let you know if I do, but why not ask Mr. Lowe?"

"I did. I just thought if you helped with the hiring you might remember someone he'd forgotten."

"Sorry, but no."

"What about Miss Wisely?"

Mr. Black blinked several times. "I know there are some who want to see women get a fairer shake in life, but to hire one on as manager of a glass plant when she's done nothing but —"

David interrupted him with a laugh. "Pardon me, but my brain had jumped to another topic entirely, and I expected you to read my mind. I meant, what do you know of Miss Wisely?"

Mr. Black widened his eyes, but then smiled. "Oh, well, she's the only child of Freewill Church's former pastor. The family works at Mr. Lowe's orphanage now."

"Anything more . . . personal about her?"

Mr. Black closed his eyes as if trying to locate information within a mental filing cabinet. "She's generally thought of as a sweet girl. Some question her involvement with the red-light district's children and her solitary trips into the area, but those tend to be people who have things to hide." Mr. Black shrugged. "Other than that, she seems a touch icy."

"Icy? I would've said . . . *wary."*

"Oh? The men I know who've attempted to court her have come away describing her as quite cool." He crossed his ankles. "So you're wanting to pursue her yourself?"

"Uh . . . no." He'd only met her three times. Of course, an intriguing woman was always a potential helpmate, but not just any woman could join the Kingsman family.

So why had he asked Mr. Black about her anyway? He pulled at the hair at the nape of his neck. "I met her under unusual circumstances and was curious. So she's only icy to men who show interest?"

The secretary paused for a second, looking off into space yet again. "That's likely a fair assessment. I only know of two men who've tried to court her, though they never had a chance. They were turned down flat."

"Only two?" How could a woman as captivating as Miss Wisely only garner the interest of a couple men?

"Yes. A woman that tall can be intimidating, I suppose."

"She might be taller than most women, but she doesn't tower over everybody."

"Truthfully, I don't know much about her beyond what I hear. But if you're looking to pursue her, perhaps the hearsay will help you figure out how to approach her."

He doubted any approach would work. She was likely older than he was and had obviously not succumbed to his charm. Not that he was seriously thinking about it. "Would you mind not mentioning this conversation to anyone? I don't want to make things awkward for anybody. I mean, it's unlikely I'll be around long enough to court a woman anyway."

"All right." Mr. Black shrugged, then pointed to the contract on the desk. "Did you want me to wait until you've read that before I leave?"

Oh yes, the contract.

After a quick glance through the first page, it looked as if the terms were exactly as discussed. If they were, he might be tempted to holler *Hallelujah*. Saving five percent might not seem like a fantastic deal, but when a plant crated and shipped thousands of glass bottles every month, five percent off lumber would raise his profits quite nicely. "I won't keep you. If everything's as we discussed, I'll sign and return it through a courier tomorrow. If not, I'll come by to schedule a meeting to renegotiate."

"Very well, sir." Mr. Black dismissed himself with a nod.

David sank into the chair and stared blindly at the paper, a little worried he'd find a problem within one of the contract's terms that would keep him from signing the bottom line, possibly creating an impasse with Mr. Lowe. He needed this factory running within budget quickly, and then he needed a promise of profit on the horizon. Hopefully this contract would be the beginning of an avalanche of breakthroughs. His father would soon hear how he'd not sold the factory as instructed, and the only way to keep the man from traipsing down here in a lather would be to have this factory well on its way to selling for a whole lot more than his father expected.

"May I see Mr. Kingsman?"

Had that been the voice of a tall angel?

He'd been stewing over how he'd mucked up the Saturday lunch thing with Miss Wisely but hadn't figured out what to do to make up for disappointing her. He'd thought he would have plenty of time to figure out something since he'd considered it unlikely their paths would cross often. But then paperwork had stolen all of his brain power — as it should have. He was here to make the best business deal he'd ever made, not interrogate pretty ladies.

What did he really need to know about her anyway?

At least she hadn't acted as if she hated him at Lowe's yesterday.

"Is he expecting you?" The man who took care of the factory's invoices sounded unreasonably irritated. He might become even more irritated when his boss gave him a lecture on how to treat people who dropped in. She could've been a customer.

"No, but I was hoping to see him if he's available. If not, I'd like to schedule a meeting."

"I'm not his personal secretary."

"Well then, could you point me to the

man I should ask?"

"He doesn't work here anymore."

"I see . . ."

David got up and opened the door wide. "Miss Wisely, I believe I'm the right man to ask, and I have time. Please come in."

She picked up a fancy little basket from Mr. Jarvis's desk and came toward him, giving him a look that was almost . . . admiring? What had he done to deserve that?

She entered his office, and he quickly glanced at his reflection in the office door's window. He looked about normal. He shut the door and gestured for her to sit. "What might I do for you today?"

She sat and then set the basket beside her before artfully arranging her skirt about her legs. The dresses he'd seen her in previously had reminded him of his late aunt's gardening clothes. But this yellow dress with black dots and wide black trim, though simple, accentuated her dark hair topped with a fashionable straw hat. She looked like summer. It was indeed very warm for the end of September.

"You told me the other day that you and your father are in business together?"

He frowned. He'd rather discuss anything except business with her. He was fed up to his ears with business. "Yes, we're Kingsman & Son. We own a few factories and . . ." It was best to not let her know exactly how wealthy he was. That information always seemed to turn a woman's smile artificially sweet, and he'd sort of enjoyed the flash of suspicion in Miss Wisely's eyes the last three times they'd met.

When was the last time an eligible woman hadn't fawned over him? "Let's just say, we have enough work to keep ourselves busy."

She fiddled with how her skirt lay across her knees. "I know you heard my proposal to Mr. Lowe yesterday, so I'd like you to be the first businessman in the area given the opportunity to help Teaville get a women's home. I saw your genuine interest in the children this past Saturday. Few men would have been so at ease in such a group. It seems you have a heart for the downtrodden — and therefore, I can't think of anyone better to be my first supporter." She flashed him a big gooey sort of smile.

He rubbed his eye. "In Kingsman & Son, the emphasis is more on *Kingsman* than *Son*. I might be a businessman, but it's my father's dreams and ambitions that run the show, and I'm afraid he would not support a women's home."

And that gooey smile disappeared. "So you have no say whatsoever?" She looked around. "I thought you were running this factory on your own. Or is your father here?"

"He's not. I didn't say I have no say. I'm just explaining that my father is the one who steers the company. He's not happy when the rudder decides to make independent moves." *Not happy* was an understatement, actually. "When I do decide to go against him, I have to think through whether it's worth pushing against the man." Like this factory. Right now he was only half sure improving the business before selling it was worth the trouble.

Though the time away from Father had plenty of other advantages. Hopefully when he returned home, the other arrangement his father wanted to force upon him would no longer be in play.

Evelyn's smile came back in full force. "There's nothing more worthy than helping women and children out of the red-light district. What better way to store treasures in heaven? A return you won't see until you leave this earth, certainly, but a significant one, nonetheless. And with the district only two blocks from your factory, it would benefit your workers to have less vice within a stone's throw when you hand them their paychecks. Those who succumb to the temptations of the area are much more likely to have trouble at home, addictions, and other vices that will affect their job performance."

He had to grin. She'd come prepared. "I agree with you. But I told you I'm not intending to stay long in the area."

"That's fine. We can still use any aid we can gather, plus your joining in will help me gain more supporters. Just one *yes* can give me the momentum to get more."

"I think Mr. Lowe was talking about more than just monetary donations. He wanted actual help. I could give you something from my personal savings, but I won't be around long enough for anything more."

"But your factory will be."

He looked away from her. He wasn't certain he wanted anyone to know his intentions for the place right now. What chance did he have at snagging a new manager and keeping his less-than-happy foremen if people learned he intended to sell? And if he promised her aid beyond money, what would stop the new owner from simply upending what he set up? "I'm afraid getting involved with a women's home is not compatible with my business goals at the moment. And I doubt my personal support is the kind Mr. Lowe wants."

"As I said, you'd be just the beginning."

To get out from under a clingy female's attention, he would normally flash the grin that turned women into putty, say something flattering, then offer an empty promise of taking his time in considering the proposal. But he couldn't do that to Miss Wisely. Her heart was in this. Her eyes already registered the worry that if she couldn't gain his support, she wouldn't gain anyone else's.

Which unfortunately might be true. He was already amazed Lowe had worked against the red-light district and hadn't been ruined by the businessmen and government officials who would be opposed to such maneuverings. "I'm very sorry, Miss Wisely, but I could give you ten dollars tomorrow if you'd like to return for it."

She closed her eyes and didn't move.

He wished he could offer more, but he wasn't about to do so without thinking things through. Maybe he could figure out a way to get her a few sponsors while he stayed in Teaville.

The silence continued until he began to worry she was going to sit there in protest. But she finally stood. "All right, I'll come back tomorrow." Her reply was filled with a sad sort of pretend cheerfulness. She then picked up her basket and held it out to him. "This is for you."

He put up his hands to refuse. "Since I couldn't help you, I don't deserve whatever this is."

"It's a welcome-to-town basket." She held it out until he took it. "The moral society usually hands them out to our church's visitors, but I figured since I was coming, I'd put one together for you." She pointed to an envelope. "You'll find a one-day pass to the new natatorium in there. I don't know what Kansas City has in the way of bathhouses, but this one has a gymnasium, swimming pool, mineral water baths, and whatever sports amusements you might desire. Along with several consulting physicians, if you've a need. There's also a list of churches and a map. I marked the sections you should probably stay out of and drew stars around the places you can find the best ice cream, cinnamon rolls, steaks, and anything else I thought you might be in need of. This is Sadie's divinity candy you enjoyed so much at the Lowes' home, and here's a wool scarf."

"A scarf?" In Kansas City, autumn sometimes had unexpected cold spells, but since he was farther south, he assumed the climate would be either similar or warmer.

Winter wouldn't arrive any time soon.

"Well, one of our orphans has learned to knit, and she insisted on giving you one since she wanted you to know she'd be grateful for any help you could give us. Her mother's still in the area and hasn't cared enough to come see her, but Suzie holds out hope that she will one day."

Miss Wisely's smile was so brittle, he was afraid if she turned her lips up any higher they'd break. "I trust you'll enjoy the divinity at least."

He swallowed hard and clenched the basket as he watched her walk away. If he'd never had occasion to feel like a heel before, he definitely knew how it was to feel like one now.

If only his father wasn't an actual heel, he wouldn't have sent her off with a frown.

He stared at the monstrous amount of divinity she'd wrapped for him and the tightly rolled gray scarf in his basket. Sleeping tonight had just gone out the window. Would supporting her ministry really be worth risking more of his father's ire?

Though Father had never actually threatened to disown him, David wasn't certain which his father would choose if he had to decide between his son and his business reputation.

7

"All right, ladies. I think we've got everything covered." Mrs. Naples, the moral-society president, consulted her list. "Once Miss Wisely finishes her corner, Mrs. Gray will deliver this quilt along with our canned goods to the Higginbothams. Miss McClain is only purchasing the dictionaries for the elementary classrooms until we raise more money, and Miss Sorenson will write a draft of our petition against the new dance hall. Are there any other matters of business we need to address before we leave?"

Evelyn glanced up from her last line of stitching and across the quilting frame toward Mrs. Firebrook. It was rare for the older woman to show up to meetings since she lived out of town.

Evelyn cleared her throat. "Before we adjourn, I was hoping to bring up a ministry need." If she didn't mention it now, she'd have to travel nearly thirty minutes to talk to Mrs. Firebrook's husband about supporting the shelter. Maybe the older woman could convince her husband for her — especially since her own persuasive skills were terrible as of late.

Mrs. Naples gave a prim and proper nod, as if she were the head of state giving permission for her to proceed. Though Mrs. Naples was a touch too serious, she was shades better than their former president, who'd been difficult to please and hypocritical.

Evelyn took a deep breath and forged ahead. "I was thinking that it's time to resurrect Mr. Lowe's ministry to the soiled doves of this town."

Stella Sorenson, the newest member of their group, gave her the most bewildered look, and Evelyn almost laughed. The pretty young blonde seemed to be even more uptight than their president — down to every strand of her Gibson girl hairstyle being perfectly arranged and every inch of her dress starched.

How much had Stella heard about the orphanage? At one time the mansion's use had been the talk of the town, but thankfully, rumors and speculations had settled down. "Before the mansion was turned into an orphanage, Mr. Lowe had tried to use the home to help women who wanted to leave the red-light district and find respectable work."

Mercy McClain leaned forward from her seat near Mrs. Firebrook. "That sounds . . . quite daring. Why did he quit?"

Evelyn smiled at the other new member of the group, whose own beautiful blond hair framed curious green eyes. Mercy was a wonderful addition to their moral society, always willing to help, even though it took her longer to do the projects assigned since a birth defect had left her with a missing right hand. But Mercy never let her handicap keep her from volunteering for anything and everything. The exact opposite of prim and proper Stella. Though Stella surely had her good points . . . it would just take more time to discover them, evidently.

"Well, the town wasn't too fond of the idea. So the Lowes compromised with an orphanage for the district children instead. However, I think it would be better if there was no need for it at all. What better way to turn the mansion back over to the Lowes than to help the mothers of these children leave the district and keep their families together?"

Mrs. Naples huffed. "I think that's a lot of time spent on something that likely won't happen."

"That doesn't mean we shouldn't try."

Mrs. Naples raised her eyebrows and sniffed.

Evelyn kept right on going. After what happened with their last president, she wasn't about to sit quietly in the corner anymore. Mrs. Little had almost destroyed their group with her conniving ways, her harsh judgment toward others, and her suppression of the group members' good ideas. Though her son and husband were now in prison, she'd somehow evaded jail time, despite the evidence against her, leaving the group to limp along for a while in a humiliated gloom.

"I'd like to build a women's home in the district where the soiled doves can be educated or learn a trade so they can start a new life elsewhere, but Mr. Lowe wants at least two local businessmen to support this endeavor before he'll consider backing it. Can you ladies pray that I can find those supporters?" She looked across at Mrs. Firebrook. "Or if any of you know someone who can help, I'd love for you to persuade him to meet with Mr. Lowe for more information."

Mrs. Firebrook kept clipping loose threads as if she weren't even listening.

Evelyn sighed. "Or if anyone has an idea about where the women might go once they're ready to live on their own, that would help too."

"How do you think they'd feel about pigs?"

Now it was Evelyn's turn to scrunch up her face in confusion like Stella had earlier. She turned to Charlotte "Charlie" Gray and frowned at the woman who wore a cowboy hat most of the time. "Come again?"

"Pigs." Charlie yanked at her thread, making the tangled mess she'd created even tighter. "Harrison and I've got ten acres we aren't doing much with, so I wondered if those girls might want to help me raise pigs. I'd been thinking about getting more."

Stella sniffed as if the mention of swine alone carried their stench. "Surely you don't think taking care of dirty pigs would appeal to even the lowest of women."

"Pigs happen to be kinder and smarter than some people I —"

A thump sounded. Likely Charlie's mother, Mrs. Andrews, stomping on her daughter's foot.

Charlie cut her eyes to her mother for a second before looking back at Evelyn. "Well, if you ever have a group of women willing to work with livestock, I think I could make a go of it. Though they'd have to stay away from our ranch hands."

"Thank you for the offer, Charlie. Stella may be correct about the idea not being appealing, but I'll let them know of the offer." She could only imagine how Scott's mother would have reacted to the suggestion — instead of Amy only slamming the door in her face, she'd probably have laughed at her as well.

The clock chimed the hour, and without even so much as a look toward Evelyn, Mrs. Firebrook gathered her things and headed out the door with Mrs. Naples.

Evelyn helped Mercy clean since it was the younger woman's turn to do so. Though Mercy never wanted special treatment because of her missing hand, Evelyn couldn't let her clean alone when it took her much longer than anyone else.

After gathering their things, they headed toward the basement's steep stairs outside of the meeting room. Mercy started up first. "Have you talked to my brother's boss?"

"He works for Plotman's Bank, yes?" At Mercy's nod, she sighed. "The president adamantly told me no." She stopped at the landing. "I'd hoped Mrs. Firebrook would have volunteered to persuade her husband to help, but I'm afraid she didn't look at all inclined."

Mercy's face contorted as if she thought it obvious that Mrs. Firebrook would never feel inclined.

"Is there something you know that would keep the Firebrooks from helping?" If she had no hope in that direction, she didn't want to waste a half day's trip out to their farm.

"Oh, well no. Not really. But if they're anything like a cousin of theirs I used to know, I'd say you wouldn't have much chance. But surely just because one Firebrook isn't nice doesn't mean they're all rotten eggs."

She'd even take a rotten egg's promise of help right now.

At the church's front doors, they parted ways, and Evelyn crossed town as quickly as she could. She'd spent hours before the meeting failing to gain support for the women's home. Her parents had pushed her out the door this afternoon, encouraging her to take her time, but the businessmen she'd met with were as enthusiastic about backing her women's home as the two she'd approached yesterday and the one who'd laughed at her the day before.

Evelyn jumped onto the streetcar for a short jaunt to the town's southeast corner and disembarked a few blocks away from the mansion. As she trudged up the winding driveway, she took in the beautiful two-story portico entryway awash in the afternoon light. She'd never thought her family would live in something so grand, but then it was quite a lot of work for the privilege to do so.

With the mansion's windows open, the smell of rosemary and garlic wafted out from the kitchen. Whatever Cook was making smelled heavenly. Maybe she could convince her to make it for the district's children.

The hysterical shriek of a child from somewhere inside the mansion made her rush through the massive front door.

No one appeared in the two-story entry hall.

"Give that back!" The shrill voice of a boy came from the hallway that ran left toward the kitchen.

"Let go, Peter. This instant!" Momma's voice descended in tone but didn't hold enough conviction.

"No! I had it first." Peter's whine made Evelyn shake her head as she marched forward.

She climbed the polished stairs out of the entryway and turned left. Peter and Lawrence wrestled at the bottom of the stairway to the second floor while Momma tried to wrench them apart, her hair falling about her face, her breathing labored as she bent over and tried to grab flailing limbs. "Please stop, boys."

Evelyn gave a sharp whistle. "Stop at once!"

All three froze. The boys' hands clamped onto the wooden train engine they were fighting over.

"What did Mrs. Wisely tell you?"

Both boys looked at each other, their glares filled with hatred. These two refused to leave their mothers' long-standing feud behind.

Evelyn stepped forward and held out her hand. "Give the engine to me. Neither of you shall have it." She kept her gaze pinned on Peter, the one who would take the most prodding to give in.

"Fine!" He shoved Lawrence away, then ran up the stairs.

Lawrence handed her the toy train. Without his sister coming by to visit him, he needed a good friend — but Peter likely wasn't going to be it.

"Run along and play." She took the toy and bumped his chin. "With someone other than Peter."

Lawrence narrowed his eyes, but when she didn't soften her expression or look away, he finally dashed off through the dining room. Hopefully he wasn't heading somewhere to sulk.

Momma slumped against one of the hallway's thin side tables and smoothed the hair away from her face. "Perhaps I'm too old for this." The deep lines around her mouth made her look older than her sixty years.

Evelyn put her arm around her mother but didn't naysay her. Momma should've already been enjoying grandchildren and scaling back on hard labor, but because of her, Momma and Daddy were here.

If they left, who would replace them until Nicholas and Lydia returned to run the mansion? They weren't finished having children and didn't want to come back until their brood was old enough to stand up for themselves when children like Peter came through.

When Lydia had first been pregnant, they'd looked for half a year before realizing no one but Evelyn and her parents were willing to step in. When they'd first talked to Nicholas about coming to the orphanage, he'd voiced concern about her parents' ages, but they'd convinced him everything would be all right since Evelyn would do the brunt of the work.

But if they left, Nicholas would likely look for a young couple to replace them. What if their replacements didn't want her help? But oh, how could she leave, especially when she'd likely never have children of her own? If she left with her parents, they'd push her to find someone to marry since they certainly couldn't house her for long without Daddy taking up some kind of preaching again. But it was far easier to claim to be too busy for courting than to explain her lack of hope in the marriage department.

She'd just have to keep her parents from working so hard they exhausted themselves. Daddy had already stepped down from being pastor of their church to meet the demands of the orphanage.

"Where's Daddy?" Evelyn took her mother's arm and strolled toward the kitchen. "He normally has an easier time disciplining Peter."

"He's icing his leg again."

Which was becoming more and more frequent. "Why don't you take him to the natatorium doctors?"

Two little girls ran past, pigtails flying.

"Hey!" Evelyn hollered. "No running inside."

Vera and Florence slowed a little, but within a step or two, giggles escaped and they rushed up the stairway.

She shook her head at them but decided not to pursue; they were generally the better behaved of the lot. "Have you talked to him about the natatorium?"

"He gives me the same answer he does you. He's gone seventy-three years without fancy specialty doctors; he's not going now. Mrs. Ullrich told him they put her under a solar therapeutic lamp, and he informed her the Good Lord made the sun and wasn't charging for it."

Evelyn smiled. Her father had always preached that anything beyond the basics of life wasn't necessary, though she doubted he'd happily leave behind the mansion's elevator or the upstairs bathrooms that pumped in hot water and even steam, especially when his leg was hurting him. "How long has he been upstairs?"

"Maybe two hours."

Half the time she'd been gone? "Have you checked on him?"

Momma patted her cheek. "I did once. He's all right."

But that meant Momma had borne the brunt of the work this afternoon. "Why don't you take a break before dinner? Put

94

your feet up, read a chapter of something?"

"You're a dear, but it's almost dinnertime. I'll go see if the meatloaf is on schedule and then get your father and send down any children wandering around upstairs." Her mother hobbled off, the limp she blamed on simple old age more pronounced.

Evelyn stopped in the middle of the hall, closed her eyes, and tilted her head back.

I thought this was where you wanted me. But how can I force my parents to stay just so I can?

And it was where she wanted to be. Or at least somewhere with children.

Maybe if they had to leave the orphanage she could help the children in the district more . . . except she'd still need an income.

She'd have to talk to Nicholas. Maybe if she could find another woman without children who was looking for work . . .

What if one of the prostitutes was willing to give up her life to help here, maybe even two of them? If they needed decent jobs to support themselves, why not hire a few for this position? Though those in town might not approve, surely the idea made sense with the children's backgrounds. And it wasn't as if they had to announce to the world who their employees were. Surely they could hire them with as little fanfare as they might some spinster from out of town.

With a spring in her step, Evelyn went out to the backyard through the muggy little conservatory and called the children in to wash their hands for dinner. Maybe she could get relief for her parents, keep her job, and help one or two of these children's mothers at the same time.

She waved at the gardener, who'd apparently stayed close to the mansion's charges and opened the door wide for several of the smaller residents to file in, followed by the one girl over the age of ten who lived there. "Thank you for watching them, Suzie."

The quiet blonde, whose mental faculties were slower than most fifteen-year-olds, only nodded and followed the little ones into the downstairs bathroom.

Caroline met Evelyn in the hallway. "There's someone here to see you."

"Me?" She took a quick glance in the hallway mirror to make sure she still looked all right. "I'm not expecting anyone. Who is it?"

"He's waiting for you up front." Caroline's mouth twitched a little, and then she leaned over and caught a running little boy in the crook of her arm. "Come, Ezekiel, let's get your muddy shoes off. I got enough to clean without you adding to the mess." She flipped him over her shoulder and tickled him.

As head housekeeper, Caroline wasn't responsible for the children, but she likely figured Evelyn's guest was going to keep her busy.

Evelyn smoothed her clammy hands against her skirt, then headed for the entry-way. Was it too much to hope that one of the businessmen who'd refused to donate to her ministry had come to tell her he'd changed his mind?

If she could set up a place and fill it with women within months, maybe she could groom someone to take over for her parents sooner rather than later.

Of course, how she would find the time for that, she didn't know. She needed to talk to Queenie. Maybe there was someone who'd be interested now.

The second she turned the corner, a man stood up from the seat he'd taken. "Miss Wisely."

Goodness, the effect of Mr. Kingsman's smile didn't lessen with time or the knowledge that he plied it on everyone. "Mr. Kingsman."

He walked straight to her, those deep blue eyes difficult to look away from. "I hope I'm not interrupting anything important. I told

Miss O'Conner I could return later, but she said you'd want to see me." He flashed her a grin.

All right, this man was beyond charming.

But he would only be in Teaville for a little while — she could resist anything for a few months. "I'm willing to see you if you need to see me." Hopefully he'd come to offer his support for her women's home. However, knowing him, his stomach might have something to do with his arrival. The cook's meatloaf was deliciously pungent, and since he seemed rather attuned to food, perhaps he caught a whiff of it all the way down at his factory.

Didn't men stop eating like there was no tomorrow once they'd reached their full height?

He was a smidgen shorter than she was, so maybe he still had some growing to do. But he had to be in his midtwenties — though she doubted he was older than her — so he had to be full-grown.

Thankfully, shorter men had never shown her much interest. "What can I help you with?"

"I don't need help — well, not any you could give me — but I thought about what you said, and —"

Her heart nearly burst out of her chest.

"You're going to help me with my women's home?"

"No."

She gritted her teeth to keep from vocalizing her disappointment.

"But I thought of a way to help you with some of the children. At the picnic last Saturday — which I would like to apologize for attending without invitation — I heard you talking with Scott about two older boys living here."

"No apology necessary. But yes, two of Scott's friends live here."

"I know what it's like to be bursting for some freedom at that age, and I thought I could offer them a job at the factory. Give them some responsibility, let them earn some money."

"They have chores, and they're not in want of anything material."

"But they'll be leaving soon, yes?"

"I suppose so." Robert and Max — fourteen and seventeen years old — had only recently come to the mansion. Their mother had been murdered, but neither boy would tell Nicholas any more about their past life than that. They'd asked permission to live in the orphanage despite other boys their age forging out on their own.

"Chores are good, but there's something

99

that drives a boy to earn his own keep, have the approval of older men — and if that drive isn't there, it needs to be. I figured having a job would give them a sense of accomplishment and a small savings to help them when they left. I'd only have them work a few hours, nothing to disturb their schooling or whatever schedule they keep at the mansion. But as you said, children in the red-light district need to find a way to get out." He shrugged. "I know it's not what you wanted, but I figured I'd offer that."

"Thank you kindly, but I'll have to think on it. Talk to my parents and see —"

"Oh please, Miss Wisely." Robert's voice startled her. She'd heard the staircase creaking but had assumed those noises were from Momma and Daddy descending.

She turned to face him. "It's not polite to eavesdrop."

"I didn't mean to, but your mother told me dinner was ready." The fourteen-year-old walked toward her with his hands clasped in front of his chest. "Max and I were just wondering what we would do once we had to leave. Maybe if we showed this gentleman we're good workers, he'd hire us on permanently."

It was hard to imagine letting Robert go to work when his voice hadn't dropped nor had he grown any facial hair, though he was always looking in the mirror as if any day his upper lip would surprise him.

Momma came down without Daddy and stopped at the end of the staircase, holding Florence and Vera's hands.

Evelyn could barely handle the look of yearning on Robert's face. "Maybe we'll have Mr. Kingsman return to talk about this another time. Dinner's ready, and my parents and I should discuss —"

"Why not now?" Momma looked past both her and Robert and smiled at Mr. Kingsman. "Would you be opposed to joining us for dinner to discuss whatever this opportunity is for Robert and Max?"

"The offer smells too good to refuse."

Of course this man wouldn't turn down dinner. "I don't think we should discuss this in front of the boys. If we don't agree that it's a good idea, it —"

"Now, Evelyn," Momma said, "these boys are pretty much old enough to make their own decisions. We can guide them, but they shouldn't be shut out of the conversation."

Robert threw back his shoulders and gave her a quick nod.

How could she continue arguing after that? "All right, Momma." She put her hand out toward Robert and looked back to Mr.

Kingsman. "Let me introduce you to Robert Milligan."

"How do you do, sir?"

Mr. Kingsman shook the boy's hand heartily.

"His brother Max is likely already waiting at the table." Momma kept a hold of the girls' hands and gestured with her head. "Robert, why don't you take Mr. Kingsman into the dining room, and I'll tell Cook to prepare another plate."

"Of course." The boy beamed. "We're having meatloaf. I've never liked it before I came here, but it's good."

"I can smell that it's so." Mr. Kingsman hung his hat on the hall tree as he passed her to catch up with Robert. "So, young man, have you done any odd jobs before?" He shortened his pace to match Robert's as they turned down the hall.

Momma patted the girls' backs and told them to follow Robert and Mr. Kingsman.

"Well, sir, I used to clean the saloon where my mother worked." Robert's voice diminished as he walked farther down the hallway. "I hope you don't find that against your liking. We didn't have much choice about where we lived or who we had to be around, but we . . ."

"Who is this Mr. Kingsman?" Momma

was looking at her with a probing gaze. "And why haven't you told me about him?"

Oh no. She'd have to quickly nip that matchmaking hope in her mother's eyes. "He's one of the businessmen I approached about the women's home."

"He seems rather nice. He should sit by your father. I can sit at the other end."

Which meant Evelyn would be sitting directly across from him if she didn't move. "Why don't we put him between Max and Robert?"

"We could move them both next to you and Mr. Kingsman, if you'd like."

"I suppose." She wouldn't argue lest Momma read too much into her wanting to distance herself from the man. Besides, if Momma sat at the other end of the table, maybe Mr. Kingsman wouldn't catch that Momma was always on the lookout for a man to sweep her daughter off her feet.

Especially since Evelyn was determined to keep her feet firmly adhered to the ground.

8

David smiled and exchanged pleasantries with his factory workers as he fought against the departing crowd on his way to the shipping section. This afternoon, Robert and Max had met him at the mansion's door so eager to start their first day that he wondered if they'd slept the night before or paid any attention in school.

The orphanage's driver could have driven them, but David had wanted to personally escort them on their first day, tour the factory, and introduce them to their foreman. He'd also hoped to have seen Miss Wisely, to say good afternoon and reassure her the boys would be taken care of. He usually got along well with everyone but his father, so this strange wall she seemed to put up whenever he came near flustered him.

Though if he'd never won his father's respect in twenty-five years, why did he allow a stranger's lack of approval to niggle at him so?

Was she just upset he hadn't offered her the help she wanted? Surely not. She had been standoffish before then, and she didn't strike him as petty or manipulative. He'd been around enough of those kind of women that he could almost feel them coming before he saw them.

Maybe it was because their first meeting had been awkward. He hated not being liked. Hopefully she would realize he wasn't so bad and smile at him once or twice.

Robert and Max were hanging up their aprons as he approached, but Max was doing it one-handed. A large bandage swathed his hand and wrist.

David hurried forward. "What happened?"

Max held up his hand and shrugged. "I accidently knocked a few jars onto the floor. When I was cleaning up, someone bumped me and I fell. A few pieces scraped my knee too, but I'm fine. I'm really sorry about the five I broke though. I told the foreman I'd pay for them, but he said I didn't have to. I hope you won't fire me. But if you do, please don't fire Robert."

David clasped the young man's shoulder, already proud of him. "Thanks for taking responsibility, but the foreman's right, you're not obligated to pay me back. I calculate breakage and mishap into my business plans. If it becomes a habit though, that's when I deal with an individual worker in regard to him continuing work here."

"Oh, I won't make it a habit. I promise."

He looked over at the foreman, who was tallying the day's undertakings. The older man gave him a nod.

"Would you two like to return tomorrow afternoon?"

"Yes," they both said in chorus.

"Good. We'll ask Miss Wisely if that's all right." Hopefully the big bandage wouldn't dissuade her. Her parents had seemed happy about the brothers working, but Evelyn had been quiet throughout dinner. "Keep in mind, though, I won't keep you on unless you're doing well in school. Good workers are good students."

Robert cringed. "What grades do we have to have? I've never gotten high marks, not like Max. He's smarter than me."

"It's not the marks themselves. It's whether the Wiselys and your teacher think you're working as well as you can."

Robert relaxed, and David motioned them to follow. "Let's get you home. You've got chores, I hear."

They walked out to the factory's small

buggy used for miscellaneous deliveries and squished onto the bench seat meant for two.

The brothers informed him of all they'd done that day as the buggy rattled over the brick streets. Hopefully their enthusiastic descriptions of their mundane tasks would calm any fears the Wiselys might have in regard to Max's accident and they would allow them to return.

"Do you know what I'm going to do with my money?" Robert leaned forward to look at him around his brother, who was squished in the middle.

"What?"

"I'm going to get me a Stevens rifle."

David smiled — he'd wanted a rifle at around Robert's age. Not that his father would have ever let him have one. "What are you going to do with your money, Max?"

The young man shrugged. "I told Robert we should save everything we make. I mean, we have no parents and we can't stay at the orphanage much longer. What if we can't get good jobs? I don't ever want to be hungry again."

"Very wise, Max."

Robert sighed. "I can save money after I get a rifle."

"You could," David said. "You've got time to think about it."

"I could always sell the rifle if we got hungry."

David crossed the railroad tracks, and that kept him from responding for a bit. "Or you could keep the rifle to get squirrels and rabbits with."

"Right!" Robert jabbed Max in his side with an elbow. "We wouldn't even need money for food if I had a rifle."

"You would need bullets, but both approaches are good." David directed the bay to head up the mansion's winding driveway and couldn't help but shake his head at the thought of using such a magnificent structure as an orphanage. His own house was almost as large, though not as impressive, but definitely grander than the other houses he'd seen in Teaville. What would his father say if he turned his Kansas City estate into an orphanage? How many people would think him crazy?

But his house was only a status symbol. The boardinghouse he was in right now was comfortable enough — though the owner was no cook. Considering Mrs. Vannoster was half beside herself running a boardinghouse while caring for twin infants, he didn't understand why she'd refused to let him cook his own meals, especially after he'd volunteered to cook for everyone.

Perhaps she figured a man wouldn't know his way around a kitchen.

Perhaps it was best he not cook for the boardinghouse residents though. After they'd tasted something cooked right, the often unidentifiable glop of stew she served every other day would be even harder for the boarders to choke down.

The sound of children's laughter was followed by the sight of a group of children playing tag, weaving in and out of the wraparound porch's massive columns as they tried to catch one another. Robert jumped off the buggy before David stopped and darted across the lawn, chasing after a boy who'd stuck his tongue out at him.

When the buggy came to a stop, Max held out his good hand. "Thank you so much, sir."

David smiled as he shook it. "You're going to go far, Max. I just know it."

The young man beamed. "Maybe one day I'll be your foreman."

"You never know." Though Max struck him as being more of the quiet, intellectual type than a laborer, he wasn't about to stomp on whatever dream the young man had at the moment. He knew how demotivating it was to have one's dreams belittled. It would have been so much easier if Father had believed in him and let him discover his weaknesses and strengths with guidance rather than telling him what he was good for and chastising him any time he talked of trying something new.

He would do nothing to squash anyone's dreams if he could help it. "If I need another foreman next year, I'll see if you're still interested. Got to work hard though."

"Yes, sir." Max jumped down and walked with a swagger toward the mansion's front door.

What if he'd felt that confident at his age? Believing he had the freedom to do whatever he set his heart on?

He'd certainly not be working in a glass factory. But to step away from Kingsman & Son would be like stabbing his father in the heart. His father surely had one, even if it was tied more to status and power than his son.

What if he just admitted making a big profit with the glass factory wasn't going to be as easy as he first thought and did as his father bid?

But if David admitted to one miscalculation, it would only make Father more certain he'd cave to his other demand. And though he agreed with Father that strengthening their bond with the Lister family would benefit their business, the stakes were far too personal.

David scratched his horse's neck and left him to head inside. He probably didn't need to go in, but he wanted to explain about Max's hand and make sure they knew he wanted the brothers to return.

And partially because he wanted a connection. It looked as if he was going to be in Teaville for a while, so he needed to get out of his office and gather a few friends.

And Miss Wisely certainly intrigued him. If he had her vision, drive, and determination, he'd not be waffling on what he wanted to do with his life, simply coasting through what was expected of him.

She was certainly not doing what was expected of her — settling down and having children — and was pursuing something without any monetary promise whatsoever, and yet she didn't seem to be second-guessing herself.

The butler showed David inside, where he waited for one of the Wiselys to meet him. He could smell something like chicken and dumplings or potpies nearly ready to be served. He sniffed the air, trying to parcel out the herbs and spices he was smelling. His stomach growled, and he tried not to think about the less-than-appetizing stuff

111

his boardinghouse matron would serve.

Mrs. Wisely came around the corner. Her white hair was flattened and skewed to one side, but her smile was contagious. Did her daughter have her smile?

He hadn't so much as gotten Evelyn to crack a grin. And why did that bother him so much?

"Good afternoon, Mr. Kingsman. How did the boys do?"

"They did well." He looked past her, hoping for a glimpse of her daughter. "I wanted to let you know Max cut himself, but I think it was an accident that has little chance of being repeated. I do hope you'll allow him to return."

"If we barred the children from everything that might result in minor injuries, they'd be doing nothing but sitting in chairs all day — and even then I bet we'd have a few bumps and bruises." She smiled again. "As long as it wasn't due to negligence, I don't see us worrying too much if they wish to return."

"I believe they do, at least they've said so to me. If they don't, send me a message. Otherwise I'd love for your driver to bring them after school whenever they're able."

"Sounds good."

He licked his lips and swallowed, trying

not to think about the food here versus the food awaiting him.

Robert ran in from the hall to the right and jumped over the three steps that descended into the entryway's foyer, right toward Mrs. Wisely.

David lunged in front of Mrs. Wisely to save her from being toppled, but Robert slammed into her first.

Though she gasped and shook her head at the boy as she teetered, she seemed to take getting the wind knocked out of her in stride. "I take it you had a good day?"

Robert nodded. "Where's Miss Wisely? I want to tell her all about it."

"I'd hoped she'd met up with you in town." Mrs. Wisely's face tensed and she closed her eyes for a split second. "Hopefully she'll return in time for dinner. You can tell her then."

Robert frowned, then ran off.

Mrs. Wisely's shoulders deflated as she stared off into space.

What had made her smile disappear so quickly? "Is there something amiss with Miss Wisely?"

Her mother looked westward, as if she could see through the mansion's walls. "After lunch, Caroline wanted to make sure one of the women she'd been tending had taken her medication. Evelyn went along to check on a child they hadn't seen Saturday. They weren't supposed to be gone this long."

If Evelyn had found trouble in the red-light district, how long would they have to rescue her before she was completely ruined, or worse?

He ran a hand through his hair, anchoring his fingers in the longer hair at the nape of his neck in an attempt to keep from pacing. He shouldn't do anything to heighten Mrs. Wisely's fears. She could surely imagine as many terrible scenarios as he. "Do you know where the child she was checking on lives?"

The front door swung open behind him, and Mrs. Wisely's shoulders raised and lowered with an exaggerated relief.

Except when he turned around, it was Miss O'Conner and no one else.

The housekeeper held her hands clasped in front of her stark white apron. "Is Evelyn here?"

Mrs. Wisely strode past him and grabbed Miss O'Conner's hands. "Were you not supposed to come back together?"

"I waited for an hour at the wagon. I went looking for her but couldn't find her." The sharp green eyes that had watched him so carefully at Saturday's picnic were limper than dying grass. "I'd hoped she'd come home with Robert and Max."

Mrs. Wisely shook her head vehemently. "She would have told you that's what she was doing."

Miss O'Conner's throat swelled with an exaggerated swallow. "I know."

"I'll get Walter this instant." Mrs. Wisely rushed past David. "Is Mr. Parker available to drive?" she called back over her shoulder at the housekeeper.

"I didn't see him out there."

"Mrs. Wisely," David called after her, overtaking her before she scuttled up the stairs. "Isn't your husband's leg giving him difficulty?"

She met his gaze with reddening eyes. "He'll look for her regardless."

"Allow me." He turned to see that Caroline hadn't budged an inch. "Miss O'Conner and I will search for her, and if we don't find her within the hour, we'll send word."

"I'm not sure Walter won't head out the second I tell him, anyhow."

"Maybe he could send your driver to Mr. Lowe's and let him know what's happened. I bet he could search more easily."

"That won't stop her father from moving

heaven and earth to find her."

"If he can't, remind him he can do so on his knees."

Mrs. Wisely's mouth moved as if she wanted to speak, but she thought better of it and scurried away.

"Come, Miss O'Conner." He took the housekeeper by the elbow. "Tell me where you've been, what she said, and anything else that might help us find her."

9

Struggling with the weight of a limp twelve-year-old, Evelyn hobbled toward a tree stump in an overgrown lot, lowered the boy onto the makeshift seat, and sat beside him. The heat from Scott's body swathed in the blanket Queenie had given her was nearly unbearable. The early-autumn warmth, the layers of her own clothing, and the long blocks she'd trekked with the boy had made her sweat more than a lady ought.

Scott moaned.

"Are you all right, Scott?" She pushed the light blanket off his head to see his swollen eyes, crowded by the telltale sores of small-pox. "I'm so sorry I started dragging you around. I should've realized Queenie might not have been able to take us in."

But the boy only made garbled sounds, his head jerking as if he was having a bad dream.

"You have to be all right . . ." Her voice

died off, and she gritted her teeth to keep herself from blubbering on the street. If only she'd visited Scott and Amy sooner. But how could she have known of the misery that had visited their house?

Tears of frustration lined her eyelids. No one would dare offer them a ride, not with how Scott looked. The raised bumps on his exposed skin had already made one person who'd ventured close speed away.

She should have stayed with Scott at his little house until the doctor returned, but with Amy still lying where she'd breathed her last . . . Well, she hadn't been able to stay any longer. Oh, if only Queenie had had room for him.

But Queenie had been tending an unconscious woman, who obviously couldn't tell them if she was immune to the smallpox or not.

Where could they go? Dragging Scott around for three blocks had pushed her limits.

Tears dripped off her cheeks and onto Scott. She dug her handkerchief out of her pocket and dabbed the dampness off his bumpy face. The poor lad was hard to look at, and though he was skinny, his long frame was just too much of a burden for her to continue wandering about town. The doctor would likely scold her up one side and down the other for taking him out of isolation.

But if she was going to nurse this boy back to life, she couldn't do so in the red-light district, the orphanage, or any place with children.

Did anyone live nearby who wouldn't be put at risk, who would allow sickness into their house?

The quick clip-clop of hooves sounded down the street.

She tucked the blanket back around Scott's face and neck to hide him from view. Maybe she should take him back to his place — surely the doctor would return to take Amy away — but how could she stay overnight in the bad part of town? The townsfolk might begrudgingly give a pastor's daughter the benefit of the doubt in regard to her trips into the district, but rumors were bound to circulate if she stayed for several nights, no matter if she was tending a sick boy or not.

"There!"

She looked up at the man's shout, and almost melted at the sight of Caroline sitting beside Mr. Kingsman in an unfamiliar beaten-up buggy.

He nearly stood to stop the horse, and

Caroline swung her leg over the little buggy's edge.

"Stop!"

They both froze.

"Have you had the smallpox?"

Mr. Kingsman straightened with a wince, and Caroline shook her head. She slid back onto the buggy's seat reluctantly. "I haven't. I've not been inoculated either."

She'd been afraid of that. "I couldn't leave him alone in his home, but I don't know where I can take him. Queenie has someone with her, and even if she didn't, taking in Scott would prevent her from helping anyone else for two weeks."

"But you're immune, right?" Mr. Kingsman was holding on to the buggy's reins as if they might slip away.

"I had a mild case when I was three — don't even remember it." She put a hand against her face. "Scars are my only memory." Had he not seen them? The ones on her right cheek were the most visible, even after all these years. She sometimes caught herself making sure that side of her face was turned away when she talked to someone. Had she been doing that subconsciously with Mr. Kingsman?

"Good." He nodded as if she'd taken a huge weight off his shoulders. Then he shook his head as if he'd just gotten a snow bath. "I mean, good that you're immune, not that you have scars."

She tried to smile at his slip, but all she could do was look at him. Most people didn't seem to worry much about people they hardly knew. But here he was helping Max and Robert, attempting to converse with the children at her Saturday lunch, and now worrying about her. Quite endearing.

But she couldn't let herself like Mr. Kingsman more than any other nice person she'd met, no matter how much his smile affected her.

Scott sagged heavily against her, succumbing to the exhaustion that made him nearly delirious. "Caroline, where can I take him?"

"I don't know as many people as you," Caroline said. "I'm hardly out in society, and I can't think of a single person in the district who'd want to take him in — let alone a place *you* should stay for any length of time."

"What about your church members?" Mr. Kingsman leaned forward on the bench seat.

"The ones I know who aren't clear across town have children." Or were poor — as people would have to be if they couldn't afford to live farther away from this section of town. She couldn't ask them to feed and

121

keep her and Scott, even if they did have room for them.

Mr. Kingsman handed Caroline the reins. "I was inoculated when I was two. I'll take him to my room at the boardinghouse. I can tend him there."

"You can't give up that much of your time. Besides, I'm sure Mrs. Vannoster would not want him in her boardinghouse. Even if all her boarders are immune, she has children."

His shoulders slumped as if he were disappointed he couldn't spend weeks tending Scott.

"What about that old man your father's always talking about?" Caroline frowned down from her perch. "The one who refuses to sell his farmhouse?"

"Mr. Hargrove?" He was one of her father's good friends. He would be sympathetic, but getting to his place would be quite the walk. She turned to look at Scott's face. He was in and out of consciousness. He wouldn't be able to walk that far. "I can't imagine getting Scott all the way there." In her head, she counted the streets she'd have to travel. "Ten blocks, almost. I had a hard enough time hobbling around with him for three. And what if he can't take us in?"

Mr. Kingsman took off his coat and dropped it behind his seat into the small boot. "I'll carry him. Just tell me how to get there." Mr. Kingsman's upper body was much more filled out than she'd expected for a factory owner.

Perhaps he could carry him all the way to Mr. Hargrove's, but that really wasn't necessary. "What if you let me take Scott in your buggy? You and Caroline could return to the mansion and have Mr. Parker retrieve your vehicle — if he's immune anyway. The buggy could be scrubbed with whatever disinfectant the doctor has, so it shouldn't have to be burned."

Mr. Kingsman descended from the vehicle, then turned to help Caroline down. "I'll take Scott in the buggy. You should return to the mansion and reassure your parents. When Caroline arrived without you, your mother nearly panicked. I told her I'd search, but I'm afraid your father will be out looking soon, if he isn't already."

"But Caroline could tell them."

"Now, Evelyn . . ."

His use of her given name stopped her.

"I'll take him." He gently pulled the boy from her arms, not even cringing when the blanket fell and exposed Scott's pox-ridden face.

"Are you sure this is all right?" Caroline asked. "Should Evelyn return to the mansion after touching Scott?"

Mr. Kingsman readjusted the boy into a cradle hold. "She's naturally immune, so the only way she can spread the disease is if she touches something. So if she walks beside you without touching you, you can go into the mansion and tell her parents to get the things she'll need for the next few weeks."

Evelyn numbly nodded at Mr. Kingsman's surprising handle on the facts of smallpox as she adjusted Scott's blanket. How could she just leave the boy, even if it was just for a trip to the mansion and back?

Mr. Kingsman resituated Scott in his arms, pulling him away from her just enough that he caused her to look up at him. "If this Mr. Hargrove won't take us in, I'll wait for you there."

"Should you take Scott to the doctor first?" Caroline asked as she came closer, but not too close.

"He's seen him already. Dr. Hiller went to get the" — Evelyn glanced at Scott to make sure he still slept — "county coroner. For Scott's mother."

Was this the first time she'd seen Mr. Kingsman frown?

Though the doctor had told her Scott's mother's smallpox was too mild to have caused her demise, what else besides the disease was responsible? Amy had been quite healthy looking a week ago. "I couldn't let the doctor quarantine us there. My reputation —"

"So let's get him somewhere you can stay for a few weeks." Mr. Kingsman took Scott to the buggy and eased the boy up onto the seat. He then held Scott upright as he scooted past him to pick up the reins.

She forced her hand to let go of the corner of the blanket she'd held onto.

God, keep Scott alive. And please let Mr. Hargrove be willing to take us in.

Evelyn gave Mr. Kingsman quick directions to Mr. Hargrove's, and Mr. Kingsman gave her a nod before driving off.

Why did it feel as if she'd failed Scott more by letting him go with Mr. Kingsman than by not checking on him sooner?

"We better get back to your parents. They're worried sick."

She nodded and walked beside Caroline, though keeping quite the space between them.

Caroline shook her head. "It's too bad you don't already have your women's home. You could have easily gone there."

125

"Though it'd still be in the red-light district."

Caroline shrugged. "Then at least Queenie could have brought her patient there and helped. Make sure you ask Mr. Lowe for several sickrooms, and a birthing room too, when that time comes. You can't imagine the squalor I help deliver babies in."

"You know, you'd probably make more money being a midwife than a housekeeper."

A sad chuff escaped Caroline's lips. "Oh, I'm not a midwife."

"But you tend so many births."

"Only because the midwives are busy and others come first. And sometimes the woman I'm tending doesn't want help. Though I help anyway. Do you remember the baby I brought to the orphanage right after the Lowes got married?"

"A boy, yes?"

She nodded. "If I hadn't insisted on staying to help his mother despite her screaming at me to leave . . . I'm pretty sure she would have declared him stillborn . . ."

Evelyn tried to shut off her mind from imagining what the woman would have done to convince someone she'd had a stillborn. She wrapped her arms about herself. The ache of dealing with this section of the town was more than she could take sometimes.

"I try my best to keep tabs on the pregnant ones, make sure they know there's an orphanage, make sure someone's present."

They skirted The Line, avoiding the lines of saloons and other establishments that catered to debauchery, all gearing up for a night of revelry — and heartbreak, financial loss, and ruined lives.

The few men walking toward the district strolled by as nonchalantly as if they were going nowhere less respectable than Main Street — as if the lives of women, children, and quite a few men weren't in turmoil inside the buildings they'd soon occupy.

"How do you do it, Caroline?"

"Do what?" The older woman looked over at her for a second.

"Keep working in the district when nothing good ever seems to come from it."

"What do you call the orphanage, then? What would those children's lives be like without the chance you, your parents, and the Lowes give them?"

"But what about Scott and his mother? And the other children and doves trapped here? There's never been more than twelve children in the orphanage at a time, and they come and go so regularly. How many have we been able to keep track of? How many have run from the placements we've made? How many returned to their old haunts? A few seem to be doing all right, but the heartache and problems they still deal with . . ."

"I try not to think about that. But my sister is the reason I continue working there. If it wasn't for her, I probably would've stopped ages ago. I'm actually more amazed *you've* lasted so long. Unlike me, Queenie, and Mr. Lowe even, nothing ties you to this place. You and your family are so pure and perfect."

Pure and perfect.

Evelyn looked away from Caroline, watching her feet as they crossed a set of train tracks.

"You don't have to be so involved in the district itself, Evelyn." Caroline sidestepped a broken whiskey bottle. "You've got sufficient work at the orphanage, especially with your father slowing down. No one's going to think poorly of you if you quit — they might even think better of you."

Evelyn hugged herself, the weight of Scott's hot, lethargic body still almost palpable. She wouldn't think better of herself if she gave up on the children who weren't in the orphanage. They needed love and care just the same. And how could she forget about their families? Scott's mother had died while trapped in a personal hell she believed she deserved and could never leave.

Though Caroline was right about her having no personal connection to the red-light district, she did know how it felt to be trapped by past choices — to have no hope of ever having the future she'd dreamed of.

At least she was free enough to do something good with her life. But what did these women have? How could she abandon them simply because she was lucky enough that no one knew what she'd done?

"It doesn't matter what people think of me." No one knew enough to make a correct judgment — and hopefully they never would. "But you're wrong about me having no ties to The Line. The children at the orphanage are connected to this place — their memories, their family and friends, their hearts. How can I ignore the misery in the district when it affects them? Now that I know what it's like, how can I say I'm following Christ if I pretend to be as ignorant of the suffering as I was before? I can't fathom not trying to help."

Caroline said nothing more, and Evelyn held her peace as they continued on in silence. Caroline wasn't particularly religious. Was Evelyn's talk of Christ the reason she'd gone quiet? Or was Caroline thinking what so many others thought — that a preacher's daughter's ability to change anything about the town's red-light district was so close to nil that her labor was for naught.

10

After climbing the porch steps with care, David wished he could lay Scott on the bench beneath the window, but if Mr. Hargrove wasn't immune to smallpox, neither of them should touch anything.

With the heel of one foot, David knocked as hard as he could without losing his balance. The boy had become more lucid on the way over but wasn't capable of keeping himself upright. Hopefully this Mr. Hargrove was immune and as compassionate as the ladies said.

A slow, steady clomping sounded from somewhere inside the house. With Scott's shivering, David struggled to keep a sturdy grip on him.

He stepped back and leaned against the railing, relieved to find it sturdy.

The door's window curtain was swept aside, and a man with a creamy pink scalp barely covered by wisps of white hair peered out at them. He narrowed his eyes at Scott, who'd pulled the blanket up to hide his face. But within a second, Mr. Hargrove dropped the curtain and opened the door. The man hobbled across the threshold, leaning heavily on a cane. "What can I do for you?"

Evelyn had mentioned Mr. Hargrove was older, but David hadn't expected the man to be physically unable to help with Scott's care. "I'm here at the behest of Miss Wisely. Are you Mr. Hargrove?"

"I am, and who's this?"

"Scott Jones, a boy Miss Wisely often helps."

The man rubbed at his white bushy beard. "An orphan?"

The boy tensed, turning into David's chest as if to hide from the words.

"Yes," David said softly.

"Then why's he not at the mansion?"

"Sir, I know this is a lot to ask. But this boy is contagious and needs to be quarantined. Before I say anything else, it's important to know if you're immune to smallpox."

"Smallpox?" The man stiffened. "I haven't heard of a smallpox case around here for some time." He frowned. "I had it as a young man, when one of my girls died of it. Many, many years ago."

"I'm sorry." He held his peace as Mr. Hargrove stared off into space. The look in his eyes mirrored the one he'd seen in his father's the day he'd asked him about Frederick.

David had been only two when Frederick died. He had no recollection of his brother or the sickness that took him, but it must have been horrible since Father never spoke of his eldest son. He'd only discovered he'd had a brother when he was seven and asked his nursemaid about the inoculation scar he'd found on his arm.

Mr. Hargrove blinked after a bit and looked at Scott's long frame. "She was my only redhead, just like me. . . ." He smoothed a jittery hand over his white hair. "I suppose Miss Wisely thinks I'll take him in."

The quiver in the man's voice made David question whether or not he should. "You don't have to." He tipped his head toward the barn. "Perhaps I could set him up in the barn? I'm not sure where else we can go."

"Barn's no good. More spiders in there than anything else. Are you expecting me to care for him?"

"Actually, it seems I should, but I'm sure Miss Wisely won't let me do so alone."

Mr. Hargrove lifted his eyebrows for a moment, but then took a step back inside. "Come in, then."

David released a breath. *Thank you, Lord.* Even Scott relaxed in his arms.

The old man led them down a darkened hallway on the ground floor. The small door he opened led into a narrow room, scarcely furnished with a stripped bed, a chest of drawers, and two dainty chairs beside a half-moon table. A single cabinet card photo stood propped against an empty vase in the table's center. No pictures lined the walls, and the lone window was small and high.

"Let me get you some linens." Listening to Hargrove's slow drag-and-step retreating down the hallway, David crossed over to one of the wooden chairs and gingerly lowered them both onto its edge.

"It's so cold in here." Scott's arms and legs trembled.

The room was actually quite stuffy and warm. "Hold on." He tucked his arm around Scott lest he shiver himself off the chair and onto the floor. "We're getting you blankets."

Scott's head rolled onto his shoulder, and David felt heat seeping through his vest and shirt. He glanced around for a basin, happy to see a small washstand wedged into a corner. This room would require a lot of maneuvering for more than two people to occupy it at the same time.

"Here we are." Mr. Hargrove shuffled in and shakily worked the sheet onto the mattress with one hand since the other gripped the head of his cane.

Though he couldn't help, David struggled to stay seated while their host labored to cover the mattress.

Once the bed was made, David helped Scott onto the clean sheet. The boy simply melted into place with a moan, then curled up tight. David spread the other cotton sheet across the boy's shivering form and turned to Mr. Hargrove. "If you would show me where I can wash up, I'm hoping you could spare a few more blankets for him. I'll replace everything he touches."

"Not necessary. Grab that pitcher, and we'll get you water and rags." In the hallway, Mr. Hargrove pointed him to the kitchen sink and then hobbled down the hallway in the opposite direction.

While David scrubbed his arms, a quick rat-a-tat-tat came from the front door.

"Come in, Doctor," Mr. Hargrove's voice warbled a few moments later. "And Miss Wisely."

David stopped scrubbing. He had taken a

wrong turn here and had needed to ask for directions, but even so, she'd gotten here quickly.

"I take it Mr. Kingsman's already here with the boy?" A man's deep bass voice sounded peeved.

"He's been put in the back room."

"And you're immune?"

"I've had it."

"And where's this Mr. Kingsman?"

David dried his hands on a towel and carried it out with him. "I'm here."

Evelyn stood staring at him, her face tight with worry. He'd figured she would've rushed to find Scott first thing, but there she stood, looking at him with quite the furrowed brow. Was she worried he'd succumb to the sickness despite his assurances? Something warmed under his skin, and he gave her a smile.

She took two harried steps toward him. "The doctor says you might be at risk — that they're finding out inoculations aren't lifelong."

A hitch caught in his chest. He couldn't stop the coldness creeping across his skin at the thought of being in the same state Scott was.

The doctor, a short blond man, perhaps in his forties, came up beside her. "I can inoculate you again, but you'll need to be observed for fever."

Evelyn wrung her hands. "He says it should still work as well as the last time. That if you get the shot quickly, there should be nothing to worry about."

"Good." He nodded, wondering why she acted so worried if the doctor had said he'd likely be fine.

"I'm so sorry." Her eyes grew wetter by the second, though no tears formed.

Even if he got the smallpox, surely two inoculations would keep him alive — at least he hoped. He took a hold of her shoulder. "It's all right."

"I just wish I hadn't gotten you into this mess, but at least you're able to go home. But please call for the doctor if you feel the least bit ill."

He frowned and looked over at the doctor. "But if you'll be coming here to check on Scott, can't you see me then?"

The doctor shrugged.

"Oh no, you shouldn't stay." Evelyn's shaky voice was underlined with determination.

Would she always insist he leave whenever he spent more than a minute with her? "You'll need help with Scott."

"But Mr. Hargrove can —"

David took her arm. "There are some things" — he lowered his voice and bent his head closer as the other two men moved toward the hallway — "that a woman who's not related to a boy isn't going to be able to assist with. Mr. Hargrove isn't strong enough to be able to help in that regard."

She looked away, still wringing her hands. "This isn't good."

How would extra help not be good? "What are you worried about? Nobody is forcing me to stay here — I'm choosing to."

"I wanted Scott out of the district so I could care for him without anyone starting rumors, and now if you . . ."

She was worried about being in his company? A woman who walked the red-light district alone with her chin held high? "Mr. Hargrove's here. He's sufficient oversight. But if you're worried, you could go home and let me take care of him."

"I can't do that."

He wouldn't insist, since he'd be at a complete loss to know how to tend Scott all on his own. "Then I'll be here to relieve you when necessary and for the doctor to observe."

And they ought to return to Scott's room to hear what the doctor said. He offered her his arm. "Scott needs us."

She stared at his arm as if taking it meant committing herself to something she'd sworn off for eternity, so he dropped his arm and placed his hand against her upper back, holding out his other arm to encourage her to lead them down the hall.

She looked at him for a second, words of protest swallowed up in her eyes, but then marched forward without saying anything.

In the room, Evelyn squeezed inside, but he remained in the doorway as the doctor assessed his patient. He was sitting on the bedside beside Scott, mostly shaking his head and muttering to himself as he checked the boy's condition.

After a few moments, the doctor stood and ran a hand through his already-tousled blond hair. "I wish you hadn't moved him, since now we've got to sanitize this place too. But he's strong enough to survive another trip. I'll take him to where my nurse is caring for the man who likely gave them the smallpox. It'd be best —"

"Oh no. I . . ." Evelyn put a hand to her mouth. "I wanted to take care of him."

The doctor frowned at the interruption. "It's really not necessary. I've a nurse capable of handling this."

Did he truly intend to place the boy with the john who'd taken advantage of his mother and caused her demise? Whether she'd agreed to the man's attentions or not, putting Scott in the same room didn't sit well. David pushed off the doorjamb. "Can he not stay here? Mr. Hargrove is willing, and we have to clean and sanitize the room already. Plus I'm to be watched for fever, correct?"

The doctor turned to David. "Yes, but there isn't any reason to disrupt your lives for the likes of him. Neither of you requires isolation, though I shall inoculate you again for good measure. Do you live alone?"

"I do. Well, I live in Mrs. Vannoster's boardinghouse, but I have a room of my own."

"She won't want to assume responsibility for watching you. I'd like to see you at least twice a day for the next eighteen days. If you feel the least bit ill, even if nothing more than a cold, I want to see you immediately."

"What if someone else could observe me?"

The man's brows puckered. "That would be fine, if you could arrange that."

"I'd love to have the company." Mr. Hargrove cleared his throat. "All of them, even the boy — it's no hardship. And with the way these two are concerned for him, I'd guess the boy would rather have their care."

The doctor huffed and snapped his medical bag closed. "If that's what you want. You must all give yourself a good scrub every time you leave this room. Do not touch anything but the sink until you've washed up, and then wash the sink. When he's healed, burn everything soft he's touched. I'll give you something to disinfect the other surfaces. As for you, Mr. Kingsman . . ." He squished past Mr. Hargrove and indicated he wanted to follow David out.

David turned and started for the kitchen, assuming the man wanted to use the sink.

The doctor scuffled behind him. "If I were you, I'd take the inoculation and leave this mess behind." He set his bag on the sink's ledge and rolled up his shirtsleeves.

"And if I choose to stay?"

"I've got three cases of smallpox on my hands. I don't want the public panicking because you're wandering in and out."

"Truly . . ."

David turned to find Evelyn standing in the kitchen doorway.

She stepped into the kitchen. "I can manage. Don't trouble yourself."

Why was she insistent on doing this alone? Perhaps if she knew it would be advantageous for him, she'd stop fretting. "Truth be told, I could use the quiet time to think and pray over the business plans I'm strug-

141

gling with. I might as well help you at the same time."

When the doctor stepped back from the sink to allow David to wash, Evelyn headed back to the sickroom before he even had the chance to second-guess himself.

The doctor wiped his bag. "My office is directly across First Street from the hospital. The green-and-white building. I expect you there within the half hour. Wash up before you leave."

The front door banged shut a few seconds later.

David washed again, and after drying his hands, he went to find Mr. Hargrove. The old man was sitting in a rocker in his parlor, a foot elevated on a hassock.

"Are you all right with my staying?"

"I have plenty of room and wasn't lying about liking company. It's a big house to rattle around in alone."

He had to decide now.

He wasn't really needed at the glass factory. He'd already put his plans into place, and they were moving along as expected. "Since this is my last time out, why don't you make me a list of things to get from the store so we can minimize the risk of contaminating more of your property than necessary? If the doctor can go about his business, surely I can hand the mercantile owner a note for supplies we'd like delivered."

"Sheets and blankets aren't an issue. But I could use some groceries while we're cooped up." He grabbed his cane and dropped his foot onto the floor. "I suppose I should check the pantry and make a list."

David held out his palm to stop him from struggling to get up. "If I make the list, will you let me cook?"

The man's fuzzy white eyebrows arched high. "You want to cook?"

"Yes, sir."

He looked at him for a second before res-ituating himself back into his chair. "You any good or just trying to help?"

"My cooking's better than decent, if I say so myself."

"How are you with beefsteak?"

"I like how you think, sir. Steak it is."

Mr. Hargrove gave him a nod, then closed his eyes as if now was as good a time as any to turn in for the day.

David rubbed his hands together. Though a quarantine couldn't possibly be considered enjoyable, playing around in the kitchen might make things more endurable.

And perhaps he could coax a smile onto Evelyn's face with a well-seasoned steak smothered in mushrooms and onions. Or

143

maybe a pudding of some sort to sweeten her up a little.

At least he'd have fun trying.

11

With dark shadows of evening filling every corner, David leaned his head against the doorjamb of Scott's sickroom, staying quiet so as not to disturb Evelyn. She'd worked tirelessly for two days to keep the moaning boy comfortable. Thankfully his restless thrashing had ceased a few hours ago.

However, his flushed face, pinched mouth, and pox-ridden skin made him look anything but comfortable.

The long hours of attempting to comfort Scott and cool his skin were taking a toll on Evelyn. She hadn't changed her dress since they'd been in quarantine, probably to keep from burning more of her wardrobe than necessary. Her hair could no longer be considered up, since more tendrils escaped the coil at the nape of her neck than remained in it. The dark smudges under her eyes and the strain about her mouth seemed to have aged her overnight, yet he couldn't do anything but stare at her, mess that she was. The devotion, the concern, and the love she possessed for this poor orphan was nearly palpable, achingly so.

And there was this unexplainable pinch in his chest as he worried over her while she worried over Scott. He wanted her to sit back and breathe and rest. Yet she refused to let anyone assume Scott's care, no matter how often he or Mr. Hargrove offered, as if closing her eyes for one second would negatively affect Scott's fate. She'd only left the room to see to her own personal needs whenever he booted her out to help Scott with his.

The dinner plate he'd brought in hours earlier appeared untouched.

That a man's heart could be won through his stomach was apparently true. Mr. Hargrove had practically declared them best chums after taking a bite of the steak he'd carefully cooked to perfection. But evidently the expression held no truth for women.

The grandfather clock in the parlor chimed eleven. He'd offered to take tonight's shift when he'd brought in dinner, but she'd ignored his suggestion by reminding him to have Mr. Hargrove check his temperature.

From her position beside the bed, she

146

exchanged the rag she'd draped across Scott's neck with a cooler one. Scott moaned in complaint.

David sighed. At least she let him bring her cold water every hour without a fuss.

She had to know she wasn't going to be much good to Scott if she kept this up. He took a step into the room. "I know you stayed up with him all night last night, but you can't do it again."

She looked over her shoulder at him. "I can." But the droop of her eyelids told a different story.

"Has anyone ever told you that you're extremely stubborn?"

Almost — a smile almost glimmered on those lips, but her sleep deprivation snagged it away before he got to see it bloom.

He walked farther into the small room, stopping at the footboard. "The last time he settled into a deep sleep like this, I didn't hear a peep out of him for nearly three hours. Go take a quick nap, at least. I can switch out rags."

She shook her head as she wrung another cloth. "I'm not going to mess up another of Mr. Hargrove's bedrooms."

"You could sleep in the room I slept in next door."

She only shook her head again and returned to swabbing the boy's face.

He wanted to go over, pull her up, and drag her out so she could get the rest she needed. But the more he insisted, the more she dug in her heels. He'd never dealt with a mule before, but he couldn't imagine a creature more stubborn than Evelyn.

But for some reason, he admired her for it. What if Father knew he would never bend to his wishes, no matter what Father said or did?

David glanced at the plate he'd brought for her supper, frowning again at how little she'd eaten. What would he be doing with his life right now if he had an ounce of her tenacity? Would he have pursued cooking and owning an eatery? Would such a venture have succeeded with sheer determination?

Or would capturing one dream only make him long to grasp another?

He lowered himself onto the corner of Scott's mattress. The boy, even in sleep, looked beyond miserable. "Is there a reason you can't leave him?"

Water dripped in the basin as she wrung out a rag. She changed out another set of cloths, but then stopped and simply stared at the boy's face.

Seconds ticked by, but he held his peace, hoping she wouldn't hold hers much longer.

She pushed the rag slipping off Scott's forehead back up against his hairline, then twirled her finger in the cowlick that formed a swirl above the boy's left temple. "He was the first child who seemed to be at all changed by our ministry. He'd gotten so excited about Jesus and loved his momma so much . . . if I'd gotten to his house sooner, she might not have . . ."

. . . *killed herself.* The unspoken end of her sentence hung heavy in the room. Yesterday, Evelyn had crumpled when the doctor told them the coroner agreed that Scott's mother hadn't died of smallpox, but rather from consuming the contents of the various empty bottles on her bedside table.

He pictured the woman he'd seen for only a few minutes, swathed in yards of vibrant purple, with rosy cheeks framed by dark brunette curls.

What if he hadn't interrupted their luncheon and Amy had heard Evelyn's story about God providing a way for the believing harlot to become part of the legacy of Christ?

For a moment, the weight of his actions squeezed the breath from his lungs. But he couldn't have known what would happen, and neither could have Evelyn. "People's choices are their own to answer for. You're not at fault for her death or any other decision she made. Nor will you be responsible for whatever happens to this boy if you step away for a spell and take care of yourself."

She busied herself dabbing the perspiration off Scott's face. A few seconds later, she turned away to start dipping rags again, but not before he saw a tear trickle down her cheek.

How could he assure her that what he said was true? She was so guarded. Maybe if he opened himself up she'd feel more inclined to trust him.

A tic in his cheek pulled at his lips at the thought of exposing his faults just to get her to take a silly nap . . . and yet what if someone finally knew the truth? He had a few friends back home, but he'd never really shared his problems with them. He was more privileged, so he'd felt wrong to complain about his life.

He scrutinized Scott to make certain the boy was asleep. "There've been countless times I wanted to run away from my life. I've never wanted to kill myself, but I understand how problems can tempt someone to leave it all behind, since I've essentially just run off to avoid some of my own problems. But no matter what anyone does to me, I'm still responsible for my own actions." He closed his eyes and gritted his teeth. He ought to write Father and tell him what was happening. It was his father's property he was gambling with, after all.

Evelyn sniffed. "And what did you run away from?"

So many things. "Basically a controlling father and an unwanted bride."

"A bride?" Her face turned hard. "You're a runaway groom? A jilter?"

He leaned backward, distancing himself from her glare. She looked at him as though *jilter* was synonymous with *despicable.* "More like a runaway son-in-law. Marianne's as disinterested in marrying me as I am her, but our folks want us married. They've got their reasons — logical ones — but both of us wish they'd stop pushing."

"So why don't you just tell them no?"

"Not all of us excel at digging in our heels." He gave her a small smile, but she only turned away to tuck Scott's blister-covered arm back under his blanket. "Anyway, I'm here in Teaville to get away from my father pushing Marianne at me — or rather, my father in general."

"I'm sorry to hear you and your father don't get along." Evelyn flipped the rag over on Scott's forehead. "What about your mother?"

"She died having me."

Her hands stilled, and she turned to look at him, holding his gaze longer than she normally did. "I'm sorry."

"Don't be." He looked down, not wanting to see pity in her eyes. "I had a wonderful nanny-turned-governess, Mrs. Rice, who filled that mother-sized hole even if she was old enough to be my grandmother."

She looked at him for a second before readjusting Scott's last rag. "My parents are old enough to be my grandparents." She traced the frayed quilt's stitches. "I'm always sorry to hear about people not getting along with their parents. I don't know how I'd live without mine."

Finally, some real talking. Perhaps he would yet convince her that sleeping wasn't such a terrible thing to do. "Are your parents supportive of . . . how you're living your life?"

She shrugged. "They'd prefer me to marry and give them grandchildren, but they're adjusting to how life is going for me."

"I wish my father only wanted grandchildren, but marriage is just another way to add to the Kingsman coffers. In his eyes, it's practically a sin not to connect two affluent families and hoard the wealth. What about you? Do your parents push you toward eligible bachelors, or are you lucky enough to be left alone in that respect?"

Her eyebrows scrunched, and her mouth pinched.

What had he said wrong?

"I think I'm done with this conversation, Mr. Kingsman." She snatched a rag off Scott's neck and dipped it into the cool water, though she surely didn't need to do that again already.

He ground the palm of his hand into one of his eyes, then stood. Directing the conversation toward something other than Scott's care had gotten him back to nowhere. "If you aren't going to let me take over, can I at least bring you something? Water, tea, a book?"

"You should stop being so nice to me."

He blinked at her. *Stop being nice?* How should he respond to that? He racked his brain for a way to answer without the use of a frustrated growl. "All right, then, I'll do as you wish and leave you alone." He took her plate and made his way to the kitchen without waiting for a response.

Seemed a friendship with her was less likely than he'd thought.

He'd had a lifetime to adjust to Father deriding him no matter what he said or did, so why did it bother him that a woman he

barely knew seemed as averse to trusting
him as Father?

12

David let Evelyn's dirty plate clatter onto the sink's ledge but immediately cringed. Scott's rest shouldn't be disturbed because he was frustrated with the boy's caretaker.

"What's the matter?"

David startled. He hadn't expected Mr. Hargrove to be sitting in the parlor off the kitchen. The older man had turned in before he'd gone in to talk to Evelyn to try to convince her one last time to let him sit up with Scott for the night. "What do you mean?"

"You're shaking your head and mumbling."

He let out a sad laugh. "Just trying to figure out what's wrong with women."

"Nothing much wrong with them, actually. They're quite nice to have around." Mr. Hargrove smiled wide. "Though maybe since I had a wife and five girls, women no longer feel quite as mysterious to me as they were when I was your age."

"But did they ever tell you to stop being nice? That isn't exactly explainable behavior."

"Ah, Miss Wisely." Mr. Hargrove looked toward the sickroom. "She does seem to have a habit of pushing men away the second one shows any interest. If you're going to pursue her, you're going to have to be sneaky about it, keep her from realizing you're interested until you've won her over. Otherwise you'll likely end up fighting a losing battle."

"But I'm not pursuing her. I'm actually just trying to be nice."

"You're not pursuing her?" Mr. Hargrove looked genuinely confused.

Had he done something to give his host that impression? David scraped the food off her plate into the trash. "No."

"Oh." His wrinkled forehead furrowed. "Well, I've only noticed that behavior from her when a young man gets too eager. She's generally a warm and kind creature to everyone else."

David dumped Evelyn's dish into the sink water, and when Mr. Hargrove shuffled out, he began scrubbing. What had he done to make a kind woman act as if being considerate was wrong?

Grief did do funny things though. Maybe Scott's mother's death was hitting Evelyn harder than he'd guessed. When Mrs. Rice had died five years ago, he hadn't exactly been the easiest man to get along with for a few months. Even if she hadn't been his mother, she was the closest woman to ever being so, and he'd grieved her deeply.

If only he didn't have this innate desire to please people, he probably wouldn't be taking Evelyn's moodiness so personally. After finishing the dishes, he moved into the parlor as the clock chimed the half hour.

Mr. Hargrove, again in his chair, turned to look at him. "If you want to go back to sleep, I can wake you if I hear anything."

"No, that's all right." Scott was bound to need him soon. "But I thought you'd gone back to bed."

"Couldn't sleep, so I thought I'd come out here and pray for the boy. I can see the sunrise through this window." He pointed to the large picture window in front of him.

The line of houses across the street blotted out the horizon, so it couldn't be that spectacular of a view.

David glanced at the clock to make sure he wasn't mistaken about the time. Just past eleven thirty, as he'd thought. "You intend to be up that long?"

The man shrugged. "I might fall asleep, but there's plenty to pray about."

David settled into the seat that was now "his," took up the figures he'd been working on earlier, and put his feet on the hassock. Agonizing over the factory's goings-on would surely keep him awake long enough to hear when Scott called for him.

He frowned at the calculations he'd left off with and drummed his fingers on the armrest. Did he really need to play with these numbers anymore? He should probably start composing the letter he needed to write his father instead.

Then again, maybe he could just sit and pray with Mr. Hargrove until the sun came up. He laid aside his pencil and paper and sighed.

"What's on those papers that makes you frown so much?"

"Business projections." He leaned his head back against the headrest.

"They got you stumped?"

"Not exactly. They're lining up as I'd hoped, but I'm trying to decide if it's wise to go against what my father wanted me to do in the first place. Though I'm probably just not stubborn enough to go against him for long."

"And you don't want to do as your father

wishes?"

"I rarely do, unfortunately." He'd probably live out his life plagued with ulcers if he couldn't figure out how to reconcile himself with simply going along with whatever Father wanted. "Though after a bit of protest, I usually end up doing what he wants."

"I remember that struggle myself. But I clearly remember the day I decided to stop and become my own man." Hargrove took a sip of whatever he had in the mug beside him. "I was fresh out of high school, with grades that made my father and mother insist I was made for something grand. Law school was their choice. They didn't take into account I wasn't the kind of person who liked public speaking or dealing with crowds."

"So you didn't go to law school?"

"No, took over a cobbling business."

"I assume your parents weren't happy."

He shook his head. "Never did make much money, since I wasn't the only shoe repair in town. I had a grand time anyway, married my grade-school sweetheart and got to listen to men spill out their woes while I fixed their soles. My little girls would help me in the shop when they missed me."

He readjusted himself in his chair, his leg

obviously bothering him. "I still have clients come tell me about their lives, and my girls adore me. Just wish most of them hadn't moved away. Though I don't blame them, since I encouraged them to support their husbands wherever their dreams took them."

"And if your son-in-law's dream was to cook?"

Hargrove took the time to sip his drink before answering. "That's your dream, is it?"

He shrugged. "It was one of them."

"That smothered steak was quite good."

"Thanks." He tried not to smile like a kid at the praise. He'd cooked for his father plenty of times, and all he'd gotten were a few happy grunts. Definitely no compliments that might encourage him to pursue his silly hobby.

He leaned his head back against his chair again, taking in Hargrove's humble furnishings. Amateur paintings adorned the walls, likely his daughters' attempts at art. A few chairs that looked as old as the man who sat in them and a scratched-up table covered with books and newspaper clippings were about all the parlor contained. This man had little yet seemed more content than David or his father. "What did your parents do when you went against their wishes?"

"They got used to it."

"I'm not sure my father would. Being his only son, if I turn my back on his business, the rift between us would likely grow insurmountable."

Muffled sounds down the hallway caused him to look at the clock. Nearly twelve fifteen. He pushed out of the chair and took a look at Mr. Hargrove's mug. "Would you like me to freshen up your coffee when I return?"

"No thanks, I shouldn't even be drinking this late at night." He reached out and took a hold of David's arm. "I'll pray for you too."

His father had often said he was praying for him, but it was likely only so his son would see things his way. But Mr. Hargrove's eyes said the man truly did care about his happiness, despite only knowing him for two days.

"Thank you," he said, surprised by the lump in his throat that garbled his reply.

Scott's distant muttering grew insistent, so he left Mr. Hargrove for the back room. If Evelyn was having a hard time keeping him calm, the boy was likely in pain or burning up again. David took a quick side trip into the kitchen to grab a bucket of cold

161

water and more pain powders.

Inside the sickroom, David blinked his eyes as they adjusted to the darkness, but he saw no movement. "Miss Wisely?"

"Mr. Kings —" Scott's voice cracked and broke off.

David made his way to the end of the bed and felt for the boy's ankle. "Do I need to take you outside?"

"Just . . . need water."

Where was Evelyn? He felt for the glass on the dresser top and poured Scott a drink as the edges of things came into focus. When he turned to give the boy the glass, he found her. Her upper body lay draped across the bed, one arm hooked across Scott's middle, her breathing soft with the rhythm of sleep. He touched her back and jiggled her a bit, but she didn't so much as twitch.

Moving to the other side of the bed, he helped the boy drink. After Scott lay back, exhausted from the effort, David collected the rags that had rolled off the boy. They were quite warm. Evelyn must have fallen asleep almost as soon as he'd left.

The boy's breathing settled into an even rhythm, but his breaths were nowhere near as deep and steady as Evelyn's. She couldn't be comfortable draped as she was, but if he woke her and suggested she go lie down, she'd likely force herself to go back to her constant rag dipping.

He lit a few more candles, traded out Scott's warm rags with wet, cool ones, and then returned to the parlor. Mr. Hargrove was either asleep or deep in prayer, so he quietly collected his papers and pencil before returning to the sickroom. He settled himself in the room's other chair and watched the two of them for a few minutes, but neither stirred.

When she woke, she'd likely be mad at herself for falling asleep, but if David stayed awake until she arose, Scott wouldn't be the worse for it.

In the breathy quiet, he let himself look at Evelyn for a good long while. Her face looked peaceful in the candlelight.

This woman did what she wanted with such conviction, even if she was obnoxious about it. Would doing what he wanted bring him peace, or was he simply going to have to find peace no matter what circumstances he found himself in?

With his legs propped between the footboard's steel rails, he turned to an empty page to start his letter to Father.

Maybe if he told him what he planned to do with no hint of being willing to compromise, Father might get "used to" his choices like Mr. Hargrove's and Evelyn's parents had.

He doubted it. But he had to start somewhere.

13

Evelyn yawned, rubbed her eye, and then jerked her head off the quilt. She winced at the morning light hitting her straight in the face, but she forced her eyes to remain open so she could check on Scott.

The boy was looking down at her, his mouth attempting a smile. "Morning," he croaked.

How late was it? At least he hadn't said *good afternoon.* "How'd you sleep?"

His answer was a noncommittal shrug.

Rubbing at a crick in her neck, she looked about the room. Thankfully neither David nor Mr. Hargrove was there. Had she snored or done anything to call attention to how she'd failed to care for Scott all night long?

She reached up and tilted the timepiece on the dresser toward her. Seven fifteen. Not too late. Hopefully the men hadn't passed by the open door yet. She reached for the rags that had fallen off Scott's face. They felt wetter and cooler than she'd expected. She put a hand against his forehead. He wasn't burning up anymore, though he still had a fever.

Scott rolled his head toward her. "Water?" There was something in his clear gaze that simply melted her worry away.

"Of course." She got up to grab the pitcher, which didn't lift as easily as she'd expected. Hadn't she needed to refill it? Or maybe David had and she didn't remember. She poured Scott a glass but left it on the dresser when she saw him struggling to sit up. "Let me help you."

He looked ready to go back to sleep any second, yet he held himself up when she arranged the pillows behind him. When she brought the glass to his lips, he took it and tipped it back himself.

Despite the sores all over his face, she had to force herself not to kiss him on the forehead. He was going to make it!

The boy shakily held out the glass for her to take, smiling back at what must have been a large goofy grin on her face.

She caught a whiff of . . . bacon and a sugary smell. "Can I get you something to eat?" Mr. Hargrove had certainly tried to keep her well fed, but it had felt wrong to eat such sumptuous meals in front of Scott. Her stomach took the time to growl in protest. "More broth or something else?"

"Not now." He started scratching his cheek.

She grabbed his hand and wrapped it under the covers. "You need to leave your sores alone. They're already going to scar — don't make it worse."

He looked at the exposed part of his arm and frowned. "Are those everywhere?"

She nodded, not knowing how to respond to the utter devastation on his mangled face.

"Can I look in the mirror?"

"That's not a good idea." She pushed back the sweaty hair from his forehead, remembering the handsome face the small-pox hid. "I had smallpox when I was three. I don't remember much about it, but I do remember panicking after catching a glimpse of myself in the mirror. I'll be honest, you don't look good, but in a few days the sores will scab and fall off. The doctor says your case is fairly mild. Mine was too. And my scars aren't too bad, right?"

The boy looked over at her, and she pulled the hair back from the right side of her face. "I have quite a few in my hairline here." She moved her hands across her face as she pointed out the imperfections she'd cried over when she was younger. "They're along my eyebrow, and there's one large one that sits in the crease of my eyelid here, and over on this cheek there's a line of them. They've faded over time." And her young skin had likely recovered better than most. She wasn't certain if his getting smallpox at twelve would keep his scars from fading as much as hers, but they'd surely fade some. "And if you look at Mr. Hargrove, he's got plenty too — that's why he wears a beard." She smiled at him. "You're lucky that one day you'll have a beard to cover them up. I certainly don't have that option."

"I've never noticed your scars before."

She squeezed his arm through the sheet. "They become a part of you, and you'll stop thinking about them so much after a while." As long as the scarring wasn't horrific, anyway. Hopefully Scott's scarring would be as minimal as hers. But she'd seen older people with significant scarring and even blindness from back when smallpox out-breaks had been more devastating. "And it seems no one focuses on flaws as much as the person who has them, so though you know they're there, no one else much cares."

Though of course, no one with any sense of decency pointed out someone's scars when they saw them, so she pretended most people were like Scott and didn't notice her scars at all.

"All right, I won't look." Scott swallowed hard and dropped his gaze. "What's going to happen to me now?"

She refluffed his pillows. He hadn't spoken this much since she'd found him. "You're going to get better."

"I mean after that?" His jaw wobbled, and he looked away from her with a sniff.

She stopped messing with his bedding and sat beside him, wishing she could take his hand but not wanting to irritate his sores. "Do you have any other family?"

He shook his head, though he winced with the effort. "I don't want to be with them."

"We should probably at least inform them —"

"They never cared about me before. Can't I go to the orphanage with you?"

"Of course you can." Since he was such an independent twelve-year-old, she had worried he might not want to. Several boys his age ran around the streets without any oversight, getting into trouble, following the paths of their fathers.

"Could I stay with you forever?"

She smoothed his hair until she could muster up an answer. She couldn't promise no one would want to adopt him. That was the whole point of the orphanage, to get the children into loving, permanent homes. Granted, not many of the couples who'd come to adopt an orphan had met Nicholas's criteria, but a few children had joined a family.

Though every bit of her wanted to promise Scott she'd always be a part of his life, how could she? Nicholas never bothered interviewing anyone willing to adopt except married couples, so the only way Scott could stay with her forever was if no one wanted him, and how could she wish for that? She licked her lips and rustled up a smile. "You'll be with me as long as I'm able to be with you."

"Even if that's forever?"

"You'll not need me your whole life. Eventually you'll grow up to be a good, strong man and have a job, and maybe a family of your own."

"But I can still visit you."

"Of course, or you could write letters if you move far away."

"I won't leave you, Miss Wisely." Scott grasped her hand and tried to squeeze, though he lacked the strength. "Not ever."

A tap sounded on the door behind her. Mr. Hargrove leaned heavily on his cane and stood with a book in his free hand.

170

"May I take over? There's breakfast waiting for you."

She turned back to Scott. "Do you need to . . ." Well, she supposed he'd have asked for David if he needed help, but after such a long night's sleep . . .

"I'm fine." Scott's eyes were at half-mast, and a contented smile graced his lips.

As much as she wanted to try to get food into him before he drifted back to sleep, he wouldn't shrivel away in an hour or two.

"I've got *The Call of the Wild*." Mr. Hargrove limped farther into the room. "Have you read it, son?"

"I haven't read any books, sir."

"Well, I thought I'd read it today. Figured you might want to listen."

Scott nodded his head ever so slightly, and Evelyn took her leave.

"Good morning."

She nearly jumped out of her skin.

Mr. Kingsman stood in the hallway, looking at her far too intently. His thick blond hair looked damp and freshly combed, and he smelled like the soap Mr. Hargrove used.

When Scott had asked for a mirror, she should've thought to at least glance at herself before leaving the room. She probably looked a fright. "Good morning to you."

"You've stepped out of the room." His voice was high and bright, as if her doing so was worthy of the newspaper's front page.

Though perhaps he was simply excited about what that meant about Scott.

"Yes, I have. Scott seems to have come through the worst, and Mr. Hargrove is in there with a book. He said he left me breakfast."

Mr. Kingsman stood staring at her with that big grin of his widening across his face.

Did he find something amusing? She forced her hands to stay still despite wanting to feel if there was some lock of hair out of place or something sticking to her face. "If you'll excuse me."

"Of course." He scooted to the side of the hallway to let her pass. "I'll just go in and see if Scott needs anything, then I can come back and dish you up a plate."

"I can manage . . ." But he'd already disappeared into the room.

She went to the kitchen sink and washed up as well as she could without casting aside her clothing for something fresh and then quickly used the shiny teakettle to take a peek at her hair. She looked unkempt but not awful. Now if only she could find an actual mirror to be certain.

Mr. Hargrove's thumping cane and dragging feet grew louder, right before he showed up in the doorway. "Forgot my coffee."

"Here, let me get it." She snatched up the mug he seemed to favor. "Thank you so much for opening your home to us. Hopefully it won't be much longer before we can leave. He seems on the mend, thankfully."

"No rush. I'm glad my home is of more use than usual." He thumped forward a few more steps, grabbed hold of a kitchen chair's back, and leaned heavily upon it. "I suppose the boy's going to the orphanage with you once the doctor clears him?"

"Yes."

"How many children live there now?"

"He'll make ten." She topped off his mug.

"That'll be a lot for you to handle once your parents retire."

"Yes, but their retirement is quite a ways away. And who knows how many we'll have then."

"Perhaps several months feels like a long way off to a youngster like yourself, but it'll be here before you know it."

Carefully, so as not to scald herself, she stopped pouring her coffee but still managed to spill some on the counter. She looked around for a dishrag. "They told you

173

they're retiring?" Maybe he was only assuming.

"Last time your father came over for chess, he mentioned they'd be leaving next summer. It's been a while since he visited. His leg keeping him down?"

"It bothers him more every day, it seems." Evidently more than he'd let on.

"He still refusing to get himself a cane?"

She nodded and finished pouring her coffee, careful not to spill any more.

"Maybe I should get him one for his birthday."

"I'm not sure he'll ever use one, no matter how ridiculous he might look hobbling about." She brought over his mug and sank into the nearest chair, staring at the little bubbles atop her coffee.

He didn't pick up his mug and walk away, and she couldn't think of anything to say to fill up the silence. Hopefully he'd leave before he noticed how difficult it was to keep her jaw from quivering.

"Did they not tell you?"

She managed to give him a quick shake of her head but didn't dare look up at him.

He sighed and shifted his weight. "I'm sorry. I assumed they discussed their plans with you."

Why hadn't they? Did they have some

plan to help her stay there? Were they working with Nicholas to find replacements before mentioning it to her? "They know how much I want to stay at the orphanage, and . . . if they're not there to help . . ." She swallowed in hopes of continuing to talk without letting too much emotion bubble out. "Perhaps I won't be staying much longer."

She wrapped her hands around her mug, absorbing the heat, to focus on something besides the way her insides jittered. "Did Daddy tell you who they expected would run the orphanage after they left?" Her voice warbled, so she took a sip of coffee. Too strong. She took another drink anyway.

After a minute of silence, she stopped pretending she liked the coffee and looked up into Mr. Hargrove's pale green eyes.

"I'm sorry you heard it from me." He stroked his beard. "I assumed Walter was excited about getting to retire because you'd finally found a man you might be interested in. I expected to hear of an engagement before the year was up. I suppose that's not the case?"

"No," she whispered. She went back to staring at her coffee. Just yesterday she'd felt sorry David's relationship with his father wasn't as good as hers was with her own. She'd thought her relationship with her parents was good, but if they'd kept something like this from her, maybe she'd been completely wrong.

"Perhaps they thought you were ready to move on to something else?"

"No, this is all I want to do. They know that. They also know I can't do it alone."

Mr. Hargrove stood still for several ticks of the clock, switching his weight from his bad leg to his good. He clearly needed to get off his feet, so why didn't he leave her to sniffle in peace? He clomped a step closer and put a hand on her shoulder. "There are several good men around here, you know. Some who might even help you in the very trenches you've dedicated yourself to."

Ah, so he was going to try to fix her life by matchmaking. She'd rather enjoyed his company over the years because he'd never once attempted it. "No, I'm certain no man is willing to live with me. I mean, not with what I've chosen to do with my life."

"Don't be so sure."

She shrugged and kept her focus on the mug in her hands. If she stayed quiet, maybe he'd return to Scott before any tears splashed into her coffee.

Mr. Kingsman's confident footsteps thumped through the kitchen as he headed for the sink to wash up after attending Scott. "I see you found the coffee."

"Yes," she whispered. She needed cream to make it tolerable, but she didn't trust her voice to ask for any.

Mr. Hargrove picked up his mug but didn't walk away.

She nearly squirmed in her seat as she resisted looking at him again. But she finally gave in.

His eyes were so soft — it was as if he were looking at one of his own daughters. "They love you. Don't fret too much."

She nodded, more to let him know he could leave and return to Scott than to promise not to worry.

David brought the coffeepot over and refilled her mug to the brim, leaving no room for cream. Probably for the best. If she drank any more, she might not be able to take a nap while Mr. Hargrove read to Scott. And right now, sleeping might be the only way to settle the panic swirling inside her.

David crossed over to the stove and lit the gas burners, then clanked through the pans piled on the counter. "Seems Scott's over the worst of it. So you'll get some rest now," he said, more as a command than a question.

Usually such a tone would make her want to do the opposite, but not today. "I hope so." Though what chance was there of turning off her brain enough to sleep?

"Good — you deserve a break. Scott's mother couldn't have been more devoted to his well-being than you've been. He told me he's going to live with you at the mansion. Once the feverish fog leaves him and the reality that he lost his mother kicks in . . . Well, I'm glad he's got you to see him through."

Scott.

She wouldn't be at the mansion for very long now. Within the year, she'd likely have to abandon Scott to whoever took over the orphanage.

For some reason, she didn't think he'd be comforted by the thought that she'd visit when she could.

She folded her arms on the tabletop and buried her head in the crook of her elbow to keep David from seeing her hold back tears.

14

Evelyn pressed her head farther into her arms on the table, trying to breathe slowly and evenly. Thankfully the clanging of pots while David cooked drowned out the sound of her failed attempts to keep her sniffling at bay.

Realizing her parents had kept a secret that could possibly destroy her future was devastating, of course, but losing a day of sleep was surely the reason she was having difficulty keeping a grip on herself.

The smell of sizzling bacon made her stomach growl. She should head to the spare room and sleep off the emotions, but her stomach might start a civil war if she did. She peeked above her arm just enough to make sure David's back was turned before she fished out her handkerchief and patted her eyes.

Mr. Hargrove had told her she shouldn't worry, and maybe she shouldn't. Surely her parents knew how much working at the orphanage meant to her and wouldn't leave before formulating a plan to help her stay. Surely they weren't going to try to push her toward a man, hoping she'd get engaged, as Mr. Hargrove had assumed.

Oh, her stomach just wasn't going to be able to digest food along with the worry churning in there. Since it would be days before she could see her parents, she should just stop thinking about it. Find a distraction, something to read.

She looked around the kitchen, but there was only a leather-bound notepad in the middle of the table that she couldn't imagine belonging to Mr. Hargrove. A page near the top was poking out a bit, and on it was what looked like . . . a curtain? "Do you draw?"

"A little." David quickly crossed the room and tapped the page back inside. His hand then pressed down on the notepad as if it might run away.

"I suppose you won't let me see?"

For a few moments, he just stood staring at her, as if weighing whether or not she was worthy, making her want to see it all the more.

He sat, pulled the notebook closer, then carefully flipped through the page edges as if he might accidentally show her top-secret information. He finally slid out the drawing she'd glimpsed.

Without comment, he pushed it toward her, then left his seat as if it had suddenly gotten hot. He went to the stove and flipped bacon.

She turned the drawing around. "Why, it's Mr. Hargrove." The background was barely sketched in behind him — a few lines for the window casing, the wisp of the curtain she'd seen — but the focus of the simple pencil drawing was on Mr. Hargrove's eyes. There was something slightly off with his bearded jawline and the forehead, but only people who knew Mr. Hargrove well would likely notice. But the emotion David had captured, the wistfulness that oozed from the portrait, was nearly palpable. "This is really well done."

"Just don't say that about my steaks." He turned around to shake his spatula at her. "Medium well is as done as they should get."

She rolled her eyes at his silly joke, but that only made him smile wider.

David's eyes. Now *that* sparkle would be something to capture in a portrait.

Of course, the color of his irises was gorgeous — she'd seen that the first day. The deep blue that masqueraded as purple when the light hit them just right — that certainly couldn't be shown in a pencil sketch. And the light that always seemed to twinkle in them would be hard to capture as well — a sparkle she doubted danced in her eyes much at all. How many times had Daddy chucked her under the chin and told her to stop being so serious?

And the look in David's eyes right now . . . She couldn't imagine how she'd describe it, let alone draw it.

Oh goodness, she was staring. And why had she stopped breathing? She quickly pulled in a draught of air and looked back at the picture, hoping he hadn't noticed the stopped-breathing part.

That smile of his was going to get her in trouble.

The expectancy of his gaze bored into her. Tracing her finger along the smudged graphite shadows, she tried to think of something to say. "Well . . . this sketch is remarkable. Did he actually look like he was longing for something when you drew him, or did it just turn out that way?"

He turned back to his cooking. "He was definitely in another time or place. That's probably my best drawing in regard to a true likeness. Of course, that was because I took my time. Mr. Hargrove was willing to sit for a while."

"You ought to do these to sell."

"I've got talent, but no genius. Father proved that to me when I was about sixteen. As I said, that's one of my best. The others aren't nearly as good. But I still like to capture faces, and I've had plenty of time to try over the past few days."

"You did more of Mr. Hargrove?"

He stiffened, then put down his spatula and grabbed a hand towel. "Another one, yes."

"May I see? It might be just as good and you don't know it." She grabbed his notepad and flipped it open.

He strode across the room, slid the notepad away from her, and flipped it shut, but not before she saw a drawing that clearly wasn't of Mr. Hargrove — unless he'd drawn him in a long-haired wig.

"Was that me?"

David's lips wriggled and his hands tensed, but then he nudged the notepad back toward her. "Yes."

Since he simply stood there, she took that as an invitation to look again. Odd that he seemed so worried about it. But then, when had he drawn her?

She pulled the notepad closer and flipped

it open. There was a page filled with numbers, another drawing of Mr. Hargrove — definitely not as good. And then, the next page.

Her sleeping head lay on Scott's bed, her hair spilling out over her shoulders and onto a simplified version of a quilt. Behind her, Scott's face was in shadow, perhaps to keep from recording the sickly way he looked.

With how everything else was only roughed in, the drawing's focus was completely centered on her.

The detail was extraordinary. Fanned out eyelashes, relaxed mouth, her upper lip without that little dip in it she'd always wished God had given her, and candlelight deepening the contours of her cheekbones.

"I'm sorry I didn't ask your permission first, but it was the first time I'd seen you so peaceful. Besides, I needed something to do to keep from falling asleep."

She almost wanted to ask him for the drawing to give to her mother, but the setting was far too intimate. Though maybe she should insist he give it to her so he no longer had it in his possession. She fingered a strand of hair lying against her shoulder. Had he embellished the amount of hair that had fallen down last night, or was her hair really that undone? Before leaving Scott's room, she should have found a mirror . . . but even if she had, her reflection would be far less pretty than what was on this paper.

She gently closed the leather binder. "Seems I was caught. I'd hoped neither you nor Mr. Hargrove had noticed after I was so adamant I could care for him."

David went back to the stove. "But you did care for him. I'm sure if he needed you — even after you'd fallen asleep — you would have sensed it and awoken." He came back with a plate and slid it in front of her. "You'll be happy to know he slept quite comfortably. I only stayed there in case he woke up needing you."

His words sent a rush of heat to her eyes, and she blinked. If only she could be sure Scott wouldn't need her in the future — for she'd likely not be there.

And now she was back to frowning. After his joke about well-done steaks, she'd at least started to . . . not frown. David sat but kept himself from reaching over and tapping her chin up. "Why so glum?"

"I'm just worried." She pushed a piece of bacon across her plate but didn't take a bite.

How could one have bacon in front of them and not eat it?

Or leave extra on the stove to grow cold?

He got up to get the rest for himself. Seemed unlikely she'd want seconds if she was just going to push hers around, though he'd hoped she'd finally eat this morning. "God knows what'll happen to every one of us. No need to worry."

"I'm more worried for Scott than myself."

He scooped up the last of the bacon and found himself a napkin. "Won't he go to the orphanage with you?"

"Yes."

Then why was she troubled? He was tempted to push her to open up, but he wouldn't. She might accuse him of being nice again.

"What is this?" She pointed at the yellow mound on her plate as if baked pudding was what was worrying her most.

"Canary pudding with a simple hard sauce." It had come out quite tasty, if he did think so himself.

She pulled the mint leaf out of the curls of lemon rind on top of the pudding.

"Oh, that? Mint. Not really meant to be eaten with the pudding, but you can chew on it afterward, if you'd like."

She looked over at the pots and cups and utensils piled around the stove, then stared at his shirt.

He looked down. He hadn't brushed off

186

the flour, so he did so.

"Who made dinner last night?"

"Me."

"What was in the potatoes?"

"Those? They were only buttermilk mashed potatoes with chives, garlic, whipped butter, and sour cream. Oh, and a pinch of smoked salt."

"*Only* mashed potatoes, huh?"

Sweet mercy, he'd done it! He slapped the table so hard she jumped in her seat.

She looked at his hand on the table with wide eyes, then back up at him, her eyebrows cocked funny. "Why'd you slap the table?"

"I got you to smile." He threw out his arms. "I don't know what you found so amusing about my potatoes, but I finally got to see a smile on your face."

Her smile drooped.

Well, that was short-lived. But at least her eyes still appeared amused.

She picked up her fork and pointed it at him. "I'm sorry to break it to you, but I have smiled once or twice before."

"Not since I've met you."

Unfortunately, the gleam in her eyes now died off.

"Surely that isn't true. I'm not that . . . dour." She took a deep breath and looked blankly past him. "It has been a rough few months, and . . . next year doesn't look too promising either." She shrugged a shoulder and took a bite of bacon.

If what disfigured her lips right now was another attempt at a smile, she utterly failed.

How could bacon make someone look confused? "I used to pride myself on making people happy with my cooking, but I've never seen that reaction before. Perhaps Father was right to discourage me."

"It's good. Truly. I just wasn't expecting . . . this." She looked at the slice as if expecting to discover something other than bacon in her hand. "What did you do to it?"

"I glazed it with maple syrup."

"I'm going to assume you didn't just take up cooking because you're cooped up with us." She took another bite and hummed.

Now that was better.

Though talking about himself yesterday hadn't opened her up as much as he would've liked, since she'd seen his drawings, he might as well tell her everything about that stifled part of himself. "Whenever I became too much of a pest, Mrs. Rice sent me down to annoy Cook. However, she wouldn't tolerate having someone in her kitchen who wasn't working." He took a bite of bacon and only wished he'd been able to smoke it like she'd taught him. But at least the crispness was perfect. "I enjoyed it. But once I turned twelve, my father curbed that hobby. *'Not befitting a man of your station,'* he said. Just like my drawings. My math skills were the only thing Father deemed worthy of my spending time honing."

"I'm sorry I dredged up that memory for you." She frowned as if she could actually feel the emotions he'd gone through when he'd realized chasing his dreams was a waste of time.

For some reason, he didn't want Evelyn to feel anything at all like he'd felt that day. And if mashed potatoes could summon up a smile, then surely he could earn another with the decision he'd made last night. "You said this next year didn't look promising, but maybe it won't be as bad as you're thinking — because I've decided to help."

"Help?" Another smile didn't appear on those lips, but at least the frown had fled again.

"I've decided to become one of those partners Mr. Lowe wants you to find for your women's home."

She blinked. Repeatedly.

"Right now would be the time you should let loose one of those smiles you hoard."

189

She rolled her eyes instead. "I'm very pleased. I'd told myself I could get a women's home with or without your help, but I was beginning to think I was only fooling myself."

"Well, my help might not actually make it happen. You still have to get someone else to join in." He stared at her bacon, wishing she'd eat it before he was tempted to snatch it away. "And I'm not going to be able to do much, but I can do something. Did Mr. Lowe outline what he required of your business partners?"

At the shake of her head, he continued. "I figured I could do a few things. I could employ a few women to clean my factory after hours. I also thought I'd sponsor a day's worth of meals each week. Not sure what else I could do. Maybe give some cooking lessons if I'm still around. Can't promise I'll be in Teaville long, but I'd still sponsor the meals once I return to Kansas City."

"All right." Her eyes livened up a little. "Who do you know who might be swayed by your joining in?"

He shrugged. "You know more townspeople than I do. I don't know any of them well."

"Have you met Henri Beauchamp?"

"I take it he owns Beauchamp Flour Mill?" He passed that mill daily on the way from the boardinghouse to the factory.

"Yes."

"I'm afraid I haven't. Not much reason for a glass factory and a flour mill to work together."

She hung her head as if his not knowing one person meant defeat.

"Now, just because I don't know him doesn't mean my support might not sway him. But instead of asking this Beauchamp for open-ended support, write up a list of ways he could help. Ask Mr. Lowe what he needs from us at minimum. If you make your requests more concrete, people might find it harder to refuse. And if they can see what I'm doing isn't completely burdensome, they might be more willing to do a little something themselves."

She settled back against her seat and looked up at the ceiling as if he'd finally said something right.

At least a little of the peacefulness he'd seen on her face last night had returned.

This woman certainly had a heart for the unfortunate, and he'd do what he could to help. Hopefully he could do enough to get something going in the right direction for her before Father came and shut him down.

15

David walked up Mr. Hargrove's porch steps. The doctor had released him from quarantine three days ago, after Scott was strong enough to take care of himself, but David had argued to return to help them in the afternoons. If the doctor could come and go, surely he could do the same. Dr. Hiller had reluctantly given him permission, if David agreed to follow a complicated regimen to keep from spreading contagion.

But washing up and dealing with his tainted clothing was no hardship. When the doctor had first permitted him to leave, his heart had actually grown heavier.

Without bothering to knock, David ignored the big yellow isolation notice to the right of Mr. Hargrove's front door and barged right in. "I'm here!"

Though no one answered, he took his crate of groceries straight to the kitchen. He needed almost two hours to cook his macaroni au gratin, so he'd better start if they were going to eat before bedtime.

Mr. Hargrove had offered to pay him to cook dinner and drop it off, but he wouldn't enjoy it half as much if he wasn't with them. Not that he could have used the boarding-house kitchen anyway.

Without waiting for Mr. Hargrove, he filled a large pot with water, put in a gener-ous amount of salt, and then put it on the stove to boil.

David fished out the candy from the crate and headed to the sickroom. Scott hadn't been interested in eating much, but what child could resist sugar?

After a slight tap on the door, David poked his head into the room. "How are we doing?"

Scott smiled, and Evelyn put down the book Mr. Hargrove had started reading to the boy last night.

"I've got something for you." He walked over and handed Scott his special purchase.

Immediately when he opened the small paper bag, Scott's face brightened behind his flaking skin. He pulled out one of the striated candies with one hand while scratching his cheek with the other. "Can I have one now?"

"It's 'may I have one now,' and you should

193

wait until dinner." Evelyn grabbed the hand rubbing his cheek. "And stop scratching."

She gave Scott a look he must have gotten quite used to over the past several days, since all he did was frown back at her.

David tried not to chuckle at the glaring match going on in front of him. "Since dinner's going to be a while, a piece of candy won't hurt his appetite."

Evelyn's narrowed eyes turned on him.

He'd already figured she'd be against it, but he'd chosen his candy wisely. "They're licorice allsorts. Licorice is medicinal."

"And the sugary coconut parts?"

"Why, I think all medicine should contain sugary coconut parts. People might be more inclined to take it." He plucked one of the circular candies from the bag and folded it into Evelyn's hand. "My former nanny always said licorice could cure *all sorts* of ailments, even grouchiness. Not that she ever had to cure me of that, since I was a perfect angel."

Her lips wriggled with a suppressed smile. So close.

"Ah, there you are, David." Mr. Hargrove hobbled in, making the tiny room overcrowded in an instant. "Did you get a ham?"

He reluctantly let go of Evelyn's hand. "No, but I got fresh catfish from a kid selling his catch that I'll fry up. Better get to it."

Mr. Hargrove only moved to the side of the room to let him pass. "I came to relieve Evelyn from reading, but should we wash up instead?"

"It'll be a while. I'm sure *White Fang* would love to keep Scott company until then." He winked at the boy before heading back to the kitchen.

Before he'd even started cleaning the fish, Evelyn's hushed footfalls registered behind him, and he couldn't keep the smile off his face. She'd not bothered to wear shoes for nearly a week now.

"Do you need help?"

He'd love to have her company, but what could she do? "That'd be nice. Maybe you could grate the cheese?"

While she washed up, he broke the macaroni sticks into short pieces. He would have started some banter, but the contemplative look on her face kept him from doing so. Could he hope she'd sought him out for something?

It certainly would be nice if she did. She only talked to him when he spoke first or if she needed help with Scott. He'd gotten occasional glimpses of what she must be like behind the wall of propriety she hid behind, but she'd not completely warmed up to him. Mr. Hargrove, however, had fast become like the father — or rather grandfather — he'd always wished he had.

So many of his friends back home were business associates, which meant they were all under Father's influence. He had a few friends at his home church, but they weren't deep relationships. Perhaps his wealth and status in Kansas City had created an invisible barrier he'd not recognized.

Evelyn took down the bowl and grater from the cupboard. "So Scott's maybe a day or two away from being able to leave."

"I'm happy to hear that." He stopped plopping the noodles into the water that was now roiling. He put a saucepan onto the stove and spooned in the butter to let it soften while they waited. "I was afraid he'd be here longer, considering how little he seems to get out of bed."

"He's only staying abed for Mr. Hargrove. Though Scott enjoys listening, Mr. Hargrove is having such fun reading aloud Scott says he doesn't want to ruin the old man's fun — especially because he took us in when he didn't have to."

Pretty insightful for a boy of twelve with his background. "That child's going to turn out plenty fine."

"I hope so." Leaning against the counter with her hands folded in front of her, she stared out toward the parlor instead of grating the cheese, remaining silent as he started cleaning the fish. The few glances he caught of her might have rivaled the drawing he'd made of Hargrove for wistfulness.

"I've been thinking . . ." She repositioned herself as if uncomfortable. "What do you think about me asking Mr. Hargrove to keep Scott permanently?"

David set his knife down. "I thought the boy wanted to go with you?"

"He does, but I'm thinking it might be better if he lives here. Mr. Hargrove could use the company, and —"

"Mr. Hargrove's an old man."

"Street children are generally fending for themselves by age six. Besides, once Scott's over his illness, he won't need physical help. He'll just need a roof over his head and love."

"Doesn't the orphanage provide that?" David washed his hands — it wasn't as if he needed the fish ready any time soon.

"Well, yes. But I'm afraid Scott only wants to go because he believes I'll be there forever. If he were to get attached to Mr. Hargrove and stayed with him, then when I left the orphanage, he wouldn't be disappointed."

David dried his hands, staring out the picture window at the trees starting to turn color. She'd be leaving soon enough to disappoint Scott? The only reason she'd give up her orphanage position was likely for a family of her own.

She was no longer staring straight ahead but rather at her fingernails.

Considering she wasn't acting excited, the man she'd decided upon must not be willing to give up his career for the orphanage or take on a child like Scott.

He'd heard of men who sent their stepchildren to boarding schools or paternal relatives upon marrying. If some could do that to the children of their new brides, then it would be a rare man indeed who'd adopt the by-blows of prostitutes, regardless of his new bride's love for orphans.

Would he be willing to adopt a street child?

He knew exactly how Father would answer that question for him.

Evelyn turned to look at him, her eyes questioning.

What had she asked again? Oh, yes, Mr. Hargrove. "I don't know when you're expecting to get married and leave the orphanage, but Mr. Hargrove must be over eighty

198

years old. He may not be alive any longer than however long you'll be at the orphanage. Scott might have to deal with losing someone before he's comfortable in his new home either way."

Strangely, she smiled at him. But as much as he'd had fun coaxing little smiles from her lately — the count was now three actual smiles and five almost smiles — he didn't want to count this one.

The thought of her getting married sure wasn't making him want to smile.

"Who said I was getting married?"

So the smile had been one of amusement or incredulity? "I'm sorry." He blew out a breath and forced himself not to explore the reason his lungs suddenly worked better. "I just assumed marriage was taking you away from the orphanage, since you seem pretty driven to work there."

"Oh, I'll help at the orphanage, one way or the other, but you're wrong about me leaving those children to get married. That's something that will never happen."

Well, if that wasn't the darndest thing — his lungs cinched up again.

Mr. Hargrove was right — this woman was dead set against suitors. What was so wrong with men she'd not even consider one?

"But my parents won't be able to work there forever. Once my parents leave, Mr. Lowe will replace them with another couple, and I can't be certain I'll be able to stay on. And I certainly have never been able to save enough money for anything important, let alone enough to keep a child. Besides, Mr. Lowe won't allow a child to be adopted by a single parent. I wish I could . . ."

He stirred the macaroni noodles to keep them from clumping against the bottom of the pan as she talked on, but his ability to focus on what she was saying was hindered by what she'd said about never getting married. Though it was unusual, what did it matter if she didn't get married? His aunt had chosen to be a spinster and had remained perfectly respectable. But then, his grandfather had left her so much money she'd been given the freedom to live as she pleased.

Evelyn wasn't anywhere near that well-off. Did she have a huge inheritance coming from some far-off relative?

She shrugged at whatever it was she was saying, picked up the spoon he must have laid down, and started stirring the noodles for him. "I will certainly do whatever I can, but I can't ignore the possibility that . . ."

She kept talking while he watched her

hand stir. Had he ever met a single woman of little means who wasn't pursuing marriage? He couldn't think of any he knew who hadn't subtly, or unsubtly, let him know she'd be willing to marry into the Kingsmans' wealth.

Perhaps that was why Evelyn was so confusing. She wasn't the least bit subtle about being completely uninterested.

What would he have to do to get her to change her mind about marriage?

Wait. What was he doing thinking that?

Evelyn set down his spoon. "I might not be able to convince him — or whoever he might hire — to keep me on. So if that happens sooner than . . ."

He blinked as he tried to focus on her words. What was she talking about now? His thoughts had gone haywire.

He couldn't move to Teaville, take over an orphanage, adopt a mansion full of urchins, or anything else that might entice Evelyn to consider him. And why was he thinking about marrying her anyway? No matter how at odds he was with Father, he'd not leave one business for another he wouldn't enjoy. An orphanage was not —

"Did you hear me?"

He blinked.

She was staring right at him.

201

Stepping back, he ran his fingers through the hair at the base of his scalp. "I heard you. . . . I was just thinking about it." Sort of.

"Well then?"

She was waiting for some kind of answer? Was she waiting on his thoughts about her predicament or Scott's? "What is it you wanted to know, exactly?"

She just shook her head as Mr. Hargrove's cane thumping grew louder behind them.

"Scott's asleep, and so was my leg." Mr. Hargrove groaned as his stiff leg dragged behind him. "I needed to get out here before it failed to get me to the dining table. Don't want to miss dinner." He stopped inside the doorway and looked at them. "Am I interrupting something?"

"Uh, no." David searched for the strainer. "But it's going to be a while, sir."

Evelyn sighed and moved toward the table in a slump.

He wanted to slap himself. Here she'd actually wanted to talk to him and he'd let his stupid mind keep him from listening — which might have gotten the kind of interest from her he'd wanted.

Or maybe he didn't want.

"If dinner's going to be late, how about some Chinese checkers?" Mr. Hargrove awkwardly let himself down into a chair.

"Sounds good to me." Evelyn went into the hallway to retrieve the game they'd played most every night since Scott had taken a turn for the better.

David had never had so much fun with a silly game. He and Hargrove had talked about all sorts of things as they moved around marbles, from lighthearted to serious topics. And though Evelyn only joined the conversation occasionally, she'd played with a competitive spirit and even chuckled a time or two. He'd never felt so free to forget all his business woes and problems as he had his evenings here at Hargrove's.

Maybe that was why he was latching onto Evelyn. She was part of the tranquility he'd always craved.

Perhaps she was just meant to be a wonderful memory before he had to return to the grind of real life. If she was to be anything more . . . Well, he hadn't the time for pursuing anyone. If things were meant to be, God would have to make it so.

16

With Scott tucked under her arm, Evelyn swayed with him in the back of the wagon on their way to the mansion. Luckily, her parents had invited Mr. Hargrove to dinner to thank him for his hospitality; otherwise David likely would have insisted she ride up front.

What would she have done if she'd had to sit on the wagon seat next to him? She generally didn't have problems holding herself aloof from men, but David, well . . .

Taking in a huge draught of pure air, she focused on the entertaining story Mr. Hargrove was telling. The one about the goose that had chased him around his parents' farmhouse when his siblings had locked him out.

He'd already told them that story twice, but he was such a dear, and reliving his memories always made his face soften and his eyes light up. She couldn't bear to tell him she'd already heard it, and evidently neither could David.

She hadn't gotten up the courage to ask Mr. Hargrove to take Scott either. She didn't want to break Scott's heart. How could she take away the one thing he was looking forward to, as David had pointed out, after he'd just lost his mother?

Scott sniffed beside her, and she looked over to see silent tears streaming down his freshly scarred cheeks. She squeezed him tighter but held her words. Nothing she could say would bring his mother back, and she didn't want him to think crying was wrong.

Crying was the only thing that had gotten her through the toughest time in her life. Her youthful indiscretions were not only life changing, but emotional through and through. And she'd had to hide every single tear lest anyone ask her what was wrong. How she'd wished for someone to hold her while she cried, but she had never let anyone know.

Only tears and time would get them through the terrible way they'd both been cheated in life.

Scott sniffed and then turned to look up at her. "Do you think I could work with Robert and Max at the glass factory?"

How had she forgotten they'd started working for David? Of course, she'd not gotten to see them after their first day. Had they gone to work since then? She hadn't even asked David how things had gone. She rubbed Scott's shoulder. "Since you're twelve, I'm going to say no. But I bet our gardener would love help. He can always use a strong back to haul things around."

He nodded and then turned quiet again.

The winding driveway to the mansion snaked behind them, curling up the hill and bringing them closer to her parents.

As much as her parents' secret plans to retire had made it hard for her to have any peace while quarantined at Mr. Hargrove's, she couldn't wait to feel Momma's strong arms around her and have Daddy plant his customary kiss on her brow.

The shadow of the portico covered them, and she sighed as she stared up at her home as the wagon came to a stop. Or what she wished was her true home — she could still hope it would always be so.

"We're here." David came around the back of the wagon, and she almost wished Scott was still sickly enough that David would have to help him out of his factory's delivery wagon instead of her. But the disease hadn't taken away the boy's need to stretch his legs, and he quickly scooted to the end of the wagon bed and hopped off.

Apparently Mr. Hargrove was sprier than she'd thought too, because he was already limping toward the door.

If she was still in the dress she'd had to burn yesterday, she would've just scooted to the end as Scott had. But her mother had sent her one of her newer dresses.

David hopped into the back of the wagon and held out his hands to help her stand.

His hands were just like anyone else's, so why was she hesitating to hold them for a moment? She clamped hers into his.

They were indeed just ordinary hands, engulfing hers with a secure grip.

He heaved her up, but her heel caught on her hem. Her current inability to be aware of anything but their hands had evidently robbed her of all grace.

For a second, David wrapped an arm around her waist to help take her weight off her skirt, but just as quickly he released her. He then extended his arm and escorted her the five feet to the edge of the wagon bed.

He didn't seem bothered by how close they'd just been and jumped down only to offer up his hands again. This time to catch her waist to bring her down.

That had happened before, on hayrides

and such, but she'd paid those men little mind. Over the past two weeks, however, having been around David longer than she'd been around any man lately, besides her father, she'd become lax with how she reacted toward him.

Not that she'd done anything wrong — well . . . except, perhaps, walk barefoot around him and fail to keep her emotions locked up tight lest they get her in trouble.

David raised an eyebrow as he stood waiting, and she tensed before putting her hands on his shoulders. Her height made it a bit awkward for him to swing her down gracefully.

"I bet you're glad to be back." He let go of her, as though holding a woman's waist was an everyday occurrence, and offered his arm again.

Not that arm-holding meant much either, but she could hardly act aloof around a man she'd shared a house with a week ago, though that was her usual tactic in dealing with men. Once they caught on to her disinterest, they usually left her alone.

And yet, here David was, eyebrows raised. Waiting.

She swallowed hard and looped her arm around his. "I am happy to be home, though I'm glad I've gotten to know Mr. Hargrove better. Father's always hogged his company."

She hoped Momma and Daddy weren't watching from a window. How long had they hoped a young man as attentive and decent as David would join them for a family dinner?

She loosened her arm so that only her hand was lying on his forearm. She could not let them set their hopes on David.

"I know this might sound terrible of me, considering why we were cooped up." He put his hand atop hers as if to keep her from going farther. "But I've enjoyed the last two weeks — getting to know you and Scott and Hargrove. It's been a long time since I've felt so . . . at home. Perhaps for the first time, really. My father's idea of a family evening is talking about his grand plans for me and his business. Especially going over whatever it is I'm doing wrong that keeps him from handing it over to me immediately. Oh, and big bowls of buttery popcorn." He smirked. "I thank God for popcorn — always something to look forward to."

By the way his eyes lingered on her, she knew he was hoping she'd smile back.

And it was hard not to. She gave him a small grin, and he wriggled his shoulders a bit, as if trying to repress a victory dance.

As thankful as she was that he hadn't left her to care for Scott alone, she wasn't sure how she would handle it if he stuck around.

She could be David's friend, no question — even wanted to be — but would others encourage him to ruin their friendship and push for something more? Would her parents?

And how could she keep her mind from dwelling on him?

It was almost cruel, really, but she'd not rail against God for bringing this man to Teaville. God was hardly at fault for how her life had turned out.

Scott grabbed on to the front door's contoured handle and pulled it open. She was then able to let go of David's arm without looking rude, and yet, the widening space between them didn't give her the sense of relief she usually got when she was able to distance herself.

The second she spied her mother, she skirted past Mr. Hargrove in the entryway and into Momma's open arms. As always, her soft embrace made Evelyn forget her worries.

"How are you?" Momma pulled back and looked up into her eyes, pushing the hair off Evelyn's forehead.

210

"Scott's got no lasting side effects from the smallpox, so that's a blessing." She turned to smile at the boy. He was standing with his hands behind him, staring up at the two-story entrance. The entryway was rather awe-inspiring with its wraparound stairway curving around the fancy gasolier that sparkled above them.

When she glanced back at her mother, she saw that probing look she knew all too well. What had she done in the space of half a minute to make her mother suspect she had a secret?

But she never had been one to cave to that inquisitive stare. And no matter what she knew about her parents' plans, she wasn't going to ask Momma about her secret either. She wanted them to tell her first. "Where's Daddy?"

"I'm here." Her father started down the entryway stairs as if his leg hadn't been causing him problems for nearly a year. And after Daddy let go of the rail to head across the hall toward her, his steadiness was impressive. No visible sign of pain. "We missed you." He walked straight for her, cupped the sides of her head with his huge hands, and kissed her on the spot near her temple, the same spot he'd kissed as far back as she could remember.

She let the warmth of his love wash over her, and when he pulled back, went on tiptoe to kiss him on the tip of his nose, just as she had for years.

After giving her a huge hug, he turned around and walked back across the entryway to clap his best friend on the shoulder. "I'm glad you came. With you and Mr. Kingsman here, I'm looking forward to tonight's dinner conversation. And hello, my boy." He held out his hand for Scott as he would for any grown man. "I hear you're joining us. Can't wait to get to know you."

Scott hesitated but shook Daddy's hand — and quickly found himself in a bear hug.

Evelyn pressed her lips hard together as if that would somehow dissolve the lump in her throat. How could she continue working here without her parents?

"Come on. Dinner's ready, but we've been holding off for you, our guest of honor." Daddy turned Scott around and started off toward the hallway, his huge hand spanning the back of the boy's neck.

Scott's grin lit up his pitted face, and her love for her father only grew.

David, after a quick glance at her, followed after them, and Evelyn tugged off her gloves. "I'm glad to see Daddy's leg isn't bothering him."

"As you know, it comes and goes," her mother said.

"But it's been so long since the last time he's walked without a hitch in his step. I was beginning to wonder . . ." She turned enough to see her mother's face. "I was beginning to think it wouldn't be long before you two decided you couldn't work here anymore." So perhaps she wouldn't ask outright, but prodding wasn't out of the question.

Uncharacteristically, her mother folded her hands and stared at them for a second. But only a second. Then she walked over to help reposition the pin that had fallen out when Evelyn had taken off her bonnet. Momma disappeared behind her, letting her fingers walk along Evelyn's scalp, pushing things back into place. "You don't know how hard it was to stay here while you were at Mr. Hargrove's." She backed away to look at Evelyn's hair and gave a nod of satisfaction.

She kept her gaze steady on Momma, but her mother didn't seem to act guilty whatsoever for avoiding her unspoken question. Were they going to keep their secret from her until the last minute?

Of course, who was she to get upset over someone keeping a secret?

213

Though she was determined not to ask about theirs, she'd still agonize over all the possible future scenarios. Could she ask Nicholas about her parents' plans? But what if he didn't know? No need to upset everything before it was absolutely necessary. "I hope it wasn't utter chaos here while I was away."

"Miss McClain came several times while you were gone. She was a lot of help."

Mercy had come? Of course Mercy would. "Is she here now?"

"Yes, she'll be having dinner with us."

"Wonderful." There were just not enough opportunities to get together with friends when the orphanage took so much of her time. "And how has Peter treated her?" She couldn't imagine he'd keep his thoughts to himself. He pestered the other orphans about their freckles or their crooked noses. What hope was there that he hadn't taunted Mercy? Despite being an absolutely lovely woman, with big green eyes and voluminous blond curls, the first thing most everyone saw was her deformed right hand — or rather, the few little nubs a few inches past her elbow where her hand quit growing in the womb.

And the fact that she was twenty-three and still unmarried seemed to indicate most men were as bad as grade-school children for focusing on what was wrong with a person instead of what was right.

Momma sighed. "He's been told countless times to keep not-so-nice thoughts to himself, but trying to rid him of all his bad habits at once is overwhelming. I've decided to focus on getting him to stop adding curse words to every sentence."

"I hope Mercy isn't too upset with him."

"She's not new to being teased, but I think Peter convincing Ezekiel that she's a monster has been difficult. The boy won't even stay in the room with her."

Evelyn frowned at the thought of the cute little four-year-old refusing to share his big dimpled smiles with Mercy.

"I'm sure she'll enjoy getting to talk to you before she goes home." Momma slipped her arm around her waist as they strolled up the small staircase to the main hallway that led to the kitchen. "And we're all excited you're home. Cook made your favorites. Ham, squash soup, and strawberry shortcake for dessert."

"That sounds wonderful. Mr. Kings—" Maybe it would be better not to tell Momma that David was a far better cook than theirs. Momma didn't need any more of David's positive traits to latch onto. "I mean, Mr.

Hargrove was wondering what we'd have for dessert, and I was hoping for shortcake."

Before they made it two steps into the dining room, a flurry of blue-checked gingham and blond curls came running toward her.

"Alex?" She got down on one knee just in time to catch the girl in a big hug. "What are you doing here?"

"I thought I'd never see you again." The six-year-old curled up in Evelyn's embrace, and her thumb popped into her mouth the second she quit talking.

"I'm sure Miss O'Conner told you I'd come see you the first Saturday I was able." Though that didn't explain why Alex was at the mansion. Had Caroline and her parents invited the district children to supper? She looked up, scanning the smiling faces of the orphans in their assigned seats, but Alex's older sister, Jocelyn, wasn't there, nor were there any extra empty seats. She smiled at Mercy, who waved at her from where she was helping Vera and Florence set the table.

"I was so afraid you were going to die." The little girl nuzzled her head against Evelyn's neck. "Especially now that I get to be with you forever."

She looked over the little girl's head at her mother's slightly worried face.

Momma licked her lips. "Alexandria

decided she wants to live with us, and no one objected. We've told her that means she might get to go live with a wonderful family someday."

"But I don't want to. You told me God can do anything, so I'll just pray I get to stay with you, and I will." The girl slid her thumb back into her mouth and relaxed against her.

How could she say no to that? "You're right. God is certainly able to do anything."

And if this little one needed Evelyn so much she gave up her sister to be with her, then why wouldn't He provide Evelyn with a way to remain working here?

Mercy came over with a big smile on her face. "But sometimes God's ways are not our ways, so we have to be prepared for Him to do something we might not like, but still trust Him to get us where He wants us." She offered her good hand to Alex. "Now let's go sit so we can eat."

Evelyn slowly stood, trying not to show any emotion on her face. How could God want her anywhere but here?

She could feel David's eyes on her as she walked to her place across from him and next to Mercy.

Alex is right. You can do anything.

Evelyn put her napkin across her knees

217

and ignored her father's dinner prayer to continue with her own.

So please let me stay, if you would. And please keep David from believing anything would entice me to leave. I like him too much to ever want to have that conversation with him.

17

The sky was full of ominous clouds. Standing on the stoop of Morris, Morris, & Freedman, Evelyn considered opening her little parasol. Its beautiful floral pattern usually cheered her, so she opened it, if for no other reason than to help her focus on the positive. There were a handful of sunbeams and light blue splotches amid the gloomy clouds rolling in from the southwest; surely her own life had splotches of cheeriness ready to bust through.

She stepped off the stoop and forced herself not to walk with a slump. Though Nicholas's lawyer had not agreed to sponsor her women's home, he had offered his services for half price for any future residents needing legal help, and free services for children. He'd also been kind enough to answer a few personal questions without asking for a fee — after he assured her keeping confidences was integral to his vocation.

Though Nicholas would not consider Mr. Morris's help to be a sponsorship, it was something. That should give her hope for her next appointment — if she could ignore the derisive laughter still ringing in her ears from the five men she'd met with before Mr. Morris.

"Don't you make a pretty picture."

Evelyn took her gaze off her feet.

David, with his hands in his pockets, leisurely strolled toward her. His head was cocked to the side as he assessed her. His handsome homburg hat perched jauntily atop his thick blond hair.

Her free hand, as if it had a mind of its own, came up to cover the scars on her right cheek. She wasn't used to getting such compliments. Did he really mean it?

"That, Miss Wisely, was a compliment. They're normally viewed as good things, not anything to frown about."

"Yes." She let her hand drop and shook herself a little. "Thank you."

"I was certain today was Saturday, but you appear to be wearing your Sunday finery. Did I miss church this morning?"

"No, it's definitely Saturday."

"Did you not feed the children lunch this afternoon?"

"I did."

He looked back at her dress.

Of course, her attire was nothing like the work dresses she normally wore. The children had given her compliments on her dusky red shirtwaist dress as well. The skirt had a deep full flounce on the bottom and a slight train bordered with a band of embroidered flowers that traveled up the front and onto the shirtwaist until they parted to border its squared neckline. The cameo she wore at the base of the high-necked collar of the white undershirt had been particularly fascinating to little Jesse, who'd crawled into her lap at story time and rubbed it between his fingers. "I didn't have time to return to the mansion after lunch before my first appointment."

She could tell he expected her to keep talking, but would he be disheartened to hear that Mr. Greer and each man afterward had thought David's sponsorship of her women's home was laughable?

She couldn't have David back out.

His gaze traveled to her dress yet again, his mouth puckered with serious perusal rather than admiration.

Though she was happy there was no male interest in David's eyes, she still squirmed. She closed the parasol and put it in front of her. As puny of a shield as it was, it did get his gaze to come back up to hers.

"You know, you should wear an outfit this nice when you go soliciting for your women's home. You came to me in a plain yellow dress with black dots, but it didn't . . ." He spun one of his hands around as if he could flip the word he was looking for out of the air. "It didn't get me to take you seriously. Whenever I'm in the middle of a business deal, I wear my best. If the other man is dressed casually, I subconsciously think he's not taking the risk to my assets as seriously as he should. I'm not saying that's right — but seeing you now, I think that might have helped me take you more seriously. It also gives the illusion you're not desperate for money since you have enough of your own to wear such an ensemble."

"Well then, at least I chose appropriately today, for I *am* out looking for supporters."

"You are?"

Why did he say that as if he were surprised? "Yes. Mr. Greer was my first appointment. I just had one with Mr. Morris, and I'm on my way to see Mr. Beauchamp again." He hadn't agreed to anything at their first meeting, but he hadn't outright dismissed her either.

Hopefully, as with David, time's passing and seeing her commitment to this venture would change Mr. Beauchamp's mind.

And since Mr. Beauchamp and Nicholas used to be good friends, perhaps he'd be willing to support her mission in an effort to bridge whatever had torn the two men apart. This time, she'd hint that supporting this endeavor might be the ointment their friendship needed to start healing.

David ran a hand through his hair. "Why didn't you tell me?"

"About what?"

"That you were trying to get supporters today."

"You wanted to know?"

"I thought you believed my support would convince others."

"I did." She twirled the handle of her parasol in her hand. "I told them of your support for the women's home, but unfortunately it has yet to get me anywhere."

"But that's not what I said."

"It's not?" What had she gotten wrong?

"I told you I'd support you. Don't you think if I came with you to your appointments — to petition the men myself — it might help?"

Of course a man pleading on behalf of her project would hold more sway. "But what if it doesn't? Without Mr. Lowe's money, nothing will happen."

"That's not true. I'll still try to find a job for any woman who wants one, whether they live in the home you'll build or not. As long as they aren't living in the red-light district anymore. And I'll still sponsor a weekly meal, if not for the women, then for the children. Surely they'd appreciate another meal during the week. For now, maybe you could send food home with them, since I said I'd sponsor a whole day."

Her throat closed on her, and she had to look away from him. Had she ever expected to meet a man more generous than Nicholas? "Why are you doing this?"

"What do you mean?"

"I mean, you're not doing this just because you feel sorry for me, are you? You did tell me earlier you couldn't help."

"So if I was doing this just for you, you'd turn down my help?" The confusion in his voice made her look back at him.

"No." Of course she wouldn't turn down help for people who needed it so desperately. "I . . . I just want to be sure your focus is on the right thing."

"Why would you think it wasn't?"

Perhaps she was reading too much into this. Maybe he was just a real gentleman. Maybe he had no affinity for her above any other woman.

It would be easier to keep her heart from fluttering if he wasn't so focused on her. And she really needed to keep her heart from fluttering again. "It's just that no one else has been willing to help me — not even those who've admitted that what I'm doing is a step in the right direction — so I just wanted to make sure you were . . . committed to this project, even if I was no longer involved. I wouldn't want your support to disappear if I did."

He stiffened. "I'll pretend that the compliment I gave you earlier wasn't paid back with an unflattering assumption about me."

She grimaced and dropped her gaze to the ground. "I'm sorry." He was right, that sounded horrid. But if he knew how much she was growing to admire him, well, she couldn't stir up any romantic interest he might have.

David shifted his weight uneasily. "My father, of course, would be the sort of person you accused me of being — someone who only does something if it benefits him — and I'll admit I'm not entirely excited about informing him that I've chosen to support your ministry. Which is why I haven't offered to help with anything more. Until my father officially hands the business to me, I'm not able to make unilateral decisions. Please don't tell anyone this, but my father intends to sell the factory. If that happens, I'll return to Kansas City. But if he's adamant our business have no connection to your cause, I'll support you with my own funds."

They intended to sell the factory? She took a step back and looked at the pavement between them.

She'd known he was returning to Kansas City, but she hadn't imagined he'd sell the factory. Once he did, Nicholas wouldn't consider David's support to be that of a local businessman. She was right back to where she'd started. She still needed two sponsors. Because what were the chances David would convince whoever bought the business from him to keep the women he hired if no one else in town would touch them?

She sucked in her lower lip and looked back up at him. "How long are you going to be here again?" If he was willing to help her drum up supporters, she'd better get to it. They didn't need to know he'd be leaving Teaville behind completely.

David was fiddling with his fingers. "I don't know. Father is likely having fits over how long I'm staying, but I'm sort of digging in my heels."

She had wanted him to move away, right? So why was her heart sagging?

Because of the likelihood that the women's home would never be, of course. She'd had acquaintances move away many times before. David's leaving would be nothing different — could be nothing different.

"But if I can get you another supporter, then we'll get the ball rolling with Mr. Lowe. He doesn't seem like a man who would start a project and not see it through. So we just need to get him started."

"No, I need two more supporters. I couldn't tell Nicholas you would be supporting him long term. I know your help is temporary and not what he asked for."

"My returning to Kansas City won't keep me from sponsoring a weekly group of meals — I can do that from afar."

"But it will keep you from hiring women."

"True. Though there is a possibility I could convince Father to keep the factory. And if we do sell, if I've already hired the women, I'll work to convince the buyer to keep them. Depends on —"

"I can't count on what might happen, so I still need two more business owners." She pulled out her timepiece. "I'm afraid Mr. Beauchamp is expecting me."

"Will you let me come with you?"

She tucked her timepiece away and nodded. If David had no set plans for departure, she'd better use his influence while he was still on board.

She couldn't let this setback derail her — otherwise what could she possibly say to encourage the women who would one day come to her for help? Their attempt to get back into good society would be far harder than convincing two men to monetarily support her women's home.

And she didn't want to think about why it hurt so much to know that, in the future, David's support would be from afar.

18

Evelyn stopped in front of the five-story flour mill wedged among the other factories lining the railroad tracks. The words *Beauchamp Mills* were stenciled in big black letters above the door of the red-brick building's office entrance. David rushed up the concrete stairs ahead of her to hold open the door.

She took in a deep breath. This was her last real possibility to get an important businessman to support her women's home. If she failed, she'd personally be fine, but how could she live comfortably while other women were trapped in untold horrors and despair?

Behind the front desk, Mr. Allen looked up from his paperwork. The middle-aged man pushed his spectacles up to the bridge of his nose. "Ah, Miss Wisely, I was wondering if you'd forgotten your appointment."

"No." She smiled at the man who'd been

a part of the group of elders who'd called her father to Teaville's Freewill Church, then turned to gesture toward David. "I hope Mr. Kingsman will be allowed to join me. He's involved in the business I'm here to discuss with Mr. Beauchamp."

"I can't imagine it'd be a problem."

"Good."

Of course, Mr. Allen didn't know what she was here for, but he needed to know David was with her for business purposes and not . . . for other reasons. Mr. Allen wasn't exactly the best at minding his own business. If gossips were hens, he was their rooster.

She followed Mr. Allen toward Mr. Beauchamp's office. They stepped inside, and the bright sunlight from the large windows overlooking the train tracks toward town made her squint a little. There wasn't much to look at out the window — just a strip of grassy field separating this factory from the big, ugly brick factory to the north. This view was only slightly better than if Mr. Beauchamp had chosen a southern office, since he'd have nothing but the flour mill's large, weathered concrete tower to look at that way.

The stocky Frenchman stood up from behind a rather ostentatious desk for a mill owner. He smiled at her for a second, but his eyes skipped straight over to David. "Do come in."

She took a seat in a plain ladder-back chair, and David headed for Mr. Beauchamp, shaking hands with him across his cluttered desk. "Pleased to meet you. I'm David Kingsman."

"Henri Beauchamp. I didn't expect two visitors."

"I convinced Miss Wisely to bring me along, hoping to help her gain your aid."

"Gain my aid? Is this about the women's home again?" He frowned over at Evelyn. "Did you not understand my answer last time?" Thankfully his voice wasn't angry but confused.

"When I first approached Mr. Kingsman, he told me he couldn't help with my women's home either, but after some time, he changed his mind. I was hoping he might persuade you to do the same."

Mr. Beauchamp's plump form went rigid, and though he kept an easygoing expression on his face, his eyes dulled. He turned to David. "I'm afraid the lady's hopes are too high. I don't see any way I could be persuaded."

David took a seat, and Henri, likely confused by the fact that David didn't look at all as if the man had just shut him down, slowly lowered himself back into his big office chair.

David put an ankle of one leg across his knee and draped an arm over the back of his chair. "Did Miss Wisely mention that supporting a women's home doesn't mean you have to commit to a lot of money? There are other ways to help. She only needs a few men to support her endeavor, for Mr. Lowe has agreed to finance the rest."

"He will indeed be the main financier," Evelyn confirmed. "He just wants to be sure he has town support before proceeding. I know you two were once close, and perhaps joining him for a good cause could bridge the gap between you."

"Mr. Lowe doesn't need my support to do any good thing. I suggest you keep nagging him until he caves and helps, as he probably already wants to." Mr. Beauchamp settled back in his seat. "But if he's truly hesitant, then I don't want any part of it."

She could have bitten her tongue out. Was there any way to cover for that misstep? "You were familiar with the problem he had with the former prostitutes he kept hidden in his mansion, yes?"

"I became aware of it when everyone else did."

Was there an edge of bitterness in his voice? "And do you know his housekeeper, Miss O'Conner?"

"Yes." His voice seemed slightly more interested.

"Well, she'll be helping me with the women's home. If you don't want to support it for me, I'd ask you to support it for her. You see, her sister —"

"Is a two-faced, devious strumpet."

Evelyn's lips moved, but her voice had fled, so she shut her mouth. How should she respond to that quick and angry put-down? Considering the venom in his voice, telling him Caroline and Moira's story wouldn't gain his sympathy.

"I'm afraid some of the women you want to help deserve exactly what they get." Mr. Beauchamp stood and folded his arms across his expansive chest. "I have another appointment."

She didn't bother to look at the clock, knowing full well they hadn't been in there five minutes, let alone the fifteen she was scheduled for. "Well, thank you for allowing me to come again. If you do change your mind, let us know." Which wouldn't happen, of course, but saying it made her feel as if all hope wasn't lost.

David helped her from her seat, and after

a quick glance over his shoulder, he silently led her out.

On the mill's porch, she held onto the railing with a firm grip as she went down the stairs. Oh, to be home so she could sink into a cushioned chair, take off her shoes, and call it a day. But she had to walk there first.

"Where do we go next?" David's expectant expression was dulled by the lack of sparkle in his eyes.

"You don't think that was enough rejection for one day?" She let go of the railing and opened her parasol since the earlier dark clouds had thinned and moved north, skirting town completely. At least something about this day had turned sunshiny.

"If you're done, perhaps you could give me a list of men to talk to. I've got nothing to do until dinnertime. That's why I crossed your path. A walk about town sounded better than sitting in my room at the boarding-house."

"Mr. Beauchamp was my last person to see. I've been to all the businessmen in town twice. And they were about as movable as he. I did get Mr. Lowe's lawyer to promise aid, but not the kind Mr. Lowe would count as support for the women's home."

"This town is fairly large. I can't believe

you've been to every butcher, baker, and candlestick maker."

His reference to the nursery rhyme made her want to smile, but her heart was too heavy. "A butcher is not going to support a women's home in any capacity that would move Mr. Lowe. A few dollars here and there won't be enough. I need a real showing of support." Trickles of money could never be counted on. How long had she been trying to grow her own bank account and gotten nowhere?

"But what about the small business owners you know from church? If you could get each to pledge a little, along with prayer support, perhaps Mr. Lowe would consider a group as worthy as one."

"Two of the big businessmen I approached were from my church. They told me 'sometimes business is just business.' "

He pulled a pad of paper from under his suit coat and handed it to her. "Write their names down. Even if all I get from them is prayer support, that might be all we need. Because if we can get enough people praying, perhaps we won't have to get Mr. Lowe any support at all. God could simply spur him forward without anyone's help."

Would it work? It wouldn't hurt to try. She grabbed his pad of paper without looking up at him and pulled the little pencil out of her chatelaine. Why was he being so nice to her? No, not to her. They'd had that conversation on the way here. He seemed to be genuinely interested in helping women like Scott's mother. Which was somehow worse. Or better. She wasn't sure which, because her heart was aching to like him. No, she already liked him. A stupid tear blurred her vision, and she furtively wiped it away.

How had she not thought to ask for prayer support as she'd gone along? Did she not have enough faith that God wanted this women's home to exist?

But what was more depressing was knowing David would leave one day. A man who cared about spiritual things, who supported her even when she was a mess, who was annoyingly, absolutely perfect.

The type of man she'd hoped would come alongside her one day.

But had never come.

Until now. And it was too late.

Or was it?

"Why are you looking so glum again? Don't give up hope yet."

There might be some hope for the women's home, but not for her dreams. Well, there was a possibility of hope, but she'd kept herself from wishing for it.

But maybe she ought to do as the lawyer had recommended and find out where she legally stood — if she could humble herself and ask for the money to do so, that is. Because if there was any possibility . . .

She took a glance at David, who smiled the second she looked at him, making her stupid heart flutter. "All right." She looked back down and quickly scribbled out a few names. "These are men from my church who own a business of some sort. If you mention your connection to me, they should listen to what you have to say."

She made a quick mental note of the sun and knew she didn't have much time before she was expected back at the orphanage. "I've got to see someone before I return home. Will I see you at church tomorrow?"

He smiled as if she'd invited him to sit in the pew with her. "I'll make sure to see you."

"Then until then."

David grabbed her gloved hand and gave her a gentle squeeze. "I'm happy to take some of the burden until you find your determination again." And with that he walked off, holding up the list as he whistled.

She held the hand he'd squeezed in her other and closed her eyes, the vestiges of the warmth of his hand slowly fading.

Once the feel of his grip dissipated, she opened her eyes and found him gone.

Yes, she needed to know exactly where she stood, since her heart was in danger of going somewhere it shouldn't. No more believing the worst, no more living with uncertainty — she had to know if the tethers she'd kept around her heart were indeed as necessary as she thought them to be.

She strode as quickly as she could toward Lowe's Mining & Gas Company. Hopefully she was remembering Nicholas's schedule correctly, because if he was at his lumber mill today, she didn't have time to get that far across town without causing her parents any more hardship than she already was.

Since window shopping in this section of town wasn't appealing — plumbing supplies and hardware held no temptation — she sped along the sidewalks. When she got to the Mining & Gas Company's door, she hesitated.

Could she really ask for the amount of money this request might take? But how else was she going to get any answers? She would never be able to afford to get them herself. Nine years had passed, and she hadn't accrued a sizable savings in any sense of the word.

She forced herself to turn the handle. Putting one foot in front of the other, she made her way toward Nicholas's secretary, hoping the twitch in her cheek was not as visible as it felt. "Is Mr. Lowe in?"

Mr. Black, a tall, skinny man slightly older than she, with a very large nose and plenty of dark hair, stood up and came around his desk. "He is. Was he expecting you?"

"No, but I was hoping he might have a few minutes for me to ask him a question." If he didn't, she wasn't sure she could muster the courage to return.

Mr. Black ran his finger down a list of things in a notebook on his desk. "He has a meeting in twenty minutes, so he'll likely need to leave in ten."

"That will do   if he can spare the time, of course."

"Let me check." The secretary crossed the room, knocked on a door with a frosted glass pane in it, then peeked his head inside. "Would you have a few minutes to see Miss Wisely?"

"Miss Wisely's here to see me?" Nicholas's muffled voice sounded worried.

"Yes."

"Send her in."

The little room was less ornamental than she'd expect of a wealthy man, but Nicholas's hands gripping the back of his chair as if he were afraid it might run away kept her gaze from wandering about.

"Is my wife all right?"

Oh, since she'd never come to see him at his offices, he likely thought an emergency would be the only reason she'd show up unannounced. "I didn't mean to alarm you. As far as I know, Lydia's as tired and cranky as she was yesterday." She grinned, but she'd evidently scared Nicholas bad enough that he couldn't return the smile.

After his body relaxed, a pucker marred his brow. "Then to what do I owe the pleasure of this visit? I doubt you're interested in natural gas." He pointed her to a simple chair placed in front of his desk, but she couldn't sit.

She gripped the back of the chair, mirroring his tense posture of only a moment ago. "I need a monetary favor."

He frowned. "Is what I'm paying you inadequate?"

"No, it's perfectly adequate for someone in my position, but what I need isn't a common need. I've tried to save for it, but after a while I came to accept I would never be able to save enough. But lately . . . I've realized I have to get answers or drive myself crazy."

"Ask then, though I reserve the right to say no."

"Of course." She wrung her hands. Though most people thought Nicholas to be a miser, in truth, he was a very generous man — if he believed in the cause. Would he be willing to help? Oh, it was too much to ask. She paced to the window despite the shades being pulled. She wouldn't have needed any favors if she hadn't been so selfish and foolish once.

"You're worrying me. Is something wrong?" He came around the desk and gripped her arm, looking down into her eyes, mere inches below his. "You're my wife's best friend. If you're in trouble, I'll help you."

She had to start somewhere, didn't she? May as well start with the circumstances that would likely keep her in his debt if he chose to help. "Have my parents told you they intend to retire?"

He shook his head.

For some reason, knowing she wasn't the only one who didn't know was a bit heartening. "They didn't tell me either. But when they leave, I likely will have to leave the orphanage behind as well, along with my only source of income. So I'm afraid, if you grant me this request, I might never be able to pay you back."

"I rarely give out loans, Evelyn, especially to friends. Just tell me what you want."

Though she wanted to bolt for the door, she had to ask. But maybe she shouldn't tell him everything. "I need to hire a detective to find someone. If he's alive and you find him, I could probably pay you back."

"I told you not to worry about that; however, you should know people who skip town because of debt aren't generally known for having money."

"That's not why I need to find him, but that's all I'd like to say about that." She squirmed under Nicholas's gaze. "I'll understand if you refuse."

He stood rubbing his jaw, looking at her as if he could mine information out of her with a piercing stare. He shook his head a little, then turned to go back around his desk. "Give me what information you can, and I'll get someone on it."

She wobbled on shaky legs around the chair and sat down. "His name is James Bowden. Last I knew, he was heading toward California."

19

"Here's your mail, sir."

Mr. Pennysworth put a pile of envelopes on David's desk.

He opened his mouth to thank his newly promoted head secretary, but his vocal cords seized when he caught sight of the name on top. His fingers involuntarily curled, as if they could refuse to pick up his father's letter. He forced himself to nod at Mr. Pennysworth to dismiss him.

He'd known it would come, but since he'd not gotten a telegram or a personal visit from Father since he'd sent his letter, he'd begun to hope Father was going to let him do as he pleased.

Not that he'd ever done so before — but Father had to stop trying to manage every little thing in his son's life at some point, right?

Blowing out an exaggerated breath, David snatched up the letter and, using his index finger as a letter opener, tore the flap open in huge chunks.

He braced himself for words unlikely to brighten his day.

David,

Not even a "dear" before his name. Seems this wasn't going to be fun.

I don't know how I could have possibly been more clear. You were to sell the place, nothing more. Do you really think we need to keep a business hours away from Kansas City? We don't have time for that, and it's obviously not something worth keeping. Get it ready to sell within the month and then get back here. Perhaps you're staying away because of our fight over Marianne, but, son, it's the best for you both. It's the best for all of us. I know you two have this sentimental idea of love, but it only brings heartache. It's not like you've ever had interest in anyone else, so it's time to get your head out of those clouds and become the level-headed partner I need.

Don't make me come down there and do things myself.

He didn't even sign it.

David dropped the letter onto his desk, wishing the autumn afternoon were cold enough for a blazing fire to pitch it into. He picked it back up, ripped it into shreds, and tossed it in the wastebasket.

A month was too little time to get this factory to generate a nice profit before selling.

And Father was wrong about him having no interest in anyone else, but a month was certainly too little time to get anywhere with Evelyn. Mr. Hargrove had said she'd take time to warm up, and she had some, but it was definitely slow going.

Though he might not know her as well as he knew Marianne, he'd seen her servant's heart, her dedication to others, her willingness to work hard without the promise of reward   all admirable qualities he'd want in a wife.

Marianne had admirable qualities too, but there just wasn't this tug . . .

Did Evelyn feel anything toward him — in a way she didn't feel for anyone else?

And what was Father going to do if he didn't return within the month anyway? Disown him? No, Father might like to trample on him, but he had too much pride in his empire, and firing his only son would make him look ineffective in the eyes of those he wanted to impress.

Father could make him miserable, though — David knew that full well.

But knowing he was not living up to expectations was bearable with miles between them and a fascinating woman drifting in and out of his thoughts.

Crash!

A few men's shouts and muffled hollers coming from inside the factory made David dash through the outer office and onto the balcony. A quick look revealed a flurry of activity near a glittering sea of glass in the far north corner. After racing down the stairs, he forged his way through the onlookers, stopping at the edge of the pile of broken shards and lumber.

A few men were already attacking the pile with brooms. He quickly glanced around to make sure neither Robert nor Max was anywhere in the mess. "Is anyone hurt?"

No one seemed to hear him. When he caught a glimpse of one of his five foremen, he picked his way over to him. "Mr. Kerry, what happened?"

The balding man with the pointed eyebrows wiped his forehead with a wadded bandana as he shook his head. "They tried to stack them too high. The product hasn't been going out as quickly as usual, and with that huge order from Nettleson, we had quite the backup. They were just trying to make room."

"No one's hurt?"

He pointed to a man headed toward the washroom. "Uriah had several jars fall on his head, but the pallet missed him. He said he's all right."

Seeing that most of the men were heading back to their stations and enough were busy with brooms and dustpans, David made his way toward the man Mr. Kerry had indicated.

The man was young, perhaps his age, holding a hand to his head as he walked.

David halted him with a squeeze on the shoulder.

The man gave him an annoyed look as he turned, but quickly schooled his expression, though he winced. "Sir?"

"Are you all right?"

"Nothing more than a knock to the noggin. Got a goose egg starting." He rubbed his fingers at the back of his head, though David couldn't see anything through his curly mop. "Going to shake out my hair and clothing to make sure there aren't slivers of glass in them."

"You weren't cut?"

"I don't think so. And I need to apologize. I was the one who insisted we stack them higher. If the others tell you that, it's true. But if we don't start shipping product faster, I don't know where you want us to put everything."

"Thanks for admitting to your part in the accident, but you're right, things have gotten crowded." He had most of the product sold and was working with shipping to get them out, but they'd run across problems with the deliverymen not being able to keep up. "I'll see what I can do, but next time, if there's a question about safety, ask your foreman. I don't want anyone hurt, even if I have to cut back production."

"Yes, sir."

"When you're done shaking out your clothing, I want you to go to the doctor and have your head checked. Then go home. It's only an hour until quitting time."

"It's not that bad, sir."

"It won't affect your wages. Tell your supervisor you're not off the clock."

Uriah's jaw slid back and forth in consternation.

Why else would the man be against getting off early? "And tell the doctor to bill me. That way I'll know you went."

The man let his head drop forward in acquiescence. "All right, sir."

He watched Uriah walk off, then David

turned to see the workers had already carted off most of the aftermath. If it wasn't for three men sweeping in one spot, no one would have known something had gone wrong.

A. K. Glass's foremen were certainly doing a fine job. This place ran like clockwork. At least his decision to fire Mr. Burns had been sound. There was no reason the factory should've been losing money. When the factory produced a decent profit, he'd tell his secretary to give them a raise.

He and his father often disagreed on how best to do things, but Father was wrong about A. K. Glass's potential.

David leaned over to pick up a shard of glass that had skidded far from the mess and tossed it in the trash barrel. Though this factory wasn't worthless, it wasn't as if he wanted to keep it either. He just wanted the best price. Manufacturing glass jars was not something he was drawn to . . . though none of their business ventures back home really sparked his fancy either. However, he did enjoy overseeing their holdings, figuring out how to increase profit, and smoothing out conflict — something that affected the bottom line more than Father realized and that his son was better equipped for, though Father seemed incapable of admitting it.

Plus, back home he sometimes got to take over their hotel's kitchen whenever a cook was sick or when one quit and they looked for a new hire. A rare occurrence, but satisfying nonetheless. His father rolled his eyes when his son wasted his time with something so trifling, but he didn't raise a big stink, since he knew it was only temporary.

If things were different with Evelyn, could he be happy with a glass factory in Teaville? If he couldn't be, then perhaps he needed to stop pursuing her, for he couldn't imagine her agreeing to move with him to Kansas City.

But those questions could be considered later — he had men to oversee.

As David slowly climbed the balcony stairs overlooking the huge manufacturing floor, he mentally calculated the output schedule, shipping delays, and storage spaces already filled. There certainly was a problem. They either needed more room or a slowed production schedule. He needed the profit from offering more diversified products and speedier delivery, so where could he get more storage for cheap?

He turned into the office, and Mr. Pennysworth stood up behind his desk. "Was anyone hurt?"

"Thankfully no, and the accident has been dealt with." At his secretary's nod, David disappeared into his office and ran his hands through his hair. The shreds of his father's letter taunted him as he second-guessed himself.

Though he might not want to do what Father wanted, he didn't want to fail either. One failure was enough at the moment, and he had already failed to get any business-men to support Evelyn's women's home, though he'd convinced a few to pray about it.

Since Father had only sent a letter instead of barging through his office door uninvited, would it be too much to hope he didn't want to broadcast their fallout to those in Kansas City and actually planned to leave him alone?

20

Evelyn put a finger to her lips as Nicholas joined them in the Lowes' parlor, in case he couldn't see that his daughter had fallen asleep.

Nicholas raised his eyebrows at being shushed, but a smile quickly appeared when he noticed the dark curly head on Lydia's shoulder.

Lydia looked over her other shoulder and beckoned him closer with a tilt of her head. "We have a request."

He looked back at Evelyn as if silently inquiring if this had anything to do with the favor she'd asked of him the previous week, so she shook her head slightly.

Rubbing his chin, he came forward. "And how much will it cost me?"

Lydia rolled her eyes. "The beauty of this scheme is that it uses what people discard . . . so not much."

Evelyn scooted to the front of her seat.

"We only need somewhere to store the discards."

Nicholas sat beside Lydia on the love seat.

"Evelyn realized women leaving prostitution will need a different wardrobe." Lydia tried to stifle a yawn but failed. "We were thinking of asking the moral-society ladies and the church to collect their out-of-fashion clothing for those women. We'd need a place to store the clothing and at least one sewing machine for alterations. There's plenty of room in the mansion's basement."

He shook his head. "You could store them at the mansion, but it wouldn't be a good idea to have the women alter them there."

"You have an objection to them being inside?" Lydia looked confused. She had insisted Nicholas would champion the idea. "They'll not have contact with the children. They'd go in through the servant's entrance."

Evelyn squirmed a little. The Lowes treated her like family and had long since stopped acting formally in front of her, but she still didn't want to witness an argument.

"The staff I hired are excellent workers, and I don't want to lose them. Though they have been informed of the children's backgrounds, a few would be uncomfortable having prostitutes on the premises — even former ones."

Another reason they needed a women's home.

Would he eventually cave to the undeniable need for one, as Mr. Beauchamp assumed, even without town support? "Of course, once we have a women's home, we would store and alter the clothing there, but until then, what if Lydia or I accompanied them?"

"Neither of you have the time to sit with them while they alter dresses. I don't want to drive away the staff. I had enough difficulty filling the orphanage positions as it was."

Evelyn wouldn't argue that Nicholas had taken care in selecting the staff. Their work was impeccable, and the children were in no danger of being mistreated.

Nicholas slipped his arm around his wife and caressed his daughter's sleeping head. "Maybe you could find a place at church?"

Evelyn looked at the ceiling, trying to remember if there was a room that wasn't being used. "I could ask, but I'm pretty sure there are no empty rooms. Though maybe we could put a trunk in the room where the moral society meets."

"You do realize you'll likely get dresses

too fancy for the jobs these women would get." Nicholas settled back against his seat. "They'd need work dresses, which aren't the kind to be handed down, but rather worn until they're ready for the rag bag."

Evelyn scowled. "I still think the idea has some merit." She truly did like Nicholas, but the way he logically took the wind out of people's sails was quite annoying.

Lydia sighed, likely thinking the same thing, and then yawned again. "What did you come in here for, dear?"

He pressed a kiss to his wife's temple. "Just to see you." He put a hand to her rounded abdomen. "And to say hi to the rest."

Lydia's belly had been a fascinating distraction while they'd talked earlier. It had jolted and jiggled without rhyme or reason.

Nicholas leaned to press a kiss to her stomach. "Hello in there."

Evelyn froze, wondering if Nicholas had forgotten she was in the room.

Lydia squirmed as if she couldn't get comfortable. "Why won't you tell me if you think it's a boy or girl?"

He lifted his head and gave Evelyn a side glance before sitting up straight.

So he had forgotten she was there.

He cleared his throat. "As I recall, you

were quite annoyed that I was right about Isabelle, so I'm keeping my guess to myself."

Lydia's mouth puckered, and she squinted an eye. "But once the baby's born, you could claim you knew all along."

"To be honest, I don't have any idea this time."

Lydia's eyes widened in shock, as if that was an abnormal admission.

"All I know is that I'll love them."

Lydia's face paled. "Them?"

Nicholas threw her a grin.

"You're just trying to make me squirm."

"You wanted to know."

"But I can't have two!"

Evelyn held in her giggle over how Lydia acted as if twins would be the end of the world.

Nicholas brushed his fingers through his daughter's curls as he looked into his wife's eyes. "You've gotten large quite quickly, and your pregnancy symptoms are twice as bad as last time."

Lydia shook her head slowly, her heavy eyelids fighting to stay open. "Several ladies said they got bigger with each child, and every pregnancy is different."

"You wanted to know my guess, love." He kissed her temple. "I've got to go. I'll see you in a few hours." He disentangled himself, stood, and nodded at Evelyn before leaving.

Though Nicholas's footsteps had faded to nothing, Lydia remained still on the couch, eyes closed.

She'd known her friend was tired, but falling asleep so quickly was surprising. Evelyn gathered her things as quietly as possible. It was time to get back to the orphanage anyway.

Lydia took in a big gulp of air and opened her eyes wide. "I just can't have twins — one's tiring enough!"

"You'll be fine, Lydia. And Nicholas isn't right about everything."

"Oh, but I was so sure the last time it was a boy, and I was wrong."

"Lyd, your husband's rich. All you have to do is ask him to hire you a houseful of maids to help you take care of your brood and he will."

Lydia blew out a breath and resituated Isabelle on her shoulder. "I don't want to do that, but she's exhausting enough." Her eyes drifted closed again.

Earlier when Isabelle had fallen asleep, Evelyn had asked Lydia if she ought to nap with her daughter, but she'd insisted she'd rather visit.

She should've listened to her instinct and

told Lydia she'd return another time. "Well, I do have to get going."

Lydia's eyes fluttered open. "I'm glad you dropped by, even if we didn't get very far in figuring out how to implement your idea."

"That's all right. Maybe when we bring it up at the moral-society meeting, the ladies will have a solution." Evelyn picked up her basket. "Now I'll let you sleep."

No answer came from Lydia, and a quick glance confirmed her friend's heavy eyelids had won the war.

Evelyn quietly pulled the door shut behind her. As she treaded softly toward the front, Sadie's gauzy-capped, dark blond head poked out of the morning room's double doors. "Miss Wisely, may I speak with you?" She padded out of the room, clasping her hands tightly in front of her.

"Of course." Had Sadie been waiting for her this entire time?

"Is the Thacker boy still at the orphan-age?"

"Yes." Lawrence had been withdrawing into himself even more lately, sitting alone near the front-door window most every day, as if his sister might come strolling by but wouldn't stop unless he was waiting. Daddy had been trying to give him lots of atten-tion, but the boy wasn't responding as

258

they'd hoped.

"It's about his sister."

Evelyn clamped onto Sadie's wrist. "What do you know?" *Please, God, let it be something good.*

But considering the way Sadie worried her lip, Evelyn's heart wasn't beating with hope.

"Do you know a Miss Rosie Cheeks?"

How she hated the prostitutes' pseudonyms, highlighting their physical assets instead of who they were. "Yes, I do." Rosie was a cottage girl who made Evelyn's insides ache. She was her age, with a two-year-old girl she guarded like a she-bear. Rosie was the nicest prostitute Evelyn had met so far, though she had little education and was a bit off-kilter. "Have you talked to Rosie? Sadie, you shouldn't go anywhere near that area of town. If anyone finds out —"

She held up her hand and looked around with wide eyes. "I know. I wasn't there. But the man who lives to our east has a butler Franklin's age. They like to talk, and when I'm taking out trash, sometimes I overhear them. You know how the subject of the red-light district gets Franklin riled, and considering if he ever found out what I was . . . Well, I'm ashamed to say I took my time emptying buckets so I could listen." Sadie's shoulders sagged. "Anyway, it seems Rosie is a favorite of the master next door."

Evelyn had caught glimpses of the plumbing store owner in the district a few times, so she knew he wasn't the most upright of men. But she could've done without knowing who he "liked."

"Between Franklin's usual rants about ladies of the night, I caught that Mr. Tomberlin was put out with Rosie for not taking customers at the moment. He sent his butler to find out why. Seems she's tending a young woman with a newborn. His description of the girl makes me think it might be Lawrence's sister."

"You've seen Annette before?"

Sadie nodded. "Once when I took a batch of peanut brittle to the orphanage. The butler said the young woman had huge freckles and wild curly hair."

Those were indeed Annette's most telling features. But Annette hadn't been prostituting herself out and had claimed she would never do so.

Had that been a lie?

Evelyn tugged her gloves on. She couldn't go home until she found out. And here she was, once again leaving her parents alone to watch the orphanage longer than she'd promised. Soon they'd stop letting her go visit anyone, lest she never return. "Could you send someone to the orphanage to tell my parents I'll be late?"

"I could have Pearl do that."

"If Mr. or Mrs. Lowe get upset that she left her post, tell them it's my fault." At Sadie's nod, Evelyn went out of doors, hoping Nicholas had walked instead of taking his driver.

Indeed he had. In the quaint little carriage house out back, Mr. Parker was currying one of the horses. Nicholas had yet to buy an automobile, likely because Mr. Parker wasn't interested in learning to drive one. Nicholas seemed to enjoy walking and likely didn't want to let go of Mr. Parker since he needed a flexible job to care for his wife with dementia.

"I'm so glad you're here, Mr. Parker."

He turned with a smile, his white hair in desperate need of a trim. "Miss Wisely, what can I do for you?"

"Could you take me to the row of shacks behind the Wet Whistle?"

His smile instantly died. "It's been a long time since a lady asked me to drive her to the red-light district, and after that harrowing night, I'm not keen on doing so again."

"I bet that was Mrs. Lowe."

"Yes." He absentmindedly rotated the

brush in his hands.

"And nothing bad happened to her, right?"

He pointed the brush handle at her as if he were staring down a wayward child. "Luck was what that was."

"I only need to check on someone. I'll do it alone, if I must."

The man rubbed his forehead and moved toward the carriage. "Today's young ladies don't have a lick of sense."

Evelyn couldn't help but smile at being called young. "On the contrary, Mr. Parker, that's why we ask for your escort."

He groaned and stomped off. "Give me a minute."

Evelyn stood aside as Mr. Parker readied the carriage while mumbling under his breath. Thankfully, he chose something enclosed. If Annette could be convinced to leave her hiding place, she'd likely need to leave without being seen.

Though if there was a baby involved, was there any hope Annette could visit her brother at the mansion without causing trouble with the staff?

21

Evelyn braced herself as the carriage bumped to a stop on the rutted road in the most dismal section of the red-light district. Evelyn tried to open the carriage door, but Mr. Parker stopped her.

"I'll go knock, miss. Tell me what you're wanting to know."

She pushed open the door anyway and descended onto the packed-dirt street. "I've no need to sit in the carriage. I've been to this section of town to nurse bruised and battered women before."

Nicholas's driver frowned at her, his brow wrinkling. He stepped back and crossed his arms over his chest. "I'm not letting you out of my sight."

"All right." She patted his arm and pointed to the middle shack. "I'll be right there."

Mr. Parker looked at his timepiece and shook his head. "I should have realized how late it was before I agreed to bring you here. I'm going with you."

She wouldn't fight him. He was right — it wasn't the best time of day to visit. She forged across the littered road, but at the door of the tiny shack, she hesitated. She'd never before come without being summoned. Glancing behind her, she made certain Mr. Parker was nearby. His expression did nothing to help her find any extra courage. She made a fist and knocked anyway.

No answer.

She knocked louder.

"No one's here, or they ain't wanting company." Mr. Parker grabbed her sleeve. "Let's go."

"I'll check the windows first."

"What?"

Before Mr. Parker could stop her, she scurried over to the grimy window and peered in, hands cupped against the glass. She might see something she might wish to unsee, but if Annette was in there with a baby . . . Well, no fifteen-year-old mother should be left unattended anywhere near The Line.

No one inside.

No sounds either.

"What are you doing here?" The roughened voice of Old Hattie Williams scared Evelyn upright.

The only prostitute she knew who didn't use a fake name shook her finger at her as she came swaggering over. Of course, Old Hattie wasn't truly that old — maybe late forties, at most — but she was older than most of the women who worked the nights. "We don't need your holier-than-thou presence here." Her dark piercing eyes and pointed nose pinned Evelyn to the spot.

"Let's go, miss." Mr. Parker threaded his arm through hers and pulled her toward the carriage.

She resisted being dragged. "I'm looking for Annette Thacker. Can you tell me where she is?"

"You're wanting one of the Annies?"

"No." At least she sure hoped Annette hadn't become the fifth prostitute named Annie who worked in Teaville. "Annette Thacker, fifteen, not a prostitute."

Old Hattie threw back her head and laughed. "If you're not wanting a prostitute, you're looking in the wrong place."

"Where's Rosie Cheeks, then?"

"Beats me."

"Miss!" a voice hissed from somewhere behind her.

Evelyn turned, trying to find the hushed

yet insistent voice.

A girl of about seven dashed out. "Miss Rosie went to live at the blue shack near the cemetery last Thursday."

She squatted in front of the little blond girl with the most matted hair she'd ever seen. Her flour-sack dress was beyond pitiful. "I'm Miss Wisely. Who do you belong to?" *Please, God, let her say her mother.*

"You're the lady who feeds kids on Saturday near the glass factory, right?"

"Yes, in the empty lot with the spindly oak tree in the middle." She held out her hand, hoping the girl would come closer, but the girl only stared at her open palm. "Would you like to eat with us next Saturday?"

No answer.

"What's your name?"

The girl stared at her for a few seconds. "Lisa, and I'll think about it." With a quick pivot, Lisa rushed back toward the dying weeds surrounding the shacks.

"Wait." Evelyn stood, but Lisa was already gone.

"I take it we aren't going home until you check the blue shack." Mr. Parker's voice sounded resigned.

Old Hattie shook her head, her pursed lips and cold eyes unnerving. "You're a fool to meddle in our business."

Evelyn held out her hands to Hattie as she had to Lisa. "What if you needed help?"

"I'd get it myself."

She let her hands fall back to her sides. "If you change your mind, feel free to talk to me."

The streetwalker only glared at her before stomping off in the direction from which she'd come.

On the way to the cemetery, Evelyn stared out the carriage window, hoping there was another blue shack by the graveyard she'd forgotten about. The one she knew of was not fit to step foot in, let alone live in.

Mr. Parker slowed as they approached the small ramshackle building that teetered on the edge of oblivion. The roof was a patchwork of broken trusses with scraps of shingles hanging on for dear life, the siding owed its color to the few curls of blue paint that had yet to flake off, and all the windows had been busted by many a grade-school boy on a dare.

Near the back side of the cabin, a dark-blond woman about-faced and rushed through the waist-high weeds surrounding the structure.

Though the coach hadn't stopped yet, Evelyn turned the handle and opened the door. "Rosie!"

The blonde kept hustling for the backyard, the face of her two-year-old girl looking over her shoulder at Evelyn.

Rosie had never shied away from her before.

"Miss Wisely!" Mr. Parker pulled his horse to a complete stop, but Evelyn had already stumbled out of the coach.

She picked up her skirts and rushed into the grasses. "Rosie!"

The woman abruptly slowed and turned to face her, her expression collected and warm. "Why, Miss Wisely, I didn't expect to see you here. Did someone tell you I was sick?"

Evelyn pulled up short and frowned at the woman's almost welcoming tone. Though they'd talked about her daughter a few times and Rosie had helped her fetch a doctor for a woman once, the prostitute had never greeted her so brightly. Coupled with her running away seconds earlier, Evelyn knew something was wrong. "Why are you at this shack?"

Rosie glanced at the nearby wall that slumped in near collapse. "Well, when a landlord has a prostitute for a tenant, he doesn't think nothing about hiking rent and asking for it early. Knows you ain't going to tell the police about it and figures you got nowhere to go. But I found me somewhere."

"This isn't a place to keep a child."

"Neither was the last place I was at."

True, but at least a two-year-old wouldn't be strong enough to push on a wall and collapse the roof onto herself at the old place. "I was told —"

The faint mewl of a newborn was quickly dampened.

"What did I just hear?" Evelyn headed for the shack.

"I didn't hear anything." Rosie scurried alongside her. "But since you's here, could you take a look at my girl's teeth? I think they're 'bout to fall out, but what am I to do about it?"

Evelyn looked back at Rosie's girl but didn't stop. The little one had her thumb in her mouth and looked content enough — whereas Rosie's face was flushed and her eyes wide.

Mr. Parker jogged up. "I think I heard a baby."

"It was just my Norah."

"That wasn't a two-year-old's cry, Rosie." Evelyn shook her head at the woman's dodging. "Where's Annette?"

"I don't know an Annette."

Mr. Parker led the way to the door and

struggled to open it since the door's top hinge was loose and the bottom corner scraped into the dirt floor.

In the corner of a room not fit for rats, Annette was slumped over a pile of blankets wadded on her lap.

Evelyn rushed over and yanked the blankets off. "You'll smother the baby."

"I was just trying to keep her quiet." Annette's voice was dull and lifeless. Her eyes were encircled with shadows, and her mouth was a grim line. The girl might have just had a baby, but considering how thin she was, she certainly hadn't been eating enough to nourish herself, let alone a newborn.

"I'm sorry, Miss Wisely. I didn't know what her name was." Rosie inched toward her, her voice contrite. "All I knew was she didn't want anyone knowing where she was. I heard her screaming a few days ago, and I couldn't just leave her. She didn't know what was happening, but the baby came out all right. She's insistin' she's staying here."

"Come on, Annette." Evelyn reached for her arms. "Let's get you to the mansion. Your brother's worried about you."

"I can't go anywhere right now." She pushed herself into the corner, away from Evelyn's arms.

"Why not?" Looking around at the spiders and trash in the corners of the shack, there was absolutely no reason to stay here longer than it took to walk out.

"I can't let no one know I'm pregnant."

Evelyn frowned at her. "You're not pregnant anymore."

"Well, no, but I'm going to have to wait until my body looks normal again before I step outside. But here . . ." She wrapped the ragged red blanket around the baby and shoved the infant into Evelyn's arms. "Take her away."

"But the baby needs you, Annette."

"No, she don't. If Daniel Fish finds out I got a baby, he'll know I ain't no virgin flower, and then he ain't going to take me back as just a cleaning girl."

Evelyn looked at the poor babe who'd yet to cry again. "So this baby isn't . . ."

"Well, she certainly ain't going to be claimed by no man, but she ain't because I sold myself."

Mr. Parker's mumbling behind them clearly indicated the exact origins of this little one would make little difference in the opinion of good society.

Evelyn looked down at the babe's gaunt cheeks, her eyes a little sunken in. "Why didn't you tell me you were in trouble the last time you visited Lawrence?"

She shook her head with little energy. "You can't fix everything. I thought you'd have him adopted out already. Then I'd have followed him to make sure he got into a good family. I've heard too many girls telling about the terrible homes they got put in. I knew you were his best chance at getting a good one, but I had to be sure. But you took too long. I couldn't be found in my condition without Mr. Fish realizing I'm older than he thought and locking me up to work. I had to be able to check on Lawrence."

"Come with me and you won't have to face Mr. Fish at all." She'd have to ask Nicholas who Mr. Fish was. His wasn't a name she recognized.

"No, you take the baby and get her into a good home. Just don't tell Lawrence she's his niece. All right?" Tears were streaming soundlessly down her face. "I don't want him thinking bad of me."

Evelyn followed Annette's gaze to the child, whose movements were lethargic. She couldn't imagine giving up a child, no matter how it was conceived. But she'd never cared for a baby this young at the mansion. Although the babies were usually adopted fairly quickly, they took a lot of time to care for.

As much as she wanted to mother this frail bundle, maybe this child was God's gift to Annette, to convince her to abandon the life she was living. "Annette, this baby needs you."

"She doesn't need me." Annette hugged herself and then turned toward the corner. "I'll come visit Lawrence soon, but don't tell him, in case I can't. I'll only come if you keep the baby out of my sight."

Clearly this girl was far from ready for motherhood, but if she was in better living conditions and given some medical help, surely she'd realize things weren't as hopeless as they seemed.

Except her gaze looked so far from the here and now. Did Annette even understand what she was doing?

Evelyn held the bundle tighter and kneeled beside Annette. "What did you name her?"

"I didn't. You name her."

Tears warmed Evelyn's eyes. A baby to name? Did she even remember any of the names she used to keep in the back of her diary for future children? "No matter what has happened, Annette, God loves you. He's given you the joy of this child. Don't give up on her."

Annette only put her hands over her ears.

Rosie's hand clamped onto Evelyn's shoulder. "I think it might be best if you take the babe, Miss Wisely. It's real good of you to think Annette here can be a good mother and all, but even those of us who keep our children, well, we aren't exactly fit mothers, you know. But if she ain't wantin' it . . ."

"All right." As Annette curled up on the floor, Evelyn stood and swallowed hard before turning to Rosie. "Have you any food here?"

"That's what I been takin' care of. She's just days away from starving — almost think that's what she was trying to do to herself — but I keep insistin'."

"Good." She frowned down at Annette one last time. "I'll make sure your brother and baby get into a good family, all right?"

The girl nodded but didn't turn around to take another look at her child.

Mr. Parker held open the door, and Evelyn stepped out of the hovel, from darkness into light. The sun, low on the horizon, made her blink. She didn't know why Annette was unwilling to get out of a life she clearly had no love for, but there was hope for this little one to never be under the red-light district's influence.

This baby had hope — was Hope.

"Let's go." Mr. Parker put a hand to her shoulder. "You've got children to take care of."

22

After wiping his sweaty hands on his slacks, David knocked on the nondescript door. A door like any other, yet he'd never thought he'd knock on one like this.

"Come in," the female voice called, sultry enough to make his heart pound.

He shut his eyes and turned the knob with the same amount of reluctance he'd had when Mrs. Rice had forced him to eat liver when he was five. He'd seen Evelyn walk into a prostitute's room without any hesitation the first day they'd met. She'd walked in; she'd walked out. He could do the same, since this was the only way the tavern owner's wife would let him see Irish Mary, no matter how much he insisted he only needed to talk to her for a few minutes. And after watching the saloon for a few nights, it was evident these ladies were never allowed out.

"Well hello, stranger." A thin blonde in a

gown of iridescent green sat on a white du-
vet atop a bed that nearly filled the room.
Her legs were crossed, one foot swinging.
Her eyes flashed down him, quick and assessing. "Your first time?"

"Uh, yes," he squeaked. "I mean, no. I
mean, being in here, yes, but no to the
other. Not that I've ever been with —" Ugh,
he needed to stop before he humiliated
himself or said the exact opposite of what
he meant.

"Tongue-tied, eh?" She rose from the bed
as if she were floating toward him.

He stood taller, as if preparing for an
onslaught, and held out his hand. "I'm not
here for what you think."

Her index finger trailed down the side of
his arm as she circled around to his back.
"What can I do for you?"

"Nothing." Ugh, where had his brain
gone? Why was she circling him? He turned
to keep trouble within eyesight.

This woman looked nothing like he'd
imagined. Miss O'Conner was stocky with
curly brown hair, sharp green eyes, and —
though decent enough to look at — she
wasn't striking. This woman's blue eyes
shone out from under thick lashes, her lips
were a vivid red, and her cheeks were
artificially pink, highlighting high cheek-

bones. Her body was not as curvy as Caroline's, but with the long blond curls dangling down to her cinched-in waist, she sure flaunted the curves she had.

"I mean, I do want something. That is, if you're Moira O'Conner. I want to talk."

She stopped and her eyes turned hard. "I'm Irish Mary."

"Right. I know that."

"I don't talk, mister." She put her hand on his chest, where his heart beat in a panicked staccato, and slipped her fingers between the buttons on his shirt. "But you can talk if you want to."

He grabbed her hand and pulled it off of him as he would a leech. "I only paid to come up here because the madam refused to let me see you any other way. You don't venture out much."

"Then why don't you get your money's worth?" She wiggled his tie loose.

Goodness, with all the talk the Lowes and Evelyn did about the plights of these women, he'd expected a trapped kitten, not a hungry lioness. He grabbed her by the upper arms and held her as far away from him as he could. "Then if you'd like me to get my money's worth, tell me about you and Henri Beauchamp."

Her eyes narrowed to slits. "I don't talk

about clients."

"I'm pretty sure he isn't one of your clients."

"Then I wouldn't know him."

"Don't play dumb. I've already greased enough palms to know you're Caroline O'Conner's sister, your name is Moira, and you were involved with Henri Beauchamp before you took up this vocation." He pulled out two dollars. "Maybe this will help. All I want to know is why he seems to hate you so much."

Though she eyed the money for a second, she jerked her arms from his grip. "I don't play the information game." She glared at him, her dark eye makeup making her look more intimidating than any female who'd ever been upset with him before. Then she marched for the door.

He rushed after her, slapping his palm against the door the second she turned the knob. The door clicked right back into place. "I'm not asking for blackmail, just understanding. A friend of mine wants to start a ministry for women like you who want to escape —"

"I'm not looking to escape, mister."

"It's David. And I see that. But others do and I'm sure you know a few. Anyway, she wants a place for them to learn a respectable trade and find their way back into good society, but she needs businessmen to support her. Mr. Beauchamp seemed to be a good candidate until she started talking about you and your sister. Your name made Beauchamp almost bust his boiler, so I thought if you could clear things up with him, he might —"

"It's not my place to clear anything up."

"But think of the women who want out —"

"What happened between the three of us is up to Caroline to tell, if she so chooses, not me."

"Miss O'Conner?" He rubbed his chin, trying to remember Henri's response to Evelyn's friend's name. Had there been an emotional reaction he'd missed?

Irish Mary yanked on the door again, and he let his hand fall. She opened the door wide and turned her head toward the busy saloon floor below. "I don't trade in secrets, mister." Her voice projected out over the din. "It's too easy to beat information out of people, and I like how I look. So get out."

A few men from below glanced up with interest.

David couldn't help his flaming face despite the fact that she'd made it quite clear he hadn't gotten anything of any sort from her. "Good day, then, ma'am. I wish you well," he mumbled.

She widened her eyes at that.

The fire in his cheeks needed a good dousing, and yet he seemed stuck in her doorway. The flash of confusion on her face stayed his retreat. Could God use him now? "I can't help but believe, deep down inside, you might want a place to go if you could. But maybe you think you're too far gone."

She moved to step back inside, but he stopped her with a soft grip on her arm. "God redeems the lowest of the low, Moira. Murderers, adulterers, and prostitutes were all a part of Christ's lineage. When He walked this earth, He supped with the crowd you're involved in and offered forgiveness and a way out. He still offers that today."

She only stared up at him, her eyes hardening — if that were possible. "Thank you for the sermon, preacher. Now get back to your church."

He hesitated, but not even a glimmer of hunger for what he'd said shone in her eyes. He released her and stepped across her threshold. The door slammed immediately, hitting his heel.

Could that have gone any worse?

He tucked his hands into his pockets and

strode across the wooden balcony. He evidently needed to talk to Caroline. He hadn't asked her about Henri's reaction to her sister's name since he'd figured having a prostitute sister was burden enough.

Keeping his gaze on where he was going instead of glancing around the busy "soda fountain," David left the Dutch Tulip as quickly as he could and set out across town. He really should think about leasing a horse. He'd not expected to be gallivanting about town so much, but ever since he'd gotten tangled up with Evelyn, it seemed he was doing more walking than he usually did in a year.

And tangled up was a good description for it. His heart sure was, anyway.

Crossing the familiar roads toward the orphanage, David chewed his inner cheek. He hadn't paid much attention to Caroline, considering any time he ran across her she was with Evelyn. So how could he just walk up and prod her for what was likely a very personal story? Should he even do so? Would Evelyn be a better person to approach her? Maybe she already knew her story.

He started up the mansion's winding driveway and took in the immaculate grounds. Near the side of the mansion, two maids were beating rugs on the clothesline, and unless there were two servants of the same build, the one on the left was Caroline.

Probably a good idea to skip going into the mansion altogether. Though his heart tugged at him to at least catch a glimpse of Evelyn, he wanted to have good news for her the next time he saw her.

He cleared his throat when he got within earshot of the women. The older one with gray hair and a slim figure turned around and frowned at him. Caroline whacked her rug a few times before taking a look at who'd arrived.

She wiped her dark curly hair off her forehead with the back of her dusty sleeve. "Mr. Kingsman? What can we do for you?"

He ran a hand around the back of his neck and glanced at the other lady. Caroline seemed to understand his hesitation and put down her beater. "Why don't you tell me on the way in?" Caroline pulled her rug off the line.

"Let me do that." He grabbed the rug, but she wouldn't relinquish it.

"This is my job, Mr. Kingsman."

"And I'm interrupting your work. I don't mind carrying it."

"If you must." Caroline turned to her

companion. "I'll get the rugs from the music room." She started for the servants' entrance, and he followed.

He kept pace with her slow stride, the rug rolled up on his shoulder, bouncing with each step, but by the time they reached the door, he still hadn't come up with a good way to ask his questions.

She opened the door and ushered him in. "I know you didn't come to help me carry rugs. So what do you want?"

He dropped the rug onto the floor. "I don't know how to ask this, so I guess I'll just start. Your sister is Irish Mary, correct?"

"Yes."

Seemed she didn't find his knowing her sister was a prostitute to be strange.

"Well, last week, when I was helping Ev . . . Miss Wisely look for sponsors for her women's home, she thought her best chance of getting help was from Mr. Beauchamp."

Caroline's expression turned suspicious.

"Evelyn attempted to persuade him by telling him about your sister's story when he cut her off, vehemently so. I figured since the mere mention of your sister's name touched a nerve, I might be able to figure out why and help him get over it. I wondered if maybe she was blackmailing him or cheated him somehow, but when I saw her today, she said you were the one I needed to talk to."

"You actually went to see her?" Caroline looked incredulous.

"It was expensive, but yes, and . . ." He cleared his throat again. "She threw me out since I wasn't there for her usual services. I know this is probably none of my business, but I thought maybe you could help Evelyn get Henri's support."

Caroline only stood there, staring at the rolled rug at their feet. After a minute, she huffed. "I don't know if telling him anything will get you the sponsorship you want, but I'm done letting that man hang on to his hatred for no good reason." She turned and headed back to the door. "Perhaps I should grab my beater wand from the clothesline before we go. Smacking him upside the head might work better than me telling him anything."

David scurried after her. "That's certainly an idea, but why don't we try all the non-physical ideas we can think of first?"

She snorted, but thankfully didn't take a side trip to the clothesline, just hollered for the other maid to get the music room rugs herself.

When she headed for the front instead of

the carriage house, he frowned. "I didn't bring my factory's wagon. Do you want to see if Mr. Parker — ?"

"He's not here. Besides, I walk farther than Elm Street almost every day. Are you wanting a ride?"

Even if he wanted one, he wasn't about to say yes now. But he'd have to work to keep from sounding winded if she kept up this pace. "No."

She nodded and marched forward, down the hill.

At least the weather was brisk and would keep them cool at the pace she set. She seemed intent on getting there as quickly as possible, and if the divot in her brow and the wriggling of her lips was any indication, she was preparing quite the lecture for Mr. Beauchamp.

He greeted the few people he recognized as Caroline led them across the tracks and into the industrial part of town.

At Elm and Ninth, in the shadow of the railcar repair shop, he decided he had to say something. "Um, perhaps I'm not needed? Moira seemed to act like this was a personal thing, and if —"

"I want you there. That way Henri can't pretend he doesn't know."

Well, at least that was clear.

When they got to the flour mill, he raced up the stairs to open the door for her. Hopefully Henri was in the building, since Caroline seemed determined to attend to business immediately.

And hopefully he'd be able to escort her home with good news for Evelyn.

In the front office, Mr. Allen's desk was empty.

David looked for a bell to ring, but Caroline skirted the desk and marched down the hall.

"Come on," she called over her shoulder.

"Wait a minute. I doubt barging in on him is a good idea. He might have an appointment." He took a quick glance at the calendar on Mr. Allen's desk, but since Caroline kept walking, he abandoned the search and hurried after her. "At least —"

She pounded on the door but didn't wait for a reply before storming in.

Henri jerked in his seat and put his hands on his desk to stand. "Now, what's this — ?"

"Sit down and listen."

David froze, as did Henri in a half squatting position.

The room felt icy for no apparent reason. While Henri slowly lowered himself, David fidgeted. Should he sit too? He couldn't sit right smack in front of Henri's desk between the two of them. He glanced around for somewhere else to sit, finding a chair in the corner.

Caroline stamped forward. "You always did have a thick skull, I just never knew how thick."

David stopped halfway to the chair. If he hadn't asked Caroline earlier if she wanted him to stay, he'd be inching back toward the door.

"Miss O'Conner." Henri sat rigidly behind his desk. "You don't have an appointment, and I don't think —"

"After these past three years, I don't know why I ever thought I was in love with you."

If Henri's body hadn't already been visibly tense, the man might just have snapped.

David gestured toward the door. "Perhaps I should leave."

Caroline sliced her hand through the air as if he were a back-talking orphan. "Stay. That way this blockhead can't spread wrongful gossip or deny he knows what I'm about to tell him."

David lowered himself onto the chair's arm, perched so he could leave the second he was able.

Henri's face was a high red. "Excuse me, Miss O'Conner, but I don't let men call me names, and I won't —"

"My sister never loved you."

Henri's face blanked, and his body lost its rigidity.

"You were just someone to flirt with, like all the others. Just like she does now. I know the names you call Moira, and I can't say I disagree with you. She is the epitome of the unwholesome prostitute people like to paint all prostitutes as being. But she's done one thing worthy of admiration, and because of that, I will try for the rest of my life to convince her to leave her line of work."

Henri glanced over at him, and David shook his head. Hopefully Henri would understand he hadn't known this was coming. He should've asked her to tell him the story before they confronted Henri, but with the sound of unshed tears in Caroline's voice, he wasn't about to suggest she fill him in later.

Grasping the chair in front of Henri's desk, Caroline lowered herself onto the seat and pressed her hands together. "When we were young" — Caroline's voice softened — "Moira always got the attention."

Her change from outrage to solemnity startled him more than her declaration of love for a man far above her station.

"The boys loved her. Our parents preferred her. Even our teachers succumbed to

289

her charm, forgetting I existed. I never knew why she hated me." She stared at her folded hands in her lap. "I was not a threat to her popularity. I was dumpy and shy. Not until later did I realize it was because Daddy was more interested in her than a man ought to be in his daughter."

David stiffened and Henri ran a hand through his hair and muttered a curse.

"My lack of beauty saved me from my father's attention — until he couldn't pay a debt. Late one night, a brothel owner sent two thugs to either extract the money from him or crack his skull. We heard the scuffle outside our window, and Moira held me as I silently cried." Caroline looked up, but her eyes seemed far away. "Just when I wondered if Daddy had been killed, he groaned and begged to have his debt erased if he gave me to the brothel owner. I'd pay his debt off and then some, he'd said."

Henri pinched the bridge of his nose, and David hung his head. Evelyn had mentioned how some of the women were trapped in the life simply because one person considered them to be nothing more than chattel, but sitting beside someone so autonomous and free, imagining her being handed over like property and someone accepting her as such, defied reason.

"I figured I'd heard him wrong, but Moira tightened her grip on me. They asked if I was the blonde. When Daddy said Moira was not for sale, they told him if the brunette wasn't deemed good enough, come morning, he better have five hundred dollars." Caroline's voice petered out.

The clock ticked loudly behind them, and David got up to put a hand on her shoulder. "I'm so sorry."

She gave his hand a quick squeeze but stood and then proceeded to pace. "I started packing immediately, but Daddy came and dragged me to the basement and locked me in. My panic and fear were so intense I thought I'd surely die, but the key jiggled in the door hours later, and Daddy took me by the wrist and dragged me into an awaiting vehicle. No amount of pleading changed his mind." She crossed her arms as if cold. "When we reached the brothel, I couldn't fight him. Daddy told an older gentleman he'd come to make good on his debt. The man barely glanced at me, shrugged, and said it was a deal if Daddy had fifty bucks, since he had immediate debts of his own. How my father had fifty dollars I'll never know, but it seemed like I lived through hours of agony as he pulled out each of those ten-dollar bills. My stomach betrayed me, and I couldn't move from where he'd left me on the floor, getting sick in a heap at the brothel owner's feet.

"Hours, or maybe only minutes, passed, when I heard Moira's voice break through my sobbing. She said if the owner let me go free and put me on the next departing train, he could have her instead." Caroline's voice grew scratchy. "She was dolled up, giving the brothel owner the same coquettish looks she plied on you and countless other men."

She looked to the ceiling, blinking repetitively, her lips pressed tight. After a few seconds, she took a breath and closed her eyes. "The next few minutes were a blur, and I don't know how she got me out of there when they could have manhandled us both, but I had the wherewithal to protest. Moira wouldn't listen, told me she was built for it, I wasn't. That her living out of Daddy's reach in the brothel was the best revenge for the hell he'd put her through."

Caroline stopped pacing and hung her head. Henri just sat blinking.

David rubbed a hand down his face. He'd been so eager to help Evelyn he hadn't considered what it would cost Caroline to tell her story. But how could he have known? And would any of this change Henri's mind?

"But I don't think what she said about

herself is true," Caroline whispered, her voice nearly nonexistent. She'd moved to stand next to Henri's picture window, her reflection showing a woman whose face had aged far faster than her sister's. "Moira knew I was in love with you. It was the only reason she didn't sleep with you like she did the other boys. And you put her on a pedestal for it. I think she gave herself up to give me a chance with you, but I left town that day."

David shifted. And here he'd thought Moira playing with his tie earlier had been the most uncomfortable he'd been in his life.

"I never went back to see you. It wasn't worth getting within reach of my father when you'd never noticed me before. And what kind of sister would I be to pursue happiness when Moira had given up her own for me?"

She wrapped her arms around herself. "After my parents died in 1904, an attorney found me and helped me sell their property to pay for Moira's freedom. I told her I'd stay with her forever, locked away from the world so she could have some of the freedom she'd given me."

She turned from the window, the lines on her face more pronounced, as if she'd gained a wrinkle or two during the retelling. Her eyes somehow despairing and resolute at the same time. "I have no idea why she won't leave, have no idea if she truly wants to stay as she claims, but I know others who'd leave if they had a chance. Those who were like me but without a Moira to save them — or those who've finally seen the light. If my sister ever sees that light, I'm going to be there, women's home or no."

Caroline shook her head as she turned to stare outside again. "I never thought I'd see you again. I was so focused on convincing Moira to leave that first year I don't think I even bothered to read a newspaper. I certainly hadn't paid enough attention to the world around me to hear you'd been in Teaville for years nor realize you were friends with Mr. Lowe. If I'd known, I'd have never taken his housekeeping position." Her jaw grew taut as she tilted her chin a little. "I wish you'd never found out about Moira, but I can't believe you've been fuming for nearly three years over a woman who only ever strung you along, while you refuse to help women like me, who would've loved you if circumstances hadn't taken that chance away. I don't expect you'd ever take a second look at me, but . . ." She suddenly about-faced and walked toward the exit without even glancing in Henri's direction.

David moved to meet her, but she held out her hand. "I don't require an escort home, Mr. Kingsman. I walk alone through worse neighborhoods when I'm called to help the women. I'm not going straight back to the orphanage anyway. I've got to walk off my desire to punch Henri in the nose first." And then she was gone.

Henri rubbed the back of his neck, staring at something on his desk.

David cleared his throat and took a step forward. "The other day when you'd reacted so violently to Moira's name, I figured if I could get to the bottom of whatever caused that reaction, you might be more willing to listen to Miss Wisely's proposal. That . . ." He held out his hand as if pointing to the story still hanging heavy in the room. "That wasn't what I expected. I shouldn't have meddled."

"No, I needed to hear the story. I had no idea." Henri shook his head, his focus on something intangible. "Give me a few days to think."

If only Caroline hadn't had to rip herself apart in front of them to get that response.

23

Stifling a yawn, Evelyn tried to keep her eyes open long enough to catch the ball four-year-old Ezekiel threw. Momma had told her to go outside and get some sunshine while the baby slept, but maybe she should have taken a nap with Hope instead.

Evelyn yawned and threw the ball back to Ezekiel. How did mothers of multiple children get anything done with newborns? A few babies had come through the mansion before, but not with so many other orphans in residence. She definitely needed more coffee. Maybe she should gulp down a potful every time the wet nurse bustled up to attend Hope.

"Miss Wisely!" Ezekiel shouted, his voice clearly disappointed.

She shook her head to clear out the fuzz. "What?"

He pointed at the ball at her feet.

"I'm sorry." She rubbed a hand across her

face, bent to retrieve the ball, and tossed it to him.

He lobbed the ball back, but it went high and wide, giving her no chance to catch it. She turned to race after it before it skipped down the backyard's long sloping hill, but she stopped midstride.

David was running after the ball, easily heading it off as it gained speed.

How she wished she could run as unencumbered as a man.

How she wished David came around more often — though she absolutely shouldn't wish that.

When had he arrived anyway? He must have pulled his buggy up front and not bothered to go through the mansion.

Ball tucked under his arm, he jogged up the hill with a slight grin, and not the one he plied on every girl. No, this one was more subtle, easily missed, and yet, it made her heart pound even worse.

She put her hands to the back of her neck and pretended she was exasperated at having missed the ball when she was actually far more concerned about covering up what was surely a blush crawling up her neck. "Thank you."

"Not a problem." He raised the ball above his head. "Catch, Ezekiel."

The boy behind her screeched as the ball soared high in the sky. He growled when he missed, then chased after the ball.

Max walked out the back door and bounded down the stairs of the massive wraparound porch.

She waved at the older boy. "Why don't you play with Ezekiel?" Hopefully Robert wasn't watching through the windows. He'd probably spend the next few hours trying to finish his schoolwork, while Max had likely completed his own with no help in twenty minutes. If Robert couldn't figure out how to get his work done faster so he wasn't left inside while the others played, she was afraid he'd be forsaking school altogether and begging David for a full-time job.

Max caught Ezekiel's wild throw and then kicked the ball toward the garden. Ezekiel ran after him.

As soon as the boys were out of earshot, she turned to David. "What brings you to the mansion this afternoon?"

David stood with his hands behind his back, the smile on his face growing wider. "What do you want more than anything in the world?"

What was this game? And if it wasn't a game, how could she begin to answer? She closed her eyes to shut out his smile. Her

298

hopes regarding what might happen if Nicholas's private investigator was successful were best kept locked up tight — from everyone, including David.

Evelyn looked at him, hoping he'd gotten distracted by the children playing around them, but he stood waiting. Did she wish to be free of her secret?

No, all her reasons for keeping it still applied. Her current dilemma wouldn't be helped by revealing it. She blew out a breath. What did she want? "I want answers."

His face screwed up comically. "Answers to what?"

She smirked, hoping to hide how truly serious her reply had been. "Things I don't know, of course."

"Would knowing the answer to which businessmen have committed to sponsor your women's home suffice?"

That wasn't the answer she wanted most, but certainly one she prayed for. Of course, lately she'd been praying God would help her give up the idea if it was going nowhere. Not exactly a faith-filled prayer, but she'd certainly uttered it a time or two.

"The answer is Mr. Beauchamp and Mr. Runyan."

She screwed up her forehead. "Runyan . . .

The man who took over Mr. Hargrove's cobbling business?"

"Yes."

"But it's such a small business, and he has seven children. How much can he help?"

"He's agreed to teach a few women to fix shoes. They'd have to do the repair work at the women's home though, since his wife wouldn't agree to them helping at the shop."

"You got the Runyans to agree to that?" Warm tingles rushed down her arms. That was far better than the dollar or two a month she'd asked of men like him.

"No, Hargrove did. I was more instrumental in Beauchamp's capitulation."

"And how did you accomplish that?" She'd left his office the last time with no hope. That was the night she'd begun to pray about knowing when to give up.

He rubbed the back of his head. "Let's just say it wasn't easy or particularly comfortable, but Mr. Beauchamp's definitely committed now."

"Truly?" When he nodded emphatically, she let out a whoop.

His face lit and he spread out his arms. "I take it that was a good answer."

"It is indeed." She went straight into his open arms and squeezed him tight. "I can't believe it!"

He enfolded her in his embrace, crushing her against him. The stubble on his cheek grazed her jaw, and the scent of the castile soap in his hair tickled her nose. The hug should've lasted no more than a second, since she hadn't even meant to embrace him, yet she tightened her arms around him even more. If only she could pretend she needed no more answers than the one he'd given her, that her past hadn't happened, and that she could stay wrapped in his arms forever.

The shouts and hollers of playing children returned her to her senses.

She stepped away from him, but one of those involuntary shivers took over her entire body. The heat in her cheeks burst into flames.

He stared at her so intently the effect of that shiver threatened to erupt again.

She crossed her arms over herself, as if she were in danger — and she was in a way. Very much in danger. Oh, how she wished she'd never disobeyed her father, had never thought she knew better than her elders, had kept her future free to entertain whatever dreams came.

Did he know he was still holding out his arms as if waiting for her to return?

Did he know how hard it was not to?

Oh, how was she to act normal after that hug? She searched the ground at her feet as if some mystical answer would rise from the grass like a fairy's ring. "I'm sorry I got carried away just then."

When he didn't answer, she couldn't help but look back at him.

His wounded expression only made things worse.

What to say? She clasped her hands together and fiddled with her thumbs. Something to get his mind off of what she'd just done. "Have you told Nicholas about the support yet?"

He blinked as if confused for a second, then sucked in a breath. "No, I haven't. I figured you'd want to."

"I do. Let me get Momma to take over for me, and we'll tell him right away." She picked up her skirts and headed for the house before she had to say anything more. Before David saw anything in her eyes he shouldn't.

If he hadn't already.

She couldn't get sidetracked by her errant feelings for a man who would never be hers. No, she needed to focus on the wonderful possibilities he'd just given her for her future. So many women would be helped now.

But could she continue to keep him at arm's length after she'd just now erased that distance completely?

Of course she could. She was reading too much into what had happened. A hug between friends was nothing crazy.

Lord, help me keep my feelings under control so I don't ruin the friendship you've blessed me with. I want so very badly to keep it, even if it's just for a while longer.

She turned to look back at David.

He was still watching her but was shortly attacked from the side by little Alex. He swooped her up and spun her around.

That sweet girl's soft spot for him made Evelyn's heart melt even more. Closing her eyes, she tore herself away from the scene and forged inside.

"Momma?" she called softly as she walked into the hallway. Momma was likely upstairs with the baby, but calling and looking in every room as she made her way upstairs would keep her mind from dwelling on the feel of David's arms around her.

Thankfully her face was cooling. When she found Momma, there should be no high color left in her cheeks.

When Evelyn reached the strangely quiet nursery, Momma was knitting beside the crib. "Momma?"

She pressed a finger firmly against her lips, set down her knitting needles, and slowly pushed herself out of her chair.

Evelyn cringed at the rocker's loud squeak, but Hope didn't stir.

Momma tiptoed across the room and swung the door slightly closed behind them. "What do you need?" she whispered.

"I'd hoped you could watch the children for me, but I see Hope's still asleep." Which didn't bode well for tonight.

"What do you need to do now?" Her mother must have been trying to keep her voice sounding normal, but the teensiest bit of long-suffering colored her question.

"Mr. Kingsman and Mr. Hargrove convinced two more businessmen to sponsor my women's home. I wanted to inform Nicholas, but I can wait until he comes Saturday."

"Mr. Kingsman's here?" Her expression brightened considerably.

The heat in Evelyn's dratted cheeks returned. "Yes, he came to tell me."

Momma's eyes lit even more. "Well then, you two go tell Nicholas. I'll have Suzie sit in here, and she can tell your father when Hope wakes. He's helping Robert finish his mathematics."

"I'm not sure anyone needs to be alerted

when Hope's awake."

"She does have the lung capacity of a lion." Her mother chuckled. "But Walter won't come get her unless he knows he has to. He's never been one for fussy babies, and I doubt Suzie will be able to settle her. But we'll manage — you go ahead."

"Thank you, I'll be quick."

"Oh, take your time, honey."

Evelyn forced herself not to roll her eyes as she left the room behind her mother.

Up ahead, Caroline disappeared into the green room. She'd want to know of the good news too. Leaving Momma at the stairwell, Evelyn headed to the room where the boys slept.

She popped her head into the room full of bunk beds and sweaty socks.

Her friend was picking up discarded clothing, mumbling something about pigs and sties.

"Guess what David just came to tell me?"

Caroline straightened, her eyebrows arched, a boy's union suit dangling over her arm.

"He got Mr. Beauchamp to agree to support the women's home. Isn't that wonderful? I told you Henri has redeeming qualities."

Caroline only looked at her.

Did Caroline remember she needed two local businessmen's support? "And Mr. Hargrove got Mr. Runyan to agree to be a sponsor as well. I'm off to tell Nicholas that he can start planning now."

"That's good." But Caroline's voice was rather emotionless.

She'd expected Caroline to be at least a little excited. "It *is* good, Caroline."

"Of course it is." Her lips curved up a touch, but her smile wasn't convincing. "I'll be grateful for a safe place to nurse my worst cases."

Caroline had been quiet the past few days. Maybe the news just needed time to sink in. She'd learned to give her friend space since Caroline seemed to hate discussing her emotions, but if Caroline wasn't out of her melancholy by Saturday, she'd try to coax her into telling her what was wrong.

Evelyn left Caroline to her cleaning and hurried down the stairs. Though her quick descent had warmed her up, the autumn nights were quick to cool, so she grabbed a shawl.

Through the Tiffany glass, she could make out David's dinky buggy, so she opened the front door.

David was just to the side. The sugar-melting grin he'd given her the day they'd met spread across his face. He extended his hand. "Ready?"

She put her hand in his, letting him help her up onto her side of the buggy. There was no real harm in enjoying holding someone's hand, was there?

She let go and tucked her hands in her lap while he walked around to climb up on his side. She could enjoy a hug, a touch, a helping hand, when appropriate, but she'd have to be content with that.

After David drove them through the fenceless gate at the bottom of the driveway, he turned left.

She pointed to the right. "Nicholas is likely with Lydia at the library now."

"Actually, I saw him turn into the orchard on the way here."

"The orchard?" He was on mansion property?

David thought he needed to drive her less than a mile down the hill?

It's all right, Evelyn. He's just being nice. Nice men are a good thing.

"I'm pretty sure, so we'll check there first."

They rattled down the road, the shouts of the children spilling down the hill as they passed. Evelyn looked up but could only see the top half of the mansion.

David cleared his throat. "Henri and I

have been talking the past few days while he was debating over supporting your shelter." David held the reins loosely, as if they were on a leisurely drive. "He's a savvy business-man, has a lot of Teaville contacts, and gave me a few ideas on how to gain traction with the glass factory here. If they're as promis-ing as they sound, I was thinking" — he cleared his throat and shot a side glance at her — "that if his ideas panned out, we might not sell the factory."

She stared straight ahead, her heart frozen in her throat. "So you'd work from Kansas City and hire someone to manage the fac-tory here?"

"I could do it that way, or . . . perhaps I'd stay. There are a couple businesses Henri said were in dire straits here and could be picked up for a steal, and they'd comple-ment what I already have going."

She nodded as if such news didn't make butterflies trip over themselves in her stom-ach.

"What do you think?"

How could she not wish for David to stay unless she was truly coldhearted? Many men probably thought she was callous since distancing herself had been the easiest way to keep her heart from ever being in danger. But she'd let down her guard with David because he wasn't supposed to stay. Her insides quivered at her mistake. She'd have to get better control of her attraction to him if he moved here permanently. "I surely don't know enough to advise you on that — I'm not a businesswoman."

She didn't dare turn to look at him, but after he was silent for a spell, she took a peek.

He seemed lost in thought, his jaw and lips scrunching around as if he were talking to himself in his head.

Past the windbreak, Nicholas's apple and pear trees grew in tidy, rippling rows down to the insignificant unnamed creek that wandered onto his property, creating a marshy overgrown area and a natural border to the hayfield he let grow to the south.

Several workers stood on ladders through-out the pear-laden trees, filling baskets. Two men below were taking full baskets to a wagon and returning empty ones to the pickers. Nicholas looked out of place in his three-piece suit as he talked to a man nearly half a foot shorter in work pants and rolled-up shirtsleeves.

Nicholas must have heard their buggy, because he turned to look and waved them over.

By the time they stopped beside him, he'd

finished talking to his overseer and walked to her side of the buggy. "To what do I owe this visit?"

"Good news." At least she hoped he'd think so. She let Nicholas swing her down. "There are three businessmen who will officially support our women's home now."

Nicholas's eyebrows shot up. He looked over her head toward David, who'd remained in the buggy, leaning casually against the seat back. How could a man's nonchalant confidence make him look thirty times more handsome than he already was?

"I'm one of the men planning to help, of course. And so are Mr. Runyan and Mr. Beauchamp."

"Mr. Beauchamp?" Nicholas shot David a disbelieving look.

David nodded emphatically. "The lengths I went through to get his support were rather . . . intense. You can speak to him if you wish, but I promise, he's committed."

"He knows he'll have to work with me?"

At David's nod, Nicholas looked down at her. "I hope you realize this won't happen overnight."

"I expect you'll want to do things your way, but I also know you will indeed do it."

He gave her a grin that only made her like her friend's husband more. Lydia had softened him so much it was a wonder people still thought of him as the town's Scrooge.

Nicholas looked toward town. "The first thing we'll need to do is talk to Queenie and Caroline. They're the ones with the most access to the women and have gained their trust. However, we're going to have to be careful to keep them separated from our work. The brothel owners have allowed them to tend to the women precisely because they've posed no threat. What you and I want to do will not be popular."

How had she and Caroline not realized Queenie's ability to tend the women could be in jeopardy if she got involved with taking them out of the district?

But he was right, the women who weren't interested in escape would still need care. She couldn't live with herself if her women's home barred those who suffered from the trifling help they had now. If God hadn't seen fit to guard her in her own rebellion, she could've ended up just like them. Not because she would have voluntarily chosen to be a prostitute, but after listening to their stories, she'd realized, if a few things had been different, she might have involuntarily joined them in their misery.

Nicholas laid a hand on her shoulder and

waited for her to look at him. "We'll move slowly. We'll not do anything before we've anticipated all the problems. It could take years though."

"I was hoping it would be faster, but I understand." And since she had plenty of years to give, she'd give them gladly.

24

Checking his timepiece, David sped up. Hopefully Evelyn and Caroline hadn't yet left the mansion to feed their Saturday group of kids.

He huffed up the last of the rise. He'd not brought the factory's rickety buggy since he'd hoped to join Caroline and Evelyn on their way into town. Now, if only he could pull that off without appearing as if he'd left the buggy behind on purpose.

Thankfully, the wagon the two women used was still parked beside the mansion. He slowed down and walked up as if he were simply dropping by.

He couldn't help smiling at himself. He really was pathetic. Good thing Father wasn't anywhere around. If someone could pop the happy bubble in his chest, it'd be his father.

Caroline came down the stairs from the exit he assumed servants used to attend guests on the porch, carrying a huge pot in her hands. Even if he started jogging, she'd get to the wagon before he could, but he did speed up in case he could help Evelyn with whatever she might bring out next.

Evelyn did follow Caroline out, except whatever she carried was cuddled against her chest.

He cocked his head as he continued up the path. The package wiggled and squawked. The tiniest fist he'd ever seen popped out of the bindings when Evelyn turned to toss a blanket into the wagon.

How had he missed seeing a baby at the mansion? Especially considering the high-pitched noises it was making now. If the size of that lump was all of him or her, it was the tiniest human being he'd ever seen.

Evelyn captured the babe's angry little fist and kissed it.

He slowed, his throat growing tight for some reason.

Caroline shoved the pot onto the wagon bed and turned. She saw him and waved.

When had he stopped walking? He jogged forward.

Evelyn gave him a quick glance but continued talking to the baby in her arms whose cries became more insistent. She started jiggling the bundle as if she were trying to curdle cream.

How did this woman not want to get married and have children? His aunt had been a cantankerous woman, the kind children drew lots over to determine who would throw rocks through her windows. Aunt Martha had reserved a semi-soft spot for him, but she'd clearly had no love for children.

But Evelyn purposely surrounded herself with young people, and they adored her. And despite the screeching going on in her arms, she held the babe against herself as if she could protect it from whatever was causing it to make such awful noise.

She would undoubtedly make a great mother. But she was pretty great as she was, mothering those who'd been abandoned or orphaned. Maybe that's why she had no desire to marry, for who could replace her in the lives of all these little ones?

Perhaps it was best to leave her to it. . . .

But hang it all, seeing her with an infant only made him want to see her with one of her own someday — preferably his.

He stilled, wide-eyed at his own racing thoughts.

"Are you all right?" Caroline stepped closer to him, head cocked to the side. "You look a little flushed."

"Uh, yeah." He took a handkerchief from his pocket and swiped at his hairline. "Maybe I shouldn't have walked up the hill so quickly." Or at least his thoughts should have slowed down.

Oh, who was he kidding? He was too far gone. He might as well throw in all his chips and stop counting the risk of courting Evelyn. He'd still pray God would help him know what to do, but he had to do something more than just wait for her to show interest in him. Could it be she didn't understand he was attracted to her?

Though this woman possessed nothing Father would deem necessary for joining their family, she did possess the things he insisted David didn't have — drive and focus. Wouldn't the best person to complete him be someone with the characteristics Father admired, even if she lacked a bulging pocketbook?

He'd reveled at the feel of her in his arms last week when she'd broken through the wall that held her so aloof and given him a hug.

Henri had confirmed Evelyn had always been a standoffish woman — but then, Caroline was just as distant. Did Evelyn have a story like Caroline's that made it difficult for her to be warm? Both of them were so driven to help the unfortunate, he couldn't imagine what they'd be like if they felt free to love without reservations.

If he could somehow get her interested in him before he declared his feelings, surely her disinterest in marriage would crumble.

Though it might go achingly slow, he was going to try courting.

Not that he would dare tell Evelyn that was his intention.

"Shhh, shhh, shhhh." Evelyn kept up a refrain of shushing as he came over to take a look at the baby.

"Who's this?" Of course his voice came out frazzled since his heart was beating way faster than it should.

"Her name's Hope." She bounced the bundle around, but the baby's lower lip only curled down farther, and her face started turning red with her pitiful mewling.

"Maybe you should stop bouncing her. I don't think she likes it."

Evelyn guffawed. "It would be so much worse if I didn't. I tried that last night."

"And it was terrible." Robert jogged past them, shoved a basket onto the wagon bed, and promptly put his hands over his ears when the babe screeched louder than a cat getting its tail pulled. He looked up at David with pitiful eyes. "If I fall asleep at work next week, you'll know why. I didn't sleep at all last night."

"You did too. I took her to the basement around three this morning."

Caroline walked by, her face registering how unpleasant that must have been for her and the other servants.

Evelyn flipped the child over and held her against her arm like she was readying to iron her flat. "And I think she fell asleep a little after four, but I don't remember when that happened exactly."

Caroline put her hands on her hips. "She woke up near five fifteen, so even if she fell asleep at four sharp it wasn't long enough."

Evelyn nodded in agreement and started twisting at the waist as if she were going to slice tall grass with a baby instead of a scythe.

As much as he'd been hoping to spend some time with Evelyn, clearly someone needed her more. "Why don't I go with Miss O'Conner and let you stay here with the baby? If you take her with you, I don't think a single child will hear a word of your Bible story. Tell me which one you planned to tell, and I'm sure I can improvise."

"You don't have to do that. Lydia's here and planned to keep the baby."

"Then what can I do to help?"

"I think we're fine."

"Now, Evelyn." He had to raise his voice to be heard. "I told you I wanted to help. I have time."

"But you might scare away the children's mothers if they come, like you did with Amy. And though it might be tempting to see you care for this squalling bundle, I'm not sure I could be that mean to you." She smirked, but her eyelids were so droopy with fatigue the smile was lackluster.

He needed to figure out some way to help her since she seemed to forget that *friends* were exactly whom one should ask for help. "Well, what if — ?"

"Hey, Mr. Kingsman!" Max jogged up to them. "If I get my school done early and got permission to leave, could I have more hours at the factory?"

"I only hire good students."

"But I am. I already finished my history book."

David blinked at the young man. "But you just started school."

He shrugged. "It was interesting."

"He reads way past bedtime." Robert, who'd walked up with Evelyn's parents, shook his head at his older brother. "I told him he'd get in trouble, but he doesn't."

Evelyn tilted her head sheepishly. "It's difficult getting onto someone for wanting to learn so badly — and it's not like it's been easy to sleep here lately." She disentangled herself from the baby, who'd latched onto the pleats on Evelyn's shirtwaist, and pretended to hand the baby to her father for a second before winking at his stricken expression and then handing the writhing child to her mother.

David looked into Max's expectant eyes. "I'll tell you what. I'll talk to the teacher and see what can be arranged."

"Thank you, sir." Max smiled, then turned to help Caroline with another pot.

Robert kicked at the dirt at his feet. "Don't have to worry about getting the teacher to let me go early. I ain't never going to get ahead."

He ruffled the boy's hair. "I'll take whatever hours you can give me. You're too good a worker for me to turn down what time I can get."

"Yes, sir." Robert's chest puffed up a little before he turned to follow Mrs. Wisely back to the mansion with the crying baby.

Feeling Evelyn's eyes on him, he turned to look at her. What he saw in her gaze made him puff up his chest a little, just like Robert.

Evelyn quickly shuttered her eyes and

rushed around to the other side of the wagon.

That stubborn woman was going to climb into the wagon on her own. He strode right behind her, and when he got to her side, she looked at him with an expression much warmer than he was used to. She put her hand in his, and he helped her up.

She took her seat but kept a hold of his hand. He couldn't help but grip it tighter.

"I'll try to think of something you can help me with, David, but until then, enjoy your free weekend." And then she let go.

She waved back at her father as Caroline started the team, and David was forced to step out of the way.

Mr. Wisely's hand clamped down on his shoulder after they'd turned down the drive. "Since you're here. Want to join us for lunch? Hargrove's coming."

"How could I say no?" David summoned up a grin, as if eating dinner with a baby who could rattle the dead from their tombs sounded splendid. He took a glance back at the disappearing wagon.

"Son, I believe you've got a long road ahead of you if that's the direction you're going."

His body turned hot at being found out, and by someone so close to her. He turned to meet Mr. Wisely's assessing gaze, but the older man didn't seem opposed. Did he have an ally? "What would you suggest to make that road shorter?"

"I wish I knew. But we'll pray you figure it out." He gave David's shoulder a squeeze before letting go and heading back to the mansion. "Evelyn and I quarreled nearly every day a decade ago. One summer, when she and I butted heads more than normal, she left to visit my aunt but came back broken. My aunt wasn't of the soundest mind and probably wasn't the best person to guide her through that time in her life, but I'd thought the separation would do us good." He turned to look back, but the wagon had already disappeared. "I'd thought I'd failed her that year. I was so frazzled over so many things going on in my life that I did and said things I regret, but the woman Evelyn is today . . . I couldn't be more proud."

"So what happened over the summer to change her?"

He shook his head. "I don't know. I think she started punishing herself for her rebellion, as if she couldn't possibly deserve to be loved anymore. She's nothing but sweet now, yet ever since then, she's cocooned herself away from me." Mr. Wisely's voice cracked. "So I'll pray you can get through to her, to convince her that God doesn't want her to punish herself forever. That she's allowed to be happy."

He'd pray for the same thing. For if she wouldn't allow herself to be happy, he'd have nothing but heartache ahead.

25

"So when do you think this women's home will come about?"

Evelyn tied off her thread and looked at the moral-society president across the quilt. For the last half hour, the ladies had been discussing what they would do once Nicholas got the women's home running. They hadn't all been enthusiastic, but most offered suggestions or tried to improve upon them. Mrs. Naples, however, hadn't said a word until now.

Evelyn unwound more thread. "I don't know, exactly. Mr. Lowe said we'll take things slow so we'll face minimal opposition."

"So years, maybe?"

"Could be months, but years might be a possibility." *Oh, let it not be more than a year.* So many bad things could happen in the space of a few months, let alone years.

"Well then, I say we focus our attentions

on something we know will happen, some-thing that won't" — Mrs. Naples sniffed — "bother anyone's sensitivities."

The room grew quiet. She glanced at Momma, who nodded at her as if she knew Evelyn would say the right thing.

"I don't want to force anyone into doing anything, of course, but I hope we can all agree that the children could use our help. Mercy's suggestion of taking turns making cookies for the children on Saturday is a wonderful one. That will show them that people outside the district besides me and Caroline care for them. But I think we could still gather up donations of old clothing. Even before the home is built, the women might need them. I don't know who here might be willing to teach them to sew, but —"

"You can't possibly be suggesting we take them into our own homes to teach them?" Stella Sorenson pierced her with a stare.

"A lady's reputation could be ruined spending that much time alone with them." Mrs. Naples gave Stella a sympathetic look. "We can't ask that of our members. Giving them our clothing instead of shortening the hems for the younger girls in our families is plenty a sacrifice."

Lydia cleared her throat. "We might not

have to teach anyone. Their families and backgrounds are often just as good as ours."

Mrs. Naples's one-eyed squint indicated her disbelief, despite Lydia having worked with soiled doves and Mrs. Naples having yet to visit the red-light district. Even back when they did serenades in the area, Mrs. Naples had refused to go.

"If needed, surely two or three of us could help," Lydia continued.

No one piped up to volunteer.

Baby Hope's cries echoed down the long hallways from somewhere in the church. When Hope had awoken fifteen minutes ago, hollering as if she were alerting the world to a fire, Mercy had volunteered to take the baby. But by the sound of it, Mercy was having as hard a time comforting Hope as everyone else did. Daddy and Nicholas had only agreed to watch the orphans if they took the baby with them to their meeting.

Stella clicked her tongue. "Perhaps you two should volunteer to teach them since your reputations can't be made much worse —"

"What?" Evelyn straightened her shoulders. "No one would dare look down on Mrs. Lowe."

"Some of us do not have Mrs. Lowe's wealth, which encourages people to overlook problematic hobbies so as not to offend her." Stella shrugged and sighed as if it were a sad but true part of life. "And though you don't seem to care about getting married, Miss Wisely, those of us who want to attract respectable husbands have to be more mindful with whom we associate."

A heavy foot stomp startled everyone.

Charlie Gray squinted at Stella as if she were aiming an imaginary six-shooter right at her heart, ready to pump it full of sense. "Some sourpusses who won't lift a finger to help a kitten might grumble about Evelyn and Lydia's ministry, but their reputations aren't so tarnished we're refusing to breathe the same air now, are we? What they got isn't catching, and well, I wish it were." She tipped her head toward Evelyn. "Several of us are mighty proud of Evelyn. She does more charitable things in a month than many do their whole lives. If I weren't so busy running my ranch, I'd try to outshine her. And even then, I doubt I'd be able to."

"Then why don't you volunteer to help the prostitutes learn to sew, Mrs. Gray?"

Charlie looked at Mrs. Naples as if she'd just suggested she fly to the moon. "Out of all the ladies here, you think *I* should teach them to sew? I thought you told us last month that we were supposed to work within our gifts." She pointed at Evelyn. "If any of those ladies want to learn how to hogtie a calf, you let me know."

The women broke into a fit of giggles until the whole group was laughing — well, everyone except Stella. She was too dignified to do anything but sniffle a chuckle.

Once the laughter ceased, Mrs. Naples rubbed her neck. "I think we should move on to our next bit of business." She folded her hands in front of her. "It seems we're heading in a different direction, so I believe it's time I step down from being president and let someone else take over."

A murmur from the ladies around the quilting frame made Evelyn squirm. This was all her fault. Though Mrs. Naples wasn't the most malleable woman, she hadn't been as coldhearted as their last president. "Please, Mrs. Naples, I know I've been quite vocal about having our group help with the needs I see every day, but I haven't done so to try to take over the direction of the group."

"However, you and Mrs. Lowe are the ones with the ideas."

Momma reached over to put a hand on Mrs. Naples's shoulder. "I hope you know we're very grateful for your leadership. With how you've delegated things this past year, we've produced more quilts than expected, your bake sale raised more funds than our other efforts, and you've brought in more members than we've ever had before."

"I'm not hurt, Bernadette. I'm just old. I could keep up with the quilting project, but anything more needs to be handled by someone else."

"Why not Miss Wisely, then?" Stella's perfectly plucked eyebrows rose. Her eyes challenged Evelyn — to what, she wasn't certain.

Sometimes it was hard to like Stella. She was pretty, had her entire life in front of her, able to chase her every dream, and yet the young lady seemed to have a hard time mustering up any sympathy for those outside her circle.

But she didn't know Stella well, and perhaps she had a reason to act as she did.

"Thank you for the vote, but I'm afraid I don't have time."

"Unlike you, most of us have families to tend," said Mrs. Albert. The woman was younger than her but rarely made it to meetings since she had five children under the age of six.

"Evelyn and her parents are running the orphanage. That's as time-consuming as any family, and I should know." Lydia's face looked placid enough, but Evelyn knew she was holding back.

She smiled at her friend, thankful that not everyone believed all single people had more free time than married people.

"Well, what about you, Mrs. Gray?" Mrs. Naples stood to gather the spools and scissors lying about. "You aren't watching over any children and seem to be on board with Miss Wisely and Mrs. Lowe's ideas."

Charlie huffed. "Cattle and sheep are plenty like children, as far as I know."

"But you've got ranch hands."

"Yes, but it's still quite the workload, Mrs. Naples. You forget that I'm running the ranch, not Harrison."

Evelyn stiffened. Charlie likely didn't know Mrs. Naples often made judgmental remarks about how Harrison Gray had to be weak to let his wife run the ranch. That he worked for the school made no difference in her mind.

"Even if livestock isn't as time-consuming as children," Charlie continued, "I'll find out for myself, come February sometime, maybe March."

Lydia gasped. "Does that mean what I think it means?"

Charlie winked at her husband's former pupil. "Sure does. I'll have to learn how to hog-tie a little one of my own. We made it to four months this time, so hopefully we'll get to the end."

"It's called swaddling, Charlie, not hog-tying!" Momma chuckled.

"Oh, Mrs. Gray, what a wonderful way to end the meeting." Mrs. Naples stopped picking up notions to waggle her finger at the woman who often frustrated her with her unseemly manners. "But don't you be riding astride or hog-tying anything. You should leave that ranching stuff to your husband and hands. You don't want to be regretting things."

The rest of them all chimed in with well-wishes and well-meant, though sometimes ridiculous, advice.

Evelyn blew out a breath, thankful the attention had moved off her and onto Charlie's happy news. Next meeting they'd likely have to hash out who would take over the leadership, but at least they'd all have time to think about it now.

After giving Charlie a quick hug, she went out to look for Mercy, who must be doing all right, considering Hope's sounds were no longer outright screams. She found them around the corner. Mercy's good hand was thumping a distracting rhythm on the baby's back, the crook of her shortened arm holding Hope tight against her. "You seem to be quite good with babies. She's about as quiet as she gets when not asleep."

Mercy blew a strand of hair out of her face. "I wouldn't know, really. Most mommas aren't willing to hand me babies this tiny, afraid I'll drop them."

Evelyn took Hope from Mercy's grip. "I'm not worried, and even if I were, I think a baby this fussy might make any mother willing to hand her over to a complete stranger."

"She isn't exactly happy, is she?" Mercy gave the baby on Evelyn's shoulder a rub along her spine with the stump at the end of her arm. "Has the doctor said anything about why?"

Evelyn sighed and shook her head. "Momma insists there has to be something wrong with her, but the doctor says he sees babies like this from the district all the time. Says it's God's way of punishing the mothers."

Mercy stiffened. "And he's the doctor who tends the women there?"

"Afraid so."

She frowned and patted the baby one last time. "No wonder you want some of us to help there. What kind of hope can they have when they hear things like that?"

"The world isn't very fair, is it?"

Mercy shook her head, tucking her bad arm under her other one.

"You're welcome to come to the orphanage anytime and try to shush the baby — though all the thanks you'll get from her is a pierced eardrum."

"Perhaps I'll do that. Beats sewing one-handed." Mercy winked.

"And we'll have tea. Let's plan on that anyway, shall we?"

While discussing when would be a good time to have Mercy visit, they walked out the back to where Evelyn had left the baby carriage someone had lent the orphanage. Hope usually calmed when placed in it, though it was nearly time for her to be fed, so Evelyn would not be pushing her home leisurely. "Say good-bye to Miss McClain. It's time to get you back home so Mrs. Dewitt can take care of you."

Mercy kissed the tip of a finger, pressed it against the baby's nose, and left.

Evelyn pushed the carriage back and forth in an effort to keep Hope content until Momma and Lydia could escape the throng and join them.

A few minutes later, Momma bustled out alone.

"Where's Lydia?"

"We're to tell Nicholas to pick her up at the Grays'. She wanted to congratulate Harrison personally." Momma's smile lit up her whole face. "Oh, I'm so happy for Charlie."

"Yes, though I hope all of us pray for them really hard. I know how devastated she's been with all their losses."

"I know that feeling of devastation well, but then God gave us you." She tucked her arm around her daughter. "I had you when I was thirty-two and was just fine. We'll pray everything goes smoothly for her as well."

"I think Charlie's near thirty-eight though. She might have a rough time of it."

"Ah." Momma waved her hand dismissively. "Can't know that. With all the trouble we had, I thought my pregnancy would've been terrible, but you've been a joy since you existed." She squeezed her arm. "We'll pray God gives her this child and that he or she will make Charlie and Harrison as proud as you make us."

Heat clumped up in her throat. Momma wouldn't be saying that if she knew everything about her.

Momma patted her cheek and started off with her beside the carriage. "I think you should take the president position."

"You know how busy we are."

"But we need a spokesperson, and you're

the best at inspiring people to do things. Look how you got me and your father to take on the orphanage. And how you got three businessmen to support your women's home. None of us could have done that. If it wasn't for you and Lydia, the moral society would still just be making quilts."

"You've forgotten that Mr. Kingsman had more of a hand in getting those businessmen to agree to support the shelter than I."

"Ah, but you inspired him."

"I don't think he needed me to inspire him to be the kind of man he is."

"He is a rather fine young man, isn't he?"

"Yes." And she needed to get off this topic quickly. "But what about you? The former pastor's wife being the moral-society president would be a logical choice."

"I don't know about that. I think the pastor's daughter would be just as logical." She slowed as she waited for Evelyn to get the carriage wheels to cooperate over some busted sidewalk. "Your father is mighty proud of the upright young woman you've become, and he'd have no qualms about the direction you'd lead the group. We know you're following after God, even if you sometimes go off to places that make us pray harder than we'd like."

Oh, how her parents' praises always

gashed at her heart. If they'd known how she'd once disregarded all their advice, they'd not be so certain of her judgment.

But it was better to focus on the future. And thanks to David and Nicholas, women caught in helpless situations would have a chance. And what other woman could sympathize with them as well as she could? "Perhaps I'll be president one day, but not while everything is so busy. We'll just have to think of someone else to nominate and pray she's willing."

Enjoying the quiet that came from Hope having fallen asleep, she walked in companionable silence with her mother to the orphanage. Soon it would be too cold to push a baby around town, and Hope didn't like being swaddled, though perhaps hog-tying her would work.

Evelyn let out a breathy chuckle, imagining Charlie taking care of a baby. She was so unlike any other woman she knew. Charlie would probably be as funny with a baby as she was trying to appease her mother by attending moral-society meetings and attempting to sew well enough that Mrs. Naples wouldn't have to undo all her stitches as soon as she left.

The second they crested the rise of the mansion's driveway, a maid burst out the

front door. "Mrs. Wisely! Miss W̶
Come quick!"

Evelyn scanned the mansion's windc̶
looking for smoke, listening for wailing, b̶
nothing was alarming. She pushed the ca̶
riage as fast as it could go. "What is it, Miss̶
Mulpepper?"

"Your father — he's collapsed," she hollered.

"What?" Evelyn stopped in her tracks, but her mother fled up the hill like a spry chick.

"Mr. Lowe sent me to find Mr. Parker. We need a doctor right quick!"

Evelyn found her legs again and rushed after her mother. "Is he alive?"

"Yes." But the way Miss Mulpepper's voice ended with a questioning intonation, there was little doubt she thought his state might be temporary.

Momma ran in calling Daddy's name, a terribly sad crack in her voice.

Miss Mulpepper chewed on her lip and looked between her and the carriage house.

"Go help my mother." Finally under the portico, Evelyn grabbed Hope out of the carriage. "I'll get Mr. Parker." Careful not to go so fast that she would trip while holding the baby, she strode as quickly as possible toward the stables.

She'd just claimed she was too busy to be

society president, but how could she
a women's home and orphanage if
dy wasn't around?

*h, God, don't take him away. I don't know
at we'd do without him.*

26

David pulled in under the mansion's huge two-story portico and hopped down from the seat of his factory's little buggy. He brushed the dust off his slacks and blinked the grit from his eyes. He was completely unpresentable, but then, he hadn't been invited to the orphanage either, he'd just . . . come.

This past week, he hadn't been able to think of a reason to visit that wouldn't look like he was coming just to see Evelyn — which he was. Figuring out how to court a woman without being obvious was quite the challenge.

But then he'd remembered her mentioning it was important for the orphans to have good male role models.

She certainly wouldn't be suspicious if he came to throw a ball with Max, Robert, or Scott, tickle Ezekiel, or swing Alex until she was dizzy. Maybe he wouldn't even talk to

Evelyn much. If she had feelings for him, and he planted himself nearby, maybe she'd feel just as antsy to be closer as he did.

He strode toward the door and used the reflection in the fancy Tiffany glass insets to fix his hair with finger combing. The shouts of children sounded from out back. He knocked on the door half-heartedly, but after half a minute he headed off to the backyard. He didn't need a servant's formal welcome anyway.

The high-pitched whine of one particular young voice grew, coupled with the escalated screaming he'd heard from the baby the last time he'd been here. Surely someone needed help, so he sped up. And yet the sound of laughter and children calling out to one another belied there was anything immensely wrong.

Around the corner, a line of children walked atop one of the garden's short stone walls, and a group chased each other near the mansion. In the middle of it all, Evelyn was crouched down beside a boy of perhaps six, pinching his nose while tipping his head back, with a toddler girl wrapped up in her skirts.

But where was the baby? He looked around for the adult who was failing to comfort the infant but saw no one. The

340

closer he got, the louder the cry, but Evelyn clearly didn't have her, and with all the children's noise, he was having difficulty pinpointing any specific sound within the chaos. "How's it going?" he called out.

She turned to him, and her shoulders slumped in a sigh, though he sure didn't hear it amid all the crying and hollering. Ah, there the baby was, in the grass on Evelyn's other side, arms and legs waving furiously.

"Not good, I'm afraid." Evelyn turned her attention back on the blond boy and pushed his head back up. "Truly, Lawrence, if you don't keep your head up, you're going to be bleeding all day."

"Sorry." He tilted his head down, and Evelyn tilted it back up.

Another boy came whizzing past, and David pulled up short to keep from getting run over.

The chaser was more considerate and swerved behind him.

David bypassed Evelyn and picked up the tiny baby, amazed at how rigid her body was. He tried to bounce her as he'd watched Evelyn do the other day, but she only screamed louder.

"Miss Wisely! Peter pulled my hair." A young girl with red braids ran over and ɔurst into tears.

Somehow Evelyn got an arm around the redhead while keeping her fingers pinched on a wriggling Lawrence. "Calm down, Vera. I can't have two screamers at once."

The girl only sobbed more, though the cry sounded more whiney than hurt. "He's always pulling my hair. I don't like him at all."

"Stop crying, darling." She brought the girl's head down onto her shoulder with a one-armed hug. "That'll only egg him on."

Vera whipped her head off Evelyn's shoulder, her fists bunched up beside her. "But you never stop him! And he only gets meaner."

Evelyn tried to catch Vera's arm before she fled but missed. The defeated look Evelyn threw David was absolutely heartbreaking.

He tried bouncing the baby faster, but he'd never been so well acquainted with the word *inconsolable* before. "You can't solve all their problems, you know."

He obviously couldn't solve this baby's problem.

"I can't even solve my own." Her voice was barely audible above the din as she let go of the boy's nose but wasn't happy with what she saw and reattached herself. She tried to rise while keeping a grip on the boy's nose as he stood as well, but the toddler girl was standing on her dress. Graceful was not the word for Evelyn trying to right herself and keep hold of Lawrence's nose. "Let's get some ice, otherwise I might be holding your nose all day."

David followed after her as she shuffle-stepped toward the mansion. "Who can I give this baby to?"

She held out her arm, and the lines of fatigue creasing her forehead were identical to the ones she'd sported while caring for Scott. "I'll take her."

She might have a free arm, but she was dragging one child and steering another.

He bounced the screamer a little faster. "It's all right. I've got her."

Surprisingly, Evelyn didn't protest, just lowered her arm and kept marching Lawrence up the hill.

David tried to switch the baby so she could see over his shoulder, but she only screamed louder. "Where's your mother? If I give her the baby, I could get the ice."

"The Lowes have a walk-in icebox in the northwest corner of the basement, but you'll either have to take the baby with you or hand her to me. Unless we can find a maid who isn't busy."

"Why not your mother?"

"She's at the old parsonage with Daddy." She looked over at him, and he was struck by the vulnerability he saw there. When had she ever allowed him to see that many emotions play across her face?

"He —" Her voice cracked. "Daddy had an apoplectic fit. He's still alive, but he's a bit confused. His left arm and leg are sluggish, and he's not getting around all that well. The doctor gave us strict orders to keep him from noise and activity until he's improved. Says he should recover . . . mostly."

"I'm so sorry." David rested a hand on her shoulder, and she crossed her free arm over her chest to put her hand atop his. Her simple act of reaching out to him made his heart lift despite the news. "I wish you'd sent me a message. I could've helped."

She shrugged, dropped her hand, and moved Lawrence through the door to the conservatory. "I don't know who I could've sent. It's been total chaos here."

"Who's helping you?"

"The staff."

"I mean with the children." He raised his voice over the baby's top-of-the-lung cry.

She looked at him again, the droop of her eyelids obvious. "Just me and the staff."

344

He looked back at the children still running around outside. "Who's watching them?"

"I was."

"Scott!" he hollered. The baby startled and surprisingly quit crying.

The twelve-year-old looked up from where he was building a corral of sticks for Alex to house her two carved ponies.

"You're in charge. Keep things running smoothly out here while we go take care of Lawrence."

Scott stood up and jogged over, his face still mottled with scarring but his eyes bright with good health. He stopped in front of David and shook his head. "Maybe you should get Max. Some of them won't listen to me."

He chucked up Scott's chin. "Just keep them out of danger, all right?"

Scott nodded, and David hurried in after Evelyn.

Though Hope was only sniffling now, her little body was so rigid he was afraid she'd burst into an ear-piercing scream any minute. He dared to turn her around to get a better grip on her, bracing himself for her complaint, but Hope latched onto his thumb with a vengeance, her tongue tickling. "Do you think the baby's hungry?"

Evelyn had already made it down the foyer steps with both children still attached. "Of course she's hungry." Her voice echoed through the massive entrance. "When is she not?"

"Then where is her nurse?"

"Late again. Hey, sweetie, can you open the door for us?"

The little girl untangled herself from Evelyn's skirts and reached up as far as her arms would go to grab the handle of a door he'd never noticed, considering how well it blended into the wall. How did Evelyn expect such a short kid to open that door for them?

"It's almost dinnertime," a voice called behind him.

Caroline stood on the top of the entryway's little staircase, her apron wrinkled and wet, but she wore a rare smile.

The little girl let go of the door she'd opened, and Evelyn grabbed it before it shut.

The little sprite ran past him toward Caroline.

He turned to see the girl raise her arms up toward the housekeeper.

"Oh no, Miss Emily. You might get Miss Wisely to carry you, but you'll just hold my hand. All right?"

Emily must have been all right, because she grabbed onto her fingers, her chubby, stocking-covered legs marching beside Caroline toward the kitchen.

David turned to see that he and Hope had been deserted. He crossed over to the hidden door and ducked into the dark staircase.

The baby's shudders were clumping together, like clouds coalescing before a storm. He held her out and jiggled her, hoping to stop the tempest from coming, but it didn't work. Her little mouth turned into the largest frown he'd ever seen, and her screaming reverberated off the stone stairwell.

One thing was certain — no one could accidentally misplace this child.

"Down here, David. Mrs. Dewitt's just arrived. She'll take the baby."

"Oh thank you, sweet Jesus!" Carefully navigating down the dark steps, he kept his big hands clamped around her but held her away from his ears, hoping to save his hearing.

He'd expected a plump matronly woman to meet him at the bottom of the stairs, but the woman waiting was likely in her late twenties, with a round face and very curly blond hair pretending to be swept up into something elegant, but failing miserably. "I hope you can help her."

"I'll try my best, sir." She held out her arms but didn't smile. Not that he could imagine many people smiling if they were handed this bundle.

She disappeared down one hallway, and Evelyn was halfway down another, steering Lawrence forward quickly now that she wasn't dragging an anchor.

He started after her. "I haven't seen Emily before. Is she new?"

Evelyn called over her shoulder. "Yes, but she's not staying. Emily's mother is . . . in bad shape. Not a sight for a three-year-old, so Caroline brought her home until her mother can take her back."

He ached to tell her they shouldn't send her back at all, but that wasn't his place.

She disappeared into a doorway on the left.

She probably didn't need his help anymore, but he wasn't going to leave without making an attempt to talk to her without a handful of children crying around them. Not with the news about her father and the sleepless nights etched across her face.

Playing and talking with the boys was not anywhere near as important as making sure she was all right.

But how could she possibly be all right?

He might not have ever known his mother, but the fact that he'd never met her overwhelmed him with sadness occasionally. He couldn't imagine how he'd feel if she'd died after loving him for more than twenty years — he'd always imagined his mother would have loved him more than Father.

He was just about to turn into the room where Evelyn had disappeared, when Lawrence ran out and smacked into him.

"Whoa there." He clasped onto the child to keep him upright.

The boy looked up at him. "I stopped bleeding already." And then he slipped out of David's grip and ran off.

Evelyn didn't appear.

He strode the last few steps and looked into the doorway on his left.

She stood in the middle of the dark room. Her shoulders were slumped, her head down, and her hands pressed together in front of her as if she were awaiting her turn to kneel before the guillotine.

"Are you all right?"

"I'm tired, is what I am." She let out a long sigh, and her shoulders drooped even more. "Lawrence stopped bleeding, so I best get outside."

He wedged himself in the doorway in case she, too, thought about darting past him.

"You do know that asking for help isn't a sign of weakness?"

"I know." But she didn't even look at him, just continued staring at the floor between her feet.

He stepped into the dungeon-like room and came over to put his arm around her. "Please tell me what you need."

Her mouth trembled and her eyes started blinking exaggeratedly. "I just need my daddy."

"Oh, honey."

Her face was tense, her lips pressed tight.

He could almost feel the fountain of tears she was repressing. "It's all right to cry."

"I already have."

How like her to only let loose her tears if they affected no one but her. "After everyone's asleep, I bet. But, Evelyn, you don't have to cry alone."

Without warning, she turned into him, wrapped her arms around his chest, and sobbed into his neck.

He put one arm around her back and reached up to rest a hand against her hair, pressing their heads together. He heard himself shushing her but stopped. He didn't want her to cry alone, he wanted her to be in his arms, each and every time her life fell apart.

Her sobs escalated to the point she was nearly hyperventilating. Maybe if he made her answer some questions, she'd be forced to breathe. "When does the doctor think your father can come back?"

"Never," she squeaked between sobs.

He smoothed her hair away from where it tickled his face, then pressed his cheek against hers. "But he's going to get better, right?"

He felt her shrug in his arms, her tears slowly abating. How long until she realized where she was and pulled away? He held her tighter.

"The doctor says he thinks he'll get better." Her voice was muffled against his ear. "But that doesn't mean he will."

Her tears returned, and he gave up trying to distract her and just held her instead.

Her father had mentioned she hid her emotions from her own family, so David wasn't about to stifle them. He'd count every single tear dampening his shirt an honor.

After another minute or so, she stilled. She'd pull away soon, so he closed his eyes and held her just tight enough to let her know he cared.

After a few more sniffs, she did indeed pull away.

He kept his hand on her arm as she stepped back until it slipped down and caught her fingers. She didn't take her hand from his, but she did look away while swiping tears with her free hand.

He kept a good grip on her. "I know I can't fix your father, but what else can I do for you?"

"I've already wasted enough of your time."

Thankfully she seemed just as content to keep her hand in his as he was to hold it. "How have you wasted any of my time?"

"The women's home."

"I fail to understand."

"I won't be able to help manage it, and who else besides me is going to do so?" She looked at him with eyes glossy with sorrow. "I have to save all my energy for this place now. Even if you volunteered to come here every day after work, there's still all the other hours I have to work alone. And if I can't keep on top of things, I won't be here much longer — that's for certain."

"The Lowes aren't going to fire you because you can't run an entire household and care for a full house of orphans by yourself."

"No, but I'll be replaced."

Why would she think Nicholas would do such a thing? Certainly he would see how impossible it was to run this place single-handedly and get her some help, not fire her. But as she stood holding onto his hand alone in the dark basement, every part of her body drooping in weariness, she likely wasn't thinking clearly. Though her father wasn't dead, there was plenty to grieve and worry about. "How long ago did your father leave?"

"Three days ago." She sniffed.

And she'd likely only slept a handful of hours in that time. "What about that young lady who was here when we came back from Mr. Hargrove's? If you tell me where she lives, I can ask if she has time to help you."

"Mercy knows already." Evelyn rubbed her brow. "She came yesterday for a few hours, but she's got obligations most every afternoon."

With his hand tightly clamped around hers, he pulled Evelyn toward the door. "Are you hungry?"

She shuffle-stepped behind him. "Not really."

"Then let's get you upstairs so you can nap."

"I can't do that." She pulled away from him.

He didn't let her go. "Yes, you can."

"I can't leave the children alone."

"If you can watch them by yourself, then so can I." He walked a step but halted. "The wet nurse will keep the baby for a while, right?"

"She'll give her back in about half an hour. As I said, I can't nap."

"You can. I'll just have to figure out what to do with the baby." Hopefully he could dazzle a maid into taking the screamer.

"Maybe you could send one of the girls to get me when Mrs. Dewitt is finished with Hope?"

Good, she was actually contemplating sleep. "I could do that." But he wouldn't.

He'd stay until she woke on her own. The older children could help him figure out the after-dinner and bedtime procedures. And even if Evelyn slept until tomorrow, surely he could bunk in with the boys, even if that meant he was on the floor. And then before he headed to work, he'd talk to Nicholas about getting Evelyn help. She should not have been left unassisted for three full days in her emotional state.

Once they were out of the basement, the exuberant sounds of children in the dining area echoed down the hallway. Hopefully their voices wouldn't drift all the way to the upstairs bedrooms.

At the bottom of the grand spiraling

staircase, Evelyn put a hand on the banister, as if to ascend, but turned to him. "Thank you, David."

"My pleasure."

She smiled at him, and if he didn't already know her eyes were weighted with fatigue, he might have let her slow perusal of him warm him with hope. Though she *had* just sought his embrace and stayed in his arms beyond all propriety.

Perhaps this slow courting thing wouldn't be all that slow after all.

27

The Lowes' young butler answered David's knock. "Come in, sir."

David pulled off his hat. "Is Mr. Lowe here?"

"He is. I'll let him know you've come." He gestured to a room to the left. "Why don't you take a seat in the parlor."

David nodded and went in to wait. The first time he'd visited the Lowes, he'd been surprised that none of their furniture was for show. Though all the furnishings were of good quality, it didn't feel like the room of the richest man in town, and it was certainly nothing like the mansion's decor.

He glanced at the comfortable-looking sofa but chose to pace. Though he tended to handle confrontation well, that didn't mean he wasn't jittery beforehand.

A giggle in the hallway stopped him.

The giggle sounded again, that of a woman, not a child.

"Oh, Franklin, stop," the voice said without much conviction.

He peeped out the door and saw the butler circling behind the young housekeeper who'd made the divinity.

Franklin let his fingers trail along the back of her arm until he had a hold of her hand. He pressed his lips to her knuckles. "Until after work, *mon chéri.*"

The boy's French was pathetic, and yet her blush proved bad French might be better than nothing.

If only getting Evelyn to respond to him was that easy. David returned to the room and closed his eyes. Though outright flirting with her would likely earn him whatever was the opposite of a giggle, when things mattered, when she'd been in utter despair, she'd sought his arms. Much more significant than a giggle anyway.

"Ah, David." Lowe came into the room, dressed in black trousers, a green shirt with rolled sleeves, no tie, and was that dust in his hair? "How are you?"

"I'm doing well, but I'm worried about Miss Wisely."

"We're definitely praying for that whole family." Nicholas's expression turned solemn. "The doctor expects Walter to recover, though he's adamant he shouldn't return to the orphanage. He's afraid another collapse could prove fatal."

Precisely. He'd been told Nicholas was the most fastidious businessman there ever was, almost to the point of insisting on overseeing every little detail, so why hadn't he done better by Evelyn? "Then why has Evelyn been left to run the orphanage alone?"

Nicholas raised his eyebrows. "The staff is supposed to help her until we arrive." He crossed his arms. "Right now, we're packing what we need to return."

"Evelyn knows you're coming?"

Nicholas nodded.

"I don't understand." David sat in the chair across from him. "Then why is Evelyn acting as if she has to run the whole place on her own? Saying she'll have to abandon the women's home idea."

"Because I'll be advertising for a couple to take over the running of the orphanage." He sat on the sofa's arm. "Lydia is due to have our next child in about three months. She'd prefer to deal with the sleepless nights here and isn't ready to return to the orphanage full time."

"So Evelyn is upset because it will take a while to get permanent help?" What would be her objection to that?

"No, I think she's more worried that whoever takes over the orphanage might not want her to stay." Nicholas sighed. "I'll definitely try to hire a couple willing to have her stay on, but if the best people for the job aren't comfortable with a single young woman living with them, her position and hours might change significantly. However, none of this should affect her ability to help with the women's home."

"And if she couldn't work at the orphanage anymore, will she be paid to run the women's home?"

Nicholas blinked, then looked away, rubbing his chin. "I hadn't thought about that."

"And what about her idea of having reformed soiled doves help run the mansion?"

"I believe a man of good character being involved with the orphans is critical. There may be a soiled dove who could help during the day, but until she's proven herself . . . Right now, the only one I could confidently hire is Queenie, and she's needed where she is. I can't think of any who are still around that I could trust. And once there is a man in the house, a former prostitute couldn't live there without causing the same problems I had with the townspeople the last time I attempted it."

So everything revolved around whatever man the Lowes hired. "Well then . . ." David shifted in his seat. "How long would you be willing to hold off on advertising, if perhaps . . . some man from around here might be willing to help at the orphanage?"

Nicholas only stared at him, making David squirm all the more. Had he just said that?

"A single man and a single woman won't work."

"I understand that. But maybe . . ." David cleared his throat. "Um, how long would you wait to give Evelyn a chance to find a husband, assuming you wouldn't push her into a marriage she doesn't want?"

Nicholas steepled his hands in front of him. "I'd be willing to hold off a handful of months if there was promising movement in that direction." One of his eyebrows raised. "Is there?"

Was there movement in that direction? Yes. Was it *promising*? David sucked in air through his teeth and forced himself not to squirm under Nicholas's scrutiny. "Some. Could we wait to see how promising things get?"

Nicholas gave him a half smile, half frown. "My wife has mentioned how very closed Evelyn is to that discussion."

360

If that wasn't the truth, he'd start believing in Santa Claus again.

"She is indeed." Lydia's voice startled him, and his skin turned hot. How long had she been listening?

She slid the rest of the way into the parlor, no child in her arms. "Did I hear what I thought I heard?"

He ran a hand through his hair. "I thought people only had to worry about staff eavesdropping behind doors."

She put her hands on her hips. "So are you interested in taking over the orphanage by marrying Evelyn or not?"

He wasn't interested in running an orphanage at all, but if he wanted to win Evelyn, it might be necessary. "She's put a lot of heart and effort into the orphanage, and I don't want to see her forced to give it up — whether I'm personally involved or not." He shrugged, hopefully looking like a controlled businessman and not a lovestruck buffoon.

Lydia came over to stand by Nicholas. "Do you have a personal reason for wanting to help the children?"

Besides it being what Evelyn wanted and how he wished he could give her the world? "Nothing beyond knowing they need help. Evelyn's so focused and dedicated and right the orphanage that I want to support. I wish someone had supported me in my dreams, as insignificant as they were. But her goals are more worthwhile than anything I've ever chased after. So if my attempt to help her stay at the orphanage ends up failing, maybe we could think up something to attract a lot of people to listen to her message and fund both her and the women's home. We've gotten a few men to commit, but if we don't get more, if we can't financially support her through this, I'm afraid she'll give up."

Nicholas just watched him while rubbing the stubble on his chin.

"We can think about it." Lydia gave David an assessing look. "But I'm hoping that won't be necessary. I can't think of anyone better suited for Evelyn than you."

His face heated again. "I'm not so sure about that."

"Well, I am. But don't go too fast — you'll have to ease her into the idea."

How he wished someone had some different advice for winning Evelyn. He'd like some actual direction besides "go slow," because that wouldn't get him anywhere fast enough to save her orphanage job. He was beginning to think he'd stumbled into a really bad retelling of the tortoise and the hare.

Lydia walked over to sit on the sofa, lowering herself down gingerly with a hand to her back. "Though we've been friends for years, she's hard to get to know. Generous to a fault, except when it comes to sharing about herself. There's a hurt in her buried so deep that anytime a man gets close, she retreats."

Help me figure out some way to get closer to her. I've asked you if she's the woman I ought to pursue, but I feel like I have no confirmation. I know how I feel, but what is your plan for us?

Why is all the advice I'm getting telling me to wait when she's only got months before Nicholas looks for someone else?

"Thank you for your advice. It seems I . . . uh . . . have some planning to do." Lydia's large grin made him squirm like a schoolboy caught passing a note to a girl in front of the entire class. "I'll be going now."

After shaking Nicholas's hand, he left them behind, seeking the cooler outside air that would hopefully steal the heat from his face and neck.

Had he really just told the Lowes he'd take over an orphanage? If anything could be further from what Father desired of him, he wouldn't know what it could be.

And yet, he didn't want to turn around and tell them to go ahead and post the advertisement.

But how could he be certain marrying Evelyn and taking over an orphanage was what he ought to do with his life?

She'd let him hold her hand a few times, hugged him twice, but as Lydia said, she was still closed off, despite neither he nor Lydia doing anything to betray her trust.

Which meant someone had likely hurt Evelyn so badly she believed anyone could turn on her in a moment. Just the thought of someone doing her wrong made him want to punch the next man who dared to look at her funny.

28

David rapped the huge brass knocker on the mansion's front door. Though he heard children playing in the backyard, he couldn't skirt around to the back this time, since he'd been formally invited to dinner. Lydia had evidently come up with an idea to gain support for the women's home and wanted his opinion.

Though she probably didn't need his opinion at all. Lydia was likely only trying to give him more time with Evelyn. Which of course was fine with him, so why was he so sweaty? He rubbed his hands on his slacks.

Well, he knew why he was jittery, but this was beyond ridiculous. When the thought of marriage had been confined to his own head he hadn't been so nervous.

But now the Lowes were holding off advertising for orphanage directors because he told them he'd be willing to marry Evelyn. If she refused him, they would know.

He startled when the door creaked open.

"Come in, Mr. Kingsman." The young butler from the Lowes' house stood straight and tall, as if he'd been promoted to over-seeing a castle. "Mrs. Lowe said to send you to the music room upon arrival." The young man did such a self-important flourish of his hand to gesture to the music room that David couldn't help but silently chuckle. At least the boy was enjoying his job.

He forced himself forward, ignoring the uptick of his heartbeat.

Lydia stood when he entered and put a finger to her lips. "So good of you to come, Mr. Kingsman," she said quietly. "The baby just fell asleep."

By the window, Evelyn was keeping the rocker moving in slow motion. The baby's head was snuggled into her neck.

She acknowledged him with a small nod right before a chorus of excited children hollered outside.

Nicholas's driver had led a pony onto the back lawn, and Nicholas was hoisting a small girl up into the saddle.

Evelyn seemed quite interested in the goings-on outside. The dark circles under her eyes were lighter, and the wistful smile on her lips made him want —

"How was the walk over?" Lydia asked from behind him.

"Huh?" His voice cracked for some foolish reason. He turned around and gave his head a good shake. "Oh, fine. I drove, actually."

"And the glass factory? How goes work there?"

"All right." He looked for a chair that didn't look dainty and chose what looked like a captain's chair. The seat was unbearably hard, but he didn't want to bounce around like Goldilocks looking for something that was just right. He had a feeling no chair in the room would be comfortable anyway.

Evelyn looked at him with raised brows.

He forced himself not to swipe at his forehead. The words *I want to marry you* weren't branded there for her to see. Though the amount of sweat trickling down his temple right now would have made more sense if he had been seared by a hot poker. He fished a handkerchief from his pocket.

"I'd ring for tea and cookies, but since the babe's asleep, I'll go get them." Lydia winked at him before leaving.

He wiped at the sweat on his brow as surreptitiously as he could. Though Evelyn might not understand why he was acting so strangely, his hostess knew exactly why he was sweaty and jumpy.

"Do you know what Lydia's up to?" Evelyn asked in a whisper.

Had she noticed Lydia's wink and singsong voice?

"She's been giddy all day," she continued. "One minute she's positively dancing around, the next minute she disappears."

At least Evelyn seemed to be oblivious to Lydia's current machinations to leave them alone together. "After you told me you thought you'd be unable to volunteer at the shelter, I asked her to think of something to bring attention to your cause. Nicholas said she wanted to get our opinion on her idea this evening."

"Hmm, she hadn't said anything to me."

The clock chimed four, and he held his breath, hoping the baby would sleep through the chest-resonating bongs.

Hope only stirred slightly, but it was enough that he tensed waiting for the screams. After the clock's chiming ended, he let out his breath when the babe's eyes remained closed.

"Bad news." Lydia reappeared in the doorway. "The children ate all the cookies. Cook's making more, but I doubt they'll be ready before dinner."

Good, he'd likely choke on a cookie right now anyway, considering his body had seized up as if he were in a life-and-death situation . . . though marriage *was* supposed to be until death do you part.

"Why don't we go upstairs?" Lydia smiled as if something wonderful awaited them there. "I'd figured on visiting first, then telling you about my idea after dinner, but we could switch things around."

He shot up. "Would you like me to get your husband?"

"No, he already approves and will be more useful watching the children. Though if you two think of something more we could do, we can discuss it over dinner."

"But the baby —"

Seems that wasn't a problem since Evelyn had already gotten out of her rocker, Hope's little face still squashed in deep sleep against her shoulder.

"Come on, then." Lydia flitted out of the room as if her stomach weren't preceding her.

He let Evelyn go in front of him. Lydia bypassed the wraparound stairs in the entryway and disappeared into a doorway halfway down the hall. Following Evelyn, he stepped into a dark, narrow stairwell and climbed behind her, the plush red carpeting

369

dampening their footsteps.

The sounds of things being shoved and scooted around somewhere above beckoned them upward as they passed the second-story landing and continued higher.

He followed the ladies out onto the third floor and stopped. This was not what he'd been expecting at all. The entire floor was a handsome, wood-planked ballroom. An oval ceiling vaulted over the entire expanse and was fitted with fancy gasoliers. Why, it was large enough to be a roller-skating rink — one that could rival Carnival Park's back in Kansas City.

David's own ballroom might be prettier, with the wall of windows looking out to his garden, but it wasn't nearly this big.

The gardener and the mansion's butler were in the far southeast corner pushing a large, dusty crate, while the Lowes' young housekeeper, Caroline, and a maid he didn't recognize scrubbed the floor to their north. Another maid was on a ladder, polishing a gasolier.

"If you had lived very long in Teaville, Mr. Kingsman, you would know that my husband has never used this ballroom. Why he's never used it is a long story, but one about to end because he's agreed to let me host a charity ball — just like you read about in books." Lydia clapped her hands to emphasize half her words as if she were one of the girls outside awaiting a pony ride. "I'm planning a banquet followed by music and dance. Everyone has been dying to see our ballroom, and I'm hoping the speeches from Nicholas, the moral-society members, and some of the older orphans will gain sympathy and aid." Lydia shrugged and turned to them. "But if not, all proceeds from the evening will go to the red-light-district ministry."

"When I asked you to come up with a grand idea, you didn't disappoint." David walked out into the middle of the room, his shoes tapping against the polished wood floor. "This place is perfect. Where do these doors lead to?" He pointed to the various doorways lining the perimeter of the ballroom, which took up almost the entire third floor.

"Well, most are storage, though the east room is furnished with a few health-inducing apparatuses like you'd find at the natatorium. Then over there is the fainting room."

She crossed in front of him to open the door next to a glass one that looked like it went to a small balcony.

He'd never been allowed inside a fainting

room and hadn't one in his own home, so he crossed over to look.

The room was long, narrow, and lined with chairs, but the low ceiling made him feel claustrophobic.

Maybe fainting rooms weren't where ladies went when they felt faint, but to practice fainting. He backed out.

"Over here is the smoking balcony." She pointed to the glass door he'd noticed, then walked past the fainting room. "And down here is the room where we keep all the piano rolls. We have a little over a hundred so far."

They had a player piano and didn't even entertain? He glanced around and spotted the fancy-looking Mignon. Ah, so a reproducing piano, even better. What rolls had Nicholas collected? Likely the best, knowing him.

How strange to have this fancy ballroom and do absolutely nothing with it. He'd have to ask about why that was over dinner, or maybe he'd overhear the speculation at the party.

Lydia padded across the room and turned in front of the rounded alcove located in the center of the north wall. "And this is the music pit, with a beautiful veranda behind it, so if we leave the doors open, you can hear the orchestra out on the front lawn. So what do you think?"

"I think it's a wonderful idea." Evelyn shifted, her back arched to keep the baby somewhat reclined. He would have told her to hand the baby over, but he didn't dare. "There are plenty of well-to-do people in Teaville and nearby towns who would flock here if we do this right, and being this is the first time you've ever held a dance, we should get plenty of publicity."

"I've already picked out the musicians. They said they need two weeks to practice since they've never played together." Lydia's smile was as bright as her eyes. "Just two weeks! It'll fly by. I've got to get a menu to the hotel for them to coordinate with Cook, and we'll have dance cards printed up and we'll get the tailor to come over and fashion dresses for you and me and Sadie —"

"Sadie?" Evelyn's face drained of color. "Don't tell me Sadie is going to be giving a speech."

Sadie? David looked over at the young housekeeper working with Caroline. Wasn't that her name? What would Sadie have to talk about?

Lydia sobered. "No, not her. I'm thinking Max. He's quite articulate for his age. Hopefully the businessmen will sympathize with a young man's story. And I might try to get Florence to sing something. She's got a decent voice and is beyond delightful. Maybe they'll imagine their daughters at her age having to live the life we'll inform them of. Caroline doesn't want to speak, but Nicholas will, and I hope you will say something, Evelyn, since this is your project."

Evelyn nodded while a ringing sounded to his right. A bell high on the wall was swinging, likely being pulled by someone downstairs.

"I told Cook to ring me when she got the . . ." — Lydia's face was almost comical as her hand stirred the air while she tried to come up with what she wanted to say — "thing. I'll just leave you two to come down at your leisure. If dinner's ready before then, I'll have Cook ring again. Please stay and discuss what you think Nicholas and I could do to make this the most fruitful and wonderful party ever." With that, she scurried back down the stairs.

Could the woman be any less subtle about leaving him and Evelyn alone? He looked at the floor for a minute to get control of his smile.

"Well, then." Evelyn did a slow turn, looking around the magnificent ballroom. "I'll go see if I can put Hope down. Maybe you and Nicholas can talk about ways to improve Lydia's plan — if you can get him away from the pony rides."

So she wasn't about to let Lydia snooker them into having time alone? "But Nicholas already knows what Lydia wants to do, and she said we could discuss it at dinner. Why don't we go out on the veranda, enjoy the view before it's crowded with partygoers?"

Her eyes glanced that way, but she shook her head. "Hope's getting heavy."

"Then let me take her." Wait, did he just offer to do that?

"Oh no, I wouldn't want to move her in case we'd wake her up."

"But you'd have to do so to put her down."

She only looked at him, as if she couldn't believe he'd dismantled her excuse.

"Here." He pried the baby off her shoulder gently, attempting to drape her against his own shoulder in a similar manner. This baby heavy? She was light as a feather.

"You woke her."

"I did?" He'd have expected a fire alarm to be going off in his ear. He started to bounce a little, like Evelyn always did. Thankfully the baby only made contented-sounding grunts. "Well, she seems happy enough. Let's go look."

He held open the glass door for Evelyn with his free hand.

Outside, the beautiful remainders of autumn clung to the trees, and the long winding driveway wove through the dying grasses that sloped toward the brick street. Teaville to the north looked bigger than he'd imagined, though it was but a speck compared to the clumps of towns surrounding Kansas City.

Hope started fussing, so he jostled her more. "Have you ever been up here?"

Evelyn leaned against the wall, staring out toward town. "We bring the kids up on rainy days to run off energy."

Hope's fussing turned into a cry, so he turned her to face him and made a pouting face just like hers. "What's wrong, Hope?"

She only cried harder in response.

He jiggled her more, but with how tiny she was, he was afraid she could be jiggled too much. If only he could get her quiet again so he and Evelyn could talk. He raised his voice to overpower hers and turned her so she could see the mansion's exterior. "Do you see that pigeon on the gable there. Isn't it pretty?"

Pretty awful, perhaps, considering Hope's escalating response.

Evelyn held out her hands. "I'm sorry she

started crying on you like that. I'll take her back."

"Will you be taking her to the wet nurse?"

"No, she doesn't come until dinnertime."

He put the baby on his arm like he'd seen Evelyn do once, only making the cry more insistent. "Then tell me what you'd do to stop her."

"You want to deal with a fussy baby?" Evelyn looked as bewildered as Hope.

He shrugged. It wasn't a matter of want, exactly, because handing back this fussy little feather would probably make him sigh in relief. But if he was going to help at the orphanage, he'd have to do things like this, right? If he couldn't figure it out, then he should stop thinking about marrying Evelyn altogether. If he would be of no help, he'd not be the kind of man she'd attach herself to anyway. "I can't learn how if I don't try."

"All right." She came over and flipped the baby around and put her on his shoulder again. "I think her tummy's hurting. So I've been pressing her midsection against my shoulder while I rock her back and forth a little. Like this." She pushed Hope up a few more inches and then used his shoulder as a fulcrum for a baby seesaw.

Whether Hope liked it or simply found the whole thing strange, she settled down to rapid-fire sniffling. "How'd you get so good at understanding babies?"

She backed away, gaze pinned on Hope. "I've just watched good mothers, perhaps, but Hope isn't a typical baby. The doctor says he sees this sort of behavior with a lot of the prostitutes' infants, always fussy, some downright in distress. He says they're protesting being born to such circumstances. We had one come in a year ago, but sadly she didn't live long."

Evelyn stared at her folded hands, the memories of grief playing across her face.

"I'm sorry."

"Yes, well." She inhaled quite loudly. "Working here isn't easy, fussy babies or not. Sometimes the children who come have been abused and neglected, and they often act in strange and difficult ways. And we rarely get them placed in a home, since Nicholas is adamant he'd rather pay for them to live here for years than go somewhere they won't be loved. Many who want to adopt the children are too poor to hire servants and figure after the life the children have led, they should be happy to clean up after them."

Hope started crying again, and he looked at Evelyn in question. The shoulder seesaw had apparently lost its charm.

"I sometimes try to swing her down near my waist in a figure-eight pattern. I think it confuses her since it's not just back and forth." She demonstrated an interesting sort of dance that made him smile despite the crying going off near his ear.

He tried it, but was sure he looked the fool. And the baby's squalling continued its crescendo. Perhaps Father was right, he needed to pursue more manly hobbies, like hitting and killing things, because this sure wasn't working.

He had to be insane to not be handing Hope back to Evelyn. For why else would a man choose this?

He put Hope up against his chest, face out, so she could see the front yard. He wrapped her tight in his arms so he wouldn't drop her off the balcony. "Come on, little lady, let's find something fun to look at." He loosened one arm to point. "Look there, Hope. Can you see the pond out by those trees? I bet there are fish out there. When you get older, we should go check."

Suddenly, the baby let out a burp louder than he'd expect from something so small. And whether she'd startled herself or that had been her problem, she relaxed and went quiet. If she wasn't still audibly breathing and shuddering, he'd have wondered if he'd squeezed her too hard. "Huh! I did it."

He turned to look at Evelyn, expecting her to give him a congratulatory smile, but instead, her warm gaze made him feel like some giant had squeezed the stuffing out of him. He forced himself to suck in air. Maybe dancing around with a crying baby wasn't the most foolish thing he'd ever done.

29

Evelyn listened at the door to the room where the wet nurse was supposed to be. Mrs. Dewitt had been paid extra to stay the night to care for Hope, but even taking into account the musicians tuning their instruments and the movement of the crowd three floors above, the basement was quiet. Despite how difficult Hope was, Mrs. Dewitt had grown fond of the baby and had convinced her husband that with four boys at home, a baby girl might be a good thing. Hopefully Nicholas approved of them adopting Hope, because she couldn't imagine anyone else taking a baby that fussy.

If only Annette hadn't disappeared and could be convinced to keep her family together, but even Rosie had no idea where she'd gone after she'd given her a note for Lawrence. Thankfully, hearing from his sister had eased up the boy's melancholy, even though she'd not told him if or when she'd return.

Evelyn turned the knob and slowly opened the door. The light was on, and Mrs. Dewitt was asleep in the rocker with both children curled up on her chest. Her boy Gregory, though not much older, was nearly three times as large as Hope, and they made for a darling scene.

However, if she woke them, Mrs. Dewitt would find nothing darling about her un-needed visit.

As slowly as she'd pushed the door open, she closed it.

She fingered the filigreed paper fan the local Teaville printer had worked overtime to produce. She'd never been to a dance that required a dance card, but she was certain most weren't this exquisite. Each dance slot was on a separate little blade that could be written on when fanned out. What a beautiful thing for a woman's memory box — if there were names on it, of course.

Closing her blank fan, she headed out of the basement. The dances would start soon, and Lydia would be heartbroken if she avoided dancing entirely. Putting her card out late meant she wouldn't have to dance every dance, but hopefully there'd be enough men still filling in cards that she'd get enough dances to satisfy Lydia, especially since she'd been kind enough to pay for her gown.

But before she left the basement, she wanted to check on Caroline. Caroline had given a heartfelt talk to the men and women before dinner, but she'd curiously left out her personal connection to the red-light district. She'd never kept Moira a secret before. Had something happened to Moira that she hadn't told her about?

Evelyn tapped on Caroline's door and, upon being invited in, stepped into the small nondescript room. "I wanted to tell you that I thought you gave a good speech this evening." The rest were going to give their speeches between dance sets. Though Caroline had changed her mind about talking, she'd asked to be excused from the party.

She rocked in her rocker, a half-finished afghan draped across her lap, and glanced up for a second. "Thank you." She pulled more yarn from her skein and continued to crochet.

At Mr. Hargrove's, David had seemed worried about her lack of smiling, and if Caroline's lack of good spirits had been as persistent as hers, no wonder he'd been concerned. "Is there anything I can do for you?"

She shook her head. "There's no need to bother with me tonight."

Evelyn took a step in. "That's not true. If you need me —"

"Evelyn." Caroline gave her a motherly look, despite her only being old enough to be an elder sister. "I said I'm all right."

Evelyn rubbed her hand down the smooth surface of the door, reluctant to leave when she knew full well Caroline had been far from all right for a few weeks now. "I wish you had let Lydia commission you a gown." She played with the draping across her own bodice, marveling at the fine texture of the silk. With its blue-and-white vertical stripes, the dress made her look even taller, and the wide blue belt made her waist look tinier than her corset truly cinched her. And the quality of the silk and the Valenciennes lace about her neck and at the end of her three-quarter sleeves made it the finest thing she owned.

Not only had Lydia provided Evelyn's dress, but she'd had one made for Sadie. Caroline, however, had completely refused. "When Henri saw Sadie was attending, he asked if you were planning to change later and come up."

Caroline's stitches grew more jerky. "If Henri asks about me again, please tell him he's not obligated to worry about me. I'm a lowly housekeeper who's happy enough to have the night off, for there will be plenty for me to do come morning."

Was that a crack in her voice?

Caroline sighed and put her needlework down and tried to smile at her. "I'm sorry, Evelyn, I know you well enough to realize you want me to talk about what's bothering me, but please go enjoy yourself. We can talk later, if you'd like."

Above them, the musicians began what sounded like their first song. The soft lilt of the violins carried down to them through Caroline's open window.

Evelyn looked at her dance card and frowned at the time printed — she should have had plenty of time to get up there before the dancing started. After listening for a measure or two, it was clear the song being played wasn't a waltz. Perhaps there was an introductory set of music before the dancing began. Even so, she needed to get up there. "Do you promise to have tea with me tomorrow?"

"Yes. Now go before you miss out." She shooed her with the back of her hand and returned to her stitching.

Evelyn was loath to leave, but Caroline was right. Dinner had been over for twenty minutes and all the well-dressed guests had gone upstairs and she should already be up there. "I'll see you tomorrow." Hopefully she'd open up to her.

She backed out of Caroline's room, walked the servants' hallway, climbed the stairs, and crossed through the empty entryway. The line for the elevator to take the women up had finally disappeared, and so had Franklin, who'd acted as operator.

She left the foyer and padded up to the hallway. Surprisingly, Sadie was gliding quickly toward the kitchen. Hadn't she seen Franklin escort her into the elevator earlier?

The seventeen-year-old hadn't protested at all about Lydia wanting to outfit her in the latest ballroom fashion. Sadie's gown was made of the creamiest off-white silk with an intricate flowered lace overlay that extended into a modest train behind her. Her see-through sleeves ended at her elbows, and the amount of roses tatted into the lace made Evelyn hope Sadie had rinsed her hair in rose water to match the dress.

The girl's dark blond ringlets were piled high on her head, and an off-white band of silk and a solitary peach silk rose had been woven into her high coiffure.

She opened her mouth to call to Sadie, but a man's arm reached out of the kitchen doors and grabbed her. She yelped and disappeared.

Evelyn put a hand to her skipping heart. Had one of the guests recognized her from the district and planned to take advantage of her, at a ball meant to help such women wanting a new life? She picked up her skirts and ran after her.

She stopped in the kitchen doorway but saw no one. Not even Cook.

A giggle sounded to her left, where the butler's pantry was located.

Oh no, was Mrs. Naples right? Would soiled doves fall back into moral vice so readily that any attempts to help them were ill spent?

Evelyn crept over to the pantry door and peeked in to see Franklin holding Sadie in a very proper dance position, arms and shoulders held high, twirling her about to the barely audible music, as if they were at a royal ball.

Franklin was obviously besotted, his eyes practically melting under Sadie's huge grin.

The music ended abruptly. Perhaps the musicians were still just warming up.

Franklin twirled Sadie around one last time, stepped away, and bowed.

"Oh my goodness, Franklin." Sadie pressed a hand to her chest, her cheeks high with color. "That's the most romantic thing that's ever happened to me."

A romantic gesture Evelyn shouldn't have been privy to. She pulled back but didn't leave, in case her footsteps would ruin Sadie's moment.

"Well" — Franklin cleared his throat — "I couldn't let you go up there and dance with those fancy gentlemen before you knew what it felt like to be in my arms."

"Oh, Franklin, there's not going to be a line of men wanting to dance with me. And even if there is, a few minutes isn't enough for any man to lose his heart to a girl playing dress-up. I don't know why Mrs. Lowe insisted on me being an actual guest, but who could say no to this dress?"

A rustle of skirts sounded, and Evelyn could imagine her twirling.

"You were right to say yes." Franklin's voice turned soft and low.

The music began upstairs again.

"Now go dance the night away, princess." Franklin's smile was evident in the warmth of his voice.

Evelyn quickly pressed back against the wall, hoping neither Sadie nor Franklin would see her on their way out.

They both passed her, and the moment they exited the kitchen, Evelyn let out a breath and pressed her fingers against the slight ache behind her eyes. She would not be jealous of anyone's dream come true.

Cook's voice boomed, and Evelyn froze, her heart pitter-pattering in a more staccato rhythm. Not seeing Cook, she rushed from the kitchen so she wouldn't be caught hiding in the corner.

The hallway was already empty, and when she got to the stairs, she poked her head into the stairwell, not wanting to follow up on Sadie's heels. The only sound she could hear was music.

After a deep breath, she climbed the stairs while fiddling with her dance card. With all the elbow rubbing Nicholas and David planned to do on her behalf, would David be too busy to dance? They were just too good to her. It didn't seem right they would spend the night working hard for her project, while she simply enjoyed the ball.

On the third floor, she hesitated at the crowded ballroom's threshold. The men's tailored coats and shined shoes contrasted with the lighter colors of the women's rustling silks. The jewels dripping off the women's dresses and pinned in their upswept hair twinkled in the gaslight. They'd been dazzling enough downstairs during dinner, but in this room amid the music . . .

Franklin was right — this was a party for a princess.

Though she loved the dress she'd allowed Lydia's tailor to make for her, she would be very out of place amid this finery. She'd insisted it couldn't be fancier than something she could wear to someone's wedding.

Walking along the wall, she kept her eyes down as she made her way to the dance-card table. Only a half dozen or so cards remained. Looking at the time again, she saw there was at least fifteen minutes until the dancing started.

Lydia would not be happy if she stood against the wall all night long, so Evelyn pulled her fan-shaped card off her wrist and laid it down.

Sadie's fan was spread out next to hers, but it appeared to be blank. She fanned Sadie's out some more — only three names. Had Sadie just put down her card as well or was she being ignored? Surely most of the crowd was unaware of her housekeeping position and couldn't be shunning her for that.

"Hello there." David's baritone made her skin prickle. "Is your card still out?"

"Oh." Her heart fluttered with his nearness. "It's right here." Her hands itched to snatch her dance card off the table. Not because she didn't want to dance with him, but because she wanted to dance with him too much.

"I've been stuck conversing with Mr. Pollack since we left the dining room. He likes to hear himself talk, I think." He grabbed the pencil off the table. "I hope you won't mind if I take the dances you have left."

Her heart sputtered. "Exactly how many dances do you want?"

"All of them, of course." He fanned out her card and frowned.

She could do nothing but swallow.

"Nobody's put their name down." His eyebrows scrunched as if he couldn't imagine how her card could be blank.

"I didn't put my card out until just now. You see, most men in Teaville who had any interest in me have . . . no interest in me anymore. Only out-of-towners like yourself would bother putting their name on my card — unless they find out I'm taller."

He ran a finger down the names of the dances. "That's silly. You shouldn't have kept yourself from taking part in the dances because of that."

"Just, uh, don't take the final one." She put a hand over the last blade of her card.

He stopped and looked up at her. "That

one's been claimed?"

"Not yet, but I'm hoping someone else will take that one." Someone elderly, with halitosis and bumbling feet. That way, when she went to sleep, that dance would be the freshest in her mind and would keep her from dreaming of David.

His eyes narrowed as he looked at her, as if an X-ray might reveal the identity of the man she wanted to dance with. "Who?"

"Oh, you wouldn't know him." Which was true — she didn't know who it would be either.

He continued looking at her so intently she glanced away.

Sadie sipped punch across the crowded ballroom, her eyes fixed on where her dance card lay.

"I suppose I'll take two waltzes and the mazurka, then." He scribbled his name on the corresponding blades. "As much as I'd love to dance all night long, Nicholas has been too kind in arranging business contacts interested in talking with me."

The mazurka? How had she forgotten Lydia had put that on the schedule? She'd tried to learn that dance twice and had given up. For truly, how often did she have the opportunity to dance at all? "I should have blocked the mazurka off my card. I've never been good at it."

That made his eyes sparkle. "But I am." He finished scribbling his name and stood. "I'll see you in a few minutes."

"Wait." She stopped him by grabbing his sleeve. "I know you said you can't dance all night, but aren't you going to put your name on any more cards?"

He laid his hand atop hers. "Yours was the only card I was waiting for."

Oh how her heart was screaming to love him. But her conscience was screaming too, and she'd learned long ago which one she should follow. She closed her eyes and backed away.

"No need to panic."

What must she look like for him to say that? Could he hear her erratic heartbeat over the noise of more than eighty guests?

"You're the only lady I know here. I'm not here to meet women, but rather to drum up support. I would have danced with Mrs. Lowe, but she's sitting out."

She'd been slightly surprised Lydia had chosen to come at all. Not because some would say it was against propriety in her condition — her friend had proven years ago she could care less about society rules — but because she'd confessed to going to bed several times this past week at six o'clock.

"I'll be more effective getting you what you want by hobnobbing." He stepped closer. "Unless you'd like a few more dances?"

If there ever was a question she could emphatically answer with both yes and no, that would be it. "Perhaps we should see how our night goes first." She glanced at Sadie, who was still staring at the dance-card table from across the room. "But if you're willing, would you mind dancing with the Lowes' housekeeper? You remember her — the girl who made the divinity?"

"Yes." He scanned the room as if trying to locate her.

She tugged on his sleeve again. "Don't stare, but she's the one in the off-white silk by the punch table. This is likely the only time she'll attend a ball, and I want her memories to be good." And how could being in the arms of a man as gallant as David ever be a bad memory?

"If you so wish." He made a show of searching the crowd, as if Sadie wasn't who he'd just been looking for, then turned around and added his name to her card.

A thickset older man sidled up to David's right and grunted as he looked over the cards. Looking down on his balding head might work to erase the feel of David's hands in hers, so hopefully he'd fill in the slot for her final dance.

Though the last time David had held her hand, the sensation had stuck with her for days.

"Let me have your pencil, will you, son?" The man stuck out his fleshy palm. "Do you know which of the remaining ladies dances well?"

Leaving David to try to help the man, she crossed over to Sadie. The closer she got to the housekeeper, the more obvious it was that Sadie felt exactly as she did — out of place and ready to run.

"How are you doing, Sadie?"

"I'm ready to throw up," she said breathlessly. "All these people. What if someone recognizes me?"

"You don't look at all like the girl I got a glimpse of years ago. Besides, Nicholas wouldn't have allowed you to come if he didn't believe you safe."

Sadie's squirming didn't lessen.

"What's wrong?"

"Nothing, really. It's just that, I'm preoccupied." Sadie reached up to run a hand through her hair but stopped before she ruined it. She clasped onto the dainty gold chain at her throat instead. "I wish I hadn't agreed to attend. Even if I wasn't what I was, I'm still unfit for this company. I'm much better suited to dance a jig with someone downstairs than waltz with anyone up here."

Evelyn took Sadie's hand, which was pulling on her necklace hard enough to break it. "I saw you dance the waltz downstairs. I think you'll do fine."

Sadie's eyes widened. "Oh, Miss Wisely, I hope that wasn't untoward. I don't want to get either of us fired."

"Don't worry." Evelyn patted her hand. "I shouldn't have been watching, but when I saw a man snatch you from the hallway, I wanted to be sure you were all right. Franklin is a fine young man. You couldn't have chosen better."

"You're right, I couldn't. But I wish I'd fallen for someone I had a chance with." She looked away from Evelyn and sniffed.

"How do you know you haven't a chance with Franklin? I saw how he looked at you."

"You know his opinion on fallen women."

He'd been the first new child she'd taken into the orphanage after the Lowes left. His mother had taken out her frustrations on him, and anytime soiled doves came up in conversation, he'd never had a sympathetic word for them.

She'd actually been surprised he'd seeme
so pleasant this evening, since helping
reformed prostitutes was the reason for this
charity ball. "Maybe he's starting to see that
his past shouldn't color his thoughts about
everyone."

Sadie grabbed her necklace again and
started pulling it. "I'm still scared of the
day I have to tell him."

A huge eruption of laughter made Evelyn
look across the way at a group of men. They
were laughing at something, maybe the bald
man in the middle of the cluster whose head
was turning bright red. David was in the
group, and his smile widened when he
slanted a glance at her, his gaze warm —
hopefully only because he'd found whatever
joke had been told to be funny.

She couldn't fault Sadie for being scared
of revealing something she wished had never
happened.

But unlike her, Sadie wasn't responsible
for the horrible secret she was keeping.
"Sadie, God knows your past, and Franklin's. Though some people would look down
upon you, God doesn't, and He won't keep
good things from you because of it." Thankfully Sadie could have whatever good God
wanted to give her. "Enjoy your night and

anklin's attentions. If he can't get past ur secret when you tell him, then maybe od wants you to dream of something else."

Sadie stopped nervously scanning the room and looked up at Evelyn. "But I like that dream so much."

At least the girl was allowed to entertain her dreams. "I'm sure you do, but don't ruin your life chasing a dream God doesn't want to give you. Pray for Franklin. If he won't allow God to change his heart, your attempts will be futile."

"Thank you, Miss Wisely. I'll do more praying." Sadie looked at her empty glass. "Do you want punch?"

"No, thank you. I should probably go find Lydia now." Evelyn glanced around the huge crowd of people. She'd rather go back downstairs and check on the baby again, or do anything else that got her out of this crowd, but if she had to be here, being near Lydia would make it bearable.

She headed in the direction she'd seen David disappear. If he'd been heading back to Nicholas, Lydia would likely be nearby.

Though the windows were open and many women were employing handheld fans, the air was thick. A very good thing Lydia hadn't held a party this large in the summer.

Not seeing the Lowes, Evelyn stopped and looked around again. Nicholas was pretty tall, but she couldn't see him anywhere.

Behind her, the glass door to the smoker's balcony showed the terrace to be empty, so she pushed out into the night. Quiet drew her more than the nearness of a friend.

The cool air was too refreshing to hoard though, so she propped the door open.

Walls on both sides of her shot straight up to the roof, and the eight-foot balcony was closed in by a plain steel rail — not at all as pretty as the veranda behind the music pit, but blissfully cool. She walked to the edge and leaned out so she could see the last of the sunlight coloring the western horizon.

The remnants of the day hemmed the deep indigo sky with violet, embroidered with the black silhouettes of trees upon a far ridge. A lovely view, but she closed her eyes against it nonetheless.

God, I know that what I've been dreaming about can't be your dream for me. I'm trying so hard to do what you would have me do, and yet right now, I wish you'd change everything for me — to swipe away my mistake as far as the east is from the west. To let me be free. At the same time, I know I have to face the consequences of my misstep, but Sadie shouldn't. Please help her to never regret the choices she makes. Keep her from doing anything that will haunt her for the rest of her life. She already has enough things in her past to —

"How are you, darling?" Momma's concerned voice came from behind her. "A lot of people, isn't it?"

"Yes." So Momma had sought escape as well.

She stopped beside her at the railing, and Evelyn put her hand atop her mother's. "Hopefully that means we'll end up with one or two more supporters before the night's end."

With her free hand, Momma played with the brooch pinned to her best dress.

At least someone else in this town realized how impractical a ball gown truly was.

"You aim too low, sweetheart. Pray for a dozen supporters, at least."

"All right." She was in awe of what a woman of prayer her mother had become the last several years.

"I saw you finally put your card on the table."

And of course, if any person other than David was paying attention to that insignificant detail of tonight's party, it would be Momma.

"I've been praying that whatever is holding you back from finding someone to love can be resolved."

She squeezed her mother's hand. She had started praying for that as well, but as she had told Sadie, she had to have faith that whatever God answered was best, even if it didn't feel like it.

"Thank you for your prayers." She truly did appreciate them, but she had to get Momma onto another topic. "How's Daddy?"

"He's as good as he was this morning. You saw how he's still got that droop to his face and slurs his words, but the progress with the rest of his body makes me hope the doctor's expectation of a full recovery is correct. But even if he gets worse, I'm glad I've had the love of a good man. Though this women's home idea is wonderful, darling, if . . . life takes you elsewhere, no one will fault you."

Evelyn simply held on to Momma's hand. "How long will you stay tonight?"

"Oh . . ." The single word was laced with her mother's disappointment over Evelyn's refusal to talk about love. "I have two more people Nicholas wants me to talk to, and then I'm going home." She tiptoed up to kiss Evelyn on the temple. "I better return to the party so I can get back to your father."

Once Momma left, Evelyn stared back out at the sky, where the sparkle of the first star emerged. As a child she'd always thought the best wishing star was the first one to appear, but girlhood wishes had gotten her into a lot of trouble. Better to pray God would do as He pleased than make any wishes.

Please help me have a good time tonight. I know dancing isn't a commitment to anything, and I'd love a happy memory to put in my treasure box. I've had so few, and I know I don't deserve them, but if you could grant me an exception this once. Would it be too much to ask that Nicholas's investigator —

"Here you are."

She shook her head. Trying to pray at the biggest event in Teaville since the opening of the natatorium was seemingly futile.

David walked up beside her, dangling her fancy dance card. "They just announced the dancing will commence. Yours was the only one left on the table. I hope you remember the first one belongs to us."

"There's no way I would forget."

Sadie had told Franklin that a few minutes wasn't long enough for a woman to lose her heart.

But what happened if her heart was already lost, despite everything she'd done to save herself the agony?

She inhaled one last gulp of fresh air before David led her inside. Tonight she wanted to forget everything and enjoy the ball, like she'd told Sadie to do.

Three dances with David — only about a half hour total. Surely her heart wouldn't implode.

30

"That's wonderful." David shook hands with Mr. Pickett, who'd just promised to give him the names of some contacts in Kansas City. That wouldn't help him with Evelyn's women's home or the glass factory here, but there was always time to look for ways to strengthen Father's holdings.

The redheaded man with a full beard who'd patiently waited to talk to Mr. Pickett stepped into the small circle that had formed around the businessman from Parsons. "Good evening, Mr. Pickett. May I introduce myself, I'm . . ."

David took a step back, only too eager to be done with the night's conversations. As grateful as he was for Nicholas introducing him to these men, he was pretty much done in. He normally wasn't up anywhere near this late.

Behind him, the musicians played their penultimate song. He widened his eyes in an attempt to keep them from drooping and scanned the crowd for a Mr. Belton. All he knew about the man was that he wore glasses and had a receding hairline. Nicholas had told him he wanted to introduce them, but he'd disappeared in the middle of David's conversation with Mr. Pickett.

He smiled when he caught a glimpse of Evelyn promenading across the floor with a gentleman several inches shorter. She seemed to be somewhat familiar with this dance — she hadn't been kidding when she'd said she wasn't good at the mazurka. His bruised toes were a testament to that.

Her partner whisked her behind a cluster of dancers, so David scanned the waning crowd for Nicholas. Ah! Nicholas had caught sight of him first and was beckoning from across the room.

David put up a hand, letting Nicholas know he saw him, and wove his way between clusters of people clumped around the edge of the area they'd reserved for dancing in front of the orchestra. Once he passed the dancers, he saw Nicholas was headed toward him.

They stopped in one of the gaps in the crowd. Nicholas pulled at his high collar. "Have you had the chance to talk with Mr. Belton?"

David refrained from yanking on his own uncomfortable collar and pulled out a handkerchief to blot his forehead. Though some guests had left, the heat from the crowd refused to dissipate. "No, but I had promising conversations with Mr. Drumsfelt and Mr. Pickett."

"Good." Nicholas gestured back the way David had come. "Mr. Belton's there near the punch table."

David looked over his shoulder but shook his head, not seeing a man who fit the description he'd been given.

"The one with the older blond woman in green on his arm."

"Ah, I see him."

"I'm afraid I can't introduce you, as I'd hoped. I'm leaving."

"No problem." He sighed in relief. Mr. Belton lived in Caney. If he had to introduce himself, maybe he'd drive over on another day. Wait. "You're leaving?" Since when did a host leave before the party was over?

"We'll still be in the mansion, of course." Nicholas wiped the sweat off his own brow. "We can talk tomorrow if you'd like. Come to dinner?"

"Certainly." At least then he didn't have to come up with an excuse to come see Evelyn.

"Were any of the men you spoke to interested in our cause?"

David jiggled his head in indecision. "Perhaps Mr. Drumsfelt, but most were more interested in rubbing elbows."

"I was hoping for more conversation about the project myself, but it didn't seem many were interested." Nicholas sighed and tucked his handkerchief back in his pocket. "Tell Mr. Belton you're a friend of mine. He should remember I mentioned you. Good night, then." Nicholas thumped him on the shoulder and strode back through the crowd.

When the sea of people parted, he caught a glimpse of Lydia sitting with a curly-headed Isabelle asleep on her shoulder. Once Nicholas made it to them, he pulled his year-old daughter off his wife's shoulder and helped her up. Lydia's stomach and the size of her ball gown made the maneuver almost comical, but the second David felt like laughing, Nicholas dropped a kiss on the top of her head and slipped an arm around her shoulders. Then the three of them skirted the perimeter of the room and headed toward the stairwell.

So that was why he was leaving early.

That would never have happened with his father. As long as there was business to discuss, Father would have stayed.

Nicholas was nothing like Father. He was the only businessman David had ever seen talk business while holding his young daughter, and he'd held her as though he did it so often he didn't realize no one else brought their child to work.

Though Father would be impressed by Nicholas's wealth, his respect would end there, since Nicholas's life didn't seem to revolve around money, power, or status.

Father would call him a pushover, despite the fact that he'd assembled this huge crowd willing to listen to a radical proposal.

David hung his head. If he were to gain the admiration of one man, only to lose the admiration of the other, which would he want?

Could he give up his two-decades-long quest for his father's approval?

"Last song, ladies and gentlemen," the conductor called.

Where was Evelyn? If he could be certain she'd love him, would Father's lack of parental pride matter so much?

He scanned the last of the crowd partnering up.

In the corner near the player piano, Evelyn was sitting on a bench talking to Sadie, who was positively glowing despite the late hour. A tall redheaded man approached them, claimed Sadie's hand, and whisked her toward the ballroom's middle.

Evelyn resituated her dress, pulled her dance card off her wrist, and started fanning herself with it, not bothering to look at the names written inside. Had whoever she'd hoped to claim her last dance failed to do so?

The conductor tapped a beat upon his little podium, and the musicians started to play the last waltz. A glance back at Mr. Belton found him engrossed in conversation.

Skirting the dancers, David made his way toward Evelyn.

She was watching Sadie. Her smile, however, looked somewhat sad. Before he got within twenty feet of her she looked up at him and seemingly couldn't look away.

He couldn't look away either. When he stopped in front of her, he held out his hand. "Since it seems no one's claimed your last dance, may I?"

She finally dropped her gaze and stared at his open palm. "I was sort of hoping I was done for tonight. My new shoes have not been kind. And this heat, you'd think it was summer."

He let his hand fall back to his side, trying not to take her response as an insult, for it was quite late. "Do you need to retire to the fainting room?"

She cringed. "Oh no, it's stuffier in there than out here."

He held out his hand again. "Perhaps some fresh air, then?"

Her hand came up, and though he noted a hesitation on the way, she put her hand in his. "That would be nice."

After pulling her to stand, he led her to the portico's balcony behind the musicians. Once outside, he smiled. They had the veranda to themselves.

She let go of his arm and went straight for the railing.

He joined her, glad the music wasn't so boisterous it prevented conversation, yet was amplified enough that their conversation would be private if someone came out.

So how to take advantage of the privacy he'd stumbled upon? He looked at the sky and spotted a pinprick of movement that quickly disappeared. "I just saw a falling star." He pointed beyond the trees. "Make a wish."

She turned to look where he'd pointed. "I think you saw a reflection from someone's lantern below. There are too many clouds."

Perhaps romancing Evelyn would be as

difficult as getting Father to admit his son had any talent.

How could he get her to loosen up? He'd thought the dance would do so, but she likely should have skipped the festivities and caught up on the sleep the baby was stealing from her — not that he wasn't happy she'd attended. He'd certainly enjoyed having her in his arms as he waltzed her around the room. "Perhaps I didn't see a falling star, but since I have so many things to wish for, you can't blame me for wanting some extra help."

She looked over at him, the reflection of the gaslight behind him flickering in her eyes. "You don't need stars to pray."

"No, but wishing on stars is still fun." He stepped closer, then leaned against the railing next to her. "If you had seen the star, what would you have wished for?"

She took a step away and looked out over the front lawn. "That after tonight, the women's home would be fully funded and no one in town would oppose it."

"Well, yes, if your wishes are that serious, then prayer would be better. But you're supposed to wish selfishly on stars."

She didn't say anything for a while. "That's all I'm willing to wish for," she said softly but resolutely.

"You're too serious by half, you know."

She wrapped her arms around her waist. "My father would agree with you."

"Why?"

"Because he's been saying the same thing for years."

"No, I meant why are you so serious?"

She shrugged. "Once, I wasn't as serious and careful as I should've been, and ever since . . . Well, not all mistakes are easy to move on from."

What had her father told him that one day? That she was punishing herself for something? "What in your past makes you believe you shouldn't wish for more?"

Nothing but music answered him.

She turned from him, the lamps on each side of the portico throwing shadows across her profile. He moved so he could see her face better, studied every dip and curve. Though he knew most men wouldn't call her gorgeous, there was such a charming quality about her. Her heart was certainly lovely, but the cute nose, the long lashes, and the determined jaw made him wish he could help her find her smile more often. "What happened? Sometimes I get the feeling you think your life is beyond repair, yet you have wonderful family and friends, a job you're passionate about —"

"That is exactly why I don't need to wish on stars. I need nothing more."

It certainly was a good list. He wished he had parents as caring as hers and a job he felt as passionate about. But did she truly have no desire whatsoever for a family of her own? Not even an inkling of yearning for him? "Truly, you would wish for nothing more?"

"Well, I would, but pining for things only makes a heart sick. I'm surrounded by children who've endured more nightmarish things than I have, so I ought to be content with what I have . . . I have to be."

"But what about —"

"David." She reached over and put a hand on his arm.

Whatever he was going to ask fled his mind.

"I don't need to wish on stars because you've done better than any old star. You're the reason I've gotten my wish of a women's home. You've not only helped me, but you made it possible for the dreams and hopes of many women and children to come true. They may never know it was you, never be able to thank you, but God knows. I hope He rewards you greatly."

He reached over and clasped her hand before she let go. "I hope I can keep fulfill-

413

ing your wishes. Let me know what they are, and I'll do everything I can."

She stared at their hands, hers limp within his.

He squeezed her fingers, readying himself for her to slip her hand from his, but instead she intertwined their fingers and squeezed back. He looked back at where he'd seen that star.

As nice as a reward in heaven would be, I wouldn't mind the reward of Evelyn's heart here on earth.

When he turned back, he couldn't see the expression on her face clearly, though she certainly seemed to be looking at him intently. Could she see more of his face in the lamplight than he could see of her? What could he say that wouldn't ruin the moment, that would hint of his feelings without scaring her away?

After another minute she released his hand but continued to watch him.

"Tell me what you're thinking."

She shook her head, stepping back into a circle of light. "What I'm thinking shouldn't be said." She blinked her eyelids rapidly, her frown tight.

He scooted closer and captured her hand again. "Something to do with me?"

She turned her face away but didn't take

her hand from his. "Yes." Her voice was so breathless he might have imagined that answer.

"What?"

She just shook her head again.

He tried not to huff in frustration. After that whisper of a *yes,* she had to like him just a little bit, yet she seemed to think it necessary to tamp down those feelings. He didn't expect her to spill all her secrets just because he asked her to, but it surely wasn't emotionally healthy to keep herself bottled up either. With a finger to her chin, he gently brought her face back around. "You know you can tell me anything, right? We're friends."

The word *friends* seemed to relax her a bit, and she smiled slightly.

"Do you know how pretty you are?"

Her smile disappeared — as he should have expected. "That doesn't sound like something a friend would say. Besides, it's just the new gown and fancy hairdo."

"I'm not looking at the dress or the hair." He let his thumb caress her jaw, amazed that she hadn't backed away from his touch yet.

Many women wore "natural" makeup though they claimed they wore none, but Evelyn really hadn't worn any until tonight.

The pink in her cheeks, though a natural color, never disappeared, and the lampblack and Vaseline concoction he'd asked Marianne about once seemed to be on Evelyn's lashes.

The coloring made her prettier, he supposed, but that wasn't what stood out to him nearly as much as what she'd covered up. He'd noticed while they were dancing, and the harsh light of the lantern confirmed it.

He dared to move his hand, and she only stood there, looking straight at him as if mesmerized. He let his fingers trail along her hairline to her cheek, where he knew she had pox scars, but they were covered with some kind of flesh-colored makeup.

Masking them didn't make her lovelier, just . . . different. But no matter what she put on her face, it wouldn't change her eyes, the proverbial window to the soul, a tortured soul he longed to fix.

Her eyes closed and his heart sped up. Her lips were just inches away. Could she be wishing on a star after all? Was she waiting for a kiss?

The last notes of the string quartet slowed near the end of the song, and he leaned forward.

Her eyes flew open and she stepped out

of his reach.

And the song died.

"Oh, David."

The longing in the syllables of his name made his breathing speed up. He reached to cup her chin again, but she took another step back.

"I have to go now. Right now." And with that, she fled back to the ballroom.

His body shook slightly, and he sucked in air. Though he wanted to rush after her, he'd only embarrass her in front of a crowd — and as everyone had told him, he couldn't go too fast.

He turned to look out over the line of carriages heading off into the night, most likely headed to Lowe's hotel. When his heart settled, he looked back up to the few stars he could see. Maybe he didn't need to wish on any after all.

He'd nearly kissed her, and though she'd fled, he'd seen she wanted to kiss him too.

31

The cool of the morning hurried David through the main doors of his factory. The heavy heat of the furnaces would be welcome today, but until they were hot enough to warm the entire building, at least he was out of the wind.

The main floor of the factory was nearly empty, but off in a corner, Mr. Kerry was drinking a cup of coffee while reading the paper. David flipped open his timepiece. Did his foreman always come in this early before work?

The man must have heard the door, and after glancing up, he raised his hand in greeting.

"Good morning," David called. And it was. Every morning since the ball had been good. For the past three nights, he'd fallen asleep reliving how Evelyn had let him trail his fingers along her soft skin, how she'd looked at him with yearning, even if she hadn't acted on it.

Since then, nothing had brought his feet back down to earth — not the boarding-house's awful oatmeal, not his unending paperwork, not even an entire run of glass jars ruined.

After work yesterday, he'd gotten two more businessmen to financially contribute to Evelyn's project. For the past few evenings, he'd been following up on all the contacts he'd made at the ball. And after his talk with Queenie this morning, Evelyn's desire to help women might become a reality even before the women's home existed.

It seemed the best way to soften her toward him was to make her dreams come true. And she had softened to him over the past few weeks — she'd sought his arms when she was worried about her father, she'd watched him when she didn't think he'd notice, and on the balcony, she'd said his name in such a way he could have sworn an *I love you* lay behind the word.

And yet, she'd fled as if she were a fawn and he a huntsman.

If it weren't for Lydia's insistence that he'd be the best man for Evelyn, and Mr. Wisely's prayers that he could help his daughter open up, he'd likely have given up already.

What was he doing anyway? Marianne might never have acted as if she wanted to kiss him, but she certainly was a lot more comfortable to be around. He felt at home with her. Evelyn made him unsure of his every move.

But Evelyn's father had said it would be a long road. Did he have enough endurance for such a monumental task when he never could seem to stand against his own father for long? Could he keep going with such minimal encouragement?

Hmmph. Seems his thoughts had just plunged him back to earth again.

He took his time climbing the stairs to his office, looking out over the near-empty floor and imagining the bustle that would take over in about twenty minutes. At the top, he leaned on the railing and looked out through the little windows high up near the ceiling.

What could he do to stay in Teaville long enough to find out if he could ever scale the wall Evelyn put between them? He only had another month and a half before Nicholas planned to advertise for help. And even if he got far enough with Evelyn to have Nicholas hold off advertising, he wasn't sure he wanted to spend all day, every day at the orphanage. He did like several aspects of business — like tweaking projections, making things run more efficiently, and balancing the ledgers — all of which he'd have no chance to do at an orphanage.

Wait. Nicholas and Lydia had worked alone at the orphanage before the Wiselys took over, so what would keep him from running a business as Nicholas surely had?

He tapped the railing. He could run this factory during the day and help the orphans at night. Plus, if the orphanage was ever shut down or Evelyn decided she wanted to leave, he'd be able to provide for her without hiccup.

Nicholas never said a good male role model had to be present at the orphanage at all times. Perhaps a few soiled doves could help Evelyn during the day, as she'd once hoped.

It wouldn't be what Father wanted for his life — but was it what he wanted?

I need some advice, God, one way or the other. Help me figure out if I'm just fascinated by a woman I don't understand or whether I'm called to her for deeper reasons.

After filling his lungs with the cool air the furnaces would turn muggy within the hour, David pushed off the balcony and headed into the offices.

Mr. Elliot was already at work, a pen behind his ear, a stack of papers lying in front of him. If his invoice manager had had a family, he would've insisted the man not work so much, but since he had kept the office running so smoothly after Mr. Burns and his nephew had stomped out, David was more than willing to pay him for the extra hours.

"Good morning, Mr. Elliot."

The man looked up at him and then at his office door. "Good morning to you, Mr. Kingsman."

David leaned over to pick up a paper that had fallen to the floor, set it on Mr. Pennysworth's desk, then headed into his office.

But he stopped halfway through the door.

"Finally made it to work, eh?" Father sat behind his desk, his broad shoulders making David's chair look small. He used a pen to point at him. "I've always stressed it's best to start work an hour before everyone else — that's how you get ahead." He put down his pen and stared, his blue eyes narrowed as if trying to determine where best to stick the tip of a fishing knife to gut his own son. The man had never met a person he couldn't criticize to death.

David pressed his lips together, though his tongue itched to tell Father to return home. He turned his back on him and hung up his things. Since Father hadn't bothered to say good morning, neither would he. He'd thought today would be a good day on the way to the factory. Clearly he'd been wrong.

He pulled his flask out of his satchel. He was going to need a lot of coffee. "What are you doing here?" Thankfully his voice sounded on an even keel, despite the anxiety roiling inside him.

Father flipped over a stack of papers and picked up a folder. "When you refuse to do as I ask, what do you expect? This place should have already been under negotiation, and you haven't even put it on the market. I sent you a very explicit letter telling you we don't have time for you to fix things up."

David pointed at the ledger on the desk. "Have you looked at the books yet? I've gotten the profit margin up eight percent in just six weeks. Look at my trajectories." He stomped over and flipped open a notebook to a series of charts. "I've increased our output without hiring any more men, I've gotten seven new clients, I made several promising contacts this week, I've reinvested —"

"I'm not interested, son." Father let his

fist fall onto the desk like a heavily weighted ax.

Well, *he* was interested, and wasn't he a partner? "Of course, this business alone won't make us millionaires, but —"

"Exactly — it's not a business worth babying." Father's well-chiseled face was hard, but then, it was rarely ever soft. "What I need is the money this place will bring — as is."

"But if we reinvest our operational profits moderately to maximize —"

"Son, that's all fine and dandy in the long run, but I needed the profit from the sale. And then with the money you'd bring in marrying Marianne —"

"I'm not going to marry Marianne."

Father's gaze was as inflexible as his waxed mustache. "There's no one better suited for you."

To a certain extent, Father was right. He understood Marianne. He knew all her secrets, she understood family business, and they ran in the same circles. "But Marianne is not in love with me."

"Do you think her infatuation with your secretary matters?"

Father knew about that? "Yes, I think that matters." Though he wouldn't call it an infatuation.

"She'll get over it." Father went back to looking at whatever paper he had in front of him as if the subject was settled.

Before now, David would have simply found something else to do, and perhaps after Father had simmered, he'd quietly push for what he wanted. But that was before he'd met Evelyn. Before he knew Nicholas and Lydia and had seen firsthand that a man could be successful in business while also having a family he loved. And not just that he loved, but that he valued over his business endeavors. "Being forced to marry someone she doesn't love is not something Marianne will get over."

"Give her time."

"Even if time might help her, it won't help me. I don't want to be married to someone who doesn't love me." He licked his lips and swallowed against his tight throat. He already knew how it was to live with someone who didn't love him. How could he choose to do that to himself for the remainder of his life?

Father looked at him as though they'd never met before. "It's not as if you're interested in anyone."

David had to swallow twice before he could answer. It would be easier to keep things to himself, but he couldn't do that anymore. What kind of husband would he be if Father controlled his every dream? "That's not true."

Father stopped fiddling with the papers again. "It's not? Who are you considering? I've only heard of a few men with daughters wealthy enough down here to be in your social strata."

"She's not one of them and likely has nothing to her name."

"That's foolishness, son." He waved his hand dismissively and went back to flipping pages.

"Why would it be foolish if I love her?" He slapped a hand on the papers Father was using to ignore him. "I don't need money to be happy."

Father sighed as if he couldn't possibly believe David needed an explanation. "When considering marriage, you can't just take love into consideration. Within the year, your wife could die in childbirth, and then what would you have to show for it?"

He turned cold all the way down to his toes. His father had nothing to show for his marriage after his mother died? "Perhaps you'd have a *son* to show for it, Father."

"Well, yes, a child, but a wife?" He waved his hand in the air again. "The more you're attached to her, the harder it is when she's gone. It's not worth the heartache."

"Is that why you've treated me this way my whole life? Do you consider it my fault Mother died having me? You're getting revenge by making sure I'll never experience the love you did?"

His father blinked at him as if he wasn't sure his normally pliable son actually stood in front of him. "That love ripped my heart out, son. Business doesn't rip your heart out."

Father was indeed heartless, he couldn't argue that. "You're wrong. It's a father who cares more about his business than his own son that rips a person's heart out."

"Why do you think I do all of this?" He hit his fist against the desk. "I'm working to set you up so you can live as you deserve."

"I don't care about a large inheritance. I just want to be happy, and I can be as happy in Teaville as I can be in Kansas City — or Africa, for that matter." He closed the folder his father had been going through and took it away. "Let me have this factory. Keep the rest for yourself."

Father eyed him for a second, his mouth twitching. "No."

"And if your refusal drives me to dissolve the partnership?"

"Don't you even think about leaving me."

He pointed at him. Whether his hand was shaking from fear or anger, he couldn't tell. Both most likely.

David refused to look at Father's accusatory finger. "I thought you'd be happy to be rid of me."

"Don't be ridiculous." He waved the back of his hand at him as if their conversation had become as bothersome as a buzzing fly. "I need you to oversee the books and deal with people."

Really? Since when did Father ever *need* him? "But you've never been impressed with anything I do. You could easily replace me with someone you like better."

"Wrong, I sent you here because you were the best one to take care of this. Teaville is too small for me and my brashness. If I angered one person, I might anger them all. I've done well enough in the big city because there's plenty of people eager to make a deal there." He marched toward the window. "You could have sold this factory with ease, negotiated the daylights out of it, and left Teaville with everyone loving you. You're so inoffensive, you and the buyer likely would have become friends in the process. Me? I'd probably sell it for more than you — if I didn't manage to irritate everyone in town wealthy enough to purchase it."

Did his ears deceive him, or had Father rattled off several backhanded compliments? Did he actually think well of him in certain aspects, or was he just placating him? Did he actually love him but the only way he showed it was by creating a business empire for him? "I'm supposed to be a partner, so why didn't you tell me that was why you were sending me here? Treat me as an equal rather than bossing me around as if I'm still twelve."

He looked at David for a moment or two, his jaw moving in contemplation, then shook his head. "No, you're soft enough as it is."

Apparently expecting more than a handful of indirect praises in one day was unrealistic. "Then I'll stop being soft and tell you you're making a foolish decision. Keeping this place is smarter."

"But I need the money now." Father pushed back the hair on his forehead, pulling his wrinkled skin tight. Then he blew out a breath, and his shoulders bent inward. "I made a bad deal, son. A really bad one."

The man was just too calculating to make a bad deal. But he'd never seen his father wilt like that either. As much as David was tempted to tell him he couldn't care less, this was his father's entire world. He sat on the edge of the desk and shook his head. "Again, why didn't you tell me?"

"Who wants to admit to a failure if it can be fixed?" He stared off into space for a minute, then sighed. "If I don't come up with five thousand dollars to pay back Mr. Quaid by year's end, he'll no longer sell to us. And if anyone gets wind of why he's cutting off doing business with me, others will follow suit. That doesn't even take into account I've failed to pay the Jacobs brothers for the past two months."

If he could get this place running as it should, he could likely pay Mr. Quaid off in . . . eight months, maybe. Surely he could negotiate more time with Quaid. Unless there was more Father wasn't telling him. "Do you owe anyone else?"

"No, but it's not going to look good if we don't settle up, considering the other debts I have that have not been called in . . . yet. If others start refusing our business, the hit to our reputation would make our customers nervous and things could go downhill quickly. It's better to sell this place, pay the debt, and avoid the taint to our name completely."

Had Father been doing business like this all along? Maybe he shouldn't have been obeying Father's seemingly erratic commands without question. David took a moment to recall how involved they were with Quaid. "Why are you so concerned about Mr. Quaid supplying us anyway? If he can't appreciate how much business we've given him and grant us a bit of leniency, then maybe we should find ourselves a new supplier and scale things back. There are more important people you should try to win over than men who only look at you in terms of dollars and cents."

"Like who?"

"Like me."

Father just stared at him for a moment, then shook his head. "You'd rather us hold on to five percent of our holdings than clear our name with Quaid?"

"I'm afraid I really don't care one way or the other."

"Then what do you care about? Besides cooking and girly stuff."

David's fists clenched, wanting to prove with a jab to his father's nose just how manly he could be. "Being valued at more than five percent of your holdings, that's what I care about. Having someone be proud of what I can do, who supports me in my endeavors."

A ridge of skin popped up between Father's brows, and his mustache contorted as his mouth scrunched in confusion. "So it's all about you, then?"

"No, Father, it's all about others."

"Fine, if you want to marry someone else, do so, but I still want this factory sold by next month." He pulled a note from his chest pocket and held it out to him. "You'll have to break the news to Marianne though. She wanted you to have this as soon as I saw you."

Maybe he could end this silly business about Marianne right now. She'd told him she'd let him know when she and Calvin decided to become serious. He slipped the letter from Father's hands and tore it open.

Dear David,

I believe my dreams are only just that. Calvin won't consider me. I'm beginning to wonder if my parents are correct. Though I've fancied Calvin, you're the one I run to with all my problems and felt safe enough to talk to about my feelings for him. I can't think of anyone I'd rather have as a friend for the rest of my life than you. Perhaps we've been fighting our parents over this not because it's such a bad idea, but because we just wanted to have a say in the matter.

I'd like to talk when you get back. I

hope you're doing well for yourself. Your father is steamed, so perhaps you are. Best of luck with him.

Your Mari

"Well?" Father's eyebrows lifted.

He refolded the note and blew out a breath. If he'd gotten this letter a few weeks ago, he'd have caved — as Father seemed to expect, considering his triumphant expression.

But he didn't want to pick the easiest path anymore. He wanted to be like Mr. Hargrove when he told his parents that law school wasn't for him. He needed to forge his own path, live his own life, strive for the greatest reward — no matter how difficult it might be.

He could explain to Father that he was done capitulating, but talking with him had never truly worked. He'd have to prove himself by standing with conviction. This note didn't change the fact that he didn't want to marry Marianne. "Doesn't change anything."

Father stilled and pulled on his mustache. "It doesn't?"

Had he ever confused Father more than he had today? Hopefully the man would start trying to understand him instead of assuming he knew what his son thought.

"No, it doesn't." He looked at the clock and took in the sounds of the factory coming to life. "Now, excuse me. I need to get to work."

32

"Where do I put the dirty towels?" One of the two women David had just hired scuttled over to him as if afraid he'd manhandle her for forgetting. Kathleen had been skittish yesterday when Queenie had brought her and Bethany to meet him, and the fear that simply rolled off her made his heart ache.

He wanted to give her a hug, but knowing such a gesture would be the furthest thing from comfort for her . . . Well, how could he not wish God would come down and punish every man who took advantage of the red-light district and turned a woman into such a shell? He refrained from touching her and pointed across the factory floor. "You'll need to wash them first. You can do that in the washroom right there. Hang them up, and then tomorrow, one of my janitors will put them away in the closet. If you see any dry ones on the line, fold them and do the same."

"Yes, sir." She walked backward a few steps before turning around to scurry to the washroom.

Was she backing away so she could keep an eye on him or out of some sort of deference? It was quite unnerving, but at least Bethany acted more normal.

He walked over to where she was scrubbing the stairs. The two women would clean until nightfall, as they had last night, but he wanted to be sure they understood the list so they didn't run out of things to do. "Is there anything you need explained before I leave?"

Bethany pulled out the paper he'd given her earlier. Thankfully she could read, though Kathleen couldn't. He'd not considered what he would have done if both were illiterate.

She scanned the items. "Where's the mail room?"

He pointed up the stairs. "Third door. Don't move any papers, even if it looks a mess."

"I understand." She kept looking at him instead of going back to work.

"Is there something else I can help you with?"

She dropped her gaze onto the soapy

water glazing the stairs. "I'm not sure this is going to work, but I thank you for being willing to try."

"I don't know why it can't. I'll try my hardest if you will." Except he wasn't sure what to do come winter, since it would be best that they work after hours, and keeping the lights on later would only call attention to them working here alone. If the women's home didn't exist by then . . . he'd have to think of something else for them to do. "Remember, I want you to leave at least twenty minutes before nightfall, even if you don't finish the tasks for the day."

"Yes, sir. Thank you again." She picked up her brush and attacked the stair with a vengeance.

He'd gotten carried away trying to come up with ways to give Evelyn her dreams and gotten too far ahead of himself. When he'd asked Queenie if she knew of any women who'd want to escape the district, he'd not thought about them leaving the second they knew they could. But how could he possibly refuse to help, no matter how ill prepared he was? He'd give up all his comforts before he sent either back to her former vocation.

Without a women's home though, he'd had to find housing for them quickly, so he'd bought a tiny house that was, unfortunately, right next to the railroad tracks. It was available and cheap and nowhere near the bad part of town. It lacked charm, a floor, and windows, but they'd have a place completely their own.

"Also, remember, no overnight guests at the house without my approval." He felt bad for reminding her he would not pay for them to run a cottage house, but he didn't want any surprises either.

She colored. "Yes, sir."

Hmm, he'd thought a prostitute would be beyond blushing.

And now he understood the reservations Nicholas had about chugging full speed ahead with this ministry. So many things he hadn't thought of.

And what about the women's safety? He couldn't be around constantly. "Do you need me to walk you home each night?"

Bethany rocked back on her heels and worried her lip. "If someone recognizes us alone, we might be forced into a situation we can't escape, but if someone saw you walking us home . . . Well, I'm more concerned for your reputation than mine."

"I'll buy you something to defend yourselves with, then. And make sure you tell me if I can do anything else."

She swiped the back of her sleeve across

her face and sniffed. "Yes, Mr. Kingsman."

He reached out to give her shoulder a re-assuring squeeze but changed his mind and ran his fingers through his hair instead. These ladies didn't need to be touched without their permission ever again. "All right. Leave a note on my desk if you need anything." He'd debated last night whether they should be alone in his factory, and maybe he was a fool to let them work unsupervised, but he had to trust them.

"Good night, ladies." He nodded at Bethany and then waved at Kathleen, who'd stopped sweeping to stare at him.

He walked out of the still-hot factory into the crisp autumn air. Clicking the door shut behind him, he leaned against it for a second and blew out a breath.

He did not want to go to the hotel where Father was staying. Last night he'd visited him like a dutiful son should and endured hours of lecture.

However, Father had intended to spend today at the natatorium, hoping to attract buyers for the factory. Perhaps he should visit again, if only to discover whether or not Father had found anyone interested. Between his obligations to his father, the business, Kathleen and Bethany, and his heart, what was the wisest thing to do?

Breaking ties with Father completely might create more trouble than he could handle right now. But would staying tied to Father keep him from doing the best he could with the rest of his life?

He started his well-traveled route to the mansion. There was one major piece of information he needed before he could plan how to go forward, and to get it, he'd have to talk to Evelyn. Time was up. He might be going too fast, but his life wasn't giving him much choice.

He kept his hands in his pockets as he pushed himself forward. He likely knew her answer, but he had to have it outright. If she could be bothered to wish on a star, she'd insinuated it would have been for nothing more than getting the children and women of the district the help they needed — and he'd been doing his best to make that happen. Not just because it was her dream, but after getting to know Scott, Max, Caroline, Bethany, and all the others, how could he not get involved? How had he ignored that area in Kansas City? He'd been involved with a few charity projects back home, but he'd never once ventured into that part of town, hadn't once thought about reaching out to those in need there.

If he ended up back in Kansas City, he'd

start something to help the children and women there — Father's money would make that infinitely easier than if he forged out on his own.

But no matter what woman Father pushed him toward, he would only marry someone he could love to the fullest and who would love him back — even if the time was short.

Which meant Evelyn might not be the one for him, though his heart was tripping all over her. He wasn't going to leave before figuring out if he had any chance with her, or else he'd wonder forever.

When he reached the bottom of the mansion property, he stopped at the gate and looked up at the beautiful estate he might be living in. Not as wonderful as being in charge of his own place, but then, he wouldn't have to pay for the whopper of a heating bill Nicholas had to have. Would Evelyn want to stay here forever, or like Lydia, raise a family elsewhere but continue to help?

His insides started quivering as he forced himself to climb the hill.

How could he steel himself against getting turned down flat while drowning in hope?

By pushing forward.

By pursuing the life he wanted.

By accepting what God did or did not

have for him when he got his answer.

He climbed the stairs to the portico and clanked the knocker — perhaps for the last time.

Franklin answered but said nothing, only opened the door for him to come in.

But he couldn't cross the threshold. How could he ask Evelyn something like this with everyone watching, people listening, or children interrupting?

"Could you ask if Miss Wisely is available to talk?"

Franklin's brow furrowed. "Out there, sir?"

His throat tightened, and all he could do was nod.

Franklin left the door partially open, but not enough for David to see inside.

For five infinitely long minutes, he paced, forcing himself to breathe deep and slow in hopes of calming his wild pulse. *God, stop me if I shouldn't ask.*

The door whined open, and Evelyn stepped out with a shawl wrapped around her shoulders. "David, is something wrong?"

He'd find that out soon enough. "I came to tell you what I've done."

She stepped out farther and clicked the door shut behind her. "Oh, dear. Whatever it is, I know what kind of man you truly are. God loves you and will forgive you."

He smiled at how she immediately jumped to giving him the benefit of the doubt. He had God's love, that he knew, but whether or not he had hers was the question. "I meant that I now understand why Nicholas wanted to go slowly with the women's home, because I just forged ahead on my own and am now incredibly unsure if I've done the right thing."

There was a glimmer of a smile in her eyes. "How can helping anyone be the wrong thing?"

"If I can't follow through."

She crossed the porch to meet him. "Why wouldn't you be able to follow through?"

"Queenie sent two ladies to me yesterday willing to clean my factory and live in less-than-ideal conditions to do so. And my father showed up to sell the factory yester-day morning — but I can't turn the women out."

"Your father's here?" She sat on the low stone wall on the edge of the portico. "Why didn't you tell me? I suppose he's making things difficult?"

That was a rather tame way of putting it. He sat on the wall in front of her, knee to knee. "What would you think of me if I dissolved my relationship with my father? I'd

443

try to only break away from the business, but I can't fool myself into thinking that wouldn't break the rest of the relationship as well."

She rubbed at her chin. "Perhaps it would be a good direction. You could attempt to work on your relationship without the stress of doing business together."

"Actually, what I wanted to ask is, how would you personally feel if I took up residence in Teaville? The last time I asked, you told me you couldn't give me business advice, but I'm not asking for business advice."

She looked away, her throat visibly working hard to swallow. "Teaville surely can't compare to Kansas City."

"In some ways, no. But Kansas City doesn't have you."

She made a sound similar to that of a whimpering puppy and took a quick sideways glance at him. "Oh no, David."

He'd have mistaken the look in her eyes for someone in love if not for how her face contorted with tears. "I'm willing to stay here if I have a chance with you. I'm willing to go against my father. I'm willing to be the one who takes over the orphanage so you can keep it —"

"Please, make your decisions without any

thought to me." Her voice was scratchy and thick, and she dropped her gaze to her lap. "I thought I'd made it clear I wasn't interested in getting married."

"But I just saw how you looked at me." He tipped her face back up, but she kept her eyes shut, her lids sealed with glistening teardrops. "And the way you looked at me the night of the ball, the way you wanted to kiss me. I know you have feelings for me. What I don't know is why you hate the idea of marriage so much you don't want me to stay."

Her eyelids fluttered open. "Please don't ask me."

He took her free hand, thankful she didn't pull away. "You told me once you wanted to be friends, but you don't let anyone know what's tearing you up inside — not Lydia, not me, not your parents. How can we help you if you refuse to let us in?"

"It's a secret," she whispered.

"I want to hear all your secrets, and I want you to know all of mine." Though he didn't know what else he could tell her, since the week he'd stayed with her at Mr. Hargrove's he'd laid out everything before her . . . yet she seemed determined to keep everything from him.

"No, you don't really want to know."

"Let me be the judge of that." He pulled back the hair that had fallen into her eyes, letting his fingers trace the scars that weren't blotted out with makeup. "I promise. Whatever you're hiding, it won't make me love you any less."

"Love?" she croaked, silent tears running down her face. "You shouldn't love me, David. As you said, I'm not even that great of a friend. How could you want anything more from me?"

"Because I'm in love with everything about you. From your passion for helping others to your confounded secret."

She looked down at her lap, where her hands were strangling the fabric of her skirt. "I'm so sorry. I never meant for this to happen. I thought I was the only one in danger."

Danger? Though she sat rigidly, he kept a hold of her hand, caressing the back of it with his thumb. "What happened that keeps you locked away from us?" He'd told her the truth just now. He had dreamed up every insane possibility that might have convinced her she shouldn't get married, but none had made him feel any different. "Do you have an illegitimate child?"

She shook her head so hard, he was certain that wasn't a lie.

"A man left you at the altar? Someone

beat you up?" With every shake of her head, he rattled off another possibility. "A family member abused you? You gave yourself to a man and feel you don't deserve to get married? You had an accident that will keep you from having children? You are an adopted child prostitute?"

All she did was shake her head and close her eyelids tighter.

"Then what? Tell me. Let me help you work through it."

She slipped her hand from his and stood. "If only I'd been able to ignore your charm, stay cold, and drive you away like the others. For it'd be far better that you hated me for being a heartless woman than what I actually am."

"And what are you?"

"A married one."

His eyelids were the only thing that worked.

That . . . that was not how she was supposed to answer his proposal. A *yes,* a *no,* a *let me think about it* — but not that.

Perhaps he hadn't heard her right? He wet his lips and forced out the question. "Did you say you're married?"

She wrapped her arms around her chest as if her heart hurt as much as his did. "Maybe."

He pinched the bridge of his nose but felt nothing. His body had to be in shock, since his skin was numb. "What do you mean 'maybe'?"

"I mean, I'm not certain, but as far as I know, I am."

He looked at his feet, waiting for the sound of his heartbeat to register in his ears and confirm his heart still thumped inside his chest, though it felt as if it had burst through his ribs and left him behind. He closed his eyes and tried to piece it together. "But . . . you're *Miss* Wisely."

"Actually, I'm Mrs. Bowden." Her voice clogged and a tear slipped down her cheek.

If she'd given him any other tear-filled response he would've gathered her up and held her until her crying subsided, but how could he hold her now, knowing she was *Mrs. Bowden*?

"My parents don't even know . . . ." Her voice died, and she looked at him with eyes so sad they looked ready to fall apart. Though perhaps her eyes only mirrored the sorrow in his. "I'm so sorry, David."

He stood and walked backward until he hit a portico column.

She took a step closer, but he could only stare at her forehead.

"I always did as much as I could to

discourage any man from having an interest in me. But with you . . . I thought because you'd return to Kansas City and would only be here for a short time, that we could be friends. You were so nice, so determined to be my friend no matter how I treated you."

"I can't fault you there. You certainly did keep me at a distance. It's my own fault for ignoring your signals." Perhaps he was more stubborn than he or Father thought. Or maybe more foolish. Either way, he was definitely paying for it.

"With how I've been feeling . . . Well, there've been several times lately that I began to think I shouldn't keep my secret any longer, but I figured I'd tell people after . . . after you were gone, so you wouldn't think . . . less of me." She stood there for a moment, then slumped and turned. "I can imagine how much you hate me right now. I'm so sorry, and I understand why you'd never want to see me again."

He stumbled forward and snatched her sleeve when she headed back toward the mansion. "No. You said you were uncertain if you were married. I don't understand how that's possible, so tell me everything. I need to know."

She pulled her hand away for a second to wipe her face but placed her hand right back in his, squeezing hard enough that his shocked nerves actually felt pain.

He tugged her back to sit on the wall and sat beside her, though this time, they both faced forward, a chasm between them. The only thing that registered was the sound of the blood rushing in his ears as he stared at the mansion's front door.

After a few false starts and two throat clearings, Evelyn took a deep breath. "My father was a pastor in Topeka before we moved to Teaville. I was a rebellious seventeen-year-old when James jumped off a train with four other boys who rode the rails. He was everything my father disliked. He flirted with all the young ladies, had a disregard for authority, was the epitome of a rake. And I was the pastor's daughter — expected to be perfect simply because of who my father was. I won't get into everything I did to exasperate Daddy, but once, after one of Daddy's parishioners took him to task for how I was behaving, he called me 'a disappointment.' And to my everlasting shame, I decided to show him what a real disappointment I could be."

"I suppose James was instrumental in doing so?"

She nodded. "I just meant to make Daddy squirm. I didn't expect to succumb to

James's charm."

Fidgeting beside him, she played with her fingernails. "We got it in our heads to show him how grown up we were by eloping once I turned eighteen. If Daddy so much as got a hint, he would have stopped us. So we waited until summer. I normally spent summers in Wichita with my great-aunt. She had dementia, so I read her books and kept her entertained. I'm not sure she even understood James and I had married, not that we lived with her. She probably didn't even realize I left at night, and my business was of no concern to the servants, so they'd never thought to inform my aunt or my parents." She brought up her legs and wrapped her arms around them, like a hurt child hiding in a corner.

"But the honeymoon was over in a few short days. James turned out to be exactly what my father feared. The moment the law said I was his, he dropped all pretense. He no longer hid that he drank, smoked, and gambled. He refused to attend church with me and my aunt." She looked off into the distance as if she could see back in time. "And we fought — all the time. I knew deep down I couldn't continue my rebellious ways into adulthood, but James didn't see it that way — and why should he have? I hadn't caught his interest by acting as I'd been taught.

"James left after we'd been married five weeks. He left a note saying our marriage had been a mistake but didn't tell me where he was going." The sound of heartbreak made her voice squeak. "After all these years, I'm not even sure why he married me, but I had certainly become the disappointment I'd set out to be, and it didn't feel good at all."

David took her hand and caressed her skin with his thumb. He couldn't imagine her pain, even if his own dreams were dying an extraordinary death.

She took a few exaggerated breaths, obviously trying to keep her emotions from completely bursting. "When I went home at the end of the summer, I didn't tell them what I'd done. When Aunt Meredith died five months later, I let my secret go with her to the grave."

Except being married wasn't something you could just forget about. "Why did you never tell your parents?"

"At first I couldn't bear the shame of it, didn't want to talk about it. I'd talked myself into believing it was all their fault for their unrealistically high expectations of me and locked myself in my room. But truthfully, I'd hoped James would come back and rescue me from humiliation, and I didn't want to endure their censure in the meantime. I didn't want to hear 'I told you so.' I'd decided I'd wait until James returned with some sorry tale that would prove I was right about him being a good man deep down and that Daddy was wrong."

She fished out a handkerchief and wiped her face. "Years went by, and I realized I was wrong to not have said anything. But the longer you live with such a secret, the harder it is to bring it up when nothing could change the outcome."

"But surely something can be done." He started doing the math. "How long has he been gone?"

"Nine years."

He'd been sixteen. She'd been out of his reach before he'd even thought about marrying.

"After several years, I did check into my options. I could either try to declare him dead or divorce him on grounds of abandonment. If I couldn't find out definitively what happened to him but declared him dead, and I remarried, if he showed up later, the courts could declare my second marriage void. The lawyer said that was a risk I'd have to consider if a judge would even grant such a declaration. And as the daughter of a pastor, the very word *divorce* made me want to die inside. How much more of a disappointment could I be to my father than to become a divorcee?" She swallowed noisily and looked away.

"Have you not tried to find him?"

"He'd once mentioned mining in California, so for years, I wrote big towns along the west coast asking for lists of people in boardinghouses and hotels. Every time I had money for a stamp, I'd inquire after James, but never got a response. A few years ago, I gave up. I didn't have the money to hire someone to find out what happened to him, and letters were getting me nowhere. But recently, I did borrow money to hire an investigator, but there have been no leads."

"I'm so sorry."

She shook her head. "Don't be. Despite messing up my life forever, I'm glad I got married."

He rubbed his ear. "You're glad?" And here he'd thought James's whereabouts was what barred them from each other, not any love she still felt for her scoundrel of a husband.

"Yes. For nearly two years, I railed at God, blaming Him for not saving me from myself. But then I realized I was upset with God because He hadn't patched up my mistakes, despite me never giving Him my loyalty to begin with. During those dark days, I realized how desperately I needed Him and truly gave Him my life."

Thankfully God had gotten her attention, but what a price. "So then why'd you keep your marriage a secret after that?"

"Pride." She sniffed. "And it could hurt Daddy. We weren't rich, so there was nothing he could do to help me. Then when our church in Topeka split, it was hard enough for him to find a job when both factions were upset with him. His references weren't the best, so I just couldn't add to his problems. A spinster daughter wasn't the weighty baggage an abandoned or divorced one would be whenever new churches were deciding on calling him. Besides, I'd already acted as if nothing had happened for two years, and it was easier to continue." She shrugged.

He couldn't have done it. "How were you able to keep up such a lie?"

"I never lied." She snapped her head up. "I just never told anyone what happened."

"So you didn't tell the truth?"

"I didn't reveal a secret. Please don't argue semantics with me. It's not as if I haven't been in turmoil over it for nine years

— especially lately." Her lips quivered as she pressed them tightly together — whether in an effort to keep from railing at him or to keep from crying, he couldn't tell.

He reached over and squeezed her hand. "After nine years, not a single court in Kansas would deny you a divorce by abandonment."

She stared at his hand holding hers but didn't pull away. "I've thought about it occasionally, but I still can't do it without knowing for certain what happened to him. What if James is alive and something really awful did happen? What if he was captured by Indians or forced to work in the bowels of some mine? And while there, scared that every day would be his last, he begged God for a second chance — to be free to come home to me and be the husband he ought to be?"

He shook his head, not wanting to sympathize with her husband, but knowing what he'd want Evelyn to do if it were him. But truly, nine years had passed. "I'd say you are highly optimistic."

"Stranger stories are told every day."

"True." He couldn't deny it, though sad ones like what he was going through tonight seemed much more common.

"And if I divorced James without knowing

what happened, solely to pursue another man, what kind of vow could I promise to keep with my new husband?" She got up and turned her back to the mansion, her face dripping silent tears. "Right now, my heart is falling apart, my father's unwell, and I may very well lose my job at the orphanage, but I have to cling to the hope that God cares for me, that He only says no because He intends better for me. And yet, why has He left me in the dark? Why did He . . ." She held out her hand toward him but shook her head and looked away.

Why hadn't God let her know what happened to James this whole time? Why hadn't He stifled his feelings for Evelyn since He knew this was her secret all along?

God could have stopped his heart — it sure had stopped now.

David stared at the ground between his feet. He wasn't sure he had enough faith right now to believe God was telling them no because He intended to give them better. What could be better than a future with Evelyn? "You said you've hired a private investigator?"

"Yes."

"Maybe I could hire a better one."

She shook her head. "Nicholas is taking care of the expense. I'm sure he chose the best man he could find."

"And what has he found out?"

"Nothing so far." She let out a shaky sigh. "I'm not sure how long Nicholas will be willing to pay the man if he can't find any clues whatsoever."

His knees bobbed in nervous indecision. The investigator could give her good news, like that she was a widow. He scrunched his eyes up tight. He would not wish for a man's death! He shot up and paced. An investigator could just as easily return with no information, and she would be in limbo forever — and as much as he wanted to be with her, he'd not force a woman to go against her convictions for his pleasure.

Well, he'd come for an answer, and he'd gotten one. Given her current situation, there was no reason to stay in Teaville. "I plan to return to Kansas City shortly. My father will be selling the factory here."

"What about the ladies you hired?" She bit her lip between her teeth.

Of course, she'd be more worried about their future than her own. It was one of the reasons he loved her.

No! He wouldn't let himself love her, or rather he wouldn't let himself think in that direction anymore. Unless God worked some sort of miracle, there was no future for them. And he couldn't even pray for her to get out of her marriage without going against everything he believed in.

"I won't leave until I can figure out arrangements for them." Since he was likely going to be incapable of thinking about anything much besides his broken heart, he wasn't sure how quickly that would happen. "But I won't stay longer than necessary."

She sniffed. "I suppose I'll never see you again?"

His insides clenched. Why hold on to hope? *Hope deferred maketh the heart sick.* He wasn't sure how his heart could feel more ill than it did now, but if he was to have any hope of moving on — as he absolutely had to — he had to take the truth of God's Word to heart and try his best to avoid becoming more attached to her. "Depends on God and how our lives go, I suppose. But I'll pray you get an answer, because —" He cleared his throat to cover the fact that he'd almost told a married woman he loved her. That was an emotion he had no business expressing or feeding any longer.

He'd been right when he said her secret wouldn't make him love her any less.

But it had certainly made it so he couldn't love her any more.

"One last hug from a friend?" The tears rolling down her face were his undoing.

He brought her close, trying not to notice how good she felt in his arms. He pressed her tightly against him until he was worried he might break her. After one last sniff of her hair, he set her back. They stared at each other for a moment or two.

He couldn't tell her he loved her, but maybe she'd see it in his eyes, feel it in the pressure of his hands.

If he didn't leave soon, he'd steal a kiss — something he had no business even thinking about, for stealing it would be. "Goodbye," he choked.

He'd never thought he could hate a word so much.

After brushing away a tear falling down her cheek, he forced himself to let go of her hands and leave his heart behind.

33

David was late, but he didn't care. The buzz of factory work surrounded him while he took the balcony stairs to his office slower than molasses on a cold winter's morning. He stopped in the middle of the stairs and fished his coffee flask from his satchel before continuing up. If only they could make coffee in the office. He was going to need a lot of it.

He looked blankly out over the sea of workers as he took a drink. He ought to check in with his foremen, like he did most every morning, but things looked like they were running well enough.

Thankfully the whirl of machines and voices helped drown out the thoughts he was trying to repress. He'd done enough thinking about Evelyn last night. He'd begged God to fill his life with something else instead of Evelyn but had refused to ask Him why things had happened as they had, because he couldn't imagine how any answer would satisfy.

After screwing the lid back on, he forced himself up the rest of the stairs — to do what, he had no idea. He could probably pull himself together enough to prevent a catastrophe — maybe. But he wasn't likely to get much done. The business projections he needed to graph would likely turn into sketches of Evelyn.

He shook himself before entering the outer office, widening his eyes to look more alert. He didn't want the men questioning him on why he looked as if he hadn't slept all night. But if any of them dared, he'd send him out for more coffee. He took a deep breath, rolled his shoulders, and marched in.

Mr. Elliot didn't even look up from his desk. But Mr. Pennysworth had the gall to look at him sympathetically after just one glance.

He must look terrible to warrant that look.

"Sir?" Mr. Pennysworth came around his desk. "Are you — ?"

David handed him his flask. "Could you get me more coffee?"

The man frowned at the silver cylinder, clearly not relishing doing something outside of his normal duties. "All right. But perhaps you should know —"

"Just coffee, black. Buy me another flask. Fill that one too." He moved past him and escaped into his office.

Except he'd chosen the worst escape route in the history of the world. "Father, what are you doing here? Weren't you going to the natatorium again?"

Behind David's desk, Father was pacing with a piece of paper wadded tight in one hand. "You're late."

Normally his heart would sink at the thought of enduring another lecture about his shortcomings, but it had already bottomed out. "What's the matter now?" He crossed over to the chair reserved for clients and sank into it, tilting his head back to stare at the ceiling.

"This!" With jerky motions, Father uncrumpled the paper in his hand and pulled down his reading glasses. "James Blickey, Ira Crull, Barry Kenshaw, Adam Barrow, Alfred Baymount, Oliver Morgan, Harold Schmidt —"

"What about them?" He recognized two as workers assigned to Foreman Kerry, and one was the head janitor. A few others sounded familiar, though he couldn't put any faces to the names.

"They've all quit. Twenty-six men so far

this morning. And you weren't even here."

"Twenty-six?" A broken heart was one powerful sedative, for his heart didn't even accelerate over the likely demise of this business. Though why would they all quit in one day? He'd been doing so well, everyone seemed to be happy with his leadership. . . . "What did you do, Father?"

"I didn't do anything!" He crumpled the list again and plopped down in David's chair. "How am I going to sell this place if we're having a mutiny?"

"Let me figure out what happened." He wasn't going to let Father blame everything on him without a shred of evidence. "Excuse me."

He shoved himself out of the chair, passed through the outer office, and looked for Mr. Kerry in the sea of workers. There were definitely gaps about the place, but as he'd noted earlier, things seemed to be running smoothly. But what had prompted twenty-six men to quit the same day?

Mr. Kerry was hefting a pallet of jars onto a cart in the southeast corner.

David descended and looked around as he made his way to his most competent foreman. A few men looked at him with raised eyebrows or narrowed eyes, but most stayed focused on their work. Despite the crowd looking thinner, nothing seemed to be backed up or running amiss. How had Mr. Burns done such a terrible job running this place considering the quality of the leadership and the ethic of the workers?

"Mr. Kerry?"

The man stopped before picking up another pallet. "Yes, sir?"

He gestured for him to follow and walked out a side door.

Standing in the alley, he waited for Mr. Kerry to wipe his brow.

"Can you tell me why so many men have quit this morning? Mr. Crull and Mr. Blickey work with you, I believe."

"Yes, and I lost O'Rourke, Whitehead, and Button as well."

"Why?"

"Frankly, sir. They're up in arms about you hiring prostitutes."

He closed his eyes. How did anyone find out about that already? "They don't work here when anyone else does. No one lost their jobs because of them."

"They say they don't want to be touching what those women are touching — the principle of the thing."

"The principle of the thing?" Did they not realize that whether at a hotel or on a streetcar, they touched things people of all shapes and sizes touched?

"I'm sorry, sir. I'm afraid you'll lose a few more over the week. Some are still stewing." He looked down at his shoes for a moment, his hands clasped behind his back, but then he looked up again. "However, I don't think it's truly because the women are prostitutes, but rather because some of these men 'know' them. Their presence is like salt in a guilty conscience. Having them in the building and getting paid for decent work makes the women feel real."

"When have they not been real?"

"I once was a stupid young man." Mr. Kerry's voice lowered and he didn't quite look David in the eye. "One day, I saw what a man could do to a woman he thought unworthy of being treated as a human . . . and let's just say, when a man starts to sympathize with those affected by his vices, he can't enjoy them anymore — not unless he has no heart whatsoever." Mr. Kerry played with his wedding band. "But even so, if you want to keep from losing any more workers, it'd be best to get rid of the women."

Doing anything that would drive away good workers was a foolhardy business move — but if he turned the women out, what could they possibly do besides return

466

to the district? Runyan wasn't willing to hire them for shoe repair until there was a women's home built.

"If I may say something more, sir?"

David shrugged.

"I admire the spirit behind what you're trying to do, but it might be too much too soon."

It would certainly be easier to stop trying. But Mr. Kerry would not be the one who had to tell Kathleen and Bethany that it was too soon to help them. "When will it ever be the time to help desperate women if not now?"

The man lowered his gaze. "Good luck, then."

"Continue on, Mr. Kerry. If someone wants to quit, send them up." He left his foreman and marched through his workers without even looking at them. Which ones were grumbling? Were any on his side? Some had to be since not everyone had walked out.

But he supposed he'd asked for it. Evelyn and the Lowes had stressed anonymity would be key to helping the women have a chance to start a new life, and how could that be achieved in the same town they'd worked? He should have figured that out sooner, if he'd only stopped to recall how every businessman besides Nicholas balked at the idea of hiring the women in any capacity.

Father was still pacing when he returned to the office.

Might as well cut straight to the lecture. He put his hands on his hips and sighed. "They quit because of me."

Father said nothing, only stood there waiting.

"I hired two women to clean the factory at night. They are former prostitutes looking to reform. Evidently some men cannot bear to touch a doorknob one of these women might have cleaned, and they decided to quit."

Father moved his mouth as if trying to find words that weren't curses. "Of all the things —" He hit the wall with the side of his fist. "Son, I can't even . . ." He turned and glared at him. "I'm going to tell Fred MacDonald he can have the place for the price he offered yesterday before he finds out. Right after I fire your harlots."

So he'd already found a buyer? The quicker they could get out of this town, the better. "All right, then."

Father's head jerked. "All right?"

He held up both hands in surrender. "Do what you wish with the factory. You'll have no fight from me."

Father just stood there blinking. "Truly?"

"Yes." Perhaps he was about to actually make Father happy for once. "I'll pack for Kansas City and talk to Marianne."

"Just like that?"

What else was he to do? "Yes, just like that."

"I thought there was a woman you were interested in here."

A woman he was interested in. It sounded so normal, so mundane. The one time he'd seriously pursued a love interest, he'd chosen so badly — no, there was nothing about Evelyn that was bad . . . just unfortunate. His throat grew warm and tight, but he swallowed hard against the feeling, raised his chin, and met his father's gaze evenly. "I was mistaken."

"Then good." He turned to grab his coat off the hook. "I'll take care of this mess. You go home to Marianne."

Right, go home. But he couldn't until he saved those women somehow. "Let me be the one to tell the women they've lost their jobs."

"You'll be better at that anyway." Father buttoned his suit coat. "Before you leave, I need to tell you about the Mondale account. You can get to work negotiating that once you get home."

Yes, because after this disaster, the first thing he wanted to do was jump into business negotiations. But if he'd ever been worried about having job security, it seemed he had to worry no more. This whole thing had gone bust, yet Father wasn't even threatening to disown him.

It was a small blessing, and at the moment, he wasn't about to complain about the scraps he got.

34

Sitting beside Daddy's sickbed, Evelyn stared at her father's hand still holding hers. She hadn't looked at her parents throughout her confession, not wanting to see the pity in their eyes. The fact that he hadn't pulled his hand away, but was holding tighter, made her want to cry.

But she wouldn't. After she'd started working with the orphans, she'd decided to cry no more tears for herself. Max, Scott, Alex, and all the others had worse lives than she did, and none of it was their fault.

She'd vowed to spill tears for them and them alone.

And she'd already broken that vow this week with David.

When no one said anything, she looked up. Momma's eyes were indeed filled with the pity she'd never wanted to see. "I'm all right, Momma." Although, knowing David was leaving forever, she wasn't sure if that was the truth. Nicholas had said two weeks ago he'd gotten a report from the investigator that claimed things didn't look promising, so her situation hadn't changed — maybe never would.

She would have to be all right — in time, lots of time.

"Honey, dearest." Momma moved her chair to sit beside her. "Why didn't you tell us?"

"Early on, Daddy and I were so at odds, I just couldn't imagine what he'd do. I really thought he might disown me." She stared at the star pattern on the quilt. "Without parents or a husband, I was afraid of where I would go. Then after keeping the secret so long, it was just easier to continue doing so. I never lied, I just . . . never explained."

She took a sip of the tea Momma had brought in. "Once we started helping the orphans, I heard Nicholas advise a prostitute he was relocating that she should keep her secrets so she could go on with life. I decided I needed to stop feeling guilty for doing the same. If any man had interest in me, I ignored him until he moved on — but that didn't work with David." She played with the frayed edge of Daddy's quilt. "Anyway, without money for a private investigator, there wasn't anything I could do. And if I asked you to spend your life savings on one and he turned up nothing, I'd have ruined your life even more."

"You can't ruin our life." Momma rubbed her shoulders. "But we could have helped you live a better one if we'd understood."

Evelyn lifted her shoulders, then hopelessly let them fall. "Then I would have put you in the same position as I am whenever someone asks why I'm not married yet. Besides, once I turned my life over to God and my attitude changed, you both practically beamed at me. I didn't want to dampen your pride or explain how you'd likely never have grandchildren because of me."

Daddy tightened his grip on her hand still resting in his. "Honey, we don't love you because you are perfect or would give us grandchildren. We love you just because you're ours."

She finally looked up at her father.

His big blue eyes were glassy with unshed tears.

"So you don't look down on me now?" Her voice shook.

"I look at you as hurt, and I don't like my little girl hurt." Daddy reached over with his other hand to run a finger down her cheek where an escaped tear had trickled.

He leaned over with some obvious effort and kissed her head like he always did. "I'm just glad you finally told us. Now I'll have the privilege to pray more specifically that things will turn out all right for you. Or rather, better than all right. I want my daughter to have the best life possible — following God, being loved."

"But, Daddy, what if the investigator finds nothing? What do I do then? I've had the lawyer tell me all the options. Declaring him dead would likely be impossible since there is no known event that would persuade a judge to give me that verdict. And since I don't know where James is, abandonment isn't certain, so I figured it would be better to stay married and keep my vow until I know for certain he'd broken his."

Daddy leaned back against his pillows and closed his eyes. The ticking of the clock became audible again, and she glanced at his chest to make sure he still breathed. Seems he'd only fallen asleep. Just as she thought to turn toward Momma to see what she thought, Daddy rolled his head toward her.

"Even if you got a divorce, nothing's going to erase what you did or who you are. And if it is true that James is still alive, we'll pray for the same thing — that you will be able to live the best life possible under the circumstances."

She hung her head and sniffed back tears. Telling David about this three days ago had made her heart hurt more than when James had left, but telling her parents made her feel freer.

When she could trust herself not to cry over knowing now that she should have told them sooner, she got up and planted a kiss on Daddy's forehead, trying not to show him any pity for his droopy face when he'd not shown her any after listening to her story. "I love you, Daddy."

She went over and gave her mother a hug. "I love you too. I wish I could stay, but I can't leave Lydia alone any longer." She stood but kept a hold of her mother's hand. "Will you pray someone good will take over the orphanage? I have a feeling I won't be there much longer, for one reason or another."

"Of course we will, sweetheart. We've been praying that for a while now."

Likely ever since they'd decided to retire earlier than she'd expected. They'd never bothered to tell her about that, and since it now affected nothing, there was no reason to bring it up.

"Thank you." She grabbed the thick coat

she'd brought since the weather had turned chilly and damp and went outside to hail Mr. Parker.

He was huddled on top of the driver's seat in his oilskin, his hat pulled down low. Why he was always trying to prove he could stand the weather as well as the horses, she didn't know, but it was time to let him return to his family.

"Take me home please, Mr. Parker." She blinked at her words, since the house she'd just exited had been her home for much longer than the orphanage — and might become her home once again if whoever was hired to oversee the orphans felt it best she live elsewhere. She climbed into the carriage just as the rain let loose.

She closed the windows and leaned back against the seat.

Oh, Lord, I feel stalled. I know Daddy's always saying we don't have to know how things will work out to trust that our steps of obedience will get us where you want us to go, but I don't even know what you want from me now. I don't know what step to take.

The carriage rattled over the brick streets, and she kept her eyes closed, praying without even knowing what she was praying. Needing direction, needing hope.

The raindrops suddenly ceased on the carriage top as the vehicle stopped beneath the huge columned portico. Home.

"Hello!" A strange male voice called — at least she couldn't place the voice.

"Sir," Mr. Parker responded, and then the carriage rocked as he got down. "Has no one answered your knock?"

"They have, but they told me Miss Wisely would be arriving soon, so I said I would wait out here."

Her heart leapt into her throat. She'd just been praying God would tell her where she was to go next. Had He only been waiting for her to tell her parents her secret to give her that next step?

"It's not the nicest weather for standing about outside," Mr. Parker responded.

"No, it sure isn't."

She leaned closer to the window. Did the voice belong to James? His voice hadn't been very distinctive, and who knew what it sounded like after nine years. If Mr. Parker opened her door now, she wasn't sure she'd be able to climb out, let alone take one single step.

"But there's a baby whose scream —"

"No need to explain further, sir." Mr. Parker chuckled. "That child could drive away a pack of wolves."

"She definitely wouldn't make it pleasant

for them."

"Miss Wisely is just inside here."

"Wonderful." The man's voice was even and calm. Surely James's voice would have held some emotion.

The door opened and she caught sight of a thin man, likely in his forties, with a shock of red hair spilling out from under his hat.

Her heart started working again. Not James.

"Miss Wisely?" He came forward to help her down.

"Yes?"

Maybe he was one of the businessmen Nicholas or David had rubbed elbows with the night of the ball, but then, he could have talked to Nicholas about anything related to the women's home.

"I'm Detective Cruse." He took her hand, and she alighted.

"Good afternoon, detective." This had to be the man Nicholas had hired on her behalf. Her hands grew sweaty, and her throat tightened at the possibility this man could end years of uncertainty in a matter of seconds.

Mr. Parker climbed back up to his seat and headed for the carriage house.

"I hope you don't mind if we stay out here. Though I'm sure there are rooms where the baby's crying will not be overly loud, the fact that I can't hear the wailing out here means no one can hear us in there. Since our conversation will be of a sensitive nature, I'm assuming you'd like to keep what we talk about to yourself."

All she could manage was a nod. She followed him to the low wall on the edge of the porch and sat. The rain created a curtain of water behind them as it poured off the portico.

He sat a few feet from her, then pulled the satchel off his shoulder. "Mr. Lowe told me I should deal directly with you."

"All right." Could he not see how much she was trembling? Why couldn't he hurry and tell her what she wanted to know?

"I was hired to track down a James Bowden."

She clenched her hands so tightly, they were losing feeling. "And?"

"I found him."

35

Detective Cruse pulled out some papers and frowned at them. "I could give you these, Miss Wisely, but I think I should probably explain them first."

Goodness, couldn't he just tell her where he'd found James? Evelyn wrapped her arms around herself and shivered in the damp cold.

"It would have been helpful if you'd told Mr. Lowe that Mr. Bowden was your husband. That would have saved me time. I started looking in California, as Mr. Lowe suggested, but James Bowden resides in South Dakota, on a homestead he's had for the past seven years."

So not trapped in a mine, captured by Indians, or lying in some hospital with amnesia. Which likely meant she had indeed married the worst of men.

"He started working for a rancher by the name of Lester Finley in 1901 when his funds got low."

Two years after he'd left her. Had he gone in the direction of California at all? Seems she'd wasted a lot of stamps.

"He tried to write you in Topeka and Wichita for money, but the letters were returned undeliverable."

They'd moved by then, and Topeka was too big for the post office master to know everyone in town — not that the postmaster in any town she'd lived in would know her by her married name.

"Mr. Bowden struck up a rather . . . friendly friendship with the rancher's daughter."

Her breath stuttered out. She knew the chances of him sleeping with other women the entire time were likely high, but that didn't stop the knife in her gut at knowing for certain. Now she had grounds for divorce, not only abandonment but adultery. Still, having to go in front of the court and share such details in front of strangers made her want to curl up in a ball and hide.

Detective Cruse frowned up at the rain that came down with insistence. "At the end of 1901, he sought a divorce from you on the grounds of your abandonment."

"What?" The rain was quite loud. She couldn't have heard him right. "He said I

481

abandoned him?" At the detective's nod, she spurted, "But he abandoned me."

"Correct." He smiled.

How could he smile about that?

"However, one cannot incriminate oneself, so he chose to incriminate you. He also likely did not work very hard to find you, for if you tried to counter him and sought a divorce on the grounds of adultery, you could have made it so he would be unable to marry again."

"So . . ."

He turned the papers around on his lap and pointed at the bottom of the page. "I'm afraid you've been found guilty of abandonment and have been divorced since February 24, 1902."

Guilty? She put her hand to her throat. "So that means, I'm . . . a criminal?"

He cringed. "You're at fault anyway."

She double-checked the date. "But if he'd have written me before 1902, I would've gone to him!"

"Yes, so I checked on the legality of your divorce." Detective Cruse took the pencil out from behind his ear and walked it through his fingers. "If there was no reasonable attempt to hand you divorce proceedings, your divorce could be considered void and his second marriage annulled. However, he did the minimum the law required. He sent you notice in Topeka and another to your great-aunt in Wichita, who was dead by then. Once that proved ineffectual, he petitioned the court for a motion to allow him to publish a notice, which was granted." He took a newspaper clipping off the bottom of the stack and put it on top. "He did so in both South Dakota and Kansas, and after no response, your divorce was approved and he married the next day."

So many years ago. She rubbed her cold arms, the splash of random raindrops beginning to soak through her dress. What could she have done with so many years of freedom?

"Considering the age of Mr. and Mrs. Bowden's oldest child, I believe a judge thought it best to push the proceedings through. He likely figured you wouldn't contest the divorce anyway."

She wrapped her arms around the hollow in her middle. "The oldest child?"

"He has four now, another on the way."

Four? She'd not been married for over six years now, and he'd started a big family without even the courtesy of letting her know she could have one too?

He handed her the packet. "These are your divorce papers. You'll need them if you want to remarry. And this" — he pulled a single folded piece of paper out of the stack — "is a letter from Mr. Bowden. When I met with him, I convinced him he owed you an explanation. However, he didn't spend too much time writing it, so don't get your hopes up that it'll settle your mind much."

"Thank you," she said reflexively.

Detective Cruse cleared his throat and waited for her to look up.

"Have you found my work to be adequate?"

She nodded. He'd ended her uncertainty. What he'd done was more than adequate.

"Then if you would be so kind as to inform Mr. Lowe, I can be paid my remainder." He stood. "I'll be on my way unless you have any questions for me."

She might, but right now, her brain likely couldn't put together an intelligible sentence. "None I can think of."

"If you do, Mr. Lowe knows how to contact me." He gave her a tip of his hat and walked out into the rain to a waiting automobile she hadn't even seen.

She laid her hand atop the papers to keep the breeze from scattering them. Things were over. Just like that. If she'd only asked Nicholas to help her sooner . . . how much less of a mess would her life be right now?

She unfolded James's letter, her hand shaking so much she put it against her lap so she could decipher his script.

Evelyn,
    I'm sorry about how things went. Glad you know now. My wife and I would prefer you don't make a fuss. Give my love to your dad.

James

She stared at his last sentence with her eyebrows clean up to her hairline. Seems James hadn't changed too much, even after all these years — after what he'd done to her, he just had to take one last poke at her father.

She wadded up the note and threw it in a rain puddle.

"Are you all right, Miss Wisely?" Mr. Parker came in out of the drizzle, the rain dripping off his hat's brim. "I wanted to check on you before I went home."

"I don't exactly feel my best, but I'll be all right."

I will be all right.

She blew out a breath, emptying the air seemingly from all the way down in her toes. She would be all right. She'd be better than she'd been for nearly a decade.

"Do you need me to help you inside?"

"No." She held out her hand, and he pulled her up. "But could I bother you to take me to A. K. G.?"

"The glass factory?"

"Yes." Her breathing grew shallow, and she forced herself to pull in deeper breaths. What would David say to this? She'd broken his heart. And he might even feel differently toward her after she'd kept something like this from him. But if anyone needed to know she was no longer married, that she hadn't even been so when she'd said she was, it was him. "If driving me there wouldn't bother you too much, I'd like to go. I know it's late."

Lydia might be miffed at being left without help for so long, but Evelyn hadn't time to explain and get a ride to the factory before Mr. Parker left for home. If Evelyn came back with David, surely Lydia would understand.

"I actually didn't put the carriage away, since it's not every day a detective is waiting around." He patted her hand. "I'll be right back."

"No, I'll come with." She couldn't just stand there when she was ready to run all the way to town. Rolling up her papers and tucking them under her arm beneath her shawl, she hurried after him, avoiding puddles and keeping the drizzle off her face with a hand to her brow. She climbed into the carriage and braced herself for the ride, trying not to think about what could go wrong . . . what could go right.

However, with each dip in the road and each turn that made her slide across her seat, her heart accelerated and her stomach knotted over getting to tell David she was . . . free.

She let that word sink in. She was not only free now, but she had been free for quite some time. Guilt had weighed heavy on her ever since the night of the ball when she'd actually, for a few rebellious seconds, thought about kissing David. She'd spent nights chastising herself over that for nothing! She was allowed to imagine what his kiss would be like — and she would. He'd likely not kiss her at the factory — and of course, that depended if he'd kiss her at all after what she'd done. And what his feelings were about marrying a divorced woman.

Divorced. That word certainly didn't sink in as well as *free.*

At the factory, men were exiting, holding down their hats and rushing down the sidewalks. She waited for Mr. Parker to open the carriage door for her, unsure she had the coordination to turn the handle at the moment. He helped her down, opened an umbrella above her, and escorted her to the crowded exit.

What was she going to do when she saw David? She wanted to run into his arms and kiss him, but just because she was free to do so didn't mean she should be that forward.

They waited beside the exit for the door to clear, and then she slipped inside.

Looking around, her chest squeezed over the fact that she had no idea where she was, or where David might be.

A balding man a few feet from her took his coat off a hook and headed in her direction as he shrugged into his slicker. "Can I help you, miss?"

"Can you tell me where Mr. Kingsman might be?"

He turned and pointed at a black metal balcony, sitting like a crow's nest high over the myriad machines and stacks of glass jars scattered across the huge factory floor. "Unless he's already gone, he's likely up there. Second door. Interior office."

"Thank you."

She carefully picked her way around the obstacles on her way there — the clanging of her heels on the first step made her look to see if anyone was glaring at her for making such a racket. Only a handful of men remained in the building, most talking to each other, though a few looked busy cleaning.

With each step, she climbed faster.

She knocked on the second door but heard no answer. She pushed it open and peered inside a large office with six desks, all in different states of disarray, except for a corner one that was tidy.

Across the room was a door with *Mr. Burns* stenciled on it. Considering there were no other interior doors, it must be where David worked.

She crossed the room and gently rapped on the door.

"Come in," someone barked — not David's voice at all.

She couldn't just walk away now after knocking, and though David hadn't answered, he might still be in there. She turned the doorknob and peeked inside.

A man with David's brow and nose, but with gray hair and a much harder jaw, looked at her with a sneer. "Who are you?"

"Miss Wisely, sir." She glanced around the room, but David wasn't there. She couldn't help the huge sigh.

"What do you want, Miss Wisely?" He looked her up and down as if trying to judge her. "You aren't one of the women my son fired, are you? Because if so, you're wasting your breath coming to me. Your dismissal is final."

"David fired the women?" The only women she knew he'd employed were the prostitutes. Hadn't he said he was going to figure out how to help them stay?

Then it hit her, and she tilted her chin. "Did you just assume I was a lady of the night?"

David's father only stared at her. "And what gives you the right to address my son so informally?"

She refrained from slapping a hand over her mouth for using his Christian name — nothing was wrong with doing so between good friends. "He and I are friends. No, more than friends. Is he still around or has he left for the day?"

"You're the one he wanted to marry?" His gaze was as menacing as an unsprung mousetrap.

She gave him a slight nod. Who else had David informed of his intent? Her heart beat sluggishly for him. Since she'd kept her secret from everyone, no one would pity her for losing her chance to marry a really wonderful man. But if David had told people he wanted to propose, he'd likely been humiliated when he'd had to tell them she'd refused.

"Why are you here, then?" David's father leaned back in his chair, his hands steepled against his chin, his eyes narrowed. "He told me he wasn't interested in you anymore."

She blinked. He wasn't interested? That didn't sound like David, but then, if he was hurt enough, who knew what he might have said. "The reason I turned him down is no longer valid. I'd like to tell him so."

Mr. Kingsman shifted in his seat and roll-tapped his fingers against the desk, from index finger to pinky in successive rhythm. "Tell him what?" His eyes sharpened in on her like a hawk on a field mouse.

"I'd prefer to tell him myself."

"He's returned to Kansas City."

She wilted. "He already left?"

"Yes. To pursue Miss Lister. She changed her mind about getting engaged."

Pursue her? "Would that be Marianne?"

"Yes. She'd broken his heart going after his secretary, but she's repented of her foolishness, and they'll mend their rifts. It was too bad you were caught in the crossfire of a lover's spat."

"But . . ." Had he truly gone back to

Marianne so quickly? David had said his father held quite the sway over him, and with the way she'd broken his heart, she couldn't blame him for leaving Teaville. But had she really been the second one to hurt him, and in so short a time?

No. Hadn't he said at Mr. Hargrove's that he and Marianne were just friends?

"David told me he had no further interest in pursuing you, so I suggest you leave my son be." He waved the back of his hand at her and picked up the paperwork in front of him.

She wasn't enjoying this conversation either, but she wasn't going to leave before he knew there wouldn't be a problem if his son did choose to pursue her. "Well, of course he didn't have any further interest in me last week. He thought I was married."

Mr. Kingsman raised his head. "You told him you were married when you were not?"

"No, or maybe yes. But I didn't do it intentionally." Ugh, for so many years she'd kept from telling anyone she was married, and the one time she'd uttered it, she'd made a muck of things. "I'm actually divorced, but I didn't know that until today."

"You're *divorced*?" He asked that as if she were a child who didn't understand the term she'd used.

She straightened her shoulders and met his eyes evenly, daring him to challenge her. "Yes."

He shrugged as if that settled everything. "Our social set doesn't take kindly to divorcees — gold diggers, most of them."

"I'm not a gold digger."

"Neither was the Baroness de Stuers of the New York Astors, but she was still shunned from good society after her shameful divorce. If her own mother wouldn't allow her back into her parlor, why do you think you'd be welcome in ours? David already had concerns about your lack of fortune, and now this black spot . . . ?"

Mr. Kingsman shook his head and made a clucking sound with his tongue as if he felt sorry for her. "My son might do a lot of things I don't agree with, but he knows what is and is not acceptable. You'd lose him connections. You'd make him a laughingstock."

She took a deep breath. David had told her his father belittled his every dream. What would keep him from doing whatever he could to stomp on hers? "I don't believe you know your son as well as I do. He's not that worried about money."

"Which makes him a fool." He shook his head as if she too were a fool for thinking such a characteristic admirable. "Miss

Wisely, I understand how you could have fallen for my son, and he for you. He does tend to get wrapped up with the pitiful ones. But I will not approve of you marrying my son, and with the baggage you bring, even he would see how your connection to us would be detrimental. We didn't work our way up in society to fritter it away by attaching ourselves to a pariah."

She swallowed hard. Some people did feel that way about divorcees, but David wouldn't . . . And yet, would he have let himself fall in love with her if he'd known she was divorced from the beginning? He would certainly tell her it didn't matter now, but though it might not matter to the heart, could she live with hurting his livelihood? She certainly wouldn't help improve his relationship with his father.

"I'm sorry, Miss Wisely, but even David would see how bad of a match you'd make. Though you might throw yourself at him and prey upon his sympathies, he would eventually heed my advice. He always has, because it's good advice. I'm sorry if I'm upsetting you, but it's best I tell you now. Save yourself some humiliation and keep yourself away from my son for his own good."

She wouldn't drop her gaze from his,

despite the self-satisfied sneer on the man's face. "I'm not convinced David would actually do as you wish."

"You're right, and if you happen to actually love him, all the more reason for you to do what's best for him. You can save him from himself."

Love was supposed to be selfless. And though David's father wasn't, she certainly wanted to be.

She stood, shaking at the thought that such a man could be her father-in-law. He definitely looked down his nose at her — but that didn't make him wrong about how others would treat David if he married her. If his father acted this cold toward her now, how could she expect his business partners to treat her differently?

But David didn't think like his father, or his peers for that matter. And perhaps that was exactly why she should trust his father about how she'd truly be seen. The problems he'd face with her on his arm would pale in comparison to anything he'd face marrying Marianne, who he'd admitted was a fine lady. And how could any woman not fall in love with David?

If she told him she was divorced, he'd probably be the kind of man who'd feel duty bound to marry her after he'd already proposed.

If offering him her love would only make his life worse, perhaps it wasn't a good thing to offer at all. She'd once rushed into a marriage and lived to regret it, so how could she live with herself if she caused David to do the same?

36

"So, Miss Wisely, have you decided whether or not you want to be moral-society president?" Mrs. Albert looked at Mrs. Naples for a second before pinning her eyes back on Evelyn.

"I have given it some thought. . . ." Until the Lowes found someone to take over the mansion, she wouldn't have time. But her problem wasn't so much that she was unsure of if or when she could take over, it was the title of the position. Could she really be the *moral*-society president? In the opinion of some, a divorced woman wasn't much better than a loose woman. And though there were several divorcees in town who ran successful businesses, none had the gall to take a position of leadership in the church.

"I was thinking that instead of having a president, we could all choose to organize projects we have a passion for and the rest of us could help." She smoothed her hands atop her quilt block. "I don't mind quilting, but if I were president, I could see that project going downhill. Mrs. Naples is surely the best one to head that up. But I'd love to lead our efforts to help the women and children of the red-light district. Maybe Charlie could take control of our food distribution since she's always giving away farm animals and extra vegetables."

"Good plan. I'd much rather head a canning bee than a quilting one." Charlie tugged on her needle, and her eyes went wide. She ducked her head under the frame and groaned. "Dagnabbit, I sewed my skirt to the quilt again."

Evelyn couldn't help but chuckle with the rest of them, and even prim Miss Sorenson giggled a little. Thank God for Charlie's unfeminine charm. Though her poor sewing often set them back, at least she kept them from being serious all the time.

Charlie's cheeks and neck were bright red, yet her eyes danced while her mother worked at saving her daughter from becoming a permanent part of the quilt.

After the laughter died down, Evelyn continued. "I bet all of us have something we'd like to champion. I wouldn't be surprised if Lydia would want to head up something related to books one day."

Her friend's face brightened, and she brought up both hands, palms forward. "Actually, the last time I was out in the traveling library coach, I thought it would be a good idea to have a Bible drive. Some of the rural folks own a family Bible, but they treat it more as a family record than something to read. I'd love to see every family, if not every family member, have their own Bible."

"See?" Evelyn's smile grew. "Someone could volunteer to be a secretary to keep our ideas straight and schedule things, and so on, but we could all take part. That way no one has to bear the brunt of the work, and we all get to see something dear to our hearts get attention."

"An excellent plan. I'll fill the secretary role if no one else wants it," Momma said. She paused and looked around, but no one made a peep in protest. "So then, as secretary, I say it's time for a vote. How many agree to Evelyn's idea of parceling out projects?"

Every hand raised, except for Charlie's mother, who was busy freeing her daughter from the quilt but let out a hearty "Aye."

"I can ask the members who aren't here to get their opinions, but I doubt any of them will oppose." Momma stood. "So, meeting dismissed!"

The women started putting away their notions, and Evelyn couldn't help but beam at some of the ideas already floating around the room. Even if she never had any volunteers to help with her projects — for even she found the district uncomfortable — it seemed there would be plenty of charity projects to keep them busy.

She gave Momma a kiss and hug before leaving with Lydia.

"I knew you were the one to get this group going in the right direction." Lydia gave her a side hug.

The moment Mr. Parker shut them inside the Lowes' coach, her friend scooted forward on her seat. "Now, I've been about to die for bursting. Nicholas told me this morning David left Teaville without even a word to him. Do you know what happened?"

Evelyn squirmed. This was not the most comfortable place to spill her life's story, but likely the only time they'd have no little ears nearby. And she wouldn't keep her secret from Lydia any longer. The coach jolted forward. Thankfully Evelyn already had a good hold of the armrest.

"I just can't fathom why he left so

abruptly," Lydia continued. "He was positively enamored with you, told us he wanted to marry you."

"He did?" She picked up one of Lydia's ladies' magazines and fanned herself with it. She'd been hoping David's father had been the only one who knew he'd had those intentions.

"Well, in a roundabout way, but it was obvious enough." Lydia oofed with a rut, then settled back against her seat.

"I think he left because I turned down his proposal."

"What!" Lydia bounced in her seat again though they'd hit no bump or rut.

She couldn't look at her friend. "That can't be such a surprise. I've always said I wasn't interested in marrying."

"But that's ridiculous. I saw how you looked at him the night of the ball."

She had lied to David about wishing on stars that night — but she'd believed her wish to know how it would feel to be kissed by him to be immoral. To think, she could have kissed him. She emptied her lungs and kept her eyes on the space between them. "I know you've always wondered why I was so averse to marriage, and since that has to do with David leaving . . . I hope you'll still be my friend after I tell you what happened."

501

"I can't imagine anything you could say that would keep me from being so."

Of course not, knowing Lydia. But that didn't mean she wouldn't be hurt. "Well, the reason I turned David down was because I believed myself to be married."

Silence.

Evelyn looked up and almost laughed at the utter confusion on Lydia's face. "I'll make the story short now, but you can ask me whatever you'd like later, since I've already told my parents. When I was eighteen I married a man Daddy would've never approved of while I was at my great-aunt's for the summer. Daddy's discernment proved right, and after a month, James left me. I was too ashamed to tell anyone, but I found out he divorced me six years ago. Though he abandoned me, the court ruled I'm at fault, and I'm not going to contest it."

Lydia blinked with exaggeration, then shook her head. "You say you're divorced?"

"Yes."

"That still doesn't explain why David would leave. No man working so hard to help the women in the district would outright give you up for that."

"No, I don't think he would either, but I didn't learn I was divorced until three days after David proposed."

"So you thought you were still married?" Lydia looked up at the coach ceiling. "You've thought that for . . . ?"

"Nine years."

"Oh my, dear girl." She reached over for her hand. "Why didn't you ask us for help?"

"I did. Just last month, I asked Nicholas to find James for me. I only gave him a name and description, so he didn't know why I was looking for James, but I'm thankful your husband was willing to find him without asking questions."

"So when did you telegraph David? Have you gotten a response yet?"

Evelyn shook her head and tugged her hand from Lydia's grasp. "I . . . I haven't sent him any messages. After I learned of my divorce, I talked to his father." She swallowed against the lump in her throat. "He convinced me David would be better off marrying someone other than me."

Lydia scrunched her face tight, like a child holding in an outburst, and shook her head. "From what I've heard, the elder Mr. Kingsman might try to force David to do as he wishes, but if David wants something, he'll push back."

"I know." And that was why she wasn't certain she should start a war between them. "David won't shun me because of my divorce, but his father, the circle he does business with, those who socialize with them . . . How many will shun him because of me? He's got a bright future, which I will not ruin. He'll find someone else."

"Now, Evelyn Grace." Lydia straightened and glared at her as if she were addressing her one-year-old. "You have to let him know."

But it was too late. "He has no ties here now. The factory has been sold. The orphanage isn't his dream."

"And this exact orphanage is your dream? This particular one?"

She swallowed against the knot in her throat. Children were her dream. Whether in an orphanage or in her arms, it didn't matter.

"What about Sadie?"

What did she have to do with the orphanage? "Your housekeeper, Sadie?"

"Yes. If Franklin ever gets his nerve together to ask for her hand, would you advise Sadie to say no because there's bound to be someone better for him than a former child prostitute?"

This was in no way similar to that. "She was forced into that life. If Franklin can't see that, then he doesn't deserve her. But my marriage and its failure were my fault."

The coach stopped, and she opened up the door instead of waiting for Mr. Parker.

She'd been willing to tell Lydia her story, just as she had her parents. But they'd not prodded her about David. Why was Lydia more interested in him than the whole crazy divorce thing? How she wished Lydia was more interested in that!

Franklin opened the front door with enthusiasm. "Happy to have you return, Mrs. Lowe." He stiffened as they walked inside in front of him, holding his back straight and tall like a soldier's. "A courier brought you a letter while you were away, Miss Wisely."

Since when did she get mail from a courier? Her hands shook as she took off her gloves. Had Detective Cruse found out her divorce was invalid, or something worse?

37

Franklin retrieved the letter off the entryway table.

Evelyn struggled to get her last glove off. Who but Detective Cruse would send anything to her through a courier?

Lydia seemed to sense her tension and laid a gentle hand on her arm.

Franklin turned with a smile, evidently oblivious to her nerves, and handed it to her. "May I take your coat?" He went behind to help Lydia shrug out of hers.

"No, I'm fine." It was rather warm, but she hadn't time to bother. She flipped the envelope over in her hands.

Her stomach stopped churning — but it didn't exactly settle either. The return address was Kansas City.

David?

She took the letter opener Franklin handed her and sliced through the business stationery, wondering at the envelope's bulkiness. She pulled out several folded pages and a paper fluttered to the floor. Stooping, she picked up the escapee.

A check. For seventy dollars.

She blinked.

"Well, what is it?" Lydia queried breathlessly.

"I don't know." She unfolded the other pieces of paper, and her heart stopped. The drawing of her asleep near Scott on his sickbed pulled at her heartstrings. He'd returned it. The next two pages were also drawings. They weren't nearly as good — as David had said, he wasn't an exceptional artist — but then again, these weren't portraits he could have drawn while looking at his subject. The first was of her with baby Hope lying on her chest, rocking her to sleep in the music room. Hadn't that been the day Lydia had told them of her idea for the charity dinner?

It was strange to miss Hope's distressed cries, but when Nicholas had approved the Dewitts to take her, she'd been relieved that the baby would be better taken care of and had found a permanent home.

The next drawing was of her again, on the balcony the night of the ball. Though she knew she'd caked on the special powder Lydia had given her to cover her scars, he'd lightly penciled them in anyway.

Had he returned the pictures because he couldn't stand to look at her anymore?

"What's the bank check for?"

Lydia flipped the drawings over and saw nothing scribbled on the backs. Checking the inside of the envelope turned up a paper she'd missed.

Evelyn,

I'd pledged to cover four days' worth of food a month for your ministries. Twenty dollars will be sent each month and should cover that expense — if not, let me know. The extra fifty is for start-up costs. From now on I'll have my secretary send you the checks, but I wanted you to have my personal address.

If you hadn't heard, the two ladies who lost their positions at A. K. G. have found replacements in the big city. If any of their friends need a job, feel free to contact me here, not at the business address, and I'll see what I can do.

I understand why you don't wish selfishly on stars now. It's not very fun when you know you can't have what you want, is it? But I won't let you give up on the dreams you can pursue.

David

"What does it say?"

She handed the paper to Lydia and worked to get her coat off, worked to keep from running upstairs to her room and hiding from the pain of what was lost.

"So how are you going to answer?"

She frowned, hoping her voice would form words without betraying the tremble in her lip and the twitch near her eye. "Answer what? There weren't any questions."

"I know you like to keep your feelings tucked away, but don't tell me you aren't even going to write him."

"What would I write? There aren't any women I know of at the moment in need of jobs, and . . . I don't know what I should say." She had plenty to say, but what if she shouldn't say anything? She picked up the check for the seventy dollars and sat on the chair near the hat rack. What should the fifty dollars go to? She probably ought to hand it over to Nicholas.

"Start by thanking him for the donation." Lydia sat beside her. "And then follow that up with the entire story you've yet to tell me, ending with the very important information regarding your marital status."

Evelyn ran her fingers across the check. "But I told you on the way here, I'd only cause him problems."

"Don't leave him in the dark like James left you."

Tears pricked her eyes and her hand froze. "I . . ."

"Aren't you always telling us that when God says no, sometimes He makes you wait for something better?"

Of course that was what she often said, but sometimes He simply said no. She shrugged.

"Can't you see God guarded your heart until David came along?"

"What does that mean?"

Lydia leaned back and looked down her nose at her as if she were looking through magnifying lenses. "What would have happened if you knew you weren't married years ago?"

She looked away. "I'd have married Mr. Patterson or any of the other men people pushed at me over the years."

"Right, because you would've seen the good in them all."

"No one pushed horrible men at me. They were all fine gentlemen."

Lydia took her hand. "I love you for always wanting to see the best in people, but were any of those men better than David?"

Her throat clogged and tears threatened.

"Not for me, no."

"See?"

Without even looking over at Lydia, she could imagine the triumphant grin that lit her face. "But why would God put me through this agony?" The last several nights she'd been unable to sleep wondering about the timing. "God could have informed me of my divorce before David arrived so I could've been free to love him. The private investigator could have come the day before David proposed." She found herself crushing the bank check, so she smoothed it back out. "That makes me think God doesn't want me to marry David either."

"What I think is you've worked so hard over the years to resign yourself to the worst that you don't really believe He intends good for you."

"But David's father is right; I'm not good enough for *him*." Evelyn sucked in air to attempt to cool her face. "I thought I'd matured, that the eighteen-year-old romantic blockhead whisked away by fancy and a handsome face was long gone. But when David came along, I couldn't keep my head about me despite believing I was still married. My emotions took over, my ability to think properly —"

"Even if you had been married while David was here, you might have been tempted with attraction, tempted with lust, but you never chose to act on those feelings, right? The seventh commandment doesn't say, 'Thou shalt not be tempted to commit adultery,' but that you shouldn't commit it."

"But Jesus said anyone who simply thinks about adultery commits it."

"He said if a man looks at a woman *to lust* after her he has committed adultery." Lydia took her hand. "The sin is in the choice, not the thought that brings about temptation. Did you ever say, 'I'm going to entertain these fancies about David though I know I shouldn't?' "

She wriggled in her chair. "I certainly tried hard not to, but I don't think I truly succeeded."

"So when you fell in love despite yourself, did you act upon it?"

"No, I turned him away."

Lydia nudged her with her elbow. "You technically didn't even have to. You're allowed to entertain your feelings for David now."

"But what about the divorce?" That was certainly not what God wanted for anyone. "What about the fact that I basically hoped the detective would inform me I was a widow? What kind of Christian woman wishes her estranged husband dead?"

"So then ask God to forgive you, Evelyn. If someone wants to condemn you for it, don't worry about them if you're forgiven by God." Lydia stole her other hand and gently tugged until she looked at Lydia, whose gaze penetrated into hers. "Give David some credit — don't you think he's the kind of guy who'll love his bride like Christ loves the church?"

She was blessed to know several men like that, and David was certainly among their number. "Yes."

"Then don't you think he'd forgive you for your married past or whatever other wrongs you think you committed against him?"

"I'm actually certain he'll forgive me, but I'm afraid he'll feel duty bound to marry me since he proposed — because he is that sacrificial."

"Do you believe God forgives sins?" At Evelyn's confused nod, Lydia continued. "So once you allowed Him to do so that first time, He was duty bound to give you eternal life because He sacrificed himself for that purpose and promised to give it, but you didn't refuse to accept that gift because you were unworthy of it, did you?"

Evelyn sniffed. "No, because that would be stupid. I could never be worthy of God's gift of eternal life. I'm simply thankful for it."

Lydia jabbed her in the ribs. "Then don't be stupid with David. Don't reject his love because you don't feel worthy of it."

She didn't want to be stupid, but she wanted what was best for him too.

But if she didn't let him decide, was she any better than his father?

The clock struck the quarter hour, and she heard Nicholas hollering for the children to come inside. "But I couldn't leave you two to run this orphanage alone —"

"Do I have to buy you the ticket myself?" Lydia rolled her eyes.

Evelyn hugged her friend tight, letting out a few of the tears she'd kept imprisoned. "Yes, you certainly do because I have no money." She chuckled and pulled away, wiping the tears off her cheek. "But I'm afraid to face him. It was hard enough watching him leave the first time."

Lydia took her cold hand in her warm one. "This from someone who walks alone through the red-light district with a pistol in her pocket. You'll have an entire train ride to muster up the courage to face whatever decision he makes."

38

The carriage slowed, and Evelyn looked out the window. She'd expected to stop in front of a row of townhouses or in a quiet Kansas City neighborhood, but instead, a large house loomed in front of her. Black iron and rock fencing surrounded a yard full of trees and manicured bushes that took up half a block. The house's floor-to-ceiling windows were lit by hundreds of lights, though nightfall was more than a half hour away.

However, they were behind quite the line of carriages and fancy automobiles flowing into the property. Perhaps her driver was just stuck in traffic.

She pressed back against her seat and took a steadying breath. Hiring someone to take her to David's had cost more than she'd expected, and despite the carriage being well sprung and having cushioned seats and fur lap robes, it had been the most uncomfortable ride of her life. Taking her heart's erratic rhythm into account, she might as well have been flitting about the city in a full gallop.

The carriage turned to the left. They'd turned in with the others? She looked out the window again. They had indeed entered onto the estate grounds. In front of the house, a woman in a fancy violet dress was being helped from her carriage by a well-dressed servant. A man in a black tailcoat stepped out of the vehicle and followed her under the columned porch.

The automobile behind the couple stopped. A servant opened the passenger door for a woman in a full-length dark maroon coat and a hat so full of feathers it seemed she'd fly away if a gust of wind took her by surprise.

Evelyn dropped her gaze onto her lap and cringed at her plain outfit as they moved slowly forward. How could she step out of this carriage in such simple attire? She'd not thought to change out of her blue wool traveling suit, but then, she hadn't packed anything that would have sufficed for a gathering such as this.

Hopefully the driver had made a mistake.

The carriage stopped, and she closed her eyes, her heart in her throat. If this indeed was David's place, perhaps it would be best to tell her driver she'd changed her mind and wanted to be taken back to the hotel.

"Miss?" The driver opened the door, popped his head into the carriage, and held out his hand. "May I help you alight?"

His smile was wider than a river. Had he not looked around and seen how inadequately she was dressed? She clamped onto her lap robe, sinking her fingers into the soft fur, its warmth persuading her to stay where it was more . . . comfortable. "Are you sure this is David Kingsman's residence?"

"Absolutely. Never got to drive in here before, but I've certainly admired it in passing." His eyes narrowed and took a quick sweep of her. "You're not here for the party?"

He was simply a driver. Surely he wouldn't lock her in and drive off to keep her from attending — not that she actually wanted to attend a party. She relaxed her hands to keep from crumpling the skirt of her dress. Wrinkles would not help her situation. "I'm just a bit . . . nervous."

But if she didn't go now, she'd worry all night long about whether this party was celebrating something in particular — like an engagement — and convince herself not to return.

Surely this had nothing to do with David and Marianne. This was likely nothing more than a simple welcome-back party . . . with tuxedos.

The driver stepped farther in, and she took his hand, hoping he'd yank her out. She might not be able to exit any other way.

Though he only gently tugged her forward, her curiosity won her over.

Once she exited the carriage, the driver behind them glared at her.

Holding up traffic hadn't charmed him any.

She turned around, but her driver was already climbing back into his seat. He grabbed the reins and glanced down at her. "I'll return on the hour."

"Wait." She'd figured by then she'd know whether or not David's driver could return her to the hotel. But with a party? "Can you return in two?"

"Sure can, miss." He tipped his hat and flicked his reins. "Giddap!"

The second he pulled away, she wanted to holler at him to come back. She didn't have an invitation. How did she expect to get in? Oh, what had she been thinking?

Another row of vehicles pulled up. She couldn't just stand there in the way of all the party guests.

She kept her head down as she moved to the front door, wishing she'd at least packed her dress from the Lowes' ball. She'd still be underdressed, but at least she wouldn't be so horribly out of place. She drew in a long breath of autumn air. If only she'd had the patience to wait until morning.

One of the butlers ushering people inside stopped in front of her and scowled. "I'm afraid you're very late. The servants' entrance is on the east side of the house."

Her cheeks heated, but she nodded and hurried away from the snickering behind her. She wasn't about to argue that she wasn't a servant right now — it was probably the easiest way to get in dressed as she was. She ran a hand along the boxwood bushes running parallel to the pavement stones and the front of the house. She guessed that in bright daylight the house was gray, but maybe it was a blue. The windows on both floors were taller than she was, their rounded white cornices beautifully carved. The house wasn't quite as large as the mansion, yet David's estate felt ten times more intimidating. She'd padded through the Lowes' mansion many times in her bare feet — that building felt like home. This one felt like a fortress.

Did David really live here? Maybe he lived with his father — that certainly might explain the grandeur.

What had she been thinking coming here? David would never have to settle for her — or even Marianne, for that matter. How many women of good social standing with deep pockets had their eyes set on this estate? And it wasn't as if David himself would make a poor choice for any bride.

If it weren't for the fact that Lydia had married someone much richer than herself and had a good marriage despite their difference in social standing, she'd not even bother going inside. But she had to at least tell David the truth about her marriage and divorce. He'd done so much for her, he deserved to know.

A door opened on the side of the building, and a young man exited with a vat of something that stunk. Evelyn caught his eye, wrinkling her nose at the acrid smell.

He scowled himself. "They burned the gravy, and I got tasked with getting rid of it." He looked her up and down. "You better get in and see Mrs. Humpreys right away and get into uniform."

She forced herself not to correct him. "Can you tell me when the party will be underway?"

"Near thirty minutes, as far as I can tell. They plan to do the announcement around six thirty and eat afterwards. If it weren't for the fact that we're short staffed, I'd tell you not to bother coming in as late as you are. Brace yourself for quite the tongue-lashing and a dock in pay."

She blinked — her brain had gotten stuck on the word *announcement*. "What are they announcing at six thirty, again?"

"The engagement, of course." He rolled his eyes and sped off into the backyard that extended to the street behind them.

Engagement.

Lydia had been wrong. Either David wasn't going to wait for time to erase his feelings for her, or they hadn't been any-where near as strong as she'd thought.

Though the wind had a warm undertone, her limbs turned to ice and her feet froze to the stoop.

What should she do? Could she just walk away without seeing him, without letting him know? Would he want to know? Maybe, but what kind of person would she be to ruin another woman's life? Surely Marianne had to have feelings for him. How could she not if David was her best friend?

The servant returned with the empty bowl, and his mouth screwed to the side.

521

"Are you not going in?"

"Could you tell me if Miss Lister seems happy?"

Oh please, God, have him say he doesn't even know who Miss Lister is.

The man nodded. "I haven't seen her this happy in ages."

She closed her eyes and staggered back. She'd come all the way to Kansas City for nothing.

The servant grabbed her by the arm. "Are you all right?"

She nodded with short little jerks but refused to open her tightly shut eyes lest she disgrace herself with tears. She wanted David to be her dream come true, but not at the expense of another's. Maybe this was why God had kept the detective away until after she'd refused David.

Releasing the air she'd held, she extricated herself from the man's grasp. "I'm all right. Go on in ahead of me."

After one last look, he scurried in, likely worried he'd be reprimanded if he remained outside any longer.

Now what was she supposed to do? Hadn't David said he didn't want to marry Marianne? Was he engaging himself because he was too hurt to resist the pressure his father was likely plying on him?

Oh, if only one decision in her life could be easy!

Voices behind the door grew louder, and someone turned the knob, so Evelyn rushed past the door before it flew open, then followed the flagstones to the backyard.

Thankfully there was a beautiful garden to hide in, where she could think — but for no more than thirty minutes!

The sky was getting dim enough that the lights inside the windows illuminated the crowd.

How could she possibly stop things now?

A bench near a hedge appeared, and she made her way there. Thankfully it was warm enough that she could concentrate on something other than being cold. The wooden slats gave a bit beneath her, and she placed her elbows on her knees, her hands folded against her chin.

If she was in David's situation, what would she want? Of course, she didn't know what he felt for her now — or for Marianne, exactly — but interrupting their engagement party . . . ?

A flash of white appeared to Evelyn's right. A woman afloat in a gown of yellow and white was picking apart an orange flower, likely a calendula this late in the season.

Evelyn leaned back to try to blend in with the bench — as much as a blue dress could blend into wood anyway.

The woman smiled at her but quickly stiffened. She looked her up and down twice. "Are you lost?"

She shook her head while looking back down at her lap. She wasn't physically lost at least.

"Mind if I sit?"

Evelyn glanced at her again. The dress this woman wore was fine, and the jewels around her neck very much real — and she wanted to sit with her?

Though it shouldn't surprise her that David surrounded himself with friends who wouldn't tilt their noses up at those beneath them. He'd so willingly sat on the ground with her and the children that first Saturday, as if men in three-piece suits always ate with people most would consider unfit to shine their shoes.

She scooted over so the woman had space for her wispy, layered skirt.

The lady flicked the flower's spent stem onto the ground. "So what brings you out here?"

Why couldn't this woman be one to appreciate companionable silence? "I couldn't go in."

"And I had to get out. It's extremely hot in there. Too many people." She rubbed at the slight yellow tinge on her fingers before putting her gloves back on.

Evelyn sat forward and stared at her knees. How she wished she had Lydia or Momma here right now. They'd help her figure out what to do.

God, help me decide how to proceed. I can't think with this woman beside me, so could you make things easy and hit me with something unmistakable?

"Are you all right?" the woman beside her asked.

With such a huge decision looming over her, how could she be?

"You're holding onto the bench as if you're afraid you'll be blown away."

She let go of the bench and clasped her hands together in her lap. "Forgive me."

"Did someone hurt you?"

She shook her head. Though she might do something to hurt David, one way or another. As if doing so two weeks ago wasn't bad enough.

"I haven't seen you before. I don't know what you know about the Kingsmans, but the younger one is well known for being adamant that everyone, no matter their station, is to be treated well. So if a servant or guest here is manhandling you, you should tell your superior. That is, if they aren't the one bothering you."

Of course David was wonderful enough to stick up for his chambermaids. "It's more of a personal dilemma, actually."

"So nothing to do with work?" Her voice turned suspicious. For why else would a servant be out here doing nothing?

"No, I . . ." What did it matter what she told this woman? She'd likely never see her again. "I'm out here trying to decide if I should tell someone something or keep it to myself."

"I'm a good listener, if you'd like. Since I don't know your name, our conversation could do you no harm. Just leave out the particulars and maybe I can help."

The woman's voice held such sincere warmth, how could she not believe her?

Perhaps God had just sent her His answer — a listening ear.

"It's about a man." She sighed.

"Of course it is." The woman's words dripped with understanding. "Love tends to give us all fits."

"*Fits* is an understatement."

"Do you know how this man feels about you?"

"Yes. Well, I did."

"And does he feel the same as you do?" At Evelyn's nod, the woman turned to see her better. "So why hesitate to tell him your feelings? I'm assuming that's your secret anyway."

"Because when he offered his hand to me, I told him I was married and turned him away. But circumstances changed."

The woman hmmed, likely realizing with her choice of words, she wasn't a widow. "And now you want him back?"

"Yes." She shrugged despite the fact that there was no uncertainty in her answer.

"How long ago did he offer for you?"

"A little over two weeks ago."

The woman stiffened. "Well, that was quick."

Quick, and oh, so very long.

"So you left this other man to pursue the new one?"

She cringed. This woman had to be thinking the absolute worst of her, yet she somehow maintained a soothing tone to her voice. "No, he abandoned me years ago. He just failed to inform me he'd gone through with divorcing me as well. I didn't learn of it until recently."

"Well, if your new love can't swallow his pride over being turned down under such circumstances, then he's not worthy of you."

"I think I'm more worried I'm not worthy of him. At least his father won't think so, and I could ruin their relationship if I assert myself."

"Dear me, I know all about that." The woman exhaled so hugely the flounce on the front of her dress ruffled. "My parents chose to marry for love when they were poor — and they still love each other quite madly — but now that they've succeeded enough to flit about the wealthy set, they want me to marry for money and status. Parents are quite meddlesome, aren't they?"

Evelyn's heart warmed at the memory of her father hobbling all the way to the train station to pray with her before seeing her off. "Mine are pretty wonderful, actually. They'd want me to marry for love."

The woman sat back and folded her arms, her expression confused. "Then you should."

"But what if doing so hurts someone else?"

"I can't answer that. But are you willing to wonder your whole life?"

And there was her answer. "No. I've already spent enough of my life wondering about my position with a man."

"Oh! There you are, my dear." An older woman in layers of gray and a mound of pearls weighing down her neck walked toward them so quickly, she'd plow right through them if she didn't stop soon. "It's time to come back inside."

The woman beside Evelyn patted her knee twice. "I hope things work out for you." She stood and took the older woman's arm — most likely her mother's judging from their similar full lips, round jaws, and high cheekbones.

The older woman spent no time turning and swishing them both back the way she'd come. "The announcement is after this song, and you're out here walking."

After they were a good distance away, the older woman looked back at Evelyn for a second, then spoke more quietly — but not quietly enough. "And who was that you were talking with?"

"One of the help, I think. Though she isn't dressed like one."

"Then you shouldn't have been talking to her at all." She tsked. "She should be working, not sitting in the garden. We should inform whoever's in charge of her whereabouts."

The younger woman's voice grew fainter as they got closer to the house, where the low hum of hundreds of voices was muffled by stone and glass.

"Oh, Momma, she was having a crisis. I'm sure she'll return to work soon enough."

"You're always too easy with the help. They'll run over you if you let . . ." A door opened, and the laughter and conversation of the crowd swallowed the women's voices.

If the announcement was after this song, she hadn't time to sit here any longer.

Please, God, help me find him if I'm supposed to, but if all I'm going to do is make a mess . . .

Except, mess or not, how could she live with herself if she never told David how much she loved him?

39

Evelyn opened the big glass doors that seemed to lead into a giant ballroom, and she slipped into the crowd of attendees, hoping no one paid much attention to her.

Where should she look for David first? She hadn't much time to find him if the stranger and her mother were correct and the announcement would happen soon.

Keeping to the wall, she brushed her way past several people, trying to get somewhere she could see without having to forge into the middle of the floor that people seemed reluctant to traverse. Seems there'd be dancing tonight.

She bumped into a man in a white servant's coat. She had to look quite a ways up to see him. He had to be nearly six foot four to be that much taller than she, plus a few more inches with all that wavy dark hair atop his head.

"Can I help you, miss?"

"Uh, no."

"I think you're lost." He pointed behind her. "The entrance to the kitchen is that way. Mrs. Humpreys is going to yell at you for coming out here without a uniform."

"Actually, I was invited here by Mr. Kingsman."

The man's eyebrows scrunched, and he scanned her outfit as if she were slathered in mud.

The lady from the garden was right — it was rather warm in here. "I know my dress isn't exactly appropriate for the festivities."

The servant sniffed. "Next time, I suggest you borrow a better one so you don't insult your host. . . . If there is a next time."

"I-I'm certain you're right." What chance did she have of coming back anyway?

Before he could say anything more, she slipped into the crowd. Never before had she been so happy to be a few inches taller than most everyone in the room. If she had any hope of talking to David, she needed to spy him quickly.

If he was sitting . . . well, she'd be too late.

His blond head was nowhere to be seen, but there was a table atop a platform at the end of the room. Surely if the announcement was going to be soon, he'd be nearby.

Or at least he'd head that way.

Oomph!

"I'm so sorry." Evelyn steadied the woman she'd bumped into.

The old lady scowled and fixed her hat, which had slipped backward, exposing perfect little gray pin curls lining her forehead. "You must be more careful." She looked her over, then frowned again. "Could you get me another glass of champagne?"

"I'm sorry, but I'm on an errand for Mr. Kingsman."

"He's over there." The woman pointed to the right, near the front of the room. "After you attend him, I'd still like champagne."

She nodded and started off in the direction the lady had pointed, craning her neck trying to catch a glimpse of him. Except, what if the old woman thought she meant his father? But she didn't see him either.

Wait, there David was, standing to the side of the platform with a group of people.

And she thought her heart couldn't pitter-patter any harder.

Oh, he was handsome. She'd only seen a man dressed in such a fancy black suit with tails and slick gleaming lapels in advertisements. His white vest shone atop his white shirt, its highly starched collar stiff beneath his chin — very aristocratic. Even Nicholas had never dressed so dapper.

She stopped, clasping onto the wool jacket she wore. She'd look like a ragamuffin next to him.

A woman jostled her from behind and a waiter from the side, but she couldn't move.

David's half smile was only too charming as he talked to the woman in front of him. A petite blonde wearing a magnificent turquoise ball gown, with a sequined overlay of dark gray lace. Was that Marianne?

His gaze drifted as the woman started talking to the man next to them, and then, upon spotting Evelyn, he bolted upright and made straight for her.

She couldn't let him meet her where everyone would see their confrontation. She maneuvered for the wall behind a table full of hors d'oeuvres.

"Evelyn?" His smile was bright and charming for a second, but then disappeared. He stopped just out of her reach, his arms stiff by his sides, looking her over as if trying to ascertain whether or not her limbs were intact. "What are you doing here?"

"I know my appearance isn't the most appropriate." She gestured to the frock everyone had frowned at. "But I was hoping to speak to you."

Up near the small platform, David's father ascended the small set of stairs and turned to smile out over the crowd with an almost empty glass of wine in his hand.

David turned to look at his father on stage. "I have an announcement I'm about to make —"

"I know." But if she didn't talk with him now, it would be too late. "This is so very wrong of me, but . . ." Getting as close as she dared so as not to set the tongues of those behind them wagging, she gripped his sleeve tightly, as if she could tether him there. "I know this isn't the best time, and this is possibly even the meanest thing I've ever done, but I can't let you go up there and make that announcement until I've told you what I've come here to say."

For some reason he gave her that stupid, charming grin again. "I don't think you can purposely be mean, Evelyn."

"Though what I plan to say could make things harder for you, I need to tell you what I really wanted to say when you proposed, since this may be the last time I can, and I'm free to do so."

He only looked at her, his expression either indicating he thought her crazy, adorably amusing, or forever lost to him. Maybe all three.

She stepped in closer, hoping the music and the incoherent babble of a hundred conversations would keep her words for his ears alone. "David Kingsman, I think you are the most wonderful man I have ever met. I'd never been in love with a wonderful man before, and it hurt to not be able to tell you how much I loved you. How much I wished I could be your wife. But the thing is, I just found out I wasn't even married when you proposed, and had I known, I would have told you what I felt for you then."

He backed away so he could look at her, his brows and lips puckered. "Your husband was found dead?"

"No."

And she'd thought David's face had looked confused when she'd first told him she was married.

"James divorced me six years ago. He claimed I abandoned him so he could marry another."

"Divorced?"

Divorce certainly wasn't the prettiest word in the English language, but she'd never heard it sound so terrible.

"I know your feelings for me were likely trampled beyond repair the last time you saw me." She took a little step back. "And I also know a divorced woman is anathema in your set — your father made me fully aware of that."

His face grew hard. "My father knew this?"

"Yes." She looked across the crowd at Mr. Kingsman talking to someone on the platform. "I don't want you to think I came here to guilt you into jilting the woman you're about to engage yourself to or proposing again to a penniless divorcee. If I were being objective, I'd not have come at all. But I'm not objective. I'm in love with the best man I've ever known and it hurt to know he had no idea how much I loved and admired him. You deserve the love of a good woman, even if that's not m—"

Dink, dink, dink. The crowd quieted as several others joined in with the clinking of silverware against crystal.

"Ladies and gentlemen, thank you for coming." David's father raised his newly filled wine glass.

Evelyn blew out a breath, but the room was too quiet to continue her speech. Not that she knew what she'd have said next. Maybe it was a good thing his father had stopped her wild ramblings. She'd gotten her point across and was nearing the point of being pathetic.

David looked at his father, then back at her with a furrowed brow.

"I know everyone's eager to hear my son's announcement. Now if someone would point him this way, we won't keep you from your dinner much longer."

The crowd tittered, and Evelyn stepped back, wishing she could hide in the shadows — but there were none.

"Evelyn." He grabbed her hand. "I —"

"Why are you still down here?" A man with slicked-back blond hair and panic written across his face swooped in and grabbed David by the sleeve.

David's nostrils flared at the man who'd turned to look at her, as if trying to place her.

David shook his head. "I'm sorry, Evelyn. I've got to go." However, he still held her hand.

Would he change his mind about engaging himself to Marianne?

"David?" his father called, and the crowd murmured. "Ah, Marianne, come up. Where's my son?"

David frowned at the man beside him. "Calvin, you have the worst timing."

"You know how your father hates it when you're late. Don't make this any worse than it's already going to be." Calvin turned toward the hors d'oeuvres table and snatched up a glass of punch. He downed it and then jerked his head insistently toward the platform.

The crowd's mumblings grew louder. Any second someone would spot them.

David squeezed her hand. "Don't go anywhere."

Her heart fluttered. "Your announcement has changed, then?"

"What?" Calvin straightened and turned back to stare at her. "What are you talking about?"

David held out his free hand to Calvin. "No, nothing's changed."

The room swam. *Nothing's changed.* Oh, how she wished she'd written a letter instead.

Calvin picked up two champagne flutes and handed one to David. "Then it's time we go."

"David?" His father's voice boomed. "Has anyone spotted my son?"

"All right." David looked her deep in the eyes. "I need to get up there, but I need you to stay. Everything will be fine."

She shook her head. How could that be?

"Trust me." He looked at her lips for a second before striding away with Calvin on his heels.

Trust him? If his announcement hadn't changed, did he realize what he asked of her? She looked at the crowd, trying to find the quickest way to the exit.

The second she started to head back the way she came, David came racing back and grabbed her hand. "I think it best you go up with me."

The crowd parted in front of them, and she hurried after David, lest she look like he was dragging her. Was he going to publicly jilt Marianne and expect no one would realize the woman he'd dragged up on stage was responsible?

But he'd said his announcement hadn't changed.

At the edge of the platform, Calvin frowned at her as David towed her past.

Yes, whoever this Calvin was, he had horrible timing. Not that hers was much better. If she'd not needed Lydia to push her, she could have been here days ago.

David's father's gaze turned hard the second he noticed her. The woman in the yellow-and-white frothy gown from the garden stood beside him, her expression mildly amused, or maybe suspicious. Had she actually been talking to Marianne? Had David's fiancée unwittingly encouraged Evelyn to ruin her own engagement party?

Her stomach lurched. How she wished she were the kind of woman to faint away. After years of keeping things to herself, why had she failed now? How was she supposed to keep calm in front of a few hundred strangers?

"Sorry, everyone. Couldn't lead a toast with an empty glass." David lifted his drink, as did many in the crowd.

He grabbed another glass off the front table and handed it to Evelyn.

How could she refuse without drawing attention to herself? She took it and then he left her on the side of the platform.

She clamped the glass between two hands, hoping she'd be able to hold on to it despite her shaking. Dropping it in front of everyone would make living through this announcement only that much worse. She glanced back to the stairs they'd just climbed, but people had gathered closer to the platform. Trying to leave now would create a scene. She slowly walked backward, hoping to blend in with the wall.

He'd said to trust him, but that didn't mean she wanted to be the center of attention for whatever he was about to do.

Marianne looked positively radiant. Her smile was one that could change a room's atmosphere.

"Let's not waste another moment." David stopped in front of the crowd. "I need Mr. Hochstetler to come up."

Calvin nearly skipped up the stairs in his haste to obey.

David's father stepped forward. "Now wait —"

"I've got several announcements this evening." David's hand rose as if silencing the crowd — though the only one speaking was his father. "And the first is that we're making Calvin Hochstetler chief executive of Kingsman & Son."

The crowd murmured, and David's father's face turned as red and tight as a new cherry tomato.

Was that the announcement? Every bone in Evelyn's body warmed like melted wax. She shook her head at herself. He'd told her to trust him and she hadn't.

But didn't the servant say this was an engagement party?

David clamped his hand onto Calvin's shoulder. "After I returned from Teaville, I was impressed with how this man not only took care of our holdings but grew them. I realized how much I relied upon him and had taken his hard work for granted. Not once in Teaville did I worry about my projects with Calvin at the helm. I figured there was no reason for him to remain my secretary when he could be a far greater asset to the company."

The crowd clapped, and Evelyn took a step back in case the visible tension in David's father's every limb burst.

"But I know the announcement you've all been waiting for deals with me and Miss Lister." He held out his arm to her and smiled as she came forward. "Whom I've known longer and trust even more than Mr. Hochstetler. Who's one of the finest ladies in my acquaintance, a person who tries her hardest to love others, and a woman of both outer and inner beauty."

Evelyn quickly placed the glass on the floor before she spilled it on herself. His praise for Marianne was far beyond what he could say of her. Though she might love others, a fine, beautiful lady she was not.

"Most of you have been asking for a while now when we planned to announce our engagement, but those plans have gone awry."

Evelyn's legs nearly collapsed out from under her, and she put a hand to the wall behind her to keep herself upright.

The crowd hushed. The older couple up front, the woman being the one who'd come for Marianne in the garden, turned ghastly white.

"As much as I love my oldest friend, Marianne loves Calvin more, and I'm happy to give them their first congratulations on many years of future wedded bliss."

Marianne's mother dropped her drink. The crack of glass splintering against the floor was drowned out by gasps, murmurs, and a smattering of hurrahs.

If Evelyn could have made a sound, she didn't know what it would be. She leaned against the wall, taking a deep breath now that her lungs worked again.

Calvin raised a hand, and the crowd hushed. He put an arm around David's shoulders. "I know what a shock this is for some of you, but I'm very grateful to David, who has done more for me than most of you will ever know." He turned and took Marianne's hand and tugged her closer, placing a kiss against her knuckles. "Let's toast to David. And to him finding a woman who will make him as happy as Marianne makes me."

When the cheers stopped, David held up his glass again. "I have one more announcement. I appreciate Calvin's toast very much, for I would like to find the happiness he and Marianne have. This morning, I wondered if I ever would find that kind of love, but now, I'm hoping to be a bachelor for only a short time more." He turned with a frown, quickly scanning behind him, and her heart ratcheted up.

The second he found her standing against the wall, he threw her his breath-catching grin, though it was more a knee-weakening one now. She literally had to stagger over to the nearby chair to sit.

"Someone just told me I deserved the love of a good woman, and I hope she's correct." David gestured toward his friends. "I praised Marianne earlier for her determination and beauty, and Miss Wisely here behind me has those same qualities in abundance. Plus she's selfless, loyal to a fault, sees the best in everyone, and is the most stubborn woman I know — but stubborn in all the good ways."

Several in the crowd chuckled.

"And most importantly, I love her." He came over and kneeled in front of her, his eyes pleading, his smile replaced with the most serious expression she'd ever seen on his face. "Evelyn, would you do me the honor of making this a double engagement party? Will you marry me?"

So much for hoping not to embarrass

herself in front of all his guests, for there was nothing she could do to stop the tears.

40

The whispers from the crowd behind David grew louder, and in his peripheral vision, he saw Father coming closer. And yet, Evelyn simply sat there crying. He jiggled her hand. "Evelyn?"

After what she'd told him earlier, he knew she loved him, knew she was concerned about her divorced status, but not so much he'd thought she wouldn't accept his proposal.

Of course, if anyone in the world didn't want a public proposal, it was Evelyn, but the timing had been absolutely perfect. He, Calvin, and Marianne had all agreed their parents would keep their protests private if the whole town knew of the surprise engagement before they could object. It wouldn't keep them from grousing and complaining, but they'd likely swallow their objections in front of others and maybe come to terms with their children picking their own spouses sooner rather than later.

If Evelyn accepted his proposal right now, Father would never publicly bring up her divorced status. For if he told anyone else what a terrible match she was and she married his son anyway, he'd only hurt himself.

"Evelyn, did you hear my question?" She looked like a startled deer, if deer could produce tears.

She took her hands from his and thrust them into her pockets, panicking over whatever she couldn't find.

Considering the state of her face, he pulled out his pocket square, which she promptly snatched up.

She patted her face and took in a shuddery breath. "Could you ask me again, just in case I didn't hear correctly?"

He couldn't help his huge grin. She was so darling. "Would you marry me?" He held out his empty palms. "I have no ring, but I can take care of that later."

She nodded, and the palpable tension from the room dissipated. Calvin's voice called out, "Three cheers for good news times three!"

The shouts of the crowd and the clinking of glasses faded as he pulled Evelyn to stand. She looked so uncomfortable that he tilted her head down to plant a kiss on her forehead instead of the one he wanted to press against her lips, then enfolded her in his arms.

The moment she sagged into his embrace and squeezed him back, he knew she hadn't simply nodded to keep from embarrassing him in front of the wealthiest people in Kansas City. He nuzzled next to her ear. "I'm so glad you came to me today. Father won't dare contest this now — at least not in front of anyone." He pulled back and looked at her face, still wide-eyed and dewy. "Though the quicker we get married, the more agony you'll save me from."

In front of this crowd, he couldn't hold onto her as long as he'd like, so he stepped back to arm's length and caressed her with his eyes. "Because the arguments Father will plague me with until the day we marry will be nothing compared to the torture of waiting for you to become mine."

Her mouth trembled, and he ran his thumb across her lower lip.

Father stomped forward on the platform and raised both hands, indicating a desire for quiet. Evelyn turned to watch him, and David held his breath while the crowd settled. He'd been fairly certain Father wouldn't blast Evelyn in front of anyone, but what if he did? Evelyn didn't need another man hurting her.

If Father so much as uttered a word against her right now, he'd flatten him and then talk to Calvin about forging off on their own.

Father's face was tight, every one of his muscles wriggling as if fighting hard to comply. "I know what a surprise these announcements have been, but when the Kingsmans throw a party, we want to make sure it's going to be talked about for months." He stabbed a finger toward the small orchestra. "Play music!"

The piano player called out for his players to prepare for Strauss's *"Künstlerleben,"* and without a backward glance, Father stomped off.

Calvin stepped forward. "All right, ladies and gentlemen — here's how dinner will be served. . . ."

As Calvin explained how dinner would be held in shifts for such a large crowd, Evelyn stared at his secretary as if she needed to know the particulars. David tugged on her hand, and she looked back at him and took a deep breath. The poor thing looked as if she'd seen a ghost.

Marianne came over with a big smile, put an arm around Evelyn, and chuckled, rubbing Evelyn's arms as if trying to loosen her up. "I'm so glad your dilemma is over."

Evelyn produced a bit of a smile. "It is, isn't it."

The two had already met?

While half the room emptied, the musicians struck up the waltz. The plaintive beginning would give them plenty of time to get to the dance floor.

Calvin claimed Marianne's arm. "I think we're to lead."

David held out his hand to Evelyn. "Shall we?"

That finally seemed to jolt her out of whatever world she'd retreated into. "I'm not dressed for a dance. I'll make you a laughingstock."

"Don't be silly. You're plenty lovely, even when wearing a work dress you've worn for days, half asleep, and on your bare feet." He snaked his arm around her waist and escorted her toward the short stairs to the floor.

She looked over at him and frowned. "While that's a romantic thing to say, it's not actual truth."

"Oh no?" He held her hand tight as they stepped down the two stairs to the floor. "Did you not get back my drawing of you and Scott that I sent?"

She blushed and nodded.

"You were plenty beautiful, just as I described." Curling her arm under his, he brought her hand up, kissing the back of her glove.

While the violin and French horn finished their short dramatic piece, he led Evelyn to the middle of the floor behind Calvin and Marianne. "I bet everyone watching us can see I care not a whit for your dress. And if all they can do is grouse about it, they aren't friends I want to keep."

She stared at him as he brought her left hand up to his shoulder and then took his time getting his own left hand to its position. He kept his eyes locked on hers as he let his hand travel the length of her arm, across her upper shoulder, and down to span the area below her shoulder blade. Then he pulled her closer and stood with her but a breath away until the first waltz section began, watching the glaze of her eyes turn from uncertainty to devotion.

He had to close his eyes then, for fear he'd kiss her in front of the whole crowd and add more scandal to his choice of wife.

The feel of her, in his arms, in his home, free to love him, made his heart soar with the quickening notes of the violin. At the first measure of the lively waltz section, he took a deep breath and began to lead.

After two turns about the room, several couples joined in, but Evelyn was not nearly as loose and graceful as she had been when they'd waltzed in Teaville. He needed no other excuse to look for an exit.

The moment they neared the doors, he spied a break in the crowd and twirled her with a flourish, pulling her out the doors behind him.

He took in a gulp of the cooling evening air and held tightly to Evelyn's hand as the door closed behind them. Thankfully a quick glance confirmed they were alone in his backyard.

Evelyn shuffle-stepped at his side as he pulled her across the pavers and out of view of the windows. "Are you sure it's fitting for us to leave your own party?"

"I'm actually not worried about what's appropriate right now." He pulled her close and captured her mouth, the warmth of her lips sending a quiver through his body. That he'd been so close to being forever denied the taste of her kiss filled him with desperation, and his mouth danced with hers in an ardent frenzy.

Her back hit the wall with a soft thud, jolting them apart for a second. He began to trail kisses along her jaw. Did she know how perfectly made for him she was? From her tenacity spurring him to dig in his own heels to the sweet smell of her skin. He'd endure every agonizing moment of their friendship all over again knowing this very minute awaited him.

"David," she breathed. The sound of his name was imbued with such contentment and utter longing that his body hummed in response.

He continued laying kisses along her neck until he hit fabric. Oh sweet mercy she was soft and lovely beyond measure. And would soon be his wife.

Thank you, Lord.

She wrapped her arms tight about him, burying her head in his neck.

The desire to continue thoroughly kissing her was almost too much to bear. He forced himself to turn his face away from the intoxicating fragrance of her and held her as tightly as he could, as if the pressure of their embrace could make them one.

The sounds of the orchestra mingled with the throb of his heartbeat and Evelyn's ragged breathing.

"I never thought I'd get the chance to propose to you again," he whispered against her ear, swaying to the music, his irregular heartbeat likely messing with his ability to sway in synchronization. "If I'd have known how good you felt in my arms and under my lips . . ." He pressed another kiss right below her ear, and her responding whimper made him seek her mouth to swallow the sound up whole.

But he stopped at the taste of salt.

He pulled back, catching the tear about to fall from her cheek with his thumb. "What's wrong?"

"Nothing." She shook her head, smiling while crying. "I just didn't expect you to propose to me in front of all those people."

He smiled at the starry-eyed gaze she was giving him. "Neither did I. This party was for Marianne and Calvin. I was just supposed to act like I could be happy at some point. I didn't realize that point would be here so soon." He pressed her head against his shoulder, leaned his against hers, and closed his eyes. "Oh, sweet Lord, I'm glad it was this soon."

"But . . ." She hiccupped. "Might it be too soon? You didn't have time to think anything through."

He backed away and frowned. "What was I supposed to think through?"

"Well, my divorce." Her voice was barely above a whisper, and she dropped her gaze from his. "Your father said I would make you the social outcast of your set."

He led her toward the garden bower. "I don't care what Father thinks. I don't care about your divorce. I don't care about your dress. I don't care how scandalized we're going to make this town. I love you, and if you love me as much as you said you did earlier, I hope we can make a difference here together. Which . . ." He cringed and gripped her hand tighter. "It's you who might need more time to think things through."

He swiped the dead leaves off the bench for her, then sat beside her. "I can't leave Calvin to work with Father alone, so I won't be returning to Teaville now." He intertwined his fingers with hers, relishing the feel of her hand in his before he forged on. "But I realized after Father sold A. K. Glass that I could do plenty of good here. I always considered Father forcing me into his business as a cross to bear, but I now see it as a blessing. Though I still wish I meant more to him, all his business holdings are within my control, and will one day be mine. When Father intended to throw the two prostitutes I'd hired out on the street without even an apology, I realized the only thing keeping him from becoming a terrible man with too much power was me. But you could help me here, right? There are plenty of rough areas in town where I'm sure you'll find people in need. We could help the women from Teaville's red-light district find a life in Kansas City, maybe even —"

Her finger stopped his lips. "Wherever you are, David, that's where I'll be." Her eyes warmed him more than a thousand candles. "I've never in my life been as miserable as these past two weeks without you." Evelyn's hands gripped his lapels, and he leaned in the last inch to meet her lips again. Her kiss was deep and desperate. Her fingers curled into his suit jacket as if she were terrified he'd let her go.

Pulling back, he tipped his head down to keep her from cutting off his words with her lips. "I promise not to desert you, Evelyn. I might have to end a kiss, go to another room, stay late at work, but I'll never abandon you."

"I know." Her voice held the sound of unshed tears. "You've already proven that, before I ever had an inkling you'd stoop to marry me."

He pulled far enough away from her this time to see her entire face. "I didn't stoop. Don't you ever think that — no matter what Father may say when I'm not around." He flashed a grin. "Besides, you're too tall for me to have to do any stooping."

She grimaced. "Does that bother you much?"

"Not in the slightest. And I'll prove it." He placed his mouth against hers as tenderly as possible, relishing the fact that he could do so, for as long as he liked.

Well, not quite as long as he liked lest he get them in trouble before they married.

But he wasn't about to pull away until he'd proven that nothing about her bothered him.

She clung to him while he explored her mouth, and a sudden shiver took over her body.

Since the temperature was mild for this time of year, her shudder sent a satisfied quiver through his own frame. He broke away and nuzzled her cheek, placing kisses along those scars she'd once tried to hide, breathing in everything about her. "I hope you aren't like Marianne and want a huge wedding that will take forever to plan."

Evelyn put her hand against his chest. "No. Though I would like to marry in front of witnesses who know me this time."

He placed his hand on top of hers, pressing it harder against his ribs, as if he could get it closer to his heart. "How could anyone marry you with no intention of keeping his vows? I'd like to pummel the scoundrel."

"I wouldn't want you to." She pulled back and took a long look at his face, the huge grin on her lips and the softness in her eyes melting away his anger. "If it wasn't for James and his abandonment, I probably would not have waited for a love so true, so consuming, and so good. I know if I told you I don't deserve you, you'd object, but I'll thank God for every ounce of agony I've been through if it means I get to be yours for the rest of my life."

"No ifs about it." He hugged her closer. He might not be able to erase the agony of her past, but he would do what he could to help her forget it. "With God's help, I hope to love you so well I never give you reason to start wishing on stars."

EPILOGUE

Four months later

The sway of their carriage rolling up the Lowe mansion's drive should have soothed, but it only highlighted the unnaturally quick pitter-patter of Evelyn's heart.

"How are you feeling?" David had his arm around her, his fingers playing with the dangling strands of her hair that always refused to stay up.

"I'm nervous."

"You shouldn't be." Her husband pressed a kiss against her temple, then sat back against their seat, his ankle crossed casually over his knee.

"You're not nervous?"

"Nope." He flashed her that knee-weakening smile she'd yet to take for granted.

"Why not?" She rubbed her hands atop her skirt. So silly of her to be this anxious.

"Because you're their mother."

Mother. The court had given her that title only an hour ago. It felt so foreign, and so right. When the carriage stopped at the top of the drive, they'd get out and "meet" their son and daughter.

David laced his fingers through hers. "You'll be guiding them. So I'm not worried."

"You're too sweet." She leaned over for what would likely be their last good kiss until they returned home. Hopefully she would never tire of showing David just how much she enjoyed the affections of the man God had blessed her with for the rest of their days.

After a few seconds, David responded to the slow caress in a way she knew would get her flustered if they continued much longer.

The moment she broke away, he followed after her and kissed her more soundly.

The carriage stopped.

He groaned, his eyes flashing hot. "What a tease you are, Evie."

She gave him a quick peck on the cheek. "But you like it."

"More than you know."

Their hired driver opened the door.

As David crossed in front of her to get out, he gave her a long look that turned her insides to jelly. And she'd thought his charming grin made her toes melt.

He helped her down, the Kansas wind greeting them with fine dust and the small of new grass.

Mr. Parker pulled up behind them, and Nicholas helped Lydia exit their carriage. Lydia met her halfway to the house and looped her arm around Evelyn's. "You ready?"

Evelyn nodded, but inside the butterflies were wreaking havoc. Which was ridiculous since she used to be in charge of twelve children at a time, and they were only adopting two. But now, she'd never have to tell them good-bye.

Nicholas led them to the side door that went directly into the orphanage's office. Once inside, he motioned to the sofa in front of his desk, but no one sat. "Since you don't have much time, let me get Mercy to bring you the children."

Lydia let go of Evelyn's arm. "And let me get my baby. I want you to see how big Jake has gotten. He just started smiling and coo-ing."

Evelyn nodded mutely and watched Nicholas and Lydia walk out the door. When she'd heard Mercy and her older brother and his wife had taken over the mansion for the Lowes, she couldn't have felt more relieved. Mercy would be a wonderful caregiver to the children and they couldn't help but fall in love with her. But what if the children had become attached to Mercy and wished to stay?

David came up behind her and wrapped his arms around her torso, resting his chin on her shoulder. "Almost time."

She leaned into him, trying to absorb some of his calm.

"Come sit." He led her to the green upholstered camelback sofa, then put a hand around her neck and massaged.

A minute later, Daddy walked in the door.

"Daddy?" She left David and wrapped her father in a huge hug. "I thought you weren't going to be able to see us." The court date had been pushed back, David had to return to Kansas City for a big business deal, and Daddy was supposed to be in Oklahoma preaching a revival. He'd not been able to return to pastoring a church, but he preached in the area's little rural churches when there was a need.

He planted a kiss on the top of her head. "We rearranged things so I could be here."

She took a step back and examined his face, not a sign left of his apoplexy. Heat pricked the back of her eyes at Daddy's huge smile.

David's father had frowned at their plans to adopt so soon, and she couldn't help but wish Daddy would be the grandfather these kids knew best. "You do know anytime you want to move in with us, all you have to do is send us a telegram, or better yet, show up on our doorstep."

He kissed her on the forehead again. "We'll let you know, pumpkin."

Momma came out from behind Daddy and gave her a tight hug.

"Mr. and Mrs. Kingsman?"

Evelyn looked over Momma's shoulder to see Mercy with her good arm around Alexandria and her shortened arm nearly parallel to the ground, resting across Scott's shoulders. He must have shot up at least three inches since they'd seen him last.

Mercy smiled. "I brought your children."

My children.

Alex ran straight over and wrapped her arms around her legs.

Evelyn held out an arm for Scott. He ambled over, but then gave her a hard, desperate hug. She kissed the crown of his head, too choked up to say anything.

David's hands clamped onto her shoulders, and he steered them all toward the sofa.

She sat, and Alex curled herself up against

564

her like a pill bug. "I'm so glad you came back for me."

Evelyn sniffed. How she'd wanted to come and take all the children home. But four of the orphans she knew were already gone, two others couldn't be adopted without their surviving parent's consent, and Robert and Max wanted to finish school in Teaville.

David pulled out a small box from his pocket. "I have gifts for you two."

Evelyn raised her eyebrows. When had he gotten them gifts?

He handed Scott a small square box.

Scott sat beside her and pried off the lid. On a velvet cushion lay a pocket watch — the initials engraved on the cover were SJK, with the K large and prominent in the middle. "Scott Jonathan Kingsman," Scott whispered to himself.

Alex looked over at Scott's watch and then turned back to David. "What did you get me?"

"This." He pulled out a smaller box and opened it for her.

Inside lay a heart-shaped locket, her initials engraved on the front, just like Scott's. "These letters are for Alexandria Marie Kingsman, and if you push this button" — he opened the locket — "I put a picture of your mother and me in there for you." The tiny picture they'd taken on their honeymoon in a little shop in eureka Springs had been cut to fit.

"Can I wear it?" Alexandria turned around and picked up her braids.

He fiddled with the tiny clasp, clearly having difficulty, but Evelyn didn't bother to offer to help since she could barely see through the tears welling up. Under the influence of such a man as his father, she didn't know how David had become so caring and thoughtful, but she couldn't help but be grateful he had.

David finally got the necklace clasp to work, then kissed Alex on the back of her head. She turned around and bear-hugged him. "I've never had anything this pretty. Thank you."

"You're welcome, sweetheart."

"We have a gift for you too." Momma handed Evelyn a heavy rectangular box.

She opened it up. Her family's Bible lay inside.

"We figured you should have it now, so you can record the names of our grandchildren in it."

Evelyn had to pull out a handkerchief to keep her tears from ruining the Bible's cover. "Thank you, Momma."

Daddy walked over to David and wrapped

him in a side hug. "I couldn't be more proud or thankful for you, son. I haven't the slightest worry about the happiness of my girl and my grandkids in your care."

David turned to clamp Daddy in a hard embrace. After a few seconds, he stepped back, eyes red rimmed. "When your daughter told you that you'd be welcome to show up on our doorstep" — David's voice was raspy — "she wasn't lying. Any day, sir."

Daddy smiled at him and then stepped back to put his arm around Momma. "We'll definitely visit as often as we can. We have grandchildren to spoil."

Scott sighed beside her, his watch cover open, but he wasn't looking at the time. It looked like there was an inscription on the inside.

She leaned over to take a peek.

Love, Mom and Dad

She cut her eyes toward David, still standing beside Daddy, who was uncharacteristically rubbing at his eyes. David was right — there was absolutely no reason to be nervous raising these children, not with the father God had provided them.

Scott clicked his watch shut and swallowed it up in his hand. He looked up at

David. "Thank you, Dad."

David seemed only capable of nodding, his throat working overtime.

"Thank you too, Mom." Scott leaned over and gave her a peck on the cheek.

Mom. A title she'd thought was lost to her forever. Thank God, He really did have something better in mind for her life. He'd forgiven her missteps and rewarded her with a family that surpassed the desires of her heart. "No, thank you for agreeing to be our son." She slipped her arm around Scott's shoulders and pulled him in tight. They might not be able to give these children a perfect life — she'd had the best of parents and gotten off track — but they could give them lives filled with love, encouragement, and security.

She could sense David's eyes on her, and she looked up to give him her best smile. *Thank you,* she mouthed.

He came over and sat on Alex's other side, put his arm around them all, and then leaned over to whisper in her ear. "Whatever you wish for, love, star or not, I'll do my best to make it come true."

AUTHOR'S NOTE

For readers wondering if there was anything wrong with baby Hope, there was. However, the term Fetal Alcohol Syndrome (FAS) was not coined until the 1970s, when the detriment of alcohol consumption during pregnancy was beginning to be understood; therefore, I couldn't outright explain Hope's problem in the story.

In the early 1900s, when the temperance movement was at its peak, it was believed that the offspring of men and women who consumed alcohol were predisposed to live a life of vice. Since grown-up children and adults with FAS are in a higher risk group for being substance abusers, being in trouble with the law, and having unwed pregnancies, the assumption of the doctors of the era was not completely off base. The long-term social and behavioral problems that some people with FAS exhibit are not always under their control, considering they've had permanent damage done to their central nervous systems, and they often need intervention services to cope.

In regard to infants, as you could see in my portrayal of baby Hope, FAS often makes them irritable, inconsolable, unable to sleep well, extremely sensitive to stimuli, colicky, uncomfortable with being touched, tense, smaller than expected, and a challenge to care for. Methods my characters employed to try calming baby Hope, like swaddling, cuddling, bouncing, patting, singing, etc., may make FAS infants feel worse.

Alcohol damages preborn children more than any other drug, and no amount is safe to consume during pregnancy at any time. A pregnant mother has one-hundred-percent control of keeping her child from experiencing the long-term social and behavioral problems caused by alcohol. If you know of someone or are someone who struggles with alcohol and is pregnant, please seek out help immediately. Your local Alcoholics Anonymous should be able to point you in the right direction.

ACKNOWLEDGMENTS

My biggest thanks this time around goes to Naomi Rawlings, who prayed for me through a big life change that made this book difficult to write, was inundated by my racing to finish by deadline, and had to deal with an overwhelmed, grumpy critique partner. And who's still on board with doing this with me all over again.

My mother and mother-in-law gave up chunks of their time to watch my children so I could go hide and write this book. I'm very grateful they were willing to come even though we've added even more hours of driving for them to do so.

I want to thank my literary agent, Natasha Kern, and the Bethany team for caring about my stories and advising me on ways to make them better.

Glenn Haggerty, Heidi Chiavaroli, Julie Cowles, and Amy Parker all read this book or at least parts of it and gave me insight on how to make it better for readers. Thank you for doing so quickly and with care.

The people who pay the most for my stories are not the ones who hand over their dollars, but rather the ones who lose their mommy and wife time to the fictional world in my head. Thank you for your sacrifice and support.

I am blessed that God gave me this vehicle for my stories, and I thank Him not only for the opportunity, but for all the people He has provided to help me succeed.

ABOUT THE AUHOR

Much to her introverted self's delight, ACFW Carol Award winner **Melissa Jagears** hardly needs to leave home to be a homeschooling mother and novelist. She lives in Kansas with her husband and three children and can be found online at Facebook, Pinterest, Goodreads, and www.melissajagears.com. Feel free to drop her a note at mjagears@gmail.com, or you can find her current mailing address and a list of her books on her website.

The employees of Thorndike Press hope you have enjoyed this Large Print book. All our Thorndike, Wheeler, and Kennebec Large Print titles are designed for easy reading, and all our books are made to last. Other Thorndike Press Large Print books are available at your library, through selected bookstores, or directly from us.

For information about titles, please call:
(800) 223-1244

or visit our website at:
gale.com/thorndike

To share your comments, please write:
Publisher
Thorndike Press
10 Water St., Suite 310
Waterville, ME 04901